DATE			

The Sicilian Amulet

Other Five Star Titles
by Jo Manning:

Seducing Mr. Haywood

The Sicilian Amulet

Jo Manning

Five Star • Waterville, Maine

This novel is a work of fiction. Names, characters, places and incidents are either the product of the author's imagination, or, if real, used fictitiously.

First Edition
First Printing: March 2004

Set in 11 pt. Plantin by Ramona Watson.

Printed in the United States on permanent paper.

ISBN 1-59414-181-9 (hc : alk. paper)

This book is dedicated to the memory of a beautiful person, superlative librarian, and dear and loyal friend, Rhoda Kramer Channing, whom I knew and loved since we met as sophomores at Hunter College High School in Manhattan. Rhoda, the late library director at Wake-Forest University in Winston-Salem, North Carolina, was always supportive of and enthusiastic about my novels and short stories, never more so than when they were set in the English Regency period. She was often the first person to read anything I wrote. Rhoda, however, also had the great good taste to love Italy (especially Venice), so dedicating *The Sicilian Amulet* to her is not so much of a stretch. Her spoken Italian, by the way, was excellent—much, much better than mine, even though I grew up in a family of Sicilian immigrants and Italian and Sicilian were my first languages. (Yes, there is a difference.)

I also want to acknowledge the years of rich folk stories told to me by my Asaro, Conigliaro, Sedita, Mannino, and Lupo forebears. The character of Caterina is based on a unique and fiercely independent great-aunt who lived her life the way she wanted to live it, not how society dictated she must live it. I've imagined a good deal about Caterina while interweaving the real events of her life amongst the fantasy. Reality and fantasy, you see, are part of the lemon and rosemary-scented air one breathes in Sicily. Gods and goddesses easily co-exist with the Madonna. The past is always present and all things are possible, even—perhaps—the reincarnation of lovers. The German photographer who befriended the lovely, lonely Caterina sprang full-blown from my imagination, but, surprise, surprise, he turned out to have been a real, live human being who practiced his art in Taormina, where the last part of Caterina's story is set.

The unexplainable—call it coincidence, call it synchronicity—happens everyday, more so than any of us consciously realizes, especially, I believe, on that magical triangle-shaped island in the Mediterranean the ancients named Sicily.

—Jo Manning, 2003

Prologue

Segesta, 1990

She couldn't take her eyes off his butt.

It was his fault. He was in her line of vision, blocking out the unfluted columns of the ruined Greek temple she was attempting to draw and also the early morning sun's pale yellow light. Furthermore, his tight, tantalizing rear end had destroyed her concentration. *That* natural wonder was beautifully formed. As an artist she appreciated those taut muscles, the almost-palpable sinewy flesh. Life models in drawing class had never looked this good!

Michelangelo's incomparable statue of the young David that she'd recently seen in Florence competed with the muscular presence of this very real man on this deserted Sicilian hilltop. She sighed as a slight breeze moved across the stranger's white linen trousers, showing the barest outline of a pair of tight bikini briefs between his skin and the thin outer layer of his pants.

Now he'd put his hands in his pockets, drawing the already tight trousers even tighter against his buttocks. The corded muscles thus revealed were, anatomically speaking, a truly outstanding example of their kind. Jane was aware that the hand clutching her drawing pencil was moist with sweat. Her stomach tightened; her thighs were slack. The way her legs were trembling, she was glad she was sitting down. She couldn't repress another sigh.

He was too taken with the view, it seemed, to notice she

was sitting there, right behind him.

Embarrassed with her blatant staring, she turned back to her sketch of the unfinished temple, hoping he hadn't heard her too-audible intake of breath. She would die if he turned around; she'd also die if he didn't. An overwhelming curiosity came over her: would the full frontal of the tall, dark-haired stranger match up to the outstanding rear view?

She wanted to know.

Badly.

And was reminded of the earthy and entirely out-of-character remark her innocent little sister Jenny had passed one day when they were walking along the beach at Hyannis. Striding ahead of them was a self-conscious bodybuilder, his over-developed gluteus maximus straining against the spandex of a tiny pair of bathing trunks. "Well, I guess he proves the old saying, Jane, that you can't drive in a spike with a tack hammer," her sister had commented.

Well, that was no tack hammer. The stranger had to have some spike.

Jane Holland! She admonished herself severely. What was happening to her? Since her arrival in Italy two weeks ago, on the last leg of a summer trip with two of her best college friends, she had noted subtle changes in her demeanor, her attitudes. She had become extraordinarily sensitive to the seductive beauty of Italian males; they really turned her on. The Mediterranean combination of dark, curly hair and olive skin, sometimes paired with astonishing blue/green eyes, had caused her heart to flutter wildly.

I'm not going man-crazy, she told herself. *I'm not!*

But she hadn't wanted to go home. She had left her friends abruptly at Leonardo Da Vinci Airport in Rome, telling them she'd decided to change her ticket—despite the costly penalty—and continue on to Sicily. She couldn't help herself; it seemed that she just had to go on. And the men were definitely getting better looking the farther south she traveled.

Now here she was, on a barren hilltop in the early morning, in the presence of what had to be the most visually exciting man—rear view, at least—whom she'd come across in her Mediterranean odyssey. She couldn't take her eyes off him. She was staring at him again. This was silly. He could turn, at any minute, and catch her at it.

Stop it, Jane! Cut it out before you make a complete fool of yourself, girl!

At that instant, he turned, in response to a high, lilting female voice that came from behind where Jane sat on a flat rock surrounded by a spill of drawing materials. As he moved towards her, he was suddenly aware of her presence. He nodded, smiling, a flash of strong, even, white teeth cutting across his smooth, tanned face. Jane thought her heart would fly out of her chest and into his warm, waiting hands.

He was magnificent.

And he bore a striking resemblance to Michelangelo's David, the marble sculpture that had so enchanted her in Florence, with his straight, chiseled, aquiline nose, firm, square jaw, noble forehead . . . and those eyes! Bluer than the Mediterranean morning. The bluest she'd seen yet. Incongruous in that olive-complected face, yet, somehow, not so out of place as all that. His wiry, curling black hair tumbled over his brow. He was clean-shaven, his hair cut short over his ears and at the back of his strong neck. He had a lazy, seductive smile. It probably gets you anything you want, Jane thought. *Anything* . . .

Dazzled, her eyes held his for the briefest of memorable moments. Just enough time for him to seem to appraise her, swiftly, to take all of her in. What did he think of her looks, she wondered? Was he partial to tall, chestnut-haired, hazel-eyed American girls with high cheekbones? Then the woman who belonged to the lilting voice appeared. She spoke to him in Italian.

She was complaining, in a teasing, half-laughing tone of voice. It was obvious that they were on very familiar terms. And now she was pounding his chest lightly with two small, clenched fists. Jane couldn't help but continue to stare, noting the girl's masses of tawny blonde hair, her golden arms and legs. She was wearing a beautifully tailored little black dress, or LBD to the cognoscenti. It was one of those deceptively simple but outrageously expensive designer dresses. Short. Linen. Probably Armani. Showing a lot of golden thigh. She was gorgeous.

They were a gorgeous couple.

Jane turned back to her drawing pad. Her line of vision was now clear. The gorgeous pair walked on, away from her, together. A lump rose in her throat. *This is ridiculous! You don't know this man. Why this sudden sense of loss? Jeez, Jane, he's probably a jerk!* But she knew, somehow, that he wasn't a jerk.

And, worse, that she would never see him again.

Chapter One

The Journey Home, Italy

Jane had taken the overnight train from Rome to Palermo after leaving her friends Wendy and Sarabeth at Da Vinci airport. She'd asked them to telephone her mother from Logan when they arrived in Boston to let her know that Jane was planning to continue her trip with a week or two in Sicily. It was almost the end of June. Winter semester at Vassar didn't commence for another two months. She had the time, if not a whole lot of money.

She and her friends had planned this European trip for over a year. They had worked on campus, ringing up purchases in the bookstore, manning the reception desk at the art gallery, waitressing at The Mug, babysitting for an assortment of faculty brats. The previous summer, they'd toiled at a number of temporary jobs in Boston—working as file clerks, secretaries, and salesgirls—to save up money for their journey. At the last minute, their parents had voluntarily kicked in, impressed with their perseverance, and paid for their airline tickets. None of them had opted for a formal junior year abroad, so this four-week trip would be it, their version of the Grand Tour, the summer before senior year.

As they were art and art history majors, they crammed in all the major museums in London, Paris, and Rome, with a major side-trip to Florence that also included Siena, Pisa, Ravenna, and Lucca. They gloried in Rome, taking in the gilded opulence of the Eternal City's art, architecture, and churches. The Vatican blew them away. Jane's special goal was to visit any church graced by the work of her hero, the gifted sculptor-architect Gianlorenzo Bernini. She patiently endured a lengthy High Mass at the tiny Church of Santa Maria della Vittoria in order to gaze at what she considered to be his masterpiece, St. Theresa in Ecstasy.

Was all that for God, she'd wondered, somewhat irreverently, gazing intently at the saint's writhing, twisted limbs and contorted, passion-filled face. She wondered if anything—God or man—would ever move her half so much? Then she blushed at the thought, heat suffusing her pale face. She hoped no one in the quiet little church could read her lascivious thoughts.

They traveled through Italy by train, amused by the bizarre stories they occasionally heard from other young female college students they encountered of misadventures on the Italian railway system. These stories—which she'd observed always seemed to happen to "a friend of a friend," never to the individual relating the tale or someone that person actually knew—involved the piping of mysterious gases into compartments, rendering their occupants helpless while thieves made off with their belongings, and, in some cases, their virtue. Sarabeth, a notorious worrywart, had gotten a bit nervous, but Jane and Wendy had laughed her out of it. Their train travels were remarkably without incident.

Except for the old pervert who'd followed Jane into their second-class compartment (he had been seated in the first-class car when he spotted them, so it just went to show . . .) and attempted to fondle her breasts. Wendy and Sarabeth had swung into action, hitting him over the head with their book-loaded backpacks. He ran out whining, his tail between his legs, beating an undignified retreat. Was it just her bad luck, with all the good-looking men in Italy, that a disgusting pervert had made a move on her?

The nine-hour overnight ride from Rome to Palermo she took alone across the fabled Straits of Messina had been amusing. The very handsome conductor ("Marcello", according to the name badge pinned on to his crisply-starched dark brown uniform) had assisted two French women with their baggage when they'd stopped at the Naples station. Through the thin walls of the adjoining compartment, she could hear that they had invited him inside. There was much laughter, clinking of glasses, then the unmistakable metallic music of zippers unzipping. The compartments were barely big enough for two people behaving themselves. Three people—definitely misbehaving—must have been extremely cozy. Jane felt a bit jealous; she had no one to share her compartment that night.

She imagined that the crushing rocks and frenzied whirlpool of Scylla and Charybdis were gnashing and chomping at the underside of the boat-train as it crossed the Straits of Messina into the dark Mediterranean night, remembering the story of Odysseus's stormy journey. Suddenly, she was in the midst of that murky, foaming water, swallowing it in, enmeshed in a nightmare that was drawing her into the inky, bottomless depths of a whirlpool. She awoke in a fearful sweat to the giggles of the French women as the train made its scheduled stop at Cefalu, site of a Club Med on one of Sicily's best-known beaches.

She looked out of the small, grimy train window just in time to see the two tourists, straw hats in hand, detraining. Each, in turn, hugged the compliant Marcello for one last *bacio*. In the background, she saw the huge rock, like a great, beached, barnacled whale, that gave the city its name.

She had looked it up in one of her many memorized guidebooks. Cefalu, from the Greek *kephale,* or headland. She slumped back on the narrow bed to catch another hour or so of sleep before they reached her destination, Palermo. As she dropped off, the throaty roar of the train engaging its gears vibrated loudly, setting the wooden signs over the station platform swinging wildly.

A knock on the door. The conductor, Marcello. Telling Jane they would soon reach Palermo. *"Grazie,"* she mumbled, getting out of bed, pulling on a pair of jeans and a loose white tee shirt and slipping into leather sandals. She ambled to the small mirror over the minuscule corner sink and looked at her pale, anxious face.

What have I done?

She felt a sudden moment of panic. Mother will be furious, she thought. She never wanted me to come to Sicily. Jane shook the cobwebs from her sleep-soused brain and turned on the taps. Cold water only. She splashed some on her face and ran her damp fingers through her tangled hair. Her face was puffy from lack of sleep. She saw the warning over the sink not to use the water for drinking. Well, so much for brushing my teeth, she grimaced. Reaching into her backpack, she took out a tube of mascara and dabbed at her eyelashes in an attempt to salvage her looks, and rolled lip gloss over her mouth. Better, she thought. Not much better, but better. It will have to do until I have a proper wash-up, she promised herself.

The train jolted to a grinding stop. *Palermo.* She'd arrived.

Marcello was at the door again. She noted with amusement that his face was puffy, too, no doubt from lack of sleep, though his sleep deprivation was for reasons different than hers. He swayed towards her a bit as the train lurched forward again, suddenly, then caught himself before he could brush against her. He seemed embarrassed. Jane frowned.

What on earth does he want? she asked herself. Surely, he had enough of *that* with those two slutty French women. Then she blushed, furious with herself for reading too much into the incident. He was merely looking for a tip.

She fished a wad of crumpled, hundred-lire notes out of her back pocket. *"Grazie,"* she said aloud, while thinking, thanks a whole lot . . . for nothing. He tipped his hat gratefully. Bags at the ready, needing no assistance from a porter for her solitary backpack and battered duffle bag, Jane raced out of the car and down the platform.

A crowd of the shortest people she'd ever seen was waiting at the gates for friends, relatives, guests, a chance to be the first to board for the trip back to Rome. At five foot eight, Jane felt like a giantess.

She skirted the crowd and made for a telephone, finding a cheap *pensione* near the station on her very first try, thanks to one of her excellent guidebooks. It was a short walk. She cleaned up and went out to explore the city. Sipping *caffé con latte* at a quaint outdoor restaurant on the Via del Giardino, she began to make plans for the week. On a sudden impulse, she decided to take a bus to the ancient ruins of Segesta, which were about fifteen miles from the city.

It was still early morning and she was exhilarated with a sense of adventure at being in a new and exciting country. She would go to Segesta and sketch. Sketching was always relaxing, and she would unwind from the long train ride. And, tomorrow, or the next day, she would look up Claudia Donzini.

The next morning, she'd looked through her address book for the name of her mother's friend—perhaps her best friend. Claudia Donzini. Claudia, nee Streatham, had, years ago, while on a student Fulbright Grant to Italy, vacationed in Sicily and met her future husband, Aldo. The Fulbright and her promising career had gone out the proverbial window.

Claudia had settled down in Palermo, married Aldo (who, upon the death of his father, assumed the title of Baron), and raised a family. Just two years ago, she'd had her first book published. It was a memoir of her life as an American in Sicily, part travelogue, part history, part myth and legend, called *Apollo's Sacred Isle.* It sold decently and set Claudia on a belated, but rewarding new career path.

Jane's mother, Joanna, had told her that Claudia was now researching a new book on the history of Sicily during the Arab occupation of several hundred years ago.

As she popped a token into the telephone booth at the train station, Jane wondered how Claudia Donzini would react to her call. She hadn't seen her in a very long time. Like Joanna, Jane's mother, Claudia Streatham had grown up in New York City and attended a small private school for girls. Joanna was there on scholarship; Claudia, from a family of old New York WASPs, was well off. They'd been an unlikely duo, the immigrants' daughter and the scion of one of America's first families, but they'd become good friends.

Jane always thought it was ironic that her mother, who'd totally rejected her Sicilian heritage by marrying a New England WASP, should have as her best friend a WASP who'd married a Sicilian. Over the past twenty or so years Claudia had visited the Hollands in Boston several times, but Joanna had yet to visit Claudia in Sicily. Yes, Jane thought, Claudia's reaction will be surprise, surprise that a Holland had, finally, made it all the way to Sicily!

Claudia's reaction was pure delight. She answered the telephone on the second ring, with a slightly nasal *"Pronto?"*

"Claudia? It's Jane Holland. I'm vacationing in Sicily for the next couple of weeks, and I wanted to call and say hello . . ."

Claudia's voice boomed over the telephone. "Well, my goodness! This is delightful! Say *'hello'*, indeed! You come right over here, young lady. Let me give you directions. Are you at the airport or the railroad station?" Claudia had taken over. Jane remembered she was a take-charge lady.

Jane hesitated. "Well, I've been staying at the *Pensione* Russo, near the railroad station. I've been walking around, exploring the area, and want to do more, but, before I went too far, I wanted to see you . . ."

"Young lady, I'm insulted! Now you check out of that *pensione* and come stay with us. I can bet it has no hot water"—she was right—"so you come here and clean up. We have lots of hot water! And *you'll* be in hot water with me, my dear, if you dare to say *no*."

The woman was firm. Jane knew when to acquiesce. It wasn't that difficult. She smiled to herself. Jane liked Claudia, who was a big-boned, no-nonsense, motherly woman. She'd do it. She checked out of the *Pensione* Russo and returned to the station to look for a cab. Claudia had given her directions to the apartment.

The Donzinis lived on the Via Delle Alpi, on the western edge of Palermo, a post–World War I residential area. She'd told Jane it was a fairly short cab ride. Confident in her college-learned Italian, and having knowledge of Sicilian dialect variations thanks to stays in New York City with her mother's family, Jane approached the cab queue in front of the station.

Mindful of how few lire she had left in her pockets, Jane

remembered to inquire how much the ride would set her back. *"Quanto costa?"*

The cabbie, a rotund little man with twinkling brown eyes, full, bushy handlebar moustache, and a jaunty navy blue beret, spoke English. He seemed to appreciate her precise Italian accent, and the fare was well within her budget constraints. She got into the Fiat taxicab. On the ride, the cabbie, Giovanni Battista, asked if she might know his cousin, Bartolomeo Battista, who lived in Canarsie, Brooklyn?

Jane had to admit she didn't know him. It was amazing, she thought, how many Italians she'd met who had relatives in Brooklyn. All her Sicilian relatives lived in Little Italy, in downtown Manhattan, or in Greenwich Village. She didn't know a soul in Brooklyn! Come to think of it, she'd never even been to Brooklyn. Brookline, Massachusetts, yes, but not Brooklyn, New York.

The little cab sped through the modern end of the city. Jane had decided, from her one day in the city, that the drivers in Palermo were as crazy and death defying as the ones in Rome. No speeding restrictions seemed to be in effect. Pedestrians jaywalked at their peril.

The cabbie took the main thoroughfare, Via Roma, a broad street that ran in front of the Palermo train station, then a warren of tiny side streets that meandered and flowed through what seemed to be an older part of the city. Jane saw stately, age-weathered *palazzi* behind stone walls and wrought-iron fences. Then they were heading straight out of the heart of the city, towards a newer, less hemmed-in section on its outskirts.

Via Delle Alpi was a gracious, tree-lined street with a number of apartment buildings and spacious-looking townhouses that fronted on expansive green lawns. Claudia's

building, Number 36, was a six-storey apartment house that overlooked a small, grassy park. It was designed in the Art Nouveau style with elongated plant forms in stained and etched glass arching over the front entrance, which was set off by a handsomely-carved oak door. The hot-pink petals of a flowering bougainvillea framed one side of the impressive doorway. It was a picture postcard come to life.

Tipping the cabbie, who wished her a most enjoyable stay in Sicily and reminded her to look up his cousin the next time she found herself in Canarsie, Jane approached the front door. Almost immediately a concierge appeared behind a second, inner door of delicate etched glass. She took in Jane's unkempt appearance and pursed her thin lips disapprovingly. Jane asked for the Baron and Baroness Donzini, explaining that they expected her.

Wispy white eyebrows rising in surprise, and, perhaps, disbelief, the old woman asked Jane to wait while she went to a telephone. Jane could hear Claudia's distinctive nasal *"Pronto."* Directed by the still disapproving concierge, she took a walnut wood and wrought iron lift to the third floor, where Claudia Donzini welcomed her with arms wide-open.

Claudia hugged Jane to her ample bosom. They were about the same height, but Claudia made almost three of Jane in girth. She stood back and looked at her, beaming happily.

"I never thought I'd see the day! Come in, come in, I want to hear all about your trip, and about your mother, and the family." Claudia Streatham Donzini was as effusive as they came as she led Jane Holland into the Donzini flat, which took up the entire third floor of the building.

Jane looked around in approval. It was a beautiful, even elegant apartment with polished hardwood floors and large floor to ceiling windows that let in the warm Sicilian sun.

She noted two impressive 18th century French antiques, an eight-foot tall mahogany armoire and a rosewood-veneer table that ran the length of the foyer. Jane had a fair knowledge of American and European antique furniture. Her paternal grandmother, Katherine Holland, had a serious collection of both in her Back Bay Boston home. Grandmother Holland would not have minded owning either of those two pieces, Jane was sure.

"What a lovely apartment, Claudia," Jane said in admiration.

"Oh, we make do, Aldo and I. And when we get tired of anything, we trade it for something else at the farm in Alcamo, where the Donzini vineyards are. Now, my dear, come in and make yourself at home. You're going to want to bathe and change, I think, no?"

Jane laughed. "Well, definitely a bath! About changing, though, I'm afraid I didn't bring all that many changes of clothing with me, and what I did bring is filthy, I'm sorry to admit." Jane was uncomfortable. Her clothes were in a disgraceful state. Her hair was still greasy; lots of hot water was needed to do a good job on days-dirty hair. She suspected she looked somewhat like a refugee from a war-torn country.

Claudia laughed back, a hearty, good-natured, throaty sound. "Our three girls have enough clothes here to outfit a small school. Anna Maria is about your age and size—well, she's a bit shorter, come to think of it—but I think her closets are a good start. Come with me and pick out what you want. Oh, goodness, your visit is such a delightful surprise, I've almost forgotten all about my dinner party tonight—"

"Are you going out?" Jane queried, noting for the first time that Claudia was in her wrapper, but also in hose and elegant high-heeled shoes, her face carefully made-up.

"No," she shook her head of tousled gray-blonde curls. "Aldo and I are having a dinner party for some of his friends from the university and some of our local social set. They are all nice people, I'm sure you'll like them. And I think—" she beamed at Jane affectionately "—that they will like you. Now, let's get along and get you ready."

She bustled Jane off in the direction of the children's bedrooms, over Jane's protests of not wanting to "barge in" on the Donzinis' dinner party. "Nonsense," was Claudia's answer as she opened the door to Anna Maria's room and hustled Jane inside.

Jane wondered where the Donzini children were. She knew that there were four of them, three girls, the oldest of the four siblings, and the youngest, who was a boy. She looked around Anna Maria's large bedroom/sitting room, twice again as big as her bedroom at home in Newton, Massachusetts.

In an alcove crammed with a stereo set, fan magazines, audiocassette tapes and CDs, was a large color poster of a young Mel Gibson. Well, her taste wasn't half-bad, Jane thought. Short but hunky blue-eyed Mel was one of her favorites, too. The rest of the decor, though, was a bit too much on the flouncy, frilly, girly side for her. Too Gone-With-The-Windish to be comfortable. Jane tried to remember what Anna Maria was like. She knew she'd met her a few times. All she could recollect was a sulky-faced, spoiled little girl who didn't want to play with her and who had turned up her nose at Jane's treasured toys.

"Where are the children, Claudia?" Jane asked, as she sat on a white and gold chair facing the matching vanity table against one wall and took off her scuffed and dirty sandals, grimacing at the dust and grime she'd picked up walking in Palermo's streets that morning.

Claudia was busily riffling through summer dresses in Anna Maria's ample, well-stocked closets. "Hmmnnn? What did you say, dear? Oh, the children . . . Renato is at the farm in Alcamo with his grandmother. Rosalia is there, too. Laura is with a friend's family in Ischia for the summer . . . and Anna Maria went to Selinunte for a few days on a camping trip with friends from the university. So, Aldo and I have been all alone! It's good to have company!"

"Aldo? He's here?" Jane stripped off her soiled jeans and wrinkled tee shirt. At least my underwear is clean, she thought.

"Aldo went to pick up some of our guests. He doesn't know you are here yet. He'll be so pleased! Here, Jane, how about this?"

She held out a white pique sheath with spaghetti straps. It was simple, Jane thought, nicely cut. She worried it might be too tight in the bosom, but Claudia, sensing her concern, reassured her. "The top of this dress has always been much too loose for Anna Maria—she rarely wears it—but I think it will be fine for you."

Claudia giggled, a surprisingly light and girlish sound. "You and I have both been well endowed in the bosom department, Jane. Sometimes I've wondered if you and Anna Maria didn't get switched at birth. She's more along the size of your mother, I think."

Jane's cheeks turned pink. Her "generous" bosom had always been a source of embarrassment to her. Her mother Joanna and her little sister Jenny were small in the breast department, and the females in her father's family were all flat of chest. The women in her mother's family were A or B cups at best. Jane wore a D cup.

Where did I come from? Jane often wondered. Mother

said she was "a throwback" to some forgotten ancestress, and left it at that, while always insisting that she carry herself well, with her shoulders back and chest out, despite her attention-getting over-endowment.

Not that I ever got the attention I wanted from the boys and men that I wanted to pay attention to me, she mused. Her very cute blonde, blue-eyed, English-rose-complected little sister Jenny was the one who attracted the boys like flies, despite her A cup bra size. *So much for a big chest!* Jane would have changed places with Jenny in a New York minute.

Her thoughts were interrupted by Claudia. "Now, you do what you have to do . . . look, there's a nice robe you can borrow, take it, and I'm sure one of the girls has a pair of shoes that will go with this dress and fit you . . . and I'll see you in . . . oh, about forty-five minutes or so? But take your time! Make yourself pretty . . . not that that will be so difficult . . . and then come out to meet our guests, all right?" In one breath, she was out of the room, leaving Jane to her own devices.

Jane wondered how happy Anna Maria would be with Claudia's generosity. Her room, her robe, her dress, her shoes . . . hmmnn, Jane thought, looking through the collection on the vanity top, her makeup. Anna Maria, in addition to being a clotheshorse, also seemed to be addicted to expensive cosmetics. How nice for me! Jane thought, making a careful selection of Italian designer bath products.

Jane showered in pure bliss—she'd chosen a shower, rather than a bath, so that she could clean her hair thoroughly—in a bathroom tiled in soft, shell pink marble veined with fissures of pale ivory. The soap and shampoo she used smelled of night-blooming jasmine. She wrapped herself in a double-sized bath towel and made short work of drying her hair with Anna Maria's heavy duty, top of the line hair dryer.

She tied her mane back from her face with a beautiful tortoise-shell hairclip and began to apply foundation to her spanking clean face. Soon she was passable, possibly more than passable, even sophisticated-looking, she thought. Could she pass for more than twenty? She hoped so. Even the prissy, critical concierge might approve of the clean, sparkling new Jane that peered back from the bathroom mirror.

Chapter Two

Journeys End in Lovers Meeting

As she stepped out of Anna Maria's bedroom, Jane heard the sound of voices speaking Italian. She panicked for a minute, then, gaining the courage she needed to meet a roomful of complete strangers, she made her way to the gathering.

Claudia's and Aldo's guests were convened in a sitting room off the foyer, on the other side of the flat from the family's bedroom suites. It was a pretty room, decorated with a light, feminine touch. The upholstered loveseats and chairs were in muted shades of blue and green, made to match the floor-length silk drapes on the long windows at one end of the room.

Aldo Donzini, a big, friendly bear of a man, came over to greet Jane as she appeared in the doorway of the sitting room. He hugged her closely and kissed her on both cheeks, complimenting her on how lovely she looked, how grown-up, how sophisticated. Heads were beginning to turn in her direction. Under the artfully applied blusher, her cheeks were beginning to turn pink naturally.

Aldo turned, addressing the room at large—there seemed to be about twenty guests in all—introducing the "daughter of Claudia's dear friend from America, Jane Holland." Aldo's English was excellent; he then repeated his introduction in Italian. His friends and colleagues raised their wine goblets towards Jane in a warm toast. The goblets sparkled brilliantly, reflecting the light from the small chandelier overhead.

Jane smiled nervously as Aldo brought a glass of the wine over to her. "It's estate-bottled, Jane," Claudia informed her, "one of our best vintages. I think you'll enjoy it. *Salute!*"

As she raised the glass to her lips, she realized someone was staring her way. Her hand trembled slightly as she looked into the bluest eyes she had ever seen, the eyes she had seen yesterday morning at Segesta, the eyes of the magnificent stranger.

The man from Segesta with the gorgeous rear was looking at her from across the room.

Jane lowered her eyes, embarrassed. I'm not going to make it, she thought. *I am going to drop this very expensive wine glass and get red wine stains all over Anna Maria's white dress and all over Claudia's silk loveseats. Red wine stains, a nightmare to clean.* She turned her back on the stranger and placed the goblet, very carefully, on an antique mahogany end table. She sighed with relief.

Behind her, a low, husky voice speaking English with a slight British accent, asked, "Is something the matter?"

She turned to face the speaker with the interesting accent. Him. *It was him!* He had come up behind her. Jane gulped.

"No . . . no . . . nothing is the matter," she stammered, wondering, as she looked at his handsome face, where the sexy British inflection in his speech had come from.

"I just thought . . . You looked as though you were going to drop that goblet. I feared you were going to pass out. I'm sorry, I didn't mean to intrude . . ."

That smile again, she thought, *that lazy, seductive smile* . . . Calm yourself, Jane, you've been with good-looking men before. No, not this good-looking. Nuh-uh.

"And . . . how funny . . . have we met before? You look familiar to me, somehow. Do we know each other?"

Jane shook her head. "No, I don't believe so. I've only just arrived in Sicily. I've never been here before. Have you been in the States?"

He's forgotten that he had a glimpse of me in Segesta, she thought, her heart sinking. But I'm forgettable, and it was just a glimpse . . . and then that beautiful, leggy creature came along . . . where is she now, I wonder? Is she his wife? His fiancée? His girlfriend?

"Isn't that odd . . . no, it seems that I have known you for a very long time . . ." He shrugged his shoulders and laughed. "Well, enough of my silliness. I'm Lorenzo Bighilaterra." He held out a strong hand, the nails neatly manicured, reaching to grasp hers. "I live in Palermo. My family and the Donzinis go back—how do you Americans put it? Ah, a long way!" He smiled again.

He was charming. Utterly charming. There were butterflies fluttering madly in Jane's stomach. She didn't know what to say, where to look, what to do. His surmise had been right; she was precariously close to passing out. Her hand felt small and warm clasped in his larger one. Claudia saved her. She came over to them in the nick of time.

"Lorenzo, my dear!" They were kissing each other on both cheeks, obviously pleased to see each other. Claudia turned to Jane. "I'm so glad Lorenzo could make it tonight. I was hoping I could persuade him and Luisa to show you the sights of Palermo and its environs. You could drive to Segesta—"

Lorenzo stopped her in mid-sentence. "Of course! That's where I saw your lovely guest—Segesta, yesterday. I was there with Luisa, in the early morning . . . it was so beautiful, so peaceful . . . and she—" he gestured towards Jane "—she was sketching the temple! You are an artist."

"Well . . . I draw . . . I'm an art history major at college. This is my first trip to Italy, to Sicily. I've looked forward to it for a long time. I wanted to draw all the beautiful things I saw . . ." She was suddenly tongue-tied, shy. He had called her *lovely*. Her, plain old Jane Holland, lovely!

"I can show you a lot of beautiful things, *signorina* . . . if you would allow me."

Oh, I'll bet you could! Then, in one smooth, fluid motion, never taking his clear blue eyes from her face, he brought his full, sensual lips to her unprotesting hand, kissing it softly. *Now,* she thought, *I'm going to really pass out.*

But just as Claudia's arrival had saved her minutes before, the appearance of a young blonde woman breezing through the sitting room door kept her knees from buckling under, as Lorenzo's attention was distracted. It was the beautiful girl he'd seemed to be on such intimate terms with at the ruined temple site. *Well, here's your gorgeous girlfriend,* Jane thought, *and it's time to turn off the charm you're sending my way before she catches you at it!*

The woman entering the room did not simply enter it; she took it over. She was average height for a woman, about five foot five, but most of it seemed to be legs; long, shapely legs. She was exquisitely tanned, and the black and white of her evening outfit was calculated to make the most of her golden beauty. She wore a very short, black, draped silk skirt topped with a pristine white lace vee-necked shell that dipped precariously low and showed remarkable cleavage.

She has to sunbathe in the nude, Jane thought, fascinated by this creature, *to get such an even, no-strap look. I wonder if they nude sunbathe together?* The outrageous thought made her want to giggle. Jane was a competitive swimmer, not a sunbather, nude or otherwise, and she favored simple, one-piece Speedo swimsuits, rather tame, even grandmotherly beachwear for the Mediterranean. No bikinis for her.

Claudia was greeting the beautiful creature, interrupting her dramatic entrance. Jane meanwhile had noted that the eyes of all the men in the room were riveted on the girl, whereas the women had given her withering glances and then looked away, lips curled.

"Ah, *la cugina!*" Claudia exclaimed.

Jane's ears perked up. *La cugina.* The cousin. Whose cousin? She turned to Lorenzo, addressing him, not thinking, in Italian. *"Tua cugina?"* He nodded. They were cousins. Not spouses, not fiancés, not lovers. *Wait,* a little voice inside her cautioned, *they're European jetsetters, classic Eurotrash, a notably decadent lot. What's to prevent cousins from being lovers, too?* She felt a swift, cutting pain in her heart.

"You speak Italian," Lorenzo commented, looking at her with approval and appreciation, looking at her, she noted, in that special way an interested male contemplates an interesting female, checking her out. Lorenzo Bighilaterra was checking her out. *Her!* A thrill ran through her body. She smiled.

She responded in Italian. "I studied Italian in college. It's a beautiful language." She could tell him she was half-Sicilian now, but, for some reason, she hesitated. Not now, she cautioned herself, not now.

"And you, *signorina,* you are quite beautiful, too." He gave her a bold, intense look that made her insides quiver.

"Thank you," she whispered.

"No," he laughed, "it is I who should be thanking you, for being so beautiful, for being here tonight."

He seemed to be amused by her shy demeanor, her awkwardness at receiving compliments. She was not used to being flattered. People didn't go out of their way to call her lovely. But it seemed to come easy for this Italian charmer. She would have to watch herself. And then he was introducing her to his cousin, Luisa Strelli.

Lorenzo was aware that Luisa's English was non-existent. If there were to be any conversation among the three of them, it would have to be in Italian. He hoped the beautiful American girl's Italian had a strong command of grammar and an extensive vocabulary. If all she'd had were Berlitz-type instruction in Italian, he would have to be the translator. But he needn't have worried. The girl put out her hand and, in clear, precise Italian, began to carry on a conversation with his cousin. Luisa stopped her usual whining and looked charmed.

The young women chatted amiably, Jane complimenting Luisa on her dress, Luisa volunteering to take her clothes shopping in Palermo. Lorenzo grinned. Luisa was skilled in shopping, that was for sure. He hoped the girl had deep pockets; he knew his cousin favored the most expensive designer boutiques in Palermo! Versace, Dolce & Gabbana, Armani . . . they all knew his little cousin well.

Lorenzo sighed, chafing at all the time he was spending lately with Luisa. Sometimes he felt he functioned merely as a babysitter; the girl was so immature. But Lorenzo knew Luisa needed an alternative to the wealthy young wastrels with whom she was friendly. Family ties! Sometimes they were more burdensome than others. For the sake of his aunt and uncle, though, he would grit his teeth and bear the burden of his silly cousin.

But this *Americana,* who seemed unsettled by his sincere compliments, was a delight, if somewhat shy. It only added to her natural charm, he thought. *Perhaps she was simply nervous among strangers?* He hoped that soon he would be much less of a stranger to her, very soon indeed. He would encourage her friendship with Luisa, even though his cousin would no doubt soon drive her as mad as she was driving him.

Aldo and Claudia ushered them into the formal dining room. Dinner was commencing. Claudia made sure that the three young people were seated together and she placed Jane between the cousins.

Jane was hardly conscious of what she ate that evening, but it wasn't much. Sitting next to Lorenzo was unnerving. When she shifted in her seat, her thigh brushed up against his. She managed to carry on her end of the conversation over the chilled *consomme,* the *vitello tonnato* swathed in mayonnaise sauce and embellished with the tight buds of young capers, and the perfect baby vegetables artfully undercooked so that they were *al dente,* crunchy, in the mouth. Jane swooned over the last course, the fresh Sicilian fruit and heaps of miniature pastries—*cannoli, sfinci, rum babas*—and a whole, plump *cassata.* And during the elegant meal she had learned a lot about Lorenzo.

For one thing, he was a Prince.

Luisa had teasingly referred to him as *"il Principe,"* and he'd blushed—Jane was fascinated to see the slight reddening under his smooth olive skin—telling Louisa she was silly. He was right, she was silly, extremely so, but she was also a good source of information. A shopping expedition with Luisa, Jane realized, would reveal much about her cousin Lorenzo. Luisa was a motor mouth, that much was obvious.

"He hates to talk about himself, my cousin, the prince,"

Luisa was saying, flipping her hair and narrowing her eyes as Jane picked at the succulent piece of tuna on her fragile china dinner plate. "I'm sure you are wondering why he speaks English with a British accent, no?"

"I assume he learned English from a British tutor," Jane volunteered.

Luisa shook her tawny blonde mane vehemently. "No, no, he went to school in England. Lorenzo went to Oxford. He has—how do you say it—ah! It's called a First, in architecture. That means he made the top grades possible."

That explained his interest in my drawing, Jane thought, looking again at his strong hands, noticing now that his fingers were long, slender, tapering. He had the hands of an artist. They had something—one thing, anyway—in common.

Jane asked, "Do you work for an architectural firm in Palermo?" And she could have bitten her tongue. *Work?* The man was an aristocrat. He probably doesn't have to work. *What an unsophisticated comment, Jane Holland!* She could have kicked herself.

"I'm not with a firm," he answered smoothly. "I have my own private consulting business, specializing in restoration. If Luisa can bear to give you up, I'd like to show you what I do. I'm planning to go to the cathedral at Monreale tomorrow. I've been involved in a project there, and it's only eight kilometers from Palermo, not far. There's someone on site I have to see. Would you be interested in accompanying me there?"

There IS a God, Jane thought, *and He has answered my prayers! Thank you, thank you! Anywhere,* she thought, *I'd go with you anywhere.*

Aloud, she composed herself and responded, "I would love to." To Luisa, she said, "Can we go shopping together the day after next?"

Luisa pouted, showing her small, plump lips to advantage. Shrugging, she agreed to two days after tomorrow. She explained to Jane that she had an important luncheon engagement the day after next. She giggled, shooting Lorenzo a bold glance.

Jane caught Lorenzo frowning. Clearly, he had an inkling of whom Luisa was meeting, and he seemed not at all pleased. *Was he jealous?* Jane wondered. *Just what was the true nature of their relationship?*

Another thought occurred to Luisa. Excited, she turned to Jane. "And we can go to one of my favorite places in all of Palermo, too, the cemetery of the Capuchin Convent!" She then launched into a lurid description, over dessert, of this tourist attraction, where mummified bodies, clothed in their last bits of finery, were displayed for viewing. Jane gulped in dismay, putting the chocolate *cannoli,* untouched, back on her dessert plate.

Lorenzo wrinkled his fine brow in distaste. "Really, Luisa . . . you are too morbid." He turned to Jane. "I despise this cult of the dead. It's not at all amusing. I prefer the living myself, don't you?"

Luisa interrupted. "Oh, Lorenzo, you are never any fun! It is amusing, the brides in their wedding dresses, the gentlemen in their fancy, embroidered smoking jackets, the babies . . . It is not as if they were ever really live people . . ."

Lorenzo was having none of her explanation. "I apologize for my cousin's bad taste. She also adores the church of Santa Maria della Concezione in Rome. You may have heard of it. It is on the Via Veneto. There, the monks have arranged the bones of the dead in what they consider to be artistic and fanciful shapes. It is just another tourist attraction, can you believe that?" He shook his fine head. "I find it all revolting." He flicked his dinner napkin over his plate as if to emphasize his point.

Jane tried to make peace between the two quarreling cousins. "Actually, the two friends I was traveling with in Italy found that church fascinating. It was directly across the street from our hotel, the Alexandria. My friends spent an entire afternoon there, but I preferred to go in search of Bernini."

Jane remembered setting foot in that innocuous-looking little church and meeting a bright-eyed young monk in a stained cassock at the door. Over his shoulder she could see the bones suspended from the ceiling in the shape of a wheel. She had turned on her heels, quickly exiting, leaving Wendy and Sarabeth to their weird and ghoulish pursuits. Luisa would get along with her two friends just fine, Jane thought.

She was suddenly conscious of a flood of approval from Lorenzo. His eyes were warm. "Yes," he agreed with her, "the living, not the dead. The great Bernini's work lives. He is one of my heroes."

"Pah!" Luisa protested, as she practically inhaled one of the small *cannoli,* eating and speaking at the same time. "You two take things far too seriously. You have to have some fun in life. Lorenzo, you are becoming very boring!" She tossed her hair in disapproval of their conversation. Mollifying her, Lorenzo reached over Jane's plate and planted a kiss on Luisa's hand.

Jane thought of her hand, the hand he'd kissed earlier, the one she'd never wash again. She was drawn to this man in a way she'd never before been drawn to any man. Yes, at first it was that body, that beautiful body, with its world-class rear-end—she blushed at the thought—but, now, there was more. He was artistic, as she was; he appreciated great art. It seemed, she thought, to be his life. He was intelligent as well as charming.

What is wrong with this picture? she pondered. *He's too perfect.* The thought hit her with a jolt, unsettling her: *He's everything I want. He is everything I have ever dreamed of wanting . . .* She shivered. It was all happening much too fast, certainly too fast for a little provincial like her.

And they had a date, just the two of them, on the morrow.

That night, after all of the Donzini guests had departed, Jane lingered over an amaretto *aperitif* with Aldo and Claudia. It was too late to call Boston to tell her mother she was now staying at Claudia's, but Claudia had promised she'd speak to Jane's mother when the time zones were better aligned. Jane had placed one call to her mother already and was still bristling with what Joanna Holland had had to say.

No, her mother was not happy she was in Sicily—a country she considered primitive, backward and barbarous—and she wanted her back home soon. She used the words "sneaky" and "behind my back" and "devious" a few too many times for Jane's comfort. Get off my back, Jane had wanted to reply, enraged at her mother's unfair comments.

I'm not a six-year-old any more, I've grown up, she'd wanted to scream—had her mother forgotten she'd be twenty-one in a matter of days?—but it had seemed best to let her rant on. Ranting was one of her mother's specialties. Jane would be home soon enough to face the music in person.

Meanwhile, there was a burning question Jane had to ask Claudia. She waited until Aldo had left them alone together.

"Claudia," she began, tentatively, "Prince Lorenzo . . . he's not . . . gay, is he?" That thought had crossed her mind at the end of the evening. So much perfection had to have a price.

Claudia hooted. She looked Jane straight in the eye, her face merry. "My dear Jane, I have it on excellent authority that he is not." And then she laughed, kissing her good night and hoping she'd sleep well.

Oh, that's great, Jane thought. Whose *"excellent authority"* was that? she wondered. Claudia's daughter, Anna Maria? Jane hoped Anna Maria had never gone out with Lorenzo. Borrowing Anna Maria's clothes was one thing, borrowing one of her boyfriends was quite another!

Chapter Three

The Sicilian Amulet

Jane had trouble sleeping the night before her tryst with Prince Lorenzo Bighilaterra. Her mind was awhirl with fantasies, her body feverish. Sleep on the Rome-to-Palermo overnight train had been fitful, at best, but sleep this night was equally elusive. And she'd experienced that strange nightmare again. The dream from the train had returned, the lurid, terrifying, dream of drowning.

An excellent swimmer, Jane was unafraid of the water. She had been one of the mainstays of her high school swim team, the anchor for all their relay events. She couldn't figure it out. *Did I have too much of Baron Donzini's private stock last night?* she wondered. But, then again, that hadn't been a cause for the dream on the train.

What does a dream of drowning mean? She knew that a dream of falling meant sex; it would have been more logical, given the way her mind was going out of control these days, if she had only dreamed of falling.

Sex, yes, sex was definitely on her mind. But so was love. She felt light-headed—perhaps from eating so little from the Donzinis' bountiful table last night—but perhaps because she was falling in love. Jane had never been in love. She had no idea what it was like. *Did it feel anything like this?* she wondered. Did people fall in love so quickly? She did not really know this man at all.

Jane woke early. Lorenzo had told her he'd come by at

8 a.m. to pick her up. She breakfasted with Claudia on Donna Maria's excellent *caffé con latte* and sweet currant buns. Donna Maria, an old Donzini family servant, was the person responsible for last evening's marvelous repast.

Claudia, a woman of many talents, was hopeless in the kitchen. Evidently, Aldo had caught on quickly to this lack of culinary skill early in their marriage, and so Donna Maria had become part of their household. Jane thought it was fascinating that both her mother and Claudia were poor cooks; they were so unlike each other in so many other ways.

Lorenzo was extremely prompt. He pulled up in front of the apartment building at exactly 7:59 a.m. Jane was again garbed in Anna Maria's hand-me-downs. She suspected the clothes she'd been traveling in had been sent out by Claudia and Donna Maria to be laundered, or, possibly, burned. She was still concerned that Anna Maria Donzini had dated Prince Lorenzo. If she had, and Jane prayed fervently that she hadn't, Jane hoped he wouldn't recognize what she was wearing this morning: a white linen skirt, coming to just above the knee, and a bright orange silk short-sleeved blouse, loose and cool. According to Claudia, the day promised to be a scorcher, and she'd advised wearing natural fibers.

The prince was attired in navy blue linen trousers, the sharp seams crisply pressed. His starched white cotton shirt was open to mid-chest, revealing an intriguing bit of curly black hair that Jane was quick to note. Around his strong neck, the strength of which she also noted, there hung a fine, thin gold chain, from which dangled a most curious amulet.

In the car—he drove a sporty, bottle green late model Alfa Romeo—Jane asked him about the curious, gleaming amulet. He fingered the golden circle in his strong right hand, his left firmly on the steering wheel of the Alfa. She was fascinated by his hands, so strong, yet so sensitive. She turned her attention reluctantly away from an examination of his beautiful person to the story he was telling her.

"This," he told her, "is the *trinacria,* the symbol of the island of Sicily. The design is taken from a coin that was minted in the city of *Siracusa,* Syracuse to you, at the time of the Greeks, the era of *Magna Graecia.* You are familiar with that early period, as an art history student?"

"Yes," she answered. "I've studied the history of Sicily."

Growing up with a full-blooded Sicilian mother who was determined to hide her ethnicity by taking on the coloration of a full-blown New England WASP matron, Jane had secretly absorbed as much Sicilian history and lore as possible. In school, she had made a point of taking all the courses she could in ancient history, particularly Greek and Roman, and had studied Latin for four years in high school.

She had regretted not having the opportunity to take Greek. The Greeks had colonized Sicily, making it a part, an integral part, of *Magna Graecia,* or Greater Greece. They had flourished on the island, bringing their magnificent culture with them: art, agriculture, science, literature, music, and religion. In those ancient times, Sicily was a green, fertile, desirable island, strategically located for trading and commerce and abundant with prized agricultural produce. The gods had shed their grace on Sicily. Those indeed had been the golden days of the island's past.

The Carthaginians and the Greeks had fought over Sicily. Later, the Romans had conquered the Greeks and taken the island, absorbing it into their grand empire. Century after century, new waves of conquerors took up where the Greeks and the Romans had left off. The golden age had passed, but marking its passing were some of the world's finest remaining Greek temples, Roman ruins, Arab mosques, Norman churches, and, it went without saying, a genetically-mixed, diverse population.

Lorenzo nodded in approval at Jane's reply, continuing the story of the amulet. "My grandfather, Maurizio Bighilaterra, amassed a magnificent collection of classical antiquities, including Greek and Roman coins minted in Sicily. This particular coin from the ancient city of Siracusa was always his favorite, everyone in the family said. He had a famous goldsmith in Palermo make up reproductions in 22 karat gold for the other members of the family. When a child reached eighteen, he or she was to receive one of these amulets."

He signaled a left hand turn manually, sticking his arm out of the window, and continued. "I got this one twelve years ago and I wear it practically every day. Some, I was told, found their way into other hands—" here he paused, slanting a wide smile her way "—as tokens of love to beautiful women, we suspect. My grandfather's was not to be found at the time of his death. There were rumors that a lovely peasant from Borgetto, one of the small towns near here, got it in gratitude for an unforgettable night of love . . . but, you're blushing! I'm sorry, Jane." He had a bit of difficulty pronouncing her name. "Please forgive me. I did not mean to be coarse."

He placed his hand placatively over hers. Then he took the thick gold chain and passed it over his head, handing it and the amulet over to her so she could examine it more closely.

"Look at the design. It has a small central circle—the sun, perhaps? It's depicted with a smiling face. You see it? And three running legs, bent at the knees, Mercury-like wings at the heels, roughly forming the outline of the Sicilian coastline, a triangle, hence the *trinacria.* Highly unusual, no?"

Jane knew that Lorenzo had thought she had started to blush over his too-casual reference to a payment for a night of illicit lovemaking, but he was mistaken. What had startled her, so suddenly, was the name of that small town, *Borgetto.* That was the town her Grandmother Acquista, her mother's mother, had come from. Her maiden name had been Conigliaro.

What connection, if any, she was immediately consumed with curiosity to know, did the Bighilaterras have with that place, which had always been scathingly described to her by her mother, Joanna, as "a godforsaken little town full of Mafiosi." She bent her head to hide her confusion, pretending to look closely at the gold reproduction of the coin, her hair brushing her shoulders and covering her cheeks.

She marveled at the coin. "It doesn't seem so ancient, that's what's strange about it. It has a perky, contemporary look. It could have been designed yesterday! I've never seen an ancient coin like it. The ones I've seen are mostly profiles of emperors, depictions of animals, sheaves of grain, ordinary things of the period like that."

She turned it over. The initials MB were incised on its back.

"It was my father's; he was named Maurizio, like my grandfather."

Silently, Jane was pleased that Lorenzo had not been named after either his father or grandfather. She much preferred Lorenzo—Laurence—to Maurizio—Maurice.

He went on. "My parents died in an automobile accident in Switzerland when I was quite young. I never really knew them. I was too young to remember anything about them."

His hands tightened on the steering wheel.

Jane had noticed that he was an extremely careful driver, not prone to speeding, so unlike the majority of his countrymen. Did the memory of his parents' fatal accident haunt him? she wondered, feeling pity for his loss. Lorenzo Bighilaterra was an orphan. Prince or no, she suddenly felt acutely sorry for him.

"I was brought up by my mother's brother and his wife, the Strellis. My uncle is Luisa's father; we are first cousins, very close. I have the greatest love and respect for my uncle and aunt, but . . . don't misunderstand me, please . . . but, I have the deepest regret at having lost my mother and father. I never knew my grandfather, either. He died young."

He shook his head, the wiry black curls tumbling over his brow. "So much was lost . . . the continuity of the family was gone. It can never be replaced. Do you know what I'm trying to say?"

Jane did. She was touched by his story. She ventured to ask, "What kind of man was your grandfather? Do you know anything more about him?"

"Well, I think he must have had a good sense of humor, choosing that particular coin, but his life didn't turn out so well, you know? He and his wife didn't get on. It had been an arranged marriage. She was an heiress from Tuscany, but it was rumored that he had fallen in love with someone else, someone who'd left him and broke his heart."

He smiled tenderly at Jane. "Who knows? It could have been that peasant he gave his amulet to, if that story is at all true. At any rate, his sorrow dug deep, and he died a natural death, but far too young. My father never really knew him, just as I never really knew my father."

Jane touched his hand in sympathy. "I'm so sorry, Lorenzo. I couldn't imagine not knowing my grandparents

. . . or my parents." *Incredibly difficult though one of my parents can be,* she added silently to herself, thinking of her last telephone conversation with her mother.

Lorenzo took his eyes off the road for a few seconds and gave her a warm look. Impulsively, he said, "You are a very sweet young woman, Jane, and very lovely. Why don't you wear that amulet today? It would go nicely with your blouse."

Surprised, but pleased and touched, she looped the long chain over her head. "Thank you, Lorenzo," she told him.

As she passed the chain over her head, she felt an eerie tingle go through her body. Something more than a chain and amulet had just passed between her and Lorenzo, something linking them. *It's his long-dead grandfather's spirit,* Jane felt. Then the feeling went away, and she thought: *How silly! What could I have been thinking? What have I to do with his grandfather? It's just a piece of nice jewelry, that's all.*

Lorenzo frowned slightly, looking at the amulet nestled between Jane's breasts. "I think you would need a shorter chain . . . otherwise, it's perfect. Yes, it suits you. I like it. It looks as though you've always worn it. That's strange, isn't it?" He laughed, then seemed to shudder slightly, as if he were hit by a sudden chill breeze.

He continued to speak. "And, Jane, I have a favor to ask of you . . ."

Oh, dear, she thought, *what is coming now? What have I agreed to, symbolically, by wearing a piece of his jewelry? What local custom am I unaware of?* She was beginning to panic. But, no, it was all right. He was explaining himself.

"I'd like your permission to call you Gianna. I'm sorry, but I have a bit of trouble pronouncing your name." He laughed, trying to explain the problem to her. "You know that there is no J in the Italian language, and no way to pronounce H, either. Your name, both your names, actually, are difficult for me, despite all the years I spent in England speaking English. Do you mind?"

Jane thought he was incredibly charming. *Anything,* she thought, *you can call me anything you want, as long as, my dear, dear, Lorenzo, you continue to call me.* Aloud, she answered, "No, how could I mind? Gianna is a lovely name, and, yes, just forget the Holland part altogether!"

"A lovely name for a beautiful young woman," he added, looking straight ahead and watching the road, which the Alfa was now climbing. He shifted gear.

His clean, chiseled profile could very well have come from one of those Greek coins, and it was still, to her bedazzled senses, not unlike the classical head of Michelangelo's perfect statue of David. She was beginning to fantasize again, wondering if, in the nude, the rest of Lorenzo would match that perfect head, that perfect rear end, that extraordinary . . . Quickly, she checked herself. *I'm about to visit a cathedral,* she thought, *and these unbidden, lascivious thoughts are crowding my brain.*

What is wrong with you, Jane? she chastised herself. *But he called you beautiful,* a tiny, pleading voice inside her protested. Jane wondered if he really meant it. *He could be the kind of man to whom flattery comes as naturally as breathing,* she thought. He was a European male; she had no experience of his type, none at all. She was worried, tensing up. She knew she was ill equipped by both lack of sophistication and proper background to handle a man like Lorenzo. *I'm a baby, a mere infant, when it comes to a man like this,* she thought. *He is out of my very restricted, very narrow league.*

She sighed, fingering the carved gold amulet, feeling the incised initials, MB, on the flesh of her thumb.

"Thank you," she whispered, responding to his compliment. She saw him smile.

To hide her growing confusion, she took one of the trusty, well-read guidebooks from her backpack, which she had taken with her in the car, and began to read about the cathedral at Monreale. Aloud, she read, in English, "*Santa Maria la Nuova,* the most beautiful Norman church in Sicily and one of the architectural wonders of the Middle Ages, erected in 1172–76 by William II . . ."

Lorenzo looked over at her as he finished parking, pulling smartly on the safety brake. "You can put that Blue Guide away, *cara.* You're going to have the billion-lire Lorenzo Bighilaterra tour. I know the cathedral better than I know my own *palazzo* on the Via Loro."

Obediently, cowed by his air of authority, she shut the guidebook and packed it away. She removed an eyeglass case from the backpack and took out a pair of sunglasses. It was bright and hot in the cathedral precincts. The sun was already hinting at the kind of day that was ahead, a typical Sicilian summer scorcher.

Jane looked up at the imposing bulk of the cathedral. She knew and loved cathedrals, although she was hardly a regular church-going person. They represented to her an all-but-disappeared age of faith, a time when each and every Christian participated in the mysteries of God and religion, when the church calendar impinged on and was an essential part of one's daily life, and when the erection of a cathedral was the tangible expression of this ongoing, sincere, and vital faith.

The building of a cathedral had involved the whole of a medieval town or city. Indeed, as she knew had been the case at Monreale, the town had evolved around the building of the cathedral. No town had existed on this spot prior to the erection of the church.

And everyone around was part and parcel of its creation. The actual building of the edifice could encompass much more than a mere one or two generations. Those involved at the beginning might not necessarily live to see it completed. Their grandchildren might, but there was no guarantee of that, either. But there had never been any question, or so Jane had concluded from all her research and reading on the subject, that the cathedral would not be finished.

That central fact was at the heart of their faith. And so the architects, the masons, the carpenters, the artisans of all kinds, the workers in stained glass, the artists, the supporting services of farmers, butchers, bakers, seamstresses, candle-makers, coopers, wheelwrights, tavern keepers, the great mass and variety of humanity and skills, had all worked together to bring about this monument to the greater glory of God. Jane couldn't think of any modern endeavor that was even halfway up to these standards of cooperation. No, the age of cathedrals and unquestioning faith was, she thought sadly, long past.

Her bittersweet musings at an end, Jane turned to Lorenzo, who was also looking up at the cathedral. His eyes, she was surprised to see, were glistening. *You love this place,* she told him, silently. Her heart gave a little tug as he took her hand simply, without ceremony, and they went up the time-worn steps together and then through the great bronze entrance doors. Before they went in, he turned her about, a strong hand on each of her shoulders, to look at the cathedral square from the very top of the steps.

"Do you feel it?" he whispered. "Do you feel the presence of this place? Sense the holiness?"

She nodded, greatly moved. He squeezed her hand and she imagined rather suddenly that their souls fluttered towards each other, tentatively, shyly, meeting as if they had met once before in another time, but in this same place. *Jane, take hold of yourself,* she cautioned, shaken by the power, the strength, of the strange feeling. She shuddered as a chill breeze brushed her face.

Once inside the cathedral, Lorenzo became *il professore,* the learned lecturer, a docent to Jane's art history student. "These doors," he told her, "are attributed to da Pisa, and were completed in 1186." He stopped to dip two fingers in a basin of holy water and to make the sign of the cross. Jane followed suit, figuring, when in Rome, do as the Romans do, and when in Sicily, likewise.

She was stunned at the expanse of the interior. The exterior of Santa Maria la Nuova was rather plain, she knew, unornamented, typical of 12th century Norman churches. The inside, however, was breathtaking in its span—it seemed to go on forever. Lorenzo was informing her that the dimensions of the interior were one hundred meters by forty meters, leading her to a spot where she would have an unobstructed view of the nave.

There was gold and color everywhere. She was washed in gold from the glittering mosaics that showered their radiance upon her. She had to gasp in pure admiration. She remembered one afternoon two years ago in the early spring, at Vassar, when the Art Department had an elderly German gentleman, an expert in the mosaics of Monreale, present a slide show in one of the lecture halls. Those slides of the mosaics hadn't begun to prepare her for the actual sight of them. They were magnificent, almost unreal.

Lorenzo squeezed her hand again; she squeezed his back this time. Jane wondered what would have occurred if Lorenzo Bighilaterra, *il Principe,* had been the lecturer at school that day instead of that ancient, wizened German scholar? Would her fellow female art students have torn his clothes apart in a Dionysian frenzy, as if he were a Greek god come to life, or a rock star? He would surely have been a tempting morsel.

She concentrated on the mosaics on the south side of the nave, pushing her frivolous fantasy aside for the time being, taking note of the pillars, obviously of Roman origin, in that area. The mosaics there told the story of the Creation, then continued along the west side and also to the north with the teachings of Jesus and the ministries of Saint Peter and Saint Paul. Lorenzo was pointing all of this out to her as they walked slowly up the side aisle toward the choir.

In the apse was the glorious, sweeping figure of Christ in benediction, dominating all else. *"Christus Benedicens,"* Lorenzo whispered in awe. Below the Christ, the Madonna, all the saints, apostles, and angels filled in the rest of the space. It was overwhelming. Jane felt she had to sit down to take it all in, to absorb it more fully, to allow it to surround her. Lorenzo agreed, leaving her to sit quietly in a front pew while he went off to conduct his business with the chief restorer, who was working on a piece in one of the side chapels.

In a little while, she felt the urge to sketch, and took out the small drawing pad she always carried in her backpack and a box of charcoal pencils. She began to stroke in a few lines. *When I'm home in Boston again, or back at school, I'll have these sketches to remind me of this afternoon,* she told herself. *That's how I'll know it all really happened, that it wasn't a dream.*

Lorenzo had still not returned. She took her sketchpad and walked back to the slender Roman pillars she had noticed when they first came in. She was certain she could identify the goddesses on the capitals, and she felt like drawing them also. Yes, she was right: Ceres and Persephone, the Earth goddess and her lost child, the two gods most closely identified with Sicily, after, of course, the god Apollo.

When she had completed the sketch and looked back towards the pew, she saw that Lorenzo must have completed his business. He was now sitting quietly where she had been, leaning forward in the pew, elbows on knees, chin in hands, oblivious to the world, as if he were the only person in the cathedral. She almost hated to interrupt his reverie.

But he was eager to continue his lecture about the mosaics, which became very technical and almost too difficult for her to follow. He lapsed into Italian vocabulary with which she was for the most part unfamiliar, but the gist of what he was saying was that Monreale's mosaics were flowing, freer, less static than the norm in the Byzantine tradition of mosaic art. There was a richness and life about them, he said, that appealed directly to the observer. The artist, Lorenzo explained, spoke to the human beings coming after him through his great artistry and talent.

"Or *her* great artistry," Jane added, remembering that, while medieval artists were, by and large, anonymous, it was a known fact that there were a number of women among them. Lorenzo nodded in agreement. "You are absolutely right, *cara*." He seemed to look at her with approval again.

Before they left the church, Lorenzo pointed out "your English saint, Thomas Becket." There he was, that brave challenger of the rights of kings, far from home, in a Sicilian cathedral that was at once an amalgam of pagan, Christian, and oriental influences and styles. Yes, the great cathedral at Monreale seemed to say that Christianity at one time embraced the entire known world.

They left the incense-and-lily-scented nave and paid a small fee to enter the Treasury and go up the tower steps for a view Lorenzo insisted was not to be equaled. The morning was keeping its promise and was now much hotter, but there was a sweet-smelling, citrus-accented breeze on the roof. The gentle cooing of mourning doves could be heard, as well as the susurration of a large grove of date palm trees nearby as their drying fronds brushed against each other gently.

The view from the roof was laid out as if it were an architectural blueprint, with the 12th century Benedictine cloister spread out next door to the cathedral. The site nestled in the valley of the *Conca d'Oro,* or golden seashell, the mountainous sea-kissed coast that is northwestern Sicily. The brilliant sunshine overlay all, lighting the vista just as the gilded mosaics lit and dominated the church's interior. It was a stunning sight. Sicily was all golden sun, Jane thought.

Lorenzo couldn't take his eyes off Jane as she took in the vista. She had put her arms up to keep the long strands of her hair from blowing in her face. The breeze was strong as it beat against her curvaceous limbs. She was a sight to behold, he thought, with the wind whipping the silk blouse against her chest, outlining her magnificent breasts with his golden amulet swinging provocatively between them. Amazed, he thought, she is so natural, so unaware of the effect of her beauty, the wonder of her lithe body.

His eyes took in the beautiful sight, until, overcome, he could stand no more and acted instinctively, impulsively, perhaps not too wisely, as primal urges got the better of him.

⋆ ⋆ ⋆ ⋆ ⋆

Stifling a low groan, Lorenzo took her in his strong arms and kissed her, slowly and masterfully. She relaxed in his grip and succumbed to the moment, feeling the crispness of his chest hairs spiking through the fragile silk of her blouse. His powerful hands were all over her, in her mane of hair, on the small of her back, caressing her buttocks. She felt herself melting into him, their souls entwining just as their bodies were. He released her, looking deep into her eyes, stroking her flushed cheeks. She was mesmerized by him, by his passion, his intensity, his powerful presence.

He sighed, then whispered, "My angel, I've wanted to do this since the moment I saw you again at the Donzinis . . ."

She couldn't speak, not one word; she just looked up at him in wonder, then buried her hot face in the crook of his shoulder and neck. He kissed the top of her bare head, holding her tight against him. Her heart was beating erratically and her arms were wound around his waist. I'm in a dream, she thought wildly, an impossible, wonderful dream, at the top of a medieval tower, in the arms of a handsome prince.

The lyrics to the song Snow White sang in the first Disney film she'd ever seen came back to her, the promise that some day a prince would appear, the answer to her dreams . . . and now here he was, in the flesh, and here she was, in his arms. *None of this can be real, can it?* she wondered. *Any time now,* she thought, *I'll be waking up. But not too soon, please, not too soon.*

Lorenzo had tipped back her head, his strong hands framing her face, and was kissing her again. This was a more demanding kiss. Their mouths were open to each other, their tongues groping, frenzied, hot. Jane was moaning in pleasure; sounds she had never heard herself make before were coming from her throat. Lorenzo thrust a hand under her skirt, very lightly stroking the warm flesh between her legs. Fire burned her flesh.

She gasped, but didn't stop him. *Anything,* she thought wildly, completely out of control, *anything, you can do anything you want. Don't stop, my love, not now, not ever.* Her body was soft and yielding against his. She wanted this. But then the stiffness of his arousal against her belly set off a sudden, instinctive reaction of panic and she moved away from him, as if frightened by the reality of his need. Lorenzo hesitated as she recoiled in apparent alarm, then he removed his hand from the hot, moist place between her thighs. *Why had he stopped?* He pulled her skirt down and smoothed it over her body.

He looked into her eyes and then stroked the stray tendrils of hair back from her flushed face. "We should go now," he whispered, releasing her from his grasp. She nodded.

Hand in hand, they went down the stairs, back to the church. The still, dank air in the cathedral felt cool against her burning skin, cool after the searing episode between her and Lorenzo on the roof. Her thoughts were racing. She didn't know what to think.

Though his wandering hands had been extremely bold, surprising her, she had not wanted him to stop. *Why had he?* But her inexperienced body had betrayed her, turning away in alarm from his worldly, knowing caresses. It was her fault, she had led him on, but he was too much of a gentleman to force himself on her. Her face blazed. She felt like a fool, stupid and naive. She fingered the amulet nervously, hoping he would not think badly of her.

Lorenzo unlocked the doors of the Alfa. With foresight, he had parked it so it was under the shade of some cypress and blood-orange trees, but the interior was less than cool. He cautioned her to slide carefully onto the warmed leather upholstery. He said nothing else; he was strangely quiet.

"Are we going back to Palermo?" she asked, her voice near tears, breaking the silence.

"Is that what you want, Gianna?" His face looked pained. His voice was flat. He waited for her answer.

"No, Lorenzo," she shook her head, "that's not what I want." She looked at him boldly, hoping he understood what she felt.

Did he? His face relaxed and he dazzled her with his warm, wide smile. His voice was soft. "Actually, I would like to take you back to the place where we first saw each other . . ."

"Segesta?"

He nodded. "Yes, it's so close . . . and I want to see it with you. I had planned to go alone that day, but Luisa insisted on joining me for the ride." He made a sour face. "It was a disaster! My sophisticated little cousin is not one for ancient temple sites, as you can imagine. They bore her. So, except for my seeing you there, *cara,* the visit was spoiled. Your soul is like mine, I think. We react with our hearts to the same things, no?"

"Yes," she whispered, near tears with the strong emotions she was feeling for him, wanting to be back on that roof, in his arms, knowing she would not flinch from him this time, worrying that he would never lay those wonderful hands on her willing body again.

"Then, let's go! But, first, before you die of thirst, let me take you to a place I know, on the water. We can get something to eat, also."

Chapter Four

Return to Segesta

He drove west, then due north to the seashore. It was a modest fishing shack they pulled up to, the kind of place where she, her little sister and her parents would stop at on Cape Cod for plain boiled fresh lobsters, lobster rolls, and crabs, a place that was unpretentious, clean, inviting, the type of simple establishment that had been in abundance when Jane was growing up, before the proliferation of the golden arches everywhere in America. There was a strong salt smell in the air, underscored with the unmistakable, smoky aroma of fish cooking on an open grill. A number of small fishing boats were pulled up onto the white sand, cobweb-like string nets fluttering over their sides in the light breeze. Jane had the strong impulse to go running into the surf, as if she were a child again.

The proprietor, a thin middle-aged man with a much-lined face, was all smiles, despite his missing front teeth. He was wiping his large, calloused fisherman's hands on a clean white apron wrapped twice around his middle and he greeted Lorenzo warmly. They chatted amiably for a while, discussing the menu, then he disappeared into the fishing shack, coming back with two cold bottles of *acqua minerale* and two straws. He led them to a table in back of the shack—there were four small wooden tables set up for business—and then disappeared again inside the little house.

Jane leaned back in an old deck chair, feeling wood

splinters against her clothes. She breathed in the familiar tangy, salt sea air, running her fingers through her mass of long hair, shaking it out in the breeze.

Lorenzo smiled as he watched her. She had taken off her sandals and was wriggling her bare toes in the white sand. She was so natural, relaxed, no artifice at all. He relished the sight of her, wanting to enfold her in his arms again. But, no, it was too soon. She had been skittish with him, though she'd seemed to want his attentions.

Had he so badly misinterpreted her signals? Was he losing his touch? Now, that was alarming! *Or was she as inexperienced, as sexually naive, as her behavior implied?* He smiled inwardly. It had been a long time since he'd been with an inexperienced female. It was a refreshing change. The demanding, sexually predatory women in his set wearied him. Sex, money, status, that was all it was. Did anyone see him for himself? Had anyone ever seen him for himself? This American girl, what did she want from him? And what did he desire from her?

He spoke, "It's too hot to eat much, so I've just ordered *tutte pesce,* a sampling of the catch of the day. We'll try a little bit of several treats from the bounty of *mare nostrum,* our mother the sea. Is that all right with you, *cara?*"

Jane nodded. Another adventure. She had a feeling that, for the eventual lucky woman, life with Lorenzo would be a constant adventure, never dull. She wondered, idly, how come he was still a bachelor? *He* was the catch of the day, she sighed to herself, as far as she was concerned. No, he was the catch of her life. *I should be so lucky,* she thought. But she knew, all too well, that desirable men like Lorenzo, handsome, wealthy men with prestige and status, did not turn up every day in the lives of ordinary girls like her. Not outside of romance novels, anyway.

The owner brought out a crab salad, served in its shell, for them to pick at, then a plate of raw sea urchins with lemon. Jane, squeamish, made a face at the putrid-looking orangey-yellow goo that Lorenzo said was the urchin roe. She didn't want to taste it, but he laughed at her and insisted that she give it a try, holding the fork to her mouth as if he were the mommy and she the picky baby. It was delicious. *Why do I question him?* Jane wondered. He seemed to know what was good, even when it looked pretty bad.

A pancake-sized omelet of fried whitebait was next, crunchy and delicate, then *tuna carpaccio,* paper-thin raw slices of tuna swathed with lashings of fresh lemon. The meal ended with the sharing of a small grilled piece of icy-white swordfish, its surface crisscrossed with the hatch-marks of the hot grill rack. The meal was perfection: enough to satisfy any hunger pangs, not enough to overstuff one on a hot day. They finished their mineral water and took their leave. Lorenzo placed a hefty tip in the owner-chef's hand and thanked him for the excellent food. He smiled his gap-toothed smile and wished them both God-speed.

"I wasn't sure that fellow was still in business," Lorenzo commented as they got back into the Alfa. "My uncle used to take me and Luisa here when we were children. He remembered me from those days and asked me if you were Luisa."

"Luisa and I don't look at all alike. She's so blonde and beautiful," Jane protested.

"Sweet, silly girl." Lorenzo leaned forward and kissed her tenderly on the mouth. "Luisa is nothing compared to you, nothing."

Jane could taste the fresh fish and tangy lemon on Lorenzo's breath. She wondered if she had died and gone to heaven. Her lips tingled from his soft kiss. Miraculously, he didn't seem angry with her for her childish behavior at the cathedral.

They continued westward on the same road that had brought them to Monreale, climbing steadily as they drove. They passed by the turnoff for Partinico and went to the right after the sign for Calatafimi. A small hand-lettered placard on a pole pointed towards Segesta. The countryside was all hills, lovely and green, the ashy green of a dry landscape. She remembered it from the bus ride of two days ago. And there it was, in the distance, the abandoned temple, a ghostly white pile of stones shimmering in the torrid afternoon sun, capping the top of the highest hill for miles.

Rummaging in her backpack, she retrieved Margaret Guido's guide to Sicilian archaeological sites. Lorenzo gave her a short look, shook his head, and admonished her, "Gianna, I told you, you are with me. You don't need that." He chuckled.

Embarrassed at her gaffe, she put the guide away, taking out her sketchbook and pencil instead. The temple was getting closer. Now she saw it, now she didn't, as they proceeded up the narrow, winding road to the ancient site. Jane recollected how the bus from Palermo had lumbered coming up this hill, wheezing and groaning as if it would expire.

Jane was sketching furiously, the tip of her pink tongue between her teeth, concentrating on the sight ahead. Lorenzo knew immediately, instinctively, that she had drawn this way since she was a young child, filling drawing pad after drawing pad with small, complex sketches. He had been the same way; his notebooks of childhood drawings filled a shelf in his bedroom. He'd kept them, often thumbing through them, and he knew somehow that she'd kept hers, too. He smiled at her ferocious single-mindedness, silently comparing her behavior, so akin to his, to that of his spoiled cousin the other day.

Luisa had insisted he turn the radio on full blast to an Italian pop station as they drove to Segesta. Her eyes, behind the designer sunglasses she favored, were closed, her fingers snapping in time with her chewing gum to the blaring music. The ethereal temple site was really of no interest to her. She could have been anywhere for all that it mattered to her. Lorenzo could have throttled her. He found that he often had the urge to throttle her these days. If there were not the strong family bond between them, he was sure he would not have wasted a moment of his time in her company.

Lorenzo talked as Jane drew. "The great German poet Goethe wrote about Segesta, did you know that, *cara?* In his great book of Italian travels, it was. I came up here once by myself and saw an old German couple, dressed for strenuous hiking, each carrying a large staff, sitting on rocks next to the temple and reading Goethe in the original language. I thought that they must have been comparing his descriptions to what was here now. And they were probably surprised to find it hasn't changed much. I was rather impressed by their dedication. They had probably traversed, on foot, the very path he'd taken before this modern road was built. People walked up here or came by donkey from Calatafimi in those days. It must have been romantic, if rather long and tiring."

He had turned off into the parking lot for the site. They were alone except for one other car. The shimmering sun was high, too hot for most tourists, even those interested in romantic archaeological sites. Jane took her pad and pencil with her as she got out of the Alfa. They walked together towards a footpath that led up to the temple. It was lined, as if purposely landscaped that way, with a very large type of cactus or succulent plant.

Jane pointed to the silvery green vegetation—the plants were about three or four feet high and about half as wide. "What are these, Lorenzo?" she asked him.

"Aloe. You know, aloe vera plants. You have them in your country, I'm sure."

"Yes . . . but not so huge!" Jane was astonished. Back home in Newton, Massachusetts, her mother kept a small aloe vera plant in a pot on the kitchen windowsill. Aloe was a handy and excellent topical ointment for burns.

But these plants were monsters, Jane marveled, as she inspected them closely. "Oh, look!" she called to Lorenzo, pointing out scratches on the broad, fleshy, barbed leaves. Lovers had written their names on the plant surfaces: Paolo e Anna, Rosa e Salvatore, Tonio e Beatrice . . . *You can find graffiti everywhere,* she thought, bemused.

Lorenzo pointed out a sign nearby, in several languages, that warned of severe fines for anyone caught writing on the aloe. She was glad to be with a law-abiding gentleman, but she would have been thrilled to see him whip out a Swiss Army knife and inscribe "Gianna e Lorenzo" on a large succulent leaf. But he wasn't about to do it, not today. She sighed.

Lorenzo put his arm across her shoulder as they walked up the path towards the temple. He was in his professorial mode again, lecturing her about the site, about the tragic history of the city of Segesta.

"I've always thought this was such a beautiful, romantic, but ultimately very sad place. The setting, here on top of this hill, is exquisite, as are the settings of all the classical sites in Sicily, but the history of this place is terribly brutal."

They had reached the top of the hill. He stretched his arms out wide, encompassing what she could see of the entire site. "Three hundred meters above sea level, once home to thousands of souls, a particularly unlucky people."

They sat down on one of the large flat rocks facing the temple, gazing at its stony silence. Jane asked, "Is it true that it was deliberately left unfinished?"

Lorenzo nodded, not taking his eyes from the building. "Yes, the roof was never put on and the columns were left rough and unfluted, but the entablature and the pediments are intact. There are thirty-six columns. We think that the architect was an Athenian, but there is a good deal of mystery and speculation surrounding this place. Every classical scholar seems to have a theory. It does, of course, add to the mystery, to the aura of the site. Was it left unfinished on purpose? If so, why?"

As Lorenzo spoke, Jane sketched the outlines of the lonely Doric temple, once intended for worship, now open to the elements. She cocked her head to one side, asking him, "Who were the Segestans?"

Lorenzo smiled. "Actually, they were the Elmyians, a mixture, some think, of the Greeks and the Trojans. This was called Egesta then, around thc 12th century B.C. The Elmyians made a number of bad alliances—as I said, they were a particularly unlucky people. First, they sided with the Greeks, then with the Phoenicians, then with the Romans. All their switching back and forth marked them as untrustworthy, even traitorous. They were entirely destroyed in a horrific, bloody way by a despot named Agathocles around 330 B.C., and bands of marauders in the centuries that followed had a go, each in his own turn, at what was left. Even the Arabs vandalized the site. There's supposed to be a city buried under here, did you realize that?"

Jane shook her head. She was fascinated by the story of the unlucky city and its inhabitants. "No one has dug it up yet?" she asked him.

"Not yet. But the theatre was excavated. It's a bit of a walk . . . Let's go back to the car and drive there. That is, if you want to see it? It's another beautiful view, facing north, looking over the hills and the sea."

She was game. He held his hand out to her and helped her off the rock. She swayed towards him as he helped her up. She could feel the tips of her nipples brush his chest, and her breath caught in her throat, knowing he could not help but feel their hardness too. They paused, conscious again of the intense and natural pull of their bodies towards each other.

"Gianna," Lorenzo whispered.

"Yes?" she answered back. She could hardly breathe, with his nearness.

He moved away from her, picking up her sketchpad and pencil from the rock, holding them for her. He was trying to say something, something that was evidently not easy for him to say. "*Cara,* back at the cathedral . . . on the roof . . . that was inappropriate of me. If I offended you, I am truly sorry."

"You could never offend me, Lorenzo," she whispered, looking into his strained face. She reached up and kissed him lightly on the lips. He took her in his arms and held her for a little while. Then he let her go, and, holding hands, they made their way back to the car. It was as if a cloud had been lifted from his brow, and she was walking on air, her sandaled feet barely skimming the ground.

The theatre, a kilometer or so east and a little north on the temple, was on another hill, Monte Barbaro. The road that led to it was literally over the buried city, now almost forgotten, once home, as Lorenzo had put it, to "thousands of souls."

The semi-circular Greek-style amphitheatre was sixty-three meters in diameter with twenty rows of seats, according to Lorenzo. It looked out over a spectacular view of small, then larger, bare hills—once probably forested—and out to a blue expanse of water, the Gulf of Castellamare.

Lorenzo and Jane picked their way down the rows of broken seats, finally settling on a perfect place to enjoy the view.

Jane pulled out her drawing pad, while Lorenzo, to her left, assumed the stance he'd had in the nave at Santa Maria la Nuova; elbows on knees, chin cupped in his hands, seemingly hypnotized by the silent beauty of the view. *Is he imagining this place as it once used to be?* Jane wondered. *Has he become one of the audience, reacting to the colorfully-garbed players in their masks and costumes, hearing them once again reciting their rhymed lines in loud, confident voices, waiting expectantly for the appearance of the deus ex machina to solve all the problems of the mere humans strutting the stage?*

He stretched, sighed, and, leaning back on his elbows onto the grassy, rocky outcroppings, seemed to make a decision for both of them. "Gianna, *bella,* I have to get you something to drink before you perish from this heat. You must be thirsty—I know I am—come! There's a tourist *caffe* nearby." He pointed vaguely into the near distance. "Shall we get ourselves a bottle of cold *acqua minerale?*"

While Lorenzo ordered water for the two of them, Jane availed herself of the facilities. She looked with surprise and pleasure at the bright-faced young woman who stared back at her so boldly in the mirror of the restroom, a far cry, indeed, from the anxious little pinched face that had been hers in the mirror on the train. *Something wonderful has happened to me,* she rejoiced. *I've undergone a sea change!* Ever the pessimist, she wondered, *Will it last?*

At the table, as they shared a large bottle of icy cold San Pellegrino mineral water, Jane thanked Lorenzo for showing her such unforgettable places. "I will always remember today," she told him.

And not only Monreale and Segesta, or that quaint, tiny shack by the sea, but your mouth and arms as we clung together on the roof of the cathedral, with your hands touching my body in so many new and unexpected ways and setting it on fire . . . What she was thinking must somehow have transmitted itself to him. He took both her hands in his and kissed them, palms up. She shivered at the sensual sensation, her toes curling.

"Gianna," he whispered, "dine with me tonight. I want so much to take you to an elegant restaurant—to wine and dine you, as you Americans say—and to take you dancing. Do you dance, *cara?*" At her nod, he smiled, "Good! Then bring your dancing shoes, too. I want to give you a lovely evening."

Jane couldn't believe her ears. The idyll was not going to end, not yet. She hadn't bored him to tears and driven him away with her naivete, her lack of worldliness. *No, this suave, handsome, sophisticated young Sicilian aristocrat likes me,* she thought, *and he wants to be with me. Where has all this good fortune come from?* she asked herself, her heart beating wildly. *And, more important, when would it end?* What if it never ended? Could she dare hope? Was it the someday of Snow White's plaintive little song, and was this the prince who was meant for her? Across all of time and space, had she found him? Had he been looking for her, also? It was bizarre, but he was the soul mate she'd ached for all the years of her young life.

As if he could read her very innermost thoughts, he was now looking at her with those intense, bluer-than-blue eyes, locking glances with hers, saying, "I just can't let you go, now that we have found each other. It's so strange, *cara*." He laughed, shaking his head as if in wonderment. "But I feel that, somehow, I have known you before. In another life, perhaps?" Now his gentle smile was broad. "Do you believe in reincarnation, like the Hindus do?"

"You think we might have known each other . . . perhaps hundreds of years ago . . . as artisans, maybe, working on the mosaics of the Cathedral at Monreale?" She was playing this sweet game with him, enjoying every minute of it, every minute of his company. He had not let go of her hands.

"Yes." He nodded in agreement. "Or perhaps thousands of years ago. We could have been lovers in Egesta, Elymians, fleeing for our lives as the city was sacked. What do you think?" He was gripping her hands tightly, wondering what her response would be to his suggestive words.

She was flushing. *Lovers, he had said lovers* . . . Her voice was low as she answered him. "I don't know, Lorenzo, I don't know about those things. But I do know that—" she took a deep breath "—that I can't let you go, either." Her head was bent close to his as they sat together in the little *caffe*. They were both still, overwhelmed by an emotion neither of them had as yet named or acknowledged to the other. It was all happening very, very fast. *Too fast?*, she

wondered. She felt exhilaration mixed with fear.

Jane looked up and saw little beads of persp Lorenzo's smooth upper lip. She was seized by th reach out with her tongue and lick each drop slow the salt from his body, to suck it, draw it deepl To draw him deeply into her. It was very hot, and heavy, the sudden strong smell of citrus– ange, bergamot—and Mediterranean herbs—w mary?—surrounding them, becoming overwhel drug-like in intensity.

Ever so gently, Lorenzo leaned towards h her on the lips. She closed her eyes. He slowl from her, got up, and helped her to her feet. lire on the table and they walked back to the felt like rubber; if he had not been holding about the waist, she was sure she would ha

They were both silent on the short Palermo, to the Donzinis, but Lorenzo had hand. He helped her out of the car, gave h peck on the cheek, whispered, "*Ciao, bella* nine," and he was gone. The sleek little Al of dusty bottle green from their ride across went roaring down the Via Delle Alpi, inner city. Jane floated on a cloud of pure the flat.

Claudia was in her small, untidy study, back on her mop of gray blonde hair, page book in her hand. Blue pencils were scatt French baroque desk and a half-drunk c perched precariously on one of its curv

"Jane," she greeted her, "I didn't thi hours. Did you have a good time with

How could Jane even begin to tell h

ried. "I don't think I have ever had such a good time with nyone, Claudia." *Not in my whole entire uninteresting life,* ne thought. "And, later tonight, we're going out to dinner, nd maybe dancing."

Claudia was peering at Jane's face, her head tilted to one de. *Oh, Lord!* Jane panicked. *What does she see?* But no, laudia was not seeing into her heart.

"You've gotten a little bit of sunburn, do you realize at? Let's find some cream for that pretty skin. So, dinner d dancing, huh? Aren't you the lucky girl? My Anna aria would give up a year's allowance to share a paltry *ge-o* with Prince Lorenzo!" Claudia was bustling and fussing over Jane as she spoke.

Jane stopped her, reaching for her firm, plump hands. laudia, please, stop, just a minute. You have got to tell more about him. Everything. I want to know every-g."

Claudia seemed taken aback by the sudden seriousness er young houseguest's tone. "Oh, my dear, you're not ing all misty-eyed about our Prince, are you? Well, let's lown, then . . . But, first, let me get that face cream. have a complexion to die for, and we have to take care ." Off she sped in the direction of her daughter's bath-1.

ne sighed and sat down heavily on the blue velvet chair to Claudia's desk. Her mother's friend was soon back, ng creams. First, she creamed off the powder and er Jane had been wearing, wiping the residue with soft tissue. Then, she smoothed on a slightly tingling, ing green paste, instructing Jane to let it do its work hour or so before washing it off with cold water.

hat feels wonderful. What is it?" Jane asked. Claudia p the glass jar, turning it so that Jane could read the

label, which pictured a stylized drawing of a familiar-looking green plant. "Aloe Vera Cream . . . For Beautiful Complexions," Jane read, thinking, *What a small world! Here's aloe vera again.*

Claudia screwed the lids onto both jars of cream. Jane was at her immediately. "Now, about Lorenzo . . ."

"Oh, my, you are eager!" Claudia smiled. "Well, I told you, didn't I, that Aldo's family has known his for generations? No? Well, the Donzini land, their estates, were not far from each other. The Bighilaterras owned a good deal of property, property they have managed to retain over the years, good, agricultural land, near Montelepre, Bagheria, Borgetto, those areas . . ."

Engrossed in her story, Claudia had not noticed the startled look on Jane's face when she mentioned Borgetto. *That town again! It keeps coming up!* Jane pondered the thought, then put it out of her mind as she paid attention to what Claudia was saying about the Bighilaterras, Lorenzo's family.

"They are quite wealthy. Part of it, of course, is that they have always married well—"

Did Jane imagine that Claudia shot a meaningful glance at her here?

"—bringing more and more wealth into the family. One ancestor even married an Altavilla, and you just don't get any higher in Sicilian society, my dear, that's the old Norman aristocracy! Lorenzo has inherited it all, as sole heir, the Montelepre estate and lands, the gorgeous 18th century *palazzo* in town, hundreds of years of accumulated furniture, paintings, jewelry, his grandfather's priceless collection of Greek and Roman antiquities . . ."

She stopped, glancing Jane's way again, her attention riveted by the amulet and chain gleaming on the girl's chest. "Hello . . . what's this?" she questioned her, as she leaned forward and took the *trinacria* in hand, examining it closely.

Jane had completely forgotten about the amulet. "Oh, it's Lorenzo's," she explained. "He wanted me to wear it today. I forgot to return it to him. He said it was some kind of family heirloom, belonging to his father . . . or his grandfather . . . I forget who. It's really unusual, isn't it? And beautiful."

Claudia nodded. "Yes, the Bighilaterras have a lot of pretty baubles. This is very fine, heavy, old gold, Jane." She was intrigued.

"So . . . Lorenzo is very rich." Jane was eager to get her back on the track. "Is he a playboy?"

Claudia shook her head vigorously. "No, he's a fine young man—serious, decent, intelligent, a strong sense of family—*not* a playboy. He does, however, spend too much time with his cousin Luisa's crowd, a bunch of spoiled and bratty jetsetters, in my opinion, with no ambition and fewer brains, but I think that's because he feels he has to keep an eye on that flighty young woman. They are first cousins, you know. Lorenzo was raised by her parents, so they are as close as brother and sister. What did you think of her, Jane?"

Jane pictured that incredibly beautiful young woman, the tawny mane of hair, the big brown eyes, flawless skin, little bit of a tip-tilted nose, that enviably slim and gorgeous body. Luisa Strelli was the kind of woman who gave other women inferiority complexes. Too beautiful, too perfect . . . well, maybe not *that* perfect! "She's gorgeous, no doubt about it, but a little dim, maybe?" Jane ventured.

"A *lot* dim, I think," Claudia agreed. "I'm sure that's why Lorenzo worries about her. She seems to lack judgment, taking up with an odd assortment of men. I guess that by spending so much time with her crowd, Lorenzo is protecting her, in his way, but the poor boy must be bored to death by those rather simple-minded rich kids!"

Jane was touched by Lorenzo's concern for his cousin. "I think it's wonderful, though, that he cares so much about her. I've never met anyone who is so caring like that, so sensitive."

"Well, my dear, I've always had a soft spot in my heart for the boy. That's why it gets me so upset when I hear . . ." Claudia stopped in mid-sentence. It was clear she had started to say something she now wished she hadn't.

"When you hear *what,* Claudia?" Jane wasn't going to let her get away that fast.

Claudia looked weary all of a sudden. The corners of her mouth drooped. "When I hear gossip, stories about him that he doesn't deserve."

If this scene had been a comic strip, a cartoon, right about now a light bulb would be going on directly over her head, Jane thought. "When I asked you yesterday if he was gay," she persisted, "and you answered that you had it on excellent authority, you said, that he wasn't, whose authority was that, Claudia?"

"Jane, I had no business making that comment; it was buying into a nasty piece of gossip about Lorenzo. It's just that . . . well, it struck me as such a funny question then . . . with what's being said about him." She seemed truly embarrassed now, as if sorry she had gone so far.

Jane prodded her, gently. "You are going to have to tell me all of it, Claudia. I have to know, I really have to—"

"Look, Jane, Lorenzo's name is always being coupled with a young woman's. They throw themselves at him, my dear. There are a lot of disgruntled young females around who, finding that they can't get anywhere with him, perhaps get even, in a way, by spreading rumors that have no basis in fact. The latest to come out of the rumor mill is that his most recent girlfriend had to go to Switzerland for an abortion. The story was that he got her pregnant but refused to marry her." Claudia's blue eyes were troubled, her voice low.

"Do you believe it?" Jane had to know the worst.

Claudia was adamant. "No, I do not! I just don't think he's the sort of man who gets involved in such a situation. He's not cold-hearted, nor is he stupid. And I don't, for a minute, believe the girl who is spreading the rumor. She's a complete ninny. Lorenzo would never have had anything like that to do with her. If she went to Switzerland at all, she went for the parties and the skiing, not for an abortion."

"Who told you the story, Claudia?"

"Anna Maria. She got it from a friend of the girl's, supposedly. And here I am, repeating it to you, even though I say I don't believe it!" She shook her head at her own folly.

"But there have always been all kinds of stories about Lorenzo and women. He does break a lot of hearts. Is that what you are trying to tell me?"

Claudia put a hand on Jane's shoulder, kneading it gently. "Yes, dear, he is a heart-breaker. I have to admit that. He's a lovely young man, I do like him, but don't let him break *your* heart, Jane. Go out with him, have fun, amuse yourself, give yourself some nice memories to take back to Boston with you, but guard your heart, my dear. Guard your heart."

Jane nodded. Claudia was very kind and had spoken to her like a concerned, caring mother, she knew that. *You're supposed to warn me about the Big Bad Wolf, Mommy, but none of it matters, not now, not any more. You're warning me not to fall in love with the prince, but it's too late, can't you see?*

Aloud, Jane said, "I think I'll go rest up now. It's been a busy day and I have a big date tonight. I'll see you later, Claudia . . . and thank you for what you told me. I do appreciate it."

Claudia looked as though she was not at all happy with what she had felt it was necessary to tell Jane. The look on her face seemed to say that being a mother was never easy. She bit her lower lip and nodded, adding, "Jane, do you want anything to eat before your nap? Donna Maria made some excellent asparagus frittatas for lunch."

"No, Claudia, thanks." Jane's voice was slightly muffled, coming from Anna Maria's bedroom. "I have to leave room for that excellent dinner Lorenzo promised me tonight."

As the bedroom door shut, Claudia remembered that she had forgotten to tell Jane that she'd spoken to her mother Joanna earlier. Oh, well, Claudia thought, no sense ruining her afternoon. Joanna had been quite disagreeable, insisting that Claudia tell Jane to cut her holiday short.

But Claudia had decided to let Jane enjoy the time with Lorenzo. The girl didn't need to have to put up with her mother's nonsense, her nonsensical ranting and raving. Let Jane have some good memories of her stay in Sicily. She was a sensible girl. She'd take precautions. And Lorenzo, whatever his faults, could be counted on to show a girl a good time. He was a prince of a guy, Claudia thought.

Chapter Five

Dancing in the Dark

Jane napped well. No wet nightmares of churning water disturbed her sleep. Despite the turmoil in her mind and heart, it was the first real, solid rest she'd had since Rome. Poor Claudia! The dear woman had tried to be tactful, but she had been overly delicate in her terminology.

"Guard your heart, Jane," she'd told her. Guard your heart . . . quite a euphemism for warning her not to jump into bed with Prince Lorenzo Bighilaterra, as so many young women, to their eventual disillusionment, evidently had. *Is she that delicate, that oblique, when she gives advice to her daughters?* Jane wondered sleepily, before falling off.

A sharp knock on the bedroom door woke Jane up at six p.m. It was Claudia, calling "Don't sleep your enchanted evening away!" Jane jumped out from under the cool white damask sheets, grabbed Anna Maria's silk bathrobe, and made for the bathroom.

In addition to jasmine-scented ovals of hand-milled soap and shampoo, there was foaming jasmine bubble bath. Jane reveled in the sweet, slightly decadent fragrance and soaked in her bath until the water had turned cool and her skin was in danger of shriveling. She rinsed out her hair with the shower attachment and conditioned it with a colorless, odorless cream. She felt splendidly cossetted and refreshed, ready for anything. Ready for Lorenzo.

Was Lorenzo bathing now? Shaving? Brushing his hair?

Her blood warmed as she imagined these intimate activities . . . and his naked body. She wanted to scrub that strong back, those . . . *Oh, dear.* Claudia, she thought, had good reasons to worry about her. Jane was not doing a good job at all of guarding her heart, her feelings. In fact, she was failing miserably.

She left the bathroom steamy with jasmine scent. Her long hair was turbaned in a soft, fluffy towel, her body draped in an enormous bath wrap of puckered white cotton.

Claudia was systematically going through the clothes in Anna Maria's marvelous closets, not unlike a saleswoman at Lord & Taylor, one of Jane's favorite department stores in Boston, looking for *"the"* dress for one of her best customers. "There you are, dear. I was just wondering which of these would be most elegant—and flattering—for tonight. How do you feel about chiffon?"

Jane felt just fine about chiffon. The particular creation Claudia was holding up for her approval seemed to be a bit daring for what Jane knew of Anna Maria. It was a creamy light pink, the color of a seashell's interior as it changes from deepest rose to whitest white. The style was reminiscent of a Greek toga in the way the bodice crossed over the breasts. And it reminded Jane of something else.

Yes, it looked like the dress that Marilyn Monroe wore in the movie *The Seven Year Itch,* the one that whirled so daringly about her bare legs and showed too much white panty when she stood over that subway grating. The crossed bodice dipped low, the skirt just capped the knee. Dreamy-eyed, Jane held the dress against her and looked into the floor-length mirror set in the bedroom doorway, imagining herself as the blonde sex symbol.

Claudia was being extremely generous. In addition to the dress, she loaned Jane some of her own good jewelry:

pearl drop earrings and a matching short necklace. Their slight pinkish cast complimented the cocktail dress. And, lo and behold! From the deepest recesses of her daughter's closet, Claudia fished out a pair of pink leather high heels, delicate, sandal-like, with criss-crossed straps, completing the ancient Greek fashion statement. Jane was overwhelmed. She felt like a princess.

And the prince was due to arrive at any moment. Someday, as in Snow White's plaintive song, had indeed come for Jane Holland.

At exactly 8:58 p.m., Lorenzo's shiny, divested-of-dust, bottle green Alfa Romeo was at the curb. Claudia and Aldo wished the young couple a good evening, and they were off. Both the Donzinis seemed to be taken with how handsome Jane and Lorenzo looked together. Aldo commented to his wife that they seemed *"made for each other."* Claudia had to agree, while still worried for Jane in her heart.

Lorenzo opened the door of the Alfa for Jane, whispering, "*Ecco bella* . . . behold beauty . . . you look incredible tonight." Jane felt the warm blood flood her capillaries, causing her sensitive skin to redden in a blush.

"I'm so glad you think so," Jane whispered back into his ear, her lips gently brushing his skin. Lorenzo thought her lips were as soft as he imagined the wings of angels to be. He gently passed a finger down her cheek, feeling its warmth. He was a very lucky man tonight. He cautioned himself to bide his time with the shy young American, though his blood was already hot for her and he wondered how good his self-control actually was.

Women had come and gone in his life, most with few regrets, but this one . . . He had not expected this gift. It was eerie. He did not know yet how it would end, but

Jane Holland was becoming an interesting diversion, if not more.

Jane thought Lorenzo looked incredible. He was wearing a tuxedo. Yes, she knew for a fact that most men looked wonderful in tuxedos—even the principal of her old high school, all 350 pounds of him, on her high school prom night—but Lorenzo was resplendent. She was convinced, however, that it was no contest. Lorenzo looked better than most men to begin with.

And his eyes! Tonight his eyes seemed to her the color of the blue so favored by Renaissance painters, the shade they achieved by grinding lapis lazuli to make it into a pigment. Such a deep, yet bright, blue. She loved his eyes. If eyes were truly "the mirrors of the soul," what a magnificent soul Prince Lorenzo must have.

She spoke. "Where are we going? Is it a surprise?" She saw that they were heading west out of the city again.

"A restaurant on the sea, in Mondello Lido. *Il Golfo di Palermo*. I hope you will like it. There's a nightclub nearby, where we can go to dance, if you feel like doing that."

He downshifted and she saw the road sign indicating Mondello Lido. They took the street marked Via Piano di Gallo and drew up at the seaside restaurant.

It was a spectacular night. A bright golden moon hung over the dark water, its light shimmering and dancing on the gentle shush of the waves washing onto the beach. A long pier extended into the gulf, culminating in a restaurant upthrust on strong wooden columns and festooned with tiny white lights. Bold black calligraphy spelled out the name: Gabbiano.

They walked across the wooden pier bathed in cool moonlight. The night was scented with the ubiquitous floral aroma of night-blooming jasmine, the scent of the soaps and perfumes favored by Anna Maria. Jane thought: *This evening smells like me.*

She felt very much at one with the environment. So far, she was pleased to discover, nothing Sicilian was at all strange to her. *It was almost,* she thought in wonder, *as if she had been here before.* When? In her dreams? In a past life? *Weird!* Her sensitivity to her surroundings amazed her and puzzled her, too. What of a past life? Could such a thing be possible? Was Lorenzo's little joke about reincarnation perhaps not so silly after all?

At Gabbiano, the restaurant, she saw that Lorenzo seemed to be suppressing a smile as he saw with what eagerness Jane was attacking her food. She was embarrassed when she realized he was looking at her, an amused look on his face.

She felt she had to explain. "Lorenzo, I haven't eaten for days. I usually don't eat like this, but there was no food at all on the overnight train from Rome to Palermo—although the booking agent had assured me the opposite—and I've had nothing much to eat at the Donzinis . . . and . . ."

Lorenzo, sensing her embarrassment, laid a finger gently over her protesting lips. "Quiet, *bella,* eat all you want to! I find your gusto, how shall I say it . . . adorable." *And I would love,* he thought, *to swallow you up just as you are swallowing up this food.* He thought her positively delicious, a confection in that creamy pink dress. The phrase "good enough to eat," or its Italian equivalent, flitted across his mind. "Buon appetito, *cara,*" he toasted her, chuckling.

In short order, he saw her go through a tray of assorted *antipasti,* olives, celery hearts, *caponata,* then a *primo piatto* of angel hair pasta in a light cream sauce, a *secundo piatto* of hare roasted with olive oil and sprigs of fresh rosemary and thyme, *carciofi alla Romagna,* a salad of mixed baby field greens dressed with balsamic vinegar, a champagne sorbet and half of Lorenzo's dessert, a *tiramisu.* He shook his head in wonder.

Accompanying the meal he had chosen, with the assistance of the wine steward, a very dry white wine, a full-bodied red, and a fine, sweet Marsala. All of the wines he picked, he informed Jane, were Sicilian-grown-and-bottled.

Still determined to tease her about her hearty appetite, he asked, innocently, "And, Gianna, do you eat in your dreams, too?"

She looked perplexed. What a strange question, she thought. Dreams, again. *No, my dreams have all been of falling or drowning these days,* she said to herself. She would have preferred, she thought, dreams of eating. But, no, according to Lorenzo, dreams of eating were not necessarily good dreams to have.

"I had a nursemaid when I was a child," he said, "a simple village girl who put me to sleep with folktales, tales learned, I'm sure, at her grandmother's knee, cautionary tales, as most folktales are. Before going to bed, she always warned me not to eat anything in my dreams, not even if tempted. It would be bad luck, she said."

A slight chill went through Jane's body. When she was a little girl, she remembered, her nonna, her Grandmother Acquista, nee Conigliaro, had told her the same thing. *I believe that I am, indeed, of this island,* Jane thought, fascinated. But she kept her thoughts to herself. She had still not told Lorenzo her mother's forbears were Sicilian and from this very place.

No, Lorenzo still did not know her heritage, had no inkling that she was part Sicilian. For all he knew, she was just another eager young American student of art who had learned Italian in college. Why was she doing this? To appear more exotic to him, perhaps? To be more interesting, say, than a girl like Anna Maria Donzini, who, like Jane, was also of half-Sicilian parentage? She really didn't know.

"Now," Lorenzo went on, slipping into his professorial persona, instructing her. "I think I have figured it out, this caution against eating in one's dreams, and it is particularly Sicilian. Are you familiar with the myth of the Earth goddess, Ceres, and her daughter, Persephone?"

Jane nodded. She knew that the English word cereal was derived from Ceres. She was the goddess responsible for the Earth's growing things, its vegetation. When Ceres's young daughter, Persephone, was abducted by Hades, god of the underworld, Ceres, in pain and grief, neglected her duties, and, as a result, the earth lay barren.

Alarmed, the god Zeus prevailed upon Hades to bring the girl back to her mother. Hades agreed, but, because Persephone had made the mistake of eating six pomegranate seeds while in the underworld, she was condemned to spend half the year underground in Hades, half above ground on Earth. That was the neat explanation of the ancients for the phenomenon of the seasons. When Persephone was above ground with her mother, Ceres was happy and the earth bloomed. When she was forced to go underground with Hades, Ceres was in despair, vegetation died off, and the earth cycled into the cold barrenness of the winter season.

"Well," Lorenzo continued, "it came to me one day when I was at the reputed site of Persephone's abduction by Hades. It's supposed to be at Lake Perugusa, near Enna. I thought the ancients most probably equated sleep with death—the loss of consciousness. If you eat in your dreams, you're doomed to Hell, the underworld, as poor Persephone was. No more for you the rainbow-colored wildflowers of the open fields and deep green forests, but, rather, pallid meadows of asphodel forever. A grim and effective image, no? So, little one, *guardate!* Watch yourself. Confine your robust appetite to the waking hours." He laughed, signaling the waiter for the bill.

"I'll take your advice, *professore,*" Jane retorted. "And I do thank you for a lovely meal! I have to say," she continued, "that the past, and, truly, the mythological past, still lives on in Sicily. Segesta and all the other ancient ruins serve as effective reminders."

"How true, *cara.* We Sicilians seem doomed never to forget our past, that's for sure. Well, as long as we have futures, it may not matter so much, I think."

Playfully, he stroked her neck, his long, sensitive fingers working his way up to her earlobe and caressing it. She luxuriated in his touch, half-closing her eyes, tempted to purr like a contented kitten. They looked at each other fondly for a few seconds, and then he swept her up, his eyes shining, "Now, let us go dancing!"

The nightclub, La Torre, was only a short walk from Gabbiano, on the same street. Jane strolled at Lorenzo's side. Despite the good meal she had packed away, she felt as light, she thought, as a feather. The filmy chiffon pleats of her dress floated around her bare knees with each step she took.

The club was half-full. It was almost eleven o'clock, mid-week, evidently not a big night for nightclubbing in the environs of Palermo. They chose a table on the outdoor pavilion, not far from the small bandstand and convenient to the dance floor.

And what was the band playing as they entered the club? A medley of Frank Sinatra's greatest hits. Old Blue Eyes was popular in Sicily, Jane guessed, and the music suddenly reminded her of home. Her sister was a big Sinatra fan, while her mother, typically, had no use for him.

Jane was not surprised that Lorenzo was a fabulous dancer. *What didn't this man do well?* she wondered. Jane loved dancing, but, because of her height, had found few satisfying partners. Lorenzo, topping her by at least three inches, was just right for a dancing partner.

And he led firmly. Jane knew she had an annoying habit of trying to lead; no chance of that with Lorenzo at the helm. What she lacked in grace he made up for with his technical skill. She thought that they were not exactly Fred and Ginger, the two of them, but okay, definitely okay.

They danced to everything. Jane was surprised to learn she could do the mambo, the tango, the cha-cha, and the waltz. Her specialty was a fast jitterbug or lindy, followed by the fox trot, and they did those, too. It was exhilarating and great fun. She had not enjoyed herself like this in a very long time. It was going to be difficult to say goodbye to Lorenzo when the time came because, with him, all seemed possible, all seemed marvelous.

At half-past midnight they were outside, moving dreamily to the beat of the 1940s Glenn Miller classic, "Moonlight Serenade," arms around each other's necks, her cheek against his chin, swaying closely in time to the sweet music. They'd had little to drink. A second round of cocktails sat untouched at their table. The sweet intoxication was with each other.

"Gianna?" It was a question, softly uttered against her smooth cheek.

Her answer was ready, given without hesitation, "Yes."

All this dancing, she knew, was but a vertical prelude to a horizontal desire. She'd heard that somewhere. Well, getting horizontal with Lorenzo was what she wanted now, both wanted and feared, but wanted much more than feared.

She took off her dancing shoes as they left the nightclub and walked on the cool bare sands of the beach, back to the car. The gritty crunchiness of the sand was not an unpleasant sensation. Jane had no idea of where they would be heading next, but it didn't matter. Nothing mattered to her now but being with him.

Lorenzo followed the sea road north, in the direction of Capo Gallo. They were past the little town of Mondello and soon in Capo Gallo, where he parked the Alfa in a cul-de-sac next to a secluded wooded area. Lorenzo removed a blanket from the trunk and they made their way down to the deserted beach. There were no signs of human habitation. On the near slope of Monte Gallo, Jane saw what appeared to be a crumbling medieval ruin, some sort of watchtower.

Shoes in her left hand, her right arm about Lorenzo's waist, she walked with him down to the water's edge. Lorenzo carefully spread the blanket on the sands and took off his tuxedo jacket. Jane placed her shoes next to it. He undid his tie. They sat side by side on the blanket, arms wrapped around each other, and gazed at the golden gleaming moon.

Jane was reminded of a film she'd seen before leaving the States, an Italian film that was a series of vignettes about the effect of the moon on human beings. In one of the episodes, a young man who was unwittingly exposed to too much moonlight when he was a child is condemned to be powerless when the moon is full. He has to instruct his young bride to lock her door against him on the evenings of the full moon, to keep him outside while he goes mad, moon mad. Jane asked Lorenzo if he had seen the film. He nodded.

"The husband was a werewolf, no?" he asked.

"Maybe just moonstruck, what we call *loony* at home. Some people think that the moon can make them do strange things, turn them into lunatics, so to speak," Jane explained. She was a moonchild herself, she realized, born under the sign of Cancer. Would tonight's magical moon have a strange effect on her?

"There is a thing I would like to do tonight, *bella,* and it is not so very strange," he whispered, lifting the hair from the back of her neck, stroking her neck with his strong fingers, kissing her where her neck met her shoulders. "You are so beautiful," he told her, as she sighed with pleasure at his deft and knowing touch.

Tenderly, he pulled down the bodice of her dress. She shivered slightly, bare-breasted in the cool lemon light of the watching Sicilian moon.

"Are you cold?" he asked her.

She shook her head. She couldn't speak, not a word. A tense excitement ran through and took control of her body, paralyzing her vocal cords. Lorenzo put his head down to her quivering breasts, sucking gently on her nipples, which had become erect, sensitive to each gentle flick of his moist and expert tongue. Her belly tightened. She felt the juices running between her thighs. Emotions she couldn't name had completely overtaken her. She was losing control.

No one had ever done to her what he was doing now, what she wanted him to keep doing. She put her hands to his head, running her fingers through his hair, grasping the curls tightly in her excitement. Small cries of animal pleasure escaped from between her lips.

He was lowering her back against the blanket, covering her with his body, kissing her with passion on her neck, her face, and on her mouth. A mouth that was sweet, yielding, and open to his probing, knowing tongue. He tasted her lips, her teeth, her tongue, so eager now for his.

Lorenzo wanted to claim her entirely as his own, from her sweet eager mouth to those heavenly firm and thrusting breasts, to that secret throbbing place between her thighs that he longed to explore with his insistent manhood, which was engorging rapidly as his burning flesh responded to hers. There had been many women, but never such an immediacy of desire, such a flashing, searing, intensity of passion so quickly. He wanted her now as he could not remember, could not imagine, wanting anyone else.

He was overcome by desire. There were no words for what he was feeling as his body eased itself into hers.

Jane clung to Lorenzo, about to lose all control, swept away in a flood of emotions utterly foreign to her. There was nothing to guide her through this passage. She felt the iron hard evidence of his desire for her, huge, pulsing, demanding, between her parted legs. She froze.

Lorenzo stopped, concerned. Leaning on his elbows, he looked down into her face, asking, "*Que suceso, bella?* What is wrong, dearest?"

Jane could only shake her head. She burst into tears, mortified, not knowing what was happening to her.

Lorenzo tenderly pulled the dress over her exposed breasts, covering her. He took a large white linen handkerchief out of his pants pocket and slowly mopped the tears on her face. "It's all right," he consoled her, "don't be upset. Nothing is going to happen that you do not want to happen, also."

But she *had* wanted it to happen—or thought she did. *What is wrong with me? What am I scared of?* Jane asked herself silently, weeping into Lorenzo's handkerchief. She blotted the tears on her cheeks, ashamed of her childish outburst. He was never going to have anything to do with her again. She had frozen twice with him, first on the cathedral roof and now here on this beach. She was an idiot; she didn't deserve his attention, his lovemaking.

"I'm sorry, Lorenzo. I don't know why this is happening. I feel so . . . so stupid . . ." She wadded up the handkerchief and gave it back to him.

Lorenzo folded the wet piece of cloth carefully and put it away in the pocket of his tuxedo jacket. He addressed her in a soft voice, trying to soothe her, not sure why she had rejected his intimate caress, wondering anew at her sexual experience or lack thereof, wondering if she was frigid.

"Gianna, believe me, it's all right. Look, I'll take you back to Palermo now. Tomorrow, maybe we can talk about this . . . now, you are too upset. I care for you very much, but perhaps this is all too fast for you. I'm so sorry, I did not know you weren't ready for . . . Gianna, look at me, don't be ashamed, please, *cara* . . ."

He didn't know what to say. If she was frigid, there was not much he could do. If she was inexperienced, he could learn to go slower, until she was ready to make love with no fear.

He'd put his hand under her chin, tilting it towards him, framing her flushed, wet face tenderly. She could see that the concern in his face was unfeigned; it was sincere, tender. *He cares for me,* Jane thought, *he really does, and I . . . I am just a big baby. I don't want to go back to Palermo. I want to be here with him, all night, under this loving moon. Oh, Lorenzo, I won't be scared any more,* she promised herself through her fears, desperate not to lose him.

"I care for you, Lorenzo, and I don't want to go back to Palermo. I want to stay here, with you. It's just that . . . that I've never," she stammered.

She was a virgin! Now it all made sense to him.

Before she had a chance to finish her confession, his mouth was on hers again, soft and undemanding. Lorenzo made up his mind that he would go as slowly as he had to in order to quiet her fears. He traced her lips with his tongue, then released her, assuring her that he wouldn't hurt her, that she only had to tell him when to stop, and he'd stop.

"We will—as you Americans say—play by your rules, *cara.* Is that all right? Will you be all right? I'm not going to force you. Do you trust me?"

She nodded. And then, surprising herself even more than she surprised him, she stood up and slipped off Anna Maria's dress and Anna Maria's lace underpants. She handed Claudia's pearl earrings and necklace to him and asked him to put them in the pocket of his tuxedo jacket. Then she was ready for him, only him, on that blanket, on that beach, under that all-seeing moon.

Lorenzo was flabbergasted. This shy virgin! He was prepared to soothe her, calm her down, keep his hands above her neck if need be, and then take her back to the Donzinis, none the worse for wear to her virtue. She had surprised him totally. But the night could still be a disaster if he wasn't careful, if he didn't proceed slowly.

As he stripped off his clothes, to join her on the blanket, he thought: *this, Lorenzo, will be the ultimate test of your skill as a lover, this skittish virgin who seems to want you, despite her trepidation, so very, very much.*

He wanted her, too, never so much as right now, as she lay there magnificent in her nakedness, her pale skin radiant in the moon's luminescence, her long legs slightly parted and raised, at the same time revealing and concealing her sex, her slender arms outstretched to him, ready to enfold him onto herself, to take him to her with—and he was suddenly very sure of this, humbled and profoundly moved by the depth of her feelings—with great passion and love.

"Gianna, there is no one, there has never been anyone, as beautiful as you, *carissima,*" he whispered as he gently and slowly lowered himself onto her waiting body. He felt her slight tremble as his skin met hers, and he paused to take the next cue from her, his sweet virgin love. She arched her back, raising her hips slightly to meet his body more closely, not fearful now, wanting him so much, yielding, yielding. Becoming one. Their souls locked.

As they had before.

High above the reunited lovers, the benign moon looked down.

Chapter Six

Promises and Lies

Jane awoke late the next morning to the sound of shouting voices. It took her a minute or two to remember where she was and just exactly who she was.

Her name was Jane Holland, she was twenty years old, twenty-one in a matter of days, and in the Palermo flat of her mother's best friend, Claudia Streatham Donzini. Last night had been the most memorable of her life. Magical. Unreal. She was madly, wildly, totally in love. With Lorenzo Bighilaterra. Her prince.

Her subconscious, virginal fear that penetration would be painful had been groundless. She'd felt no hurt, no pain, just the power of their mutual need. She had been transported into the exquisite realm of the senses, her very nerve ends afire, acutely sensitive to the needs of her body and mind, wanting only to satisfy her desires again and again. None of the books she'd read, none of the experiences related by her more worldly friends, had prepared her for this, for what had happened between her and Lorenzo.

Their bodies had moved to a secret rhythm and nothing they did with or to each other was alien. It was as if, she thought with wonder, two missing parts of a long-lost puzzle had come together again. She didn't have the words to describe their lovemaking. It was in another dimension, beyond words, a dimension dominated by the five senses. She'd flowed into him, tasting, touching, feeling, inhaling

. . . And she had not wanted it to stop.

But they had to stop. Lorenzo wanted to take her back to his palazzo, to tuck her into his bed, keep her with him forever, but reality intruded, and he realized that the Donzinis expected him to bring Jane back. They'd set no curfew, she'd been given her own keys to the apartment building and their flat, but it had been clearly understood that she would be returning. Lorenzo did not want to alienate his good family friends. They would meet the next evening. They had so much to talk about, so many plans to make together.

Jane remembered it had been impossible to say goodnight to him. They had clung together in his sports car for a good hour on the Via Delle Alpi as dawn broke. Finally, Lorenzo had taken the first step, escorting her to the door of the building, kissing her goodnight once more, repeating the name of the bar in the city where they would meet. From there, he planned to take her to his Via Loro *palazzo,* to cook her a meal, a meal he would take great pains to prepare, one she'd never forget. He was planning to satisfy all of her appetites, he teased, chucking her under the chin. And then he was gone.

So much, she thought, for guarding her heart. That heart was now his, his heart hers. She had no doubt that he cared for her as deeply as she cared for him. *It's happened,* she told herself. *This is the reason I came here, why I was drawn so mysteriously to Sicily. It was fate.* She hadn't fought it; she'd gone with the flow, and this was the sweet, sweet result. Now that they had found each other, she would never leave him. She knew in her heart that he would never leave her. She felt it with every sensitive fiber of her being.

Her tender musings were interrupted again by shouting voices. She paid closer attention. Those voices were raised in anger. What was going on? It was Claudia and a younger voice . . . Anna Maria? *Had she returned?* How could she scream at her mother that way? Jane wondered, alarmed at the high decibel count of that shrill, uncontrolled voice.

Jane scooped Anna Maria's filmy pink chiffon dress from the floor where she had so carelessly tossed it and hung it hurriedly on a padded hanger, smoothing down the wrinkled pleats. She shook the evening sandals over a wastebasket, loosening the last few grains of sand from the beach, and inserted them into a shoetree. Claudia's jewelry was on the dresser, in good condition, all the pink pearls glossy and intact. Next to the pearls was a small, velvet-encased jewelry box.

Lorenzo had given it to her when they parted last night, a surprise gift. It was a thick gold chain to wear with his *trinacria* amulet. He wanted her to have the amulet, to wear it for the duration of her stay in Sicily, but to exchange this shorter chain for his. She had been deeply moved by the gesture, knowing how much the amulet meant to him. He told her it would bring her good luck, as it had brought him good luck, meeting her. It took just a minute to substitute the gold chains. She tucked his chain in her change purse, to return to him that night. Her heart beat wildly against her ribs in the excitement of knowing she'd be with him again soon. *Life,* she thought, *was so very, very good!*

She'd almost forgotten Anna Maria's underpants! There they were, on the dresser. She'd never borrowed anyone else's underwear, being a fastidious young person, but she'd felt that the occasion last night had deserved better than Lollipops, that American brand of plain white cotton she was used to wearing. No, she had needed lace, Anna Maria's sexy lace bikini briefs. Now she couldn't give them back. They'd been used and bore physical traces of last night. She would wash the delicate lace in cold water and mild soap and she'd keep them as a memento. She would buy the girl a new pair of fancy panties.

Hurriedly, she threw Anna Maria's silk paisley bathrobe on over her nakedness and slunk quietly to the closest bathroom to wash her face. She picked up a bottle of mouthwash and quickly rinsed out her mouth with the mint-flavored liquid. She pulled her hair back it into a make-do ponytail. She was now prepared to check out the battling Donzinis. She had a sinking feeling that she knew what they were arguing about: *her*.

The fighting seemed to have ceased. Aldo Donzini had gotten between Claudia and Anna Maria and was admonishing his daughter severely. Although he struck her as a big, gentle teddy bear of a man, Aldo was not, Jane thought, someone to be trifled with. Anna Maria's face was sulky, stormy; Claudia's was red, angry.

"And that is no way, *cara mia,* to talk to your mother!" Jane heard Aldo saying in a firm voice as she came into the bright kitchen. "You apologize right now, *questo momento,* is that clear? Or you go to your room for the rest of the day and do your sulking in there. Make your choice!"

Anna Maria was hardly cowed; she was having none of it. "And how, Papa, can I go to my room? You have put that *Americana* in there! Mama has allowed her the run of my closets."

"Stop it, Anna Maria, stop it right now!" This was Claudia speaking, the angriest Claudia that Jane had ever seen. She couldn't help thinking that if Anna Maria had had the law laid down to her years ago, put over a pair of parental knees (perhaps both pairs of knees), she wouldn't be such a brat today. For the girl was behaving like a total little brat.

Aldo was thoroughly pissed off, Jane saw, and looked as though he was about to take his daughter by the shoulders and give her a good shake. Then Anna Maria spotted Jane and lunged right at her, almost knocking her down. She was clawing at the paisley bathrobe on Jane's back.

"That's mine! How dare you!" she screamed, tearing open the bathrobe, embarrassing Aldo with a flash of Jane's naked white thigh. At this juncture, Claudia hauled off and struck her daughter. The force of the slap resounded in the big kitchen, echoing off the white walls. Anna Maria collapsed heavily on the blue slate floor in a spate of loud, angry tears, kicking her heels against the slate.

Claudia reached over and retied the silk robe around Jane's waist, smiling, seeming her old placid self again, asking, "Jane, dear, did you have a good time last night?" It was just as if things were normal, this totally manic morning in the Donzini household. And, suddenly, they were . . . normal, that is. The air had been cleared.

While Jane apologized profusely and sincerely to Anna Maria for causing her unhappiness over the use of her wardrobe, Aldo announced that he was driving to Alcamo for the peace and quiet of the vineyards. He would spend the day quietly, watching the grapes grow. He kissed his wife goodbye, gave Jane an affectionate, fatherly pat on the cheek, pointedly ignored his daughter, and was out the door. Claudia, now serene as ever, bustled about making a pot of fresh filtered coffee.

Jane mollified Anna Maria by insisting on taking her shopping to replace the underwear she had borrowed, and to buy herself a robe so that Anna Maria could have hers back. Evidently, the disputed robe was a much-prized Liberty of London print, something Anna Maria never allowed anyone else—even her two sisters—to borrow. Jane couldn't quite understand that, she and her sister Jenny always traded off clothes, but she nodded as if she understood completely.

While Anna Maria went off to wash her tear-stained face and to change her clothes—she had only arrived an hour or so earlier from Selinunte, where she had been camping at the site of the temple grounds with friends—Claudia discussed Jane's date with the prince. Jane told her only what she felt was prudent for her to know. The rest she locked up in her heart. Claudia admitted that she'd had no idea when Jane had returned; she and Aldo had slept quite soundly through the night knowing that Jane was in good hands.

Jane marveled at how Claudia and she got on so wonderfully together while her own mother and she were always at odds. She pondered if indeed there really had been a mix-up at the hospital, as Claudia had teased earlier, and that Claudia was her biological mother, and Joanna was Anna Maria's. *No, there's not that much fairness and justice in the world,* she concluded.

Anna Maria rejoined them, her sullen face still a little puffy, a red mark on her cheek where she had been so roundly slapped. She was wearing American jeans and a tee shirt of the singer George Michael. Jane saw that the girl was really into teen pop culture and all set to go shopping in downtown Palermo.

Jane studied Anna Maria's face closely. She was not an unattractive girl, but her face seemed to be set in a permanent sullen pout. It occurred to Jane that the argument this morning might have been compounded by the fact that Anna Maria had been told that Jane had been out with Lorenzo. *Jealousy?* It was a possibility. Jane would have to watch her step with Anna Maria. The girl was dangerous, a mischief-maker and spreader of nasty gossip. She decided she would be nice to Anna Maria, but cautious around her. *Very cautious.*

Jane dressed in jeans, too, and a silent white tee shirt, speaking for no one, an advertisement for nothing. She and Claudia's daughter would shop and have lunch downtown. It was just after the noon hour. Jane remembered, also, that she had a tentative date to go boutique shopping with Luisa Strelli the next day. *What a waste,* she thought, *to be with these two vastly uninteresting women when I could be with Lorenzo instead.*

She didn't have all that much time left in Sicily. The most she could get away with—if her mother didn't make too much of a fuss—was drawing it out to two more weeks, but that was pushing it. She had to get back to Boston, look for a job in what was left of the summer, and try to make some spending money to get her through the winter term at Vassar.

She realized, with a start, that she was not looking forward to going back to school, she who had always loved school so much, who hadn't shed one tear her first day of kindergarten. *She wanted to stay in Palermo.* There was too much, all of a sudden, to think about. It had hit her suddenly, taking her by surprise, but she knew she was hopelessly in love. Last night had changed her life completely. *What did the Italians call it? Un culpo di fulmine,* a bolt of lightning. That was exactly what it was, how it felt.

Anna Maria and Jane took a cab to Palermo's main shopping drag, Corso Vittorio Emmanuele. Their first stop was a fancy lingerie boutique, where Jane replaced Anna Maria's lace bikini briefs with a much more expensive pair. Anna Maria was delighted. Jane also bought more underwear for herself. The Lollipops days were over. She was going to get used to lace, lace and silk. Lorenzo was worth it, she decided, and so was she!

She also purchased a plain white cotton robe to use for the rest of her stay with the Donzinis. Peace with Anna Maria was accomplished. Yes, buying things for the brat definitely put her in a much better humor, and when Jane said she would treat her to lunch, Anna Maria accepted with alacrity and even a smile.

They went to an outdoor *caffe* on the Cortile Santa Caterina and ordered pizza and Diet Cokes, the food and soft drink of choice, Jane noted, of Palermo's young idle set, many of whom were lounging at the marble-topped bistro tables in no hurry to go anywhere or to do anything. Jane meanwhile was counting the hours until she saw Lorenzo once more, blissfully playing over and over again in her mind's eye the incredible lovemaking of the night before. She sighed audibly.

Anna Maria scowled. She brought up the subject, unbidden by Jane, of the prince. She was brutally direct. "You know, *cara,* Prince Lorenzo Bighilaterra has an extremely bad reputation. He is a womanizer. My mother was very wrong not to have warned you, not to have kept you from going out with him."

"She did warn me, Anna Maria. Look, I like him. He's a charming, considerate man. We are enjoying each other's company." *And he's my lover, you little brat, and I hate to hear you talk about him, so can it!* Jane wished she could add aloud. It bothered her to hear his name being uttered by this surly adolescent.

Anna Maria waved away Jane's defense of Lorenzo. Her voice was heavy with disdain. "Listen, Jane, my mother likes him because he pays her a lot of attention, comes to her parties, kisses her hands, gives her compliments. She has no idea, none, of what he is really like! I thought he was nice once, too. I would even have gone out with him."

Fat chance, Jane muttered under her breath.

"Did you say something, Jane? Well, as I was saying, I had my eyes opened. He is not at all to be trusted. He enjoys breaking girls' hearts."

"Oh, come on, Anna Maria!" Jane was really getting angry. "Idle gossip is dangerous and hurtful. You can't do that, destroy reputations on the basis of lies, half-truths, innuendo." Jane was not about to let Anna Maria go on in this annoying vein. She was going to shut her up once and for all.

Jane winced as Anna Maria raised her voice. "You and my parents . . . you are all the same! My mother shuts her eyes to all of Prince Lorenzo's scandalous love affairs, my father to the Bighilaterras and their dealings with the Mafia."

What was this? What on earth was the girl nattering on about now? Jane was suddenly hooked, despite herself. The Mafia and the Bighilaterras?

"What are you talking about, Anna Maria?" Jane challenged her.

Anna Maria looked smug. "His grandfather . . . everybody knows the story . . . he was shot in a Mafia territorial war. Their properties are in the heart of Mafia country here. Borgetto, Montelepre, Partinico, Bagheria . . . the Bighilaterras have always been hand-in-glove with the Mafiosi, since the end of the 19th century. But, no, my father, he insists it can't be so.

"Why? Because the Bighilaterras are aristocrats, related to the cream of Sicilian society, very rich, own so much property, have such nice manners? You are all such dupes. And *you,* the only reason he's after you is because you are American, new in town. You're the flavor of the week, Jane, that's all. When you leave, there'll be someone else. There always is. You're no different from all the others he has duped and dumped."

She was vicious, but Jane, though her ears burned and she would gladly have strangled Anna Maria right there, over her cheese and anchovy pizza and Diet Coke, let her prattle on. She refused to believe Lorenzo was a womanizer. A man had to care very much, she was sure, to make the kind of tender, gentle love he had made to her. It couldn't be pretense, it couldn't be faked. No, she wouldn't, couldn't believe that! She trusted him with all her heart and mind and soul. But the Mafia thing . . . Jane made up her mind to ask Aldo about that. She didn't like the sound of that, not at all, and she wanted to know more about it, to set her mind at ease.

Not wanting to listen to Anna Maria any more, shutting her ears to the venom spewing from her mouth, letting the girl blather on, Jane cast her eyes over the midday crowd in the street as she sipped at her ice-cold Coke. A familiar-looking car drew up to the curb alongside the outdoor *caffe,* right in front of the fancy-looking restaurant with the elegant awning that she and Anna Maria had walked by before, the Conca d'Oro. It was a shiny bottle green sports car, an Alfa Romeo. Jane's heart stopped. She knew that car. She knew that driver, too. Or thought she did.

It was Lorenzo.

Lorenzo . . . Lorenzo, her love. *With a woman.* A small, slender, very blonde, beautifully groomed older woman. She was in the front seat with him, laughing, possessively caressing his upper thigh in a languid, practiced manner. She kissed him full on the mouth and got out of the car. On the sidewalk, she half-leaned back into the window of the Alfa and called out, clearly, unmistakably, *"Ciao, bellissimo, a domani!"*

Lorenzo blew a kiss to her, a big smile on his face, and started up the engine. The roar of the Alfa's powerful motor thundered in Jane's skull, a death-knell blasting her to pieces. The woman turned and entered the restaurant. She was elegant, beautiful, a socialite, clearly on intimate terms with Lorenzo. Too intimate. *Too, too intimate.*

Anna Maria was sulking. "You're not listening to me, Jane!"

Jane wanted to shake her, to scream at her to shut up. *Shut up, you brat, shut up!*

I've just died, have some respect for the dead, Jane wailed to herself as her world fell apart. *This can't be happening,* she thought, *not now, not like this,* as she put her hands over her face and wept her heart out, the sobs coming up from some wet, hidden place deep inside her.

Anna Maria blanched, thinking she had possibly gone too far in her vituperation. "I'm sorry, Jane," she apologized, contrite. "What did I say? Please don't cry! Everyone is looking at us! This is embarrassing! Please, please, stop!"

Jane stopped crying and wiped her eyes with her hands. She pushed away her lunch. How could she eat? Anna Maria, hating to see good food she was not paying for go to waste, finished off everything. She was now more than eager to placate Jane, however, worried and knowing full well that her mother would whale the tar out of her if she saw Jane upset. Jane's uncontrollable sudden outburst of tears seemed to have completely unnerved Anna Maria.

"Do you want to go back home to the Via Delle Alpi?" Anna Maria asked in a plaintive voice, licking pizza crumbs off her greasy fingers.

Jane nodded. Palermo had suddenly become too small. She had to get away. Some swift decisions had to be made. She picked up her packages as Anna Maria hailed a taxicab.

Claudia was not at home. Anna Maria, who had been extremely nervous in the cab, breathed a sigh of relief at her mother's absence. Jane quickly packed the few belongings she had into her backpack and duffle bag. Taking one last glance around the bedroom, she spotted Lorenzo's golden amulet and its new chain on the dresser. I should leave Claudia a note, asking her to get them back to him, she thought. Then another idea crossed her mind. Yes, she told herself, it would be tit for tat.

Lorenzo had said that his grandfather had parted with his *trinacria* amulet in exchange for an unforgettable night of love with a peasant woman from Borgetto. *Would it not be fitting,* she thought, grimly, *if I, the descendant of peasants from Borgetto, kept it in exchange for last night's lovemaking?* Yes, she decided, it would be most appropriate. She hooked the chain around her neck and tucked the amulet under her tee shirt. She scribbled a short note to Claudia, leaving it with his old gold chain, which she removed from her change purse. *There,* she thought, *it's done. It's over.*

Anna Maria was worried. "You can't leave without telling Mama. She'll be angry with me. She'll think it was because of something I did, something I said."

Clearly, Anna Maria was aware of how well her mother did know her, Jane thought, listening to her whining. The little brat *had* said too much, but that wasn't why Jane was leaving Palermo. She was pleased, though, to see the little creep sweating it out, stewing in her own evil juices. Jane was feeling mean. And betrayed.

Lorenzo had betrayed her. With another woman. *An older woman.* It was all so decadent, so European; older women, younger men, like the racy novels by Colette Jane had once read. Now it made her sick to her stomach. She had seen a woman whom she believed had to be Lorenzo's mistress, seen her touch him intimately, kiss him. Jane had to put it all out of her mind or she'd go mad.

Claudia had been right, she realized, and so had the unpleasant Anna Maria. Jane was just another in what was evidently an unending line of easy conquests for the Prince, of women who had fallen for his good looks, his charm, his sexy voice, yes, even his artistic sensitivity. *I'm just another bimbo,* she agonized. *There is nothing special about me. As Anna Maria put it to her so meanly, I'm simply the flavor of the week for* il principe, *and the week is coming to an end.*

No, she thought, it hadn't taken all that much to nail her, and she had gone to her own sacrifice with quite a good deal of enthusiasm. A little art history talk, some delicious food, limpid, caring looks, talented kissing, exquisite lovemaking. Why was she such a fool? She had known, from the first, that she was way out of her league, unprepared for a first sexual experience with a man like that, a man who had obviously experienced all there was to sample.

She never really knew him, she realized, too late. That was the truth, and it hurt. It was all a girlish dream of love and romance. She hurt. She hurt badly. But the last thing she was going to do, so help her, she promised herself, was to cry one more tear over this stupid mistake, the worst of her life.

Jane could not bear right now to be in the same city with him, to know he was nearby. She was aware, knowing herself and the depth of her feeling for him, that his sweet talk could possibly ensnare her again. She could not afford to take the chance of it happening. She had to forget it, all of it, fast. In the best American tradition, she had to make a quick getaway.

"*Escolta,* Anna Maria, listen," she ordered the girl, back in control of her own destiny now, determined to rise above this setback. "I'm going to go to Borgetto, to visit my grandmother's people. I'll be back in a couple of days. Just tell your mother that something came up, that I had to change my plans, okay? And, if Lorenzo calls here, and you had better get this straight, understand? If he calls, you tell him I've gone back to the U.S. Don't you dare, and I mean this, don't you *dare* tell him I went to Borgetto. Do you get it?"

Anna Maria nodded soberly.

Jane said, "Now, this is very, very important to me, so repeat it. What is it I want you to say?"

"Tell my mother you've gone to Borgetto. If Lorenzo calls, that you've gone back home. Listen, Jane, Mama is not going to like that. She is a very truthful person."

It was clear that Jane had scared Anna Maria, first by breaking down in public and now by assuming this commanding persona who was giving her strict orders that she wanted followed to the letter. Anna Maria looked miserable.

"Good," Jane said. "Now one more thing, and please leave your mother up to me. I'll explain everything to her as soon as I can, I promise. You can assure her of that. Now, listen again, in the off chance, the extremely slight chance, that my mother calls from home, do *not* tell her I've gone to Borgetto. Say I'm taking a few days and traveling around Sicily by myself. Do you understand that?" It was extremely unlikely, Jane was certain, that her mother would call, but she wanted to take no chances.

Anna Maria looked confused, but she nodded in agreement. At this stage, Jane thought, she would agree to anything, just so Jane left, fast, before Claudia returned home. She was worried, wondering how smart Anna Maria was. *For sure,* Jane thought, *if she screws this up, I will personally come back and kill her with my own two hands.* But what else could she do? Jane had no choice but to depend on the girl—as unreliable as she appeared to be—to carry her messages.

"Now," she continued, shouldering her bags, "tell me where to get the bus that will take me to Borgetto."

Chapter Seven

Borgetto

The small, rickety green bus dropped a weary Jane off at the junction of Route Four and the outskirts of Partinico. Borgetto lay straight ahead in the late afternoon haze, a couple of miles up the hill on the rural road. The white-washed buildings of the town shimmered under the merciless rays of the hot sun, but the day was drawing to a close and evening would bring cool breezes.

Jane hoisted her duffle bag over one shoulder, adjusted her sunglasses, and made her way, with great curiosity, to the place of her ancestry. Borgetto—it literally translated into "small town"—clever, pithy, Jane thought—clung to the side of Monte Crucificio. The once-deep forest that had buffered Borgetto from the bigger town of Partinico had long since disappeared. Only a few deciduous trees remained, their long-gone fellows having fuelled the energy need of the region's peasants these last fifty or more years.

Jane's *nonna,* Benedetta Acquista, nee Conigliaro, had told her about the forest. The forest was why *nonna* had never gone to high school, which was in the larger town; she'd been afraid to have to traverse it twice a day. Her parents, who could use her labor at home, didn't push her to go to school when she balked. *She should see the forest now,* Jane thought. *Hah! Try and see it, rather!*

All Jane had to go on to locate *Nonna*'s Conigliaro relatives—*Nonno* and the Acquista side came from the other side of the island—were addresses she half-remembered from her grandmother's big black address book. As a child, on vacation in New York City's lower east side, she had amused herself by browsing through this book and asking *Nonna* questions about all the relatives still in Sicily. The strange names had fascinated her. They were people whom she'd been sure she'd never meet, would never know, yet they shared the same blood, the same ancestors, the same genes and DNA.

Maybe, she pondered, as she trudged up the dusty road, shifting her duffle from one shoulder to the other, *this is why I came to Sicily, not Lorenzo. Maybe my real fate is to meet all these people, to get to know family I would never otherwise know.* People that, if her mother Joanna had her way, she would never know.

Yes, angering her mother by coming to Sicily was one thing, but visiting Borgetto was even worse. When she had called Joanna, her mother had made it clear she was not to get it into her head to visit her Sicilian relatives in Borgetto. She had come right out and said that, characterizing them all as "lowlifes." *My mother is a snob,* Jane realized. *She can't stand being the child of immigrant peasants. She pretends to be what she is not, moving far away from her family, refusing to visit Sicily, trying to forbid me to do so.* It was all so stupid, Jane thought.

Her dad's family had been peasants too, when they'd arrived at Plymouth Rock. What set them apart from her mother's family was that they had come to America in the 1600s, and that they'd spoken English when they came. None of them had to go to night school to learn the language. *Big deal,* Jane thought, *big, stupid deal!*

She was suddenly very angry with her mother, with her rigid attitudes, her narrow-mindedness. With a start, she realized that she had never been so critical of her mother before. *Yes, Jane,* she told herself, *you've changed on this trip, you have truly changed.* Perhaps some terrible things had happened to her, but maybe she was finally growing up, and that was a good thing. It had had to happen someday.

As her sneakers scuffed the rock-strewn path into Borgetto, Jane's thoughts turned again to Lorenzo. In a few hours he would be at the Grand Albergo Hotel bar, not far from his *palazzo* on the Via Loro, wondering where she was. Lorenzo, always so prompt. How long, she wondered, would he wait for her? Would he become alarmed? Would he telephone the Donzinis? What would Claudia tell him? The worst part of this awful scenario was that Claudia was going to be really angry at Jane.

She should have had the courage to telephone Lorenzo herself before she left and broken the date. She hated him for what he had done to her, his awful betrayal of her innocent love, but she'd known she couldn't speak to him. She'd be putty, she knew, in his hands . . . those wonderful, strong yet sensitive hands. *Oh, God,* she prayed, *make me forget him, please!* To harden her heart against him, she envisioned him meeting a blonde bimbo—preferably American—at the Hotel Albergo Bar and inviting her to his *palazzo* in Jane's stead.

Yes, someone else he could seduce easily, with his looks and charm, just another exotic flavor of the week, and then he'd laugh about it with his older mistress. Yes, that's how it would go. Jane knew she was perilously close to tears again; she would have to put him out of her mind.

She had arrived at the Borgetto town limits. A stray, dun-colored dog, its poor ribs showing, came out of an alleyway to sniff her. She stroked its head and walked on, reaching the deserted town square, empty save for a solitary water tap at a dilapidated fountain trickling precious drops into the dusty street. She looked around her.

A rusted sign affixed to a stone building pointed her to the street she was seeking: Corso Roma, the street on which her grandmother's younger sister, Maria Modica, lived. Aunt Maria was supposed to own a general store-cum-outdoor-*caffe*. It shouldn't, Jane thought, looking about her, be hard to find. Nothing in this two-bit town could be very hard to find!

The Caffe Roma, dingy, small, a sorry excuse for an outdoor *caffe,* was at Numero Sei Corso Roma. Behind the bar, at a shiny brass espresso machine was a slim, rather dark-complexioned young woman. *She has to be my cousin Ninfina, Maria's only child,* Jane thought. The young woman peered in Jane's direction as she approached the *caffe*.

Jane had the eerie feeling she was the sole visitor to Borgetto in years. Not exactly one of your big tourist spots, she grimaced, glancing around her at the tired-looking two-story houses, all badly in need of fresh whitewash. As Jane's little sister might have said, it was Nowheresville.

Jane pushed her sunglasses up over her forehead, and smiled at her cousin. *"Buon giorno, Ninfina. Sono la tua cugina, Gianna. Parla Inglese?"*

Jane's slow, deliberately phrased Italian got through to the girl. She smiled back sweetly, showing tiny white teeth. *"Non parlo Inglese . . . mai lei capisco."* She came out from behind the counter and embraced Jane warmly. Jane thought it was like embracing a bird, all bones, not much flesh. She had always thought of herself as relatively slim, but, compared to Ninfina, she stocked considerably more in the flesh department.

The girl gestured Jane to a seat at one of the tables.

"Grazie," Jane responded, remembering her manners. Ninfina ran back to the bar, and parted a hanging curtain made up of jet-black and multi-colored beads. *"Mama!"* she called out, *"E Gianna. Venga! Venga subito!"*

A widow woman dressed entirely in black shuffled out to the bar. In addition to a shapeless black cotton shift and black hose rolled just beneath her bony, jutting knees, she wore scuffed, worn at the toe, black cloth slippers. No jewelry. Her two front teeth were missing and her unkempt white hair was dry and brittle, framing a deeply tanned, deeply wrinkled face. *But what a face!* Jane was stunned. The woman was beautiful.

Her eyes were a clear, unnatural-looking green, the color of the sea foam in Botticelli's "The Birth Of Venus." Her nose was straight and chiseled, her cheekbones high, sharp, and commanding. Jane thought: *she looks like no one in my mother's family in New York, but she does look . . . how strange . . . a little like me.* Jane's eyes were hazel, a very light brown, her nose straight, and her cheekbones also high. *Maybe we're both throwbacks,* Jane thought, *reminders and remainders of the many conquerors who raped and pillaged Sicily and its people through the ages.*

Aunt Maria smiled a smile of great sweetness at Jane. She seemed truly happy to see her. Both she and Ninfina fussed over her in the style of Claudia Donzini. They brought her strong, dark espresso in a tiny white china cup, marzipan cookies, fresh, plump, sugary figs from their garden. Their clucking and bustling caused neighbors up and down the Corso Roma to draw aside their curtains and stare, unabashedly, at the sneakered, blue-jeaned, tee-shirted, tall American girl, who was not a little embarrassed and red-faced from all the loving attention.

They managed to converse, after a fashion. Jane realized

that her relatives' English was nil, zero, non-existent. She suspected that there hadn't been anyone around Borgetto speaking English in a very long time, if ever. Talk about backwaters! Jane thought, recalling the Italians, yes, even Sicilians, she'd run into these last two weeks who could all manage *some* English if pressed to do so. Jane tried to enunciate her Italian clearly, using Sicilian words when she remembered them. A skeletal vocabulary was coming back to her, to make things easier.

As a rule of thumb, Jane had learned, Sicilian was like Italian except for a specialized vocabulary drawing on words from Arabic, Greek, French, and Spanish, and for quirks such as "l" becoming "d"—the word *bella* becomes *bedda*—and the use of the ubiquitous pronoun, "u", instead of the more precise male and female pronouns. But Maria and Ninfina's accent was *Nonna*'s, as familiar to Jane as her grandmother's dear face, so she really did not miss too much of what they were saying, and she was focusing on her comprehension.

The bottom line was that they were delighted to see her, full of questions about the family, questions about her trip, and they hoped she would stay with them a while. Jane remembered the saying that home is where they always have to take you back. In that way, she felt she was home.

Aunt Maria closed the *caffe* to customers and bustled back inside the tiny two-story house to make dinner. Despite her protests that dinner would be skimpy because Jane had given them no prior notice of her arrival—but they forgave her, nonetheless—Maria and Ninfina managed to prepare a most substantial and truly delicious meal: veal cutlets breaded with fresh crumbs and sautéed with green sage leaves, a salad course of milky buffalo mozzarella and juicy red-ripe home-grown plum tomatoes drizzled with clear, fruity virgin olive oil, soft cheese-flavored risotto, and a new bottle of the local red table wine.

Not to partake heartily would have been insulting, a slur on the family honor. Jane made certain no *vendetta* would result because of her lack of appetite. She played the part of famished guest well, to the best of her ability. She was, finally, in the warm, welcoming bosom of her family, where she was sure she belonged.

Fie on Lorenzo!

She would not be the sometime plaything of a callous, spoiled, cheating, lying prince, not ever.

Chapter Eight

Margherita

At dinner, the next morning's agenda had been discussed. Ninfina would drive Jane in her tiny, battered Fiat (it had been pointed out to her on the street that night, a heap badly in need of a paint job and some body work) to the top of Monte Crucificio. It was the local shrine, dedicated to the Madonna. According to Jane's relatives, it had worked a miracle for her grandmother, Benedetta, when she was a little girl. It was called the Oratorio di Romitello.

Jane had nothing in her many guidebooks concerning the Oratorio. It was evidently a very well kept secret. She wasn't all that keen on seeing it, but the path of least resistance seemed to be acquiescence, so she pretended great interest in seeing the shrine. Maria and Ninfina seemed highly pleased at her enthusiasm and did not appear to notice that it was feigned enthusiasm, at best.

Afterwards, Jane would be pretty much on her own. Ninfina had to go to Partinico to pick up the week's perishable supplies for her mother's general store, which was next-door to the *caffe* and actually the ground-level floor of their house. In the afternoon, both of them would be busy tending the store. One of the activities Jane could possibly pursue, they suggested, was visiting her dear departed Conigliaro relatives in the Borgetto cemetery.

Jane cringed, recollecting how the Sicilians of her acquaintance really got into visiting their dead weekly, if possible, and daily, ideally. Jane's grandfather, Calogero Acquista, had died three years ago. If she had a penny, she calculated, for each of her *Nonna*'s visits to his grave, she would have amassed a small fortune by now. In contrast, her paternal Grandfather Robert Holland had been cremated, his ashes scattered on Cape Cod. No gravesite to visit. Yeah, Jane thought, WASPS can be cold, but Sicilians might have had a tendency to overdo things.

Jane had spent a terrible night. A new bed was always problematic, and the narrow cot in her aunt's guest room had a thin, uncomfortable mattress. But the actual problem, once again, was her dreams. She experienced sensual, extremely graphic, erotic dreams about Lorenzo; dreams that made her writhe unsatisfied in her bed. She dreamed of his passionate mouth, of his hands opening up all of her secret places, making them his, and causing her pent-up juices to overflow. He had spoiled her forever for any other man. No one would ever match up to her first lover.

She remembered how willingly she had given herself, how eager she was for his naked body, the body she'd fantasized loving for days. He was, as she had suspected, the equal, if not the better of Michelangelo's glorious David. And he had been all hers, even if so briefly.

Hers. Yes, she had ordered herself to forget him, to go on with her life, to chalk him up to the sad experience that is every wronged woman's lot, no matter her age, but the reality of the situation was that he was in her blood. She would have to have had every drop drained from her body to get him out of her thoughts, her desires, her flesh. Did she have the inner strength to rid herself of Lorenzo? She doubted it, and she hated herself for being so weak.

She wondered how long he had waited for her at the

hotel bar before he telephoned the Donzinis? Was he worried, upset, then annoyed or angry? She thought her speculation would lead to madness. She was making herself insane. Thus passed her first sleep-tossed night in Borgetto.

Elsewhere that night, while Jane tossed and turned and most of the town of Borgetto slept tranquilly in the cool, softly scented evening breezes that blew in from the sea across grassy valleys, dissipating in the violet-hued mountains, others were at work. Pickaxes were tearing up the dense, fertile earth, shovels lifting it in great scoops and tossing it in large mounds to the side. Low, guttural voices growled to each other and dirty hands shoved wooden boxes filled with straw and soil and other unnamed things.

Some did not sleep at all that night and strange things were occurring.

Jane finally drifted off to sleep in the early hours of the morning. The harsh squawk of an infuriated rooster blasting the dawn of a new day woke her up.

Her mood, however, was sour and unhappy, and the ride up the mountain to the Oratorio di Romitello did nothing to improve it. The winding road was narrow and unpaved in many places. Along the sides, at intervals, there were neat little white crosses indicating where unlucky travelers had gone off the shoulders to their deaths. Jane shuddered at the thought of these abrupt leaps into the spread arms of eternity.

Ninfina told her that before people had cars, it had taken hours by donkey cart or by foot to get to the top. Many had walked it barefoot or on their knees, as a penance. Great-grandmother Francesca Conigliaro, Benedetta's mother, had been one of those penitents.

Benedetta, as a young child, had fallen gravely ill and was near certain death. This was before the advent of antibiotics like penicillin, medicines now taken for granted, Ninfina said. Francesca went to the Madonna at the Oratorio to beg for help. If the four-year-old girl's life would be spared, her mother would hike up the mountain barefoot every year on the anniversary of her cure. Until she was quite old and feeble, Ninfina related, Francesca Conigliaro honored her vow, for the child's high fever broke within hours of her mother making that promise.

Jane was suddenly reminded of a story that Benedetta had told her of another vow to the Virgin. Doubtless, it had been influenced by her mother's experience at the Oratorio di Romitello.

It went like this, she told Ninfina: a poor widow needed food for her starving children, and so she importuned the Madonna, through a statue of the Virgin in her church. She fervently promised that she would, in return, give the Blessed Virgin all she had—which was, in this particular case, one dried-up miserable fava bean, the sole content of her otherwise-vacant cupboard.

Now, here's the catch—when you go to ask a favor of the gods, whether the old Greek gods or the God of the Roman Catholic Italians—you have to promise something in return. Something that is important to you. In this case, that fava bean was all the poor widow had to offer. It stood between her and her family's starvation. It was a sincere promise. Well, luck arrived, in spades! When she returned to her hovel, there was a man at her door, a man to whom her late husband had lent money, years and years before. The man had become successful, and was now back to repay his debt, with interest. The widow was now a wealthy woman, rich beyond her wildest hopes.

The Blessed Virgin would now be repaid, but not, thought the widow, with that miserable dried-out fava bean, not in the face of her unexpected largesse. That, she thought, would be disrespect. She went to a goldsmith and had him fashion a fava bean out of the heaviest gold—Italian 22 karat—for the Madonna. The widow took it with her, proudly, to the little church, laying it before the bare, painted feet of the wooden icon. At once, the statue came terrifyingly to life.

Pointing an angry, accusing finger at the widow, the Virgin refused the golden fava bean, reminding her of her unkept promise, the dried-up bean. "But this is better!" the widow protested, confused.

"This was not our bargain," the Madonna countered. The widow finally caught the drift of the Madonna's displeasure and raced back to her now-full cupboard, hastily searching for and retrieving that old bean, which had become lodged in a crack. The promise had been kept, to the letter. The Madonna was satisfied. The debt was paid in full.

Jane thought it was a great moral tale. It made two things perfectly clear to anyone who heard the story. One, the gods are incredibly literal, so be careful what you promise to them. Two, they always expect to be paid back in full. You cannot cheat them, whether by too much or too little.

As the cousins came to the top of Monte Crucificio, two sights came into view. There was a simple, ruined country church, its clock tower the only part of it still standing, and a hulk of modern architecture that was the new church. Ninfina told Jane that a storm had destroyed the old country church, and, that instead of having it repaired, the townspeople had decided to build one that was newer and better than the old one. From what she could see, Jane decided that it certainly was newer, but better? The old church had been charming, the new one, however, was nondescript, even charmless.

Jane was fascinated, though, with the interior of the new Oratorio. It was plain, austere, all its walls simply whitewashed, no decoration of any kind save for offerings to the Madonna. They were garlanded with an astonishing variety of ex-votives, ranging from the sublime to the truly grotesque. She feasted her eyes on the spectacle.

There was expensive-looking gold jewelry in locked cases, letters documenting miraculous cures from mysterious diseases, before-and-after photographs of cancer patients in remission, newspaper clippings of amazing recoveries from near-fatal accidents (simply making the trip up and down the mountain, Jane thought, and getting yourself back in one piece was a miracle!), and, fascinating but horrific, a veritable Grand Guignol of body parts fashioned out of rubber, plastic, vinyl, and lord knew what else. There were realistic-appearing hearts from survivors of heart attacks, staring glass eyes from patients who had not gone blind, kidneys, arms, legs, breasts, and so on, *ad infinitum*.

Yuck! Jane turned her eyes away from the hanging body parts hurriedly, before she lost her breakfast. As her stomach settled, she saw, in an alcove, hundreds of charming tin placards, each a standard size, about one and a half by three inches, probably all stamped out by a specialized machine years ago. The placards bore people's initials and decorations of a more subtle and artistic nature of the same anatomical parts now rendered so obscenely in modern plastic and other materials. Nothing graphic, only etched or suggested, artistically.

Jane was brought back to another place, another time, but in the same Mediterranean tradition. Several summers ago, her mother the Anglophile had decided they would all go to England for a summer vacation. They had visited the museum at Bath in the south of England, once a thriving Roman city called Aquae Sulis. In the museum there had been a large collection of Roman antiquities, glass cases brim-full of the same kind of ex-votives, offerings to the gods in exchange for healing. Bath was famous for its miraculous, medicinal waters.

There were exquisitely-fashioned gold rings set with precious jewels, gold and silver coins, amulets, and, yes, tiny terra-cotta representations of breasts, limbs, heads, all parts of the body. The gratitude of the survivors, those Roman colonists saved from death, disease, and recovered from accidents, and the gratitude of contemporary Sicilians, was all one and the same. The ancient workmanship of the terra cotta, the lurid bits of plastic on the walls of the Oratorio, the initialed squares of tin, were all sincere expressions of heartfelt thanks to the gods.

Jane scanned the placards of tin. Lorenzo had been right about her name: there were no "J"s, no "H"s. Lots of "L"s and "B"s. Jane wondered, *What if I pray to the Virgin, now, here in this church?* Seems as though a bunch of folks got what they wanted. Maybe my broken heart can be healed, too. Nope, Jane, the little voice that had to be her conscience, deep inside her, cautioned, these people are believers, you aren't, why would the Virgin listen to you?

Ninfina nudged Jane out of her reverie and towards the small chapel. Women, mostly widows in black, were lighting candles and hard at prayer. Ninfina evidently had something to ask, or thanks to give. As she knelt at the altar, Jane accompanied her, lighting one of the votive candles, something she always did in a church in memory of her two grandfathers. Leaving Ninfina to her private communication with the Virgin, Jane went quietly to sit in one of the pews.

An old woman, another widow by the look of her, dressed in shapeless black a la mode de Borgetto, stared at her with intent, serious eyes. Jane smiled politely, mindful of the respect that is due to one's elders, nodding to the old woman as she entered a front pew close to the altar railing. She could feel the widow's eyes boring through her back. She was acutely uncomfortable. Staring had always struck her as extremely rude, no matter who—senior citizens not excepted—did it. *How strange!* she thought. *Who is this old lady and why is she so interested in me?*

Ninfina finally finished her prayers and joined Jane. Her black eyes snapped a look of pure hostility over Jane's shoulder, in the direction of the old woman.

"Who is that, Ninfina?" Jane queried.

Ninfina shrugged. "Your aunt, Margherita."

Surprised—*why your aunt,* thought Jane, *and not our aunt?*—Jane turned around to look, but the old widow had gone.

Jane was full of questions for her cousin in the car. It was hard work, what with Ninfina's reticence to be questioned closely about the old woman and Jane's struggles with Sicilian vocabulary, to get much information out of Ninfina. But before they got back to the *caffe,* Jane had managed to make some major inroads. The old woman was Margherita, nee Conigliaro, Jane's grandmother Benedetta's aunt.

Benedetta and Margherita were the same age. Unless you knew the Conigliaro family history, this seemed odd, but Francesca, the mother of both Benedetta and Maria, was the eldest of seven daughters, Margherita the youngest, a gift to her parents in their twilight years, what used to be called a *"change of life baby,"* that is, a pre-menopausal conception. According to Ninfina, Jane's grandmother and Margherita, her aunt, were like sisters when they were growing up. Jane was amazed. With all the many stories Nonna had told her about her family in Sicily, there had never been one mention of a Margherita. *Why?* Jane wondered.

It was a tragic story, in the time-old tradition of tragic Sicilian stories.

Margherita's older sisters had all disliked her. She was considered pampered, spoiled, too doted upon by the old parents, who called her their *"vasteneddu,"* the crutch they would lean on in their dotage. Jane thought, but kept the thought to herself, that the other sisters were jealous of Margherita, just as Claudia's daughter, Anna Maria Donzini, was of Jane, just as the Biblical Joseph's brothers were of him. Jealousy had a long tradition, too, and it was not an emotion specific to Sicily.

When the old parents died, one soon after the other, no one would accept the responsibility of the young girl's upbringing. So she was sent to an orphanage in Palermo. Jane was stunned. *How dreadful!* How could you do that to your own flesh and blood? She contrasted this behavior with Lorenzo's aunt and uncle, who took the orphaned boy in with love and a sense of duty. The Sicilians, she'd been brought up to believe by her grandmother, always took care of their own. A lie. *An outright lie.*

What a terrible story, Jane exclaimed to Ninfina. How cruel! But, no, Ninfina insisted. The reason no one wanted Margherita was because she was hard to handle, extremely spoiled. No one could control her, according to her mother, Maria. When she was released from the orphanage, she came back to Borgetto—*the last place I'd come back to!* Jane thought—and continued to cause the family a good deal of trouble.

By that time, Jane's grandmother had already emigrated to the United States, but her mother, Francesca, kept her well-informed of Margherita's doings. She was bad news, Ninfina went on, and bad luck, too. She had married, but her husband had soon died. She had no children. Her late husband's family, the Manninos, took care of her. One of her many nephews had probably driven her up to the Oratorio. None of her family had anything to do with her. Nor with those Manninos, either.

"Guardate, Gianna," Ninfina warned Jane. "Stay away from Margherita. She's bad luck, trouble." With her free hand, Ninfina made the sign Jane knew was the warding off of the evil eye, the pinky and the index finger stuck out, the rest of the fingers tucked under. Jane shuddered. That evil eye precaution always creeped her out.

Guardate. Watch yourself. It was the second time in a week that Jane had been told to watch out for herself. Three, if Anna Maria's warning was counted. *Will I be smart enough to heed the warning this time?* Jane wondered. It was hard for her to believe that old woman was evil. She didn't at all look like a bad person. In fact, she had a rather sweet face. She just looked old and frail, so very sad.

But then, Jane remembered wryly, she thought Lorenzo was okay, too, so what did she really know about people and what went on deep in their hearts?

There was nothing Jane could do to make herself useful around the house, the general store, or the *caffe.* There wasn't that much in the way of business, and Maria employed part-time help from town to assist her in both establishments. Jane had a delicious lunch of homemade bread, called pane di casa, and freshly-sliced, slightly salty prosciutto with some of Maria's sun-dried tomatoes. (She simply picked them off a drying screen in her bountiful garden and placed them on Jane's plate, moistening the tomato halves with olive oil.) Jane was, at least, continuing to eat well, here in Nowheresville. She needed to keep up her strength; this was good.

Ninfina drew Jane a map of the cemetery. I'm not really *dying* to go there, Ninfina, Jane wanted to pun, but thought better of it. Her cousin dropped Jane off in her battered little Fiat, pressing the hand-drawn map showing the family plots into her reluctant hand. Jane was not comfortable among the dead. Funerals, wakes, cemeteries, all made her very uneasy. She suppressed a sudden shudder.

As she had honestly told Lorenzo, she preferred the living. But, unwilling to offend her new-found relatives, whom she was living off these few days while she tried to heal her slashed and broken heart, she had agreed to visit the dead, and visit the dead she would. She had to acknowledge, though, that it was going to give her the creeps.

Ninfina, on the ride to the cemetery, had confided to Jane that she and her mother tried to get there at least every other day. *At least?* Nofina's father, Salvatore Modica, had passed away about ten years ago, and she kept a photograph of him on the dented dashboard of her Fiat. There were also framed studio portraits of him all over the house. Jane recalled her grandmother's comments about her brother-in-law, Salvatore. She hadn't thought much of him.

Salvatore Modica had been short and swarthy. (*"An Arab,"* Nonna called him.) He had been chronically unemployed. Nonna could not understand why her fair-complected, beautiful sister Maria of the wondrous green eyes, who, she said, could have had her pick of anyone in

Borgetto, anyone at all—as if, Jane thought, there could ever have been such a great selection in godforskaen Borgetto!—would have married an unemployed bicycle mechanic of negligible looks and too-dark skin. He had a sorry line of work. Few people, right after World War II, could afford to own bicycles, much less have them fixed.

Nonna thought it was a front for his real occupation: cigarette smuggling. It was not an innocent line of work; in those days tobacco/cigarette smuggling was controlled by the Mafia. (The Acquistas in New York City were stolidly and voiciferously anti-Mafia.) At any rate, Salvatore's suspected clandestine activities, whatever they were, which brought him such vocal overseas family censure, eventually generated enough capital to open the general store and *caffe* his wife and daughter now ran.

Jane studied the map, written in smudgy pencil, as she carefully picked her way among the well-kept tombs and mausoleums, the headstones, and pieces of old, crumbling rock. There were a number of people actively wandering about, clipping long grass on graves, filling glass jars of freshly picked wildflowers with water from an old-fashioned pump. Some were kneeling in prayer at gravesides. The scene was busy rather than somber, but Jane still felt ill at ease and out of place.

She had finally found the family plots. So much stone had eroded that it was difficult to decipher the old names. Oh, my, she saw, there they were, the Modicas, all in a straight line, small baby stones in one long row. Maria and Salvatore's stillborn-and-died-in-infancy offspring. Only Ninfina had survived birth and early childhood. They'd named them, every single one of those baby souls: Antonio, Mario, Salvatore, then three girls with the very same name, Maria Grazia. Brrrr! A chill ran through Jane. It was all so terribly sad. All those pregnancies, all those premature deaths.

She had rambled on to a neighboring plot, which was all Conigliaros. Simone and Francesca, Nonna's parents, and lots of other names that meant nothing at all to her. Somebody Lupo. Polizzi. Guida. She looked up with a start. In her path was the little old lady from the Oratorio that morning. Her Aunt Margherita—no, correction, her Great-Aunt Margherita—was standing right in front of her.

This time she was not staring into Jane's eyes, nor boring a hole into her back. She was transfixed by Lorenzo's trinacria amulet, which had escaped from under Jane's white tee shirt when she was bending over to look at the names on the tombstones and was now dangling on her chest. Margherita looked scared to death, her brown eyes wide in fear.

"Buon giorno, signora." Jane nodded a greeting. *"Como sta?"*

Margherita looked into Jane's eyes with the saddest expression she had ever seen on any human being, ever; the old woman's expression was sadder than sad.

"Caterina?" she asked.

Jane shook her head, "No, Gianna." Who had the old woman confused her with? Jane didn't think she really looked Sicilian, except for her dark hair and her longish nose, and she was certainly a good deal taller than most of the Sicilians she had met so far.

"La trinacria . . ." She pointed to the gleaming amulet. And then she started to cry. She was weeping copiously.

Jane was disconcerted. *Oh, my,* she thought, *I cry easily, but this old lady has me beat by a mile.* But then again, she realized, they were closely related.

Jane came closer to her, putting her arms around her and

letting her sob out her sorrows against Jane's chest. She was tiny, bird-like, along the lines of Cousin Ninfina. "There, there," Jane attempted to console her, "please don't cry, it's all right." Jane really had no idea if it was all right or not, but the remarks seemed appropriate to the occasion.

The old lady sighed heavily, for one so small, as if the burden was all too much to bear, and gestured to an empty stone bench nearby. Jane walked over to it with her. The torrent of tears had stopped, only to be replaced by a veritable torrent of words. Jane asked her to slow down, so she could make some sense out of what Margherita was so urgently trying to tell her, as if, at any moment, they would be interrupted and she would have to stop. The old woman seemed extremely distraught.

It seemed that Jane was the spitting image of someone named Caterina. Someone who had saved Margherita's life when she was a young girl. Someone who was living in America and had come back to Sicily. Jane had no idea who the old woman was talking about. She knew no one named Catherine. Margherita took a couple of deep breaths and attempted to speak more slowly and clearly.

Catherine, Caterina, was her older sister, one of the seven Conigliaro sisters, an aunt, like her, to Jane's grandmother and her Aunt Maria. No one had ever told Jane about this great-aunt, either. She was beginning to suspect that there were quite a number of secrets in this family and she was beginning to be more than a little ticked off.

There was a lot to tell, it seemed, and tiny old Margherita was determined to start telling it. The pain of hearing Sicilian spoken so fast was giving Jane a headache, but she persevered, her curiosity highly aroused. She kept patting the little old woman on the shoulders when she would collapse into another round of tears, and, slowly, her story took shape and form.

This is the gist of what Margherita told Jane that quiet afternoon surrounded by the quiet, sleeping dead of Borgetto. As she already knew, Francesca was the eldest of the seven Conigliaro sisters, Caterina in the middle, and Margherita, of course, was the baby. Caterina had been married young, to a local man, and had emigrated with him to America. "Brooklyn," according to Margherita. (*Where else?* Jane thought.)

Caterina was a beautiful woman and extremely strong-willed. Her husband, Giuseppe, was thin and mean. He was small-minded, jealous, constantly beating her up because he was jealous and mean. Caterina, unlike other turn-of-the-century battered wives, however, was not about to put up with such abuse.

Luckily, there were no children, so she up and left him, of her own free will, and returned to her hometown of Borgetto. She ran into immediate criticism and disapproval from the Conigliaros for deserting her husband. It just wasn't done, no matter what kind of a brute he was. Other women put up with it, she was told, and she should, too. She was setting a terrible example and embarrassing *la famiglia.* They even brought in the local parish priest in an attempt to show her where her wifely duty lay. This angered her, and it was not the only thing that made her furious. She learned that her sisters had put young Margherita into an orphanage.

They quailed in the face of her fury. She called them all terrible names, according to Margherita, venting her anger and alienating them from her forever. She marched off to Palermo and signed her baby sister out of the orphanage, literally in the nick of time. Margherita had been so lonely and depressed that she had stopped taking nourishment and was willing herself to die. The timely intervention of Caterina, back from America, had truly saved her life.

They both returned to Borgetto—*why?* Jane wondered—and went to work as house-servants for the region's wealthiest man, an aristocratic landowner, a prince, named Maurizio Bighilaterra. Upon hearing the name of Lorenzo's grandfather, Jane's mouth went dry and she felt a sharp pain in her heart. Her mind was racing madly.

Margherita tried to continue her tale, but Jane could barely pay attention. The old woman noted the girl's agitation—her face had turned pale—with some anxiety. Jane, hurriedly, lied and said she had to get back to Maria and Ninfina before they began to worry about her. At the mention of her relatives' names, Margherita's sad brown eyes again filled with tears.

"I don't even know them," she wept. "We live only three streets from each other and we do not know each other. Life is cruel, cara mia."

This is the woman whom they think is evil, Jane thought, evil and a troublemaker. They've warned me to keep away from her. *What harm can this sad old woman do to me?*

Jane hugged Margherita goodbye and kissed her withered cheek, promising to meet her in the cemetery the next day. There was a good deal more to say, and, thought Jane grimly, she guessed she would have to hear it, hear about her mother's family and their long-ago connection with the Bighilaterras. In a somber mood, Jane walked through the big old wrought iron cemetery gates and back along the dusty, rutted road that led back to town, back to the *caffe.*

Jane's head was full to bursting with questions for Margherita, but was she ready to handle the answers?

Chapter Nine

Three Men in Black

When Jane came back from her walk, she found the *caffe* busy; that is, busier than she had seen it before. Ninfina was behind the bar, grinding rich, aromatic dark-roasted coffee for *la macchina,* the espresso machine. Under her direction, Stefano, a young boy who was one of the part-time helpers, was taking small thick white china cups of the resultant strong brew to one of the tables. Now Ninfina was pouring a clear white liquid into very small shot glasses. She put the glasses on a tray and brought them to a table that already held three cups of foamy-topped espresso.

The three men in black seated there grunted gruff acknowledgement and threw back the shot glasses in swift, stiff-armed motions. Then they stirred great quantities of sugar into the tiny coffee cups and began to sip delicately at the frothy liquid. They growled in appreciation of the espresso's dark strength.

"Buon giorno!" Jane greeted her cousin. The three men turned and stared at her, insolent, appraising stares that Jane chose to ignore. She turned her back to them and asked Ninfina what *"the white stuff"* in the shot glasses was.

"Grappa," she answered. "E molto forte . . . very strong . . . tastes . . ." Here she made a gagging gesture, with her hand at her throat, as if choking herself, her tongue sticking out of her mouth grotesquely. They both burst into spontaneous giggles.

The three menacing looking men in black glanced their way again, apparently not at all amused by what seemed to be the girls' frivolity at their expense. The youngest one, who wore a red bandanna around his dirty neck, stared longest and hardest at them. Then he said something in a low growl to his companions, who both laughed, making a harsh, sinister sound that reverberated in the courtyard of the little *caffe.*

"Ninfina, who are those . . ." Jane had been about to say bozos. "I mean, who are those men?" She whispered her question behind her hand.

Ninfina whispered back, following Jane's lead, realizing that her three customers were paying inordinate attention to their conversation. "Sono i fratelli Schifosi . . . the Schifosi brothers, Guido, Nino and Alfredo. The oldest, Guido, he knew my father. They used to work together."

Jane thought: *Worked together? Repairing bicycles? Or smuggling cigarettes? Were they Mafiosi?* The Schifosi brothers were clad de rigueur for an afternoon out in Borgetto: basic black. In their case, work clothes: thick black cotton trousers, rather baggy black undershirts peeking out from under long-sleeved black denim shirts, black caps on their heads, the brims pulled down over their low, ape-like foreheads. Only the youngest—he was Alfredo, Ninfina said—sported some color, with his red neckerchief. The other two decided to stick with the black motif at their thick bull-like throats.

On their large feet—which seemed to Jane to be at least size fourteens—were heavy, laced-up construction boots, the kind that go over the ankle. All three men had a coat of dingy film over their surly, unhandsome faces, their rough hands, their unkempt, greasy hair. Jane shuddered at the condition of their horny fingernails, torn, blackened. A loathsome trio, she decided. According to Ninfina, they were loyal and regular customers.

"What exactly do they do for a living?" Jane continued to question, *sotto voce*. She imagined a road-gang, but had seen no road construction nearby, neither when she'd been on the bus, nor with Lorenzo in his car. Likewise, there had been no evidence of road construction at the top of Mount Crucificio or near the cemetery. She also had trouble reconciling the heat-retaining black costumes the brothers favored with the reality of the country's climate.

Who in his right mind, she thought, *would work in black clothing in the torrid Sicilian summer sun?* Old Guido, the eldest, looked like he'd been around for at least seventy summers or more. You would have thought, Jane pondered, that he would have caught on!

Ninfina shrugged. Clearly, this conversation about the Schifosis was not that interesting to her. "They dig," Ninfina said.

Hmmnn, they sure do, Jane agreed, as she saw, from the corner of her eye, one of the brothers groping up a hairy nostril, digging away.

"Sometimes they work on the tuna fishing boats," Ninfina continued. "It is not always easy to find work here, you know. But, I have to say, they always have lire in their pockets. Sometimes . . ." She paused.

"Sometimes, what?" Jane had the feeling Ninfina was about to say something significant.

Ninfina frowned. "Sometimes I think they keep other customers away. People don't like being around them. I hear them called malandrini."

That was a slang term, Jane knew, for bad eggs, tough guys.

"But . . ." Ninfina shrugged again. "They give us a lot of

business, so . . ." She made a helpless little gesture with her tiny hands, as if to indicate that having to make a living and relying on customers like these was their lot, hers and her mother's, and they would have to put up with it.

Jane thought: *I've always had it so easy, so has Jenny; we've been pretty pampered, compared to these people.* She was sympathetic.

Dismissing the Schifosi brothers and their kind from her life, Jane went to work behind the bar, washing out the demitasse cups and saucers soaking in the sink. She felt it was the least she, the coddled houseguest, could do. As she rinsed out the dainty filigreed espresso spoons, she could feel the hostility of someone's eyes on her. Raising her own clear hazel eyes, she stared steadily back at Guido Schifosi, who, flustered, suddenly became very interested in the contents of his drained espresso cup. Jane shrugged and went back to her washing, stacking, and wiping.

A stray thought wandered through the byways of Jane's active mind, airy and innocent as a dandelion wafted by the wind. Why such copious quantities, she wondered—as she saw them ordering another round of coffee and grappa—of keep-you-up-all-day-and-night liquid refreshment? *How were these guys ever going to sleep tonight?* Assuming that fishing and construction work were break-of-dawn activities, and that men thus engaged needed to get to bed early in order to get enough sleep, why were they ensuring that they would stay up all night, mainlining so much caffeine and alcohol directly into their bloodstreams? Well, it sure wasn't any of her concern, she decided briskly, finishing up the washing and wiping her hands on a dishtowel.

Leaving the *caffe* in the hands of the young boy, Stefano, Jane went in to dinner with Ninfina. Aunt Maria had prepared the "pasta of the three Margheritas" with a typically

Sicilian sauce of fresh tomatoes and fried eggplant, garnished with the sweet, fragrant leaves of freshly plucked basil.

Nonna made the very same dish, Jane recalled. Basically, it was a leftover special that used the odds and ends of dried pasta, *"pasta asciutta,"* putting together enough of this combination to feed your whole table. One half-pound of leftover pasta or less from a package of dried would never do to feed a large Italian family, but put together with a quarter-pound of this, a quarter-pound of that, mixing up two or three different kinds of macaroni, you could make a meal.

Jane seized upon the opportunity to use the name of the pasta dish to bring up her new-found Great-Aunt Margherita to Aunt Maria. She was all innocence as she commented, "Oh, Margherita, just like the aunt we saw today in church."

Silence. Jane could count the drops of water trickling slowly from the washer-compromised tap on the kitchen sink. The ticking of the clock in the parlor, two rooms away, was suddenly very marked. Maria glanced over at Ninfina, and then, in passionately-worded Sicilian, she made it abundantly clear to Jane that Margherita's name was not one that was mentioned in their home, not ever. She and another sister had once been involved in a shameful matter, one that had made pariahs out of the Conigliaros, once *"una famiglia respettada,"* a respected family. It had taken years, after this incident, for the family to hold its head up again in the town.

Unto two generations, Maria continued, inflamed, the shame had hung over them, even touching Benedetta, who was in America, and blackening her good name. Maria, of course, had been a very young child when all this had happened, but she'd felt the repercussions all her life. It had adversely affected her "marriageability." Jane wondered if that explained why Maria had accepted the offer of a man beneath her status, an unemployed ne'er-do-well. It had been a terrible cloud over all of them.

Jane resisted bringing up the name of Caterina into the discussion. She didn't want to let them know how much she really knew, nor that she had spoken with Margherita that afternoon, but she had to say, "She seemed like such a gentle, sweet-faced old lady."

Aunt Maria sniffed that appearances were often deceiving, or words to that effect. She passed a salad to Jane of bright red plum tomatoes dressed in olive oil and dotted with the miniature green leaves of freshly picked, aromatic oregano. The conversation had come to a quite decided end. The meal continued in total, absolute silence. Jane had obviously trod a tad too far into sensitive territory.

Jane had discovered where the land mines lay. She dipped a piece of pane di casa in the fruity olive oil dressing of the delicious tomato salad, pondering her next move.

"Zia," she began, in the same innocent tone of voice she'd used before, undaunted, "where is the house my Nonna grew up in, the house where you both grew up together? She always said it was such a beautiful home, one of the finest in Borgetto."

Maria shook her head. *"E chiuso,"* she said. "It's all closed up and I don't know what happened to the key. I looked for it the other day, as a matter of fact, and I could not find it." She turned to her daughter, asking, "Have you seen it?"

"Not for a long time, Mama. Where could it be?" Ninfina sounded puzzled.

"Is the house nearby?" Jane persisted, looking from one perplexed face to the other.

The serious expression on Maria's face changed, crinkling into a smile. She laughed. "But it's right across the street! I thought you knew that, Gianna?" Jane shook her head no. "Well, after we finish eating, go right outside and look. It is still light out."

"*Venga con mi,* Ninfina? Will you come with me?" Jane asked.

"I cannot, Gianna. I have to do the supper dishes and then go over the books with Mama. Go by yourself. It is just exactly facing this house, right across the way. The number is on the door, Numero Quattro, Corso Roma," Ninfa reassured her.

Jane promised she would wash the supper dishes for them when she got back from taking a look at the house, so that they could devote themselves to the account books. She exited Maria's house at the front door, coming, just as Ninfina had told her, face-to-face across the cobblestone street with Numero Quattro, Corso Roma. Jane realized why she had taken no notice of it before. *One of the finest homes in Borgetto?* Hardly. Not from the outside, at least.

It was tiny and nondescript, hugging the corner of the side street, overwhelmed by a much more substantial house on its right-hand side. It was whitewashed, with a dark-green painted wooden door. Jane remembered reading somewhere in a guidebook that the color of the paint on a Sicilian door was an indication of the ancestry of the family residing within. Blue was Greek. Red, Normans. Green? What was green? Or was red Arab? Now she wasn't sure.

Dwarfing the door in question was an enormous wrought-iron ring. It looked like a giant's door knocker. Or had it been the hitching post for the family donkey? Jane crossed the street and touched the ring, gently pushing it against the flaking paint drying into dust on the scarred wood of the door. Slivers of dried paint had been falling off for years, by the look of it, coming to rest on the front step. No footsteps marred the dusty flakes of paint. No one had disturbed it. No, Jane decided, no one had entered the place in years, from the outward look of it.

Out of curiosity, she peered into each of the two street-level windows. Heavy drawn shutters on the inside effectively barred her inspection of the house's interior. Discouraged, she walked around the corner. The back of the house was almost in darkness. The sun had begun to set. There were a few street lamps on the Corso Roma, but none here in the back.

Alleyways at the rear of townhouses abutted the narrow street Jane now found herself walking on. It, too, was paved with large, round, worn-down cobblestones. There was a rear entrance to Number Four, a door roughly less than half the size of the massive entrance in the front. The only ground-floor window was small, square, and quite high up, the sort of window one saw in a pantry or kitchen storage room.

Here, Jane's height was definitely an advantage. *If only I had a stepstool or a box,* she thought, *I'd have the few more inches I'd need to look into that rear window to see what I could see.* She squinted down the rapidly darkening street to see if there was anything at all she could use to give her access to that small aperture. Nothing. No trash piles in the alleyways, no broken, discarded pieces of old furniture. *Neat people, unfortunately for me,* she thought.

Soon it would be impossible to see anything. Night was falling in the country, and it would be complete and utter darkness, as only rural darkness could be. *Why didn't I bring a flashlight?* She was annoyed with herself.

Leaning a hand against the back door, thinking that she

could give herself leverage by jumping up and getting a look in the window that way—from what she could make out, it was clear, if slightly grimy, glass, no shutters or curtains masking what was inside—she was surprised to find that the old door was slowly opening on its own, squeaking eerily on its rusting hinges. *What luck!* Jane rejoiced. She couldn't wait to tell Maria and Ninfina. But, first, she'd investigate on her own, with the precious bit of twilight that was still left in the day.

Jane pushed the door more firmly, anxious to quiet its squeaking hinges, and stepped back, startled, falling flat on her rear end. Ouch! She'd been spooked. *There was someone in there.* A ghost? Oh, oh, this was scary stuff, all of a sudden, this poking around in long-abandoned houses.

Don't be silly! Jane told herself. *Go in there.* Cautiously, she stepped back into the house. *No living or dead thing is in there, Jane Holland,* she admonished herself, firmly. And she was right. The thing inside the house was not living. Nor was it dead.

It was the long white marble torso of a nude woman. It stood facing Jane, just inside the back door of her grandmother's childhood home. The statue's stone skin was smooth and shone palely in the twilight streaming through the high, small, rear window. Her Attic features were perfect: oval face, elongated unseeing eyes, straight aquiline nose, small round chin.

There had been damage to that perfection. The stone, marcelled waves of hair, brushed back from that beautiful face, was chipped in places, broken. Her arms were gone, her long, smooth legs cut off unevenly, one at mid-thigh and the other below a sculpted round knee. The torso was slightly turned, at a soft angle. Her breasts were firm and high, navel deeply indented in a round, curved belly.

It was a Greek goddess.

Jane made a guess: 5th Century, B.C., the Golden Age of Greece. She had seen her sisters reproduced by the hundreds in her art history textbooks and at the Louvre, Boston's Museum of Fine Arts, the Metropolitan Museum of Art in New York City, and the Uffizi Gallery in Florence. Jane knew her kind well. This particular specimen was magnificent.

And what, dear God, was this priceless statue doing here, in the town that time forgot, Borgetto, Sicily? What on earth was going on?

Jane's eyes had adjusted to the dimming light. Now she could see that the statue had been imbedded in a coffin-like wooden crate packed carelessly with straw and dirt. And she was not alone. Behind the goddess, a ghostly white hand broke the earthen surface of a long, rectangular box, as if beckoning Jane to explore ancient secrets. *No, thank you,* Jane thought, *I am already knee-deep in secrets, I don't need any more right now!* But this one was being thrust upon her. *Maybe I have a knack I've never been aware of before,* Jane thought, wondering at her odd luck.

She walked through the room in wonder and amazement. There had to be a good dozen crates lying about, straw and dirt littering the floor. Flat against the drawn shutters of one of the front windows was a smallish crate with damaged slats, chicken wire binding hanging loose.

She put out a hand and pulled the wire to one side, breaking a couple of slats. She pushed aside the straw and damp clay soil. Something incredible was inside this box, Jane knew, and it wanted her to expose it. The dirt insinuated itself under her fingernails and lodged there as she scratched harder inside the crate, finally touching a cold surface. The piece was terra cotta, small, less than a foot in height, not that much more around.

Red clay curls, bound up in a chignon knot at the top of the head. A woman's profile, the chin proudly thrust upward. She had wings. Jane could see them as she dug away, appearing under her hurrying hands. And . . . a fish tail! *Was this some kind of weird creature, part woman, part bird, part fish?* Jane wondered, working feverishly now to see the whole.

No . . . wait . . . the creature was seated gracefully, one long leg curled under her body, the other extended, toes pointed like a ballet dancer's. The head of the fish now began to emerge. No, not a fish, not at all. It was a dolphin. That round forehead and that pointed snout were unmistakable. The feminine creature astride the dolphin was a water nymph, a nereid, one of the fifty daughters of Nereus, the old man of the sea. She was nude. In her arms she held up a billowing piece of drapery, like a sail. The folds of the terra cotta cloth flowed, as if directed by an unseen wind. *Wow!* Jane sat back on her heels in astonishment.

She put out a hand and traced the pattern of the waves incised by the unknown sculptor under the dolphin's body. The artist had given the large beast character, from the big round eyes and smiling mouth to the imaginative, but not true to nature, fish-like scales on its back. Jane remembered an old movie she'd seen on television years ago; it was called *Boy on a Dolphin*, and starred Sophia Loren and Alan Ladd. This was its mate, the girl on the dolphin, and it was perfection. Jane liked it a whole lot better.

In her awe of the beautiful piece of sculpture, Jane had become unaware of her surroundings, a dangerous thing. Her ears had neglected to catch the squeaky hinges of the back door opening again, but she was quick enough to hear the guttural, rough voices of men. Getting to her feet swiftly, her heart pounding, she made for the front door, pulling back the latch. Would it hold? Would it disintegrate under her grasp? Her luck held.

She just barely squeezed out of the front door as the narrow, focused beam of an invading flashlight lit on the marble goddess. She hadn't had time to cover up her nereid, the woman on the dolphin. Whoever it was, coming in that back door, would know that things had been tampered with, that someone had been there.

Damn! Jane thought. But she was home free, almost, melting quickly against the hastily shut front door as she saw the unmistakable worn-down heels of the construction boots of one of the Schifosi brothers retreating into the back alley.

Jane held her breath, gulping back air. He didn't turn back. He hadn't heard her, she thought, exulting in her luck. She slunk across the cobblestone street and into her aunt's house, making her way into the kitchen.

Mechanically, beginning to breathe more normally, she started to soak and sponge the supper dishes. She could hear Maria and Ninfina talking in the front parlor, and the shuffling of papers as they went through invoices and entered them in the account books.

For the first time in almost a week of troubled nights she would have something else to think about besides Prince Lorenzo Bighilaterra and her broken heart. There was a mystery across the road and she was going to investigate it.

Chapter Ten

The Earth Yields Up Its Secrets

Spring semester Jane had taken a course with Dr. Christine Havelock, the chairman of the Art History Department at Vassar College, on ancient Greek art. Greek art became one of Jane's great passions; taking the course, to her, was the equivalent of dying and going to heaven three days a week, M, W, F, at 10 a.m. She didn't miss one class. Her term paper was Classical Greek Sculpture of the Golden Age. She'd gotten an A+ on the paper, a solid A in the course.

As she lay in the narrow bed of her aunt's austere guest room in Number Six, Corso Roma, the discoveries that she'd made that evening at Number Four made her crazed. *What did it all mean?* What were the Schifosi brothers up to? Was robbing antiquities from archaeological sites their line, so to speak, of work?

It seemed fairly obvious to Jane that they were antiquities robbers. It was, she knew from the readings in her Greek art course, a lucrative line of work indeed, a growth industry second only to the international trade in drugs, having proliferated madly in the last few years in and around Mediterranean sites. And what did it have to do with her relatives? The robbers were operating out of the house that her grandmother had grown up in. What did her aunt and her cousin know about these activities? *How did it all add up?*

It tore Jane in pieces to think that her kindly, new-found relatives, Maria and Ninfina, were in cahoots with that loathsome trio, the Schifosis. But Guido, the eldest, had been a friend of Salvatore Modica's, had worked with him. Had the late Salvatore been a participant, also, in this illicit trade? Was her too-critical mother, Joanna Holland, nee Acquista, correct when she characterized her Sicilian relatives as scum of the earth, lowlifes?

There was too much for Jane to contemplate. Everything was awhirl in her head; she couldn't think logically any more. She fell asleep only because her body willed her to do so. She was exhausted. And she dreamed. Never had she had such disquieting dreams. It seemed to her that she'd come to Sicily to dream.

That night she dreamed that she came upon the Schifosi brothers as they were digging up the torso of the Greek goddess. The statue screamed in human pain as their sharp-edged shovels glanced against her immortal body. And then the statue moved, and Jane saw it was her face. She was the statue and she was the one who was screaming in pain.

She woke up trembling, in a cold, clammy sweat. Falling back into another troubled sleep, she saw herself wandering across the bleak, lonely plains of Segesta under a dead and mottled moon, the temple white and forbidding behind her. Out of the earth, sudden and terrifying, sprang a hand, a marble hand. As Jane came closer to look, it took hold of her ankle, dragging her, screaming, into the clammy, slithery, worm filled soil. Now she was under the dirt, in the cemetery at Borgetto. Her Great-Aunt Margherita and her Grandmother Benedetta were sitting together, weeping above her grave. Their copious tears were salting the ground and seeping through the earth, bathing Jane's still, white, dead face.

The flow of salty tears became a wave, a strong, powerful wave that whipped across her face as she lay astride a gigantic dolphin in the middle of the deep Mediterranean Ocean. There were schools of dolphin all around her—bottlenose, striped, rough-toothed, spinners—as far as she could see. She stood up on her dolphin's back and removed her pleated toga, spreading it before her like a sail, the pleats smoothing out flat in the force of the wind. Fierce breeze after fierce breeze filled the cloth, whipping it and propelling her and her dolphin farther and farther from shore. The land had fallen completely away; it was a speck, then nothing, on the horizon.

Ahead, suddenly, there was a whirlpool. They were heading straight for it, no time to turn, to flee. She was sucked inside it, her lungs filling with foam, drawn deep inside its core, as the darkness engulfed her entirely. She cried out in terror!

No, she didn't cry out. It was the rooster, down the street, belligerently and rudely waking her up. Her bed linen was drenched with cold, acrid-smelling sweat. Her hair hung damp and heavy on her neck. She was a mess. *I need a bath,* Jane thought, bleary-eyed. *Would there be water?* she wondered. *Hot water, preferably, for a bath or shower today?*

Borgetto, like all the small towns in that part of Sicily, only got water three times a week. It had something to do with the Mafia's control of water rights on the western part of the island. The days that water was available, townspeople bathed quickly, then filled bathtubs and other large receptacles, buckets, basins, sinks, so that they would have water for the dry days.

It was a major pain, Jane fumed, not to have something most people take for granted available at all times. And she wondered how people could put up with criminals controlling such basic resources. She realized, more and more, how spoiled and pampered she had been, how used to the rule of law in a civilized society. These poor people were forced to make do, so they did, without complaining.

Praise God and all the saints! There was hot water today. Jane exulted in the warm, wet streams that coursed down her body. She shampooed her hair with a rosemary-scented concoction Ninfina seemed to be partial to and rinsed it out with the juice of the sweet lemons—*limone dolce*—that grew in her aunt's garden. The combination of lemon and rosemary seemed to suit her more than Anna Maria's expensive jasmine-scented soaps and perfumes. And jasmine, although a pleasing smell, was really not her.

Ninfina had made the suggestion that the lemon/rosemary shampoo—which had been used by the women in their family for generations—would be excellent for Jane's hair, both giving it shine and acting as a natural bleach to bring out the blonde highlights in her brown hair. She had also warned her to rinse it out thoroughly, as the sweet lemony smell tended to attract honeybees.

Thoughtfully, Ninfina had squeezed several lemons for Jane the night before and placed the liquid in a small plastic squeeze-bottle on the rim of the big white porcelain tub. Jane appreciated her cousin's consideration.

Breakfast was *caffe* latte and sweet rolls in the kitchen. Still playing the role of helpful houseguest, and keeping to herself, for the time being, what she had seen in the house across the street the evening before, Jane asked her aunt and cousin if she could do anything for them that day. They couldn't come up with a thing, so Jane said that she was interested in visiting the cemetery again. This pleased them. It was real strong evidence for them, Jane was sure, of family bonding.

Her reason, of course, was hardly that. Jane still envisioned cemeteries as creepy places—she shivered inwardly as her dream of the cold hand pulling her down into the even colder earth came to mind, unbidden—but she had a rendezvous planned with Margherita. There were so many things to find out, things only she could, and would willingly, tell.

She also had to telephone Palermo. She couldn't put it off any longer. No, not Lorenzo, though she ached to hear his beloved voice. She could not leave Claudia Donzini in the dark, not after all her kindnesses to Jane. Claudia had to be told that Jane was all right, and when she was planning to come back to Palermo. She had to make her apologies, too, for her abrupt and rude behavior of the past few days. Leaving the Donzini home so suddenly, the way she did, was not polite, not at all.

She had to admit to herself that she also hoped Claudia would give her news of Lorenzo. She couldn't speak to him, not yet, but she yearned to know how he was, how he had taken her sudden, emotional defection. She still hurt so badly. *When was the pain going to go away? Jane, Jane, steel yourself against him. Guardate!*

She turned to her Aunt Maria. "Zia, may I use your telephone to ring my friends in Palermo? I was staying with Baron Donzini's family, and they might be worried, since it's been a couple of days that they haven't heard from me."

Aunt Maria didn't know who Baron Donzini was, but she was clearly impressed with the title. Jane explained that the family came from Alcamo originally, and that Aldo taught Italian literature at the University of Palermo, while Claudia, his wife, was Joanna Holland's old school friend from America. They assured Jane that the telephone in the front parlor was at her disposal, and went about their daily chores, leaving her alone.

Maria opened up the general store, Ninfina went to see to the *caffe*. They seemed terribly innocent, Jane thought. Or was it simply complacency? Did they feel safe, sure that the American relative was naive, unaware of what was really going on beneath the surface of their seemingly routine lives?

Why do I suspect a sinister sub-text to all this? Jane fretted. She realized that the language barrier, perhaps, made it difficult for her to follow what was going on. She felt like a small girl again, in her grandmother's house, not fully grasping what was going on in the adult world, not fully understanding what the grownups were saying.

Jane thought she was turning into quite an accomplished liar. First, she sneaked a look into the Bagheria-Borgetto-Montelepre telephone directory (as big as a small-sized college spiral notebook), to find Margherita Mannino's exchange, remembering that she'd said she lived with her late husband's nephew on the Via Reggio. Jane hoped that the old woman had good hearing, because she feared shouting into the telephone would tip her precarious hand with Maria and Ninfina.

The old woman had great hearing, and was overjoyed that Jane had called. She arranged to meet her at the family plot at approximately 10:30 a.m., but not today, tomorrow. She apologized for the slight change of plans; she had forgotten a long-standing doctor's appointment in Palermo in her excitement over meeting Jane. She did, indeed, sound terribly excited, saying that she was bringing something to show Jane the next day. *"Ciaio, cara,"* she said as she rang off.

Now for the big one, Jane thought, as, hand shaking, she dialed through to Palermo. *Please, God, let Claudia be the one to answer . . .*

"Pronto." Yes, it was Claudia, her nasal tones ringing loud and clear. Claudia was glad to hear from Jane, but she was angry, too.

"Jane Holland," she began, "whatever got into you—"

Oh, Claudia, Jane thought, cheeks suddenly ablaze, remembering the ecstasy of her night under the full moon with Lorenzo, *you should only know. But this is really not the right time to discuss all that.*

"We have all been so terribly worried! Jane, I had no idea who your mother's relatives are, how was I going to get in touch with you, how would I know you were all right, how would we find you." There were a lot of hows. Claudia was vehement, and she had a right to be angry at her, Jane thought.

"And also, my dear, you should be aware that you have made Lorenzo Bighilaterra very upset. I cannot, for the life of me, Jane, understand how you could be so rude as to stand him up that way, planning to just leave him waiting for you at that bar when you had no intention at all of showing up. That's a rotten little game to play. What did he do to you to deserve that? No, I take that back, what has gone on between you and him is your business, and none of mine, I realize that."

Bless you, Claudia, Jane thought, silently.

"But don't get into the habit of treating people like that, Jane. There are better ways, more adult ways, to accomplish the same thing. Do you understand what I'm saying to you?"

Jane wanted, suddenly, to unburden herself to Claudia, to tell her everything. She knew she would sympathize, not be judgmental. Or was she simply looking for a shoulder to cry on? Did she want Claudia to play mommy? *Stop it, Jane, get a grip now,* she warned herself.

Aloud, she answered, "Claudia, I understand, and I appreciate what you're saying. I need some time to clarify my thoughts right now. When I get back to Palermo, maybe—"

"When are you coming back, Jane?"

"Soon, Claudia, soon." She didn't want to commit herself to a hard date. Then she could swear she heard Claudia take a deep breath, as if to steel herself for what was coming next. Jane had no warning, absolutely no time to get herself to the bomb shelter. The nuclear warhead hit her right between the eyes, dead on.

Claudia was continuing to speak. ". . . and, Jane, you should not, dear, have depended on Anna Maria to get all your messages straight, to get all those varied stories, those very different stories, to the people for whom they were intended—"

"What do you mean?" Jane didn't like Claudia's hesitant tone. Here came the guided missile, taking on speed. "She didn't tell Lorenzo I was going to Borgetto . . ." Jane began.

"Oh, yes, that she did, that she did, but that's not the worst thing she did."

Oh, no, Jane thought, as the warhead zeroed in, not that! She gulped. "My mother called. She told her I was in Borgetto, too, right?"

Blam! She knew Claudia's answer already. "I'm afraid so, dear . . . and she's coming to take you home."

Reeling, Jane was indignant as well as mortally wounded. "Take me home? *Take me home?* Am I a child? What's wrong with that woman? I can get home by myself, thank you very much!"

"Well, apparently, Anna Maria was quite indiscreet when your mother called."

That's it, thought Jane, I am going to kill that little

cretin the minute I see her again. Claudia was telling her the whole awful story now.

"She told your mother that you'd gotten deeply involved with a playboy, an older man who was in the midst of a scandal, who had a bad reputation, was a womanizer—"

"Claudia, are you serious?" Jane was shaking with anger.

"I wish I were not, dear," she replied, quietly. "Unfortunately, I didn't have a chance to speak with Joanna myself, to dissuade her from coming, to tell her that my daughter is an absolute idiot who doesn't know enough to mind her own business. I really am so sorry about this, Jane."

This is incredible, Jane thought. With all she had on her mind now, the last person she wanted to deal with was her mother. She couldn't believe her mother was coming to Sicily to bring her home. It was positively humiliating. And now, her pride in tatters all about her, in shreds around her feet and ankles, the shrapnel from the bomb having pierced her flesh, there was one more thing she had to know.

"Claudia, please tell me, what did Lorenzo have to say—about me?"

On the other end of the telephone, in Palermo, Claudia Donzini remembered the appalling events of scarcely two days ago. It had started when she'd gotten home from a luncheon engagement with Mary Lou Fanelli, another expatriate American who was one of her best friends in the city. Came home to find Anna Maria in a state, frightened, incoherent.

"Where's Jane?" she'd asked her daughter, casting an eye around the flat.

Anna Maria had started to bawl. "It's not my fault! She wanted to go!"

Claudia had taken Anna Maria by the wrist, had shaken

her. "Go where? You had better tell me everything, young lady, starting right now! Where is Jane?"

And it had all come out. Jane's peculiar outburst at lunch, her impromptu decision to leave Palermo and head for Borgetto, where her mother had relatives, her scuttling of the date with Lorenzo, her instructions to Anna Maria concerning what to tell Claudia, Lorenzo, and, in the off chance she called, her mother.

Anna Maria had just gotten off the telephone with Joanna Holland. She admitted to her mother that she'd been indiscreet, telling Joanna not only that Jane had gone to Borgetto—directly, it seemed, against the orders of her mother the other day—but that she was involved with a notorious Sicilian playboy. Joanna Holland's reaction to the news had been swift. She announced she was booking a flight immediately and coming to Sicily to take her errant daughter home, to rescue her from the clutches of the Eurotrash with whom she'd gotten herself involved.

Calmly, Claudia had released Anna Maria from her grip. Calmly, she had told her daughter, "I'm not exactly sure what your father and I are going to do about your loose, vicious tongue, Anna Maria. We are going to have to give this a great deal of thought. Just because you may not be punished right away, do not, for a minute, think that you will escape punishment. Is that very, very, clear?"

A suddenly contrite Anna Maria had nodded unhappily, tearfully, as Claudia had continued. "Did you relay Jane's message to Lorenzo?"

Anna Maria shook her head, numbly. "Not yet," she sniffled.

At that, Claudia, staring down her daughter, asked, "What will you tell him?"

Anna Maria sensed that there was only one correct answer to this question, "Whatever you think I should tell him, Mama?"

"Very good, Anna Maria. You will tell Lorenzo that Jane wanted him told that she had gone home, to the States, but, that in reality, she has gone to Borgetto. Further, that this was something she explicitly did not want him to know."

At that moment, as if by pre-arranged signal, Lorenzo called to confirm their plans, his and Jane's, for the evening. The time was then about 3:30 in the afternoon. Anna Maria answered, relating the message from Jane, edited by Claudia. Before Lorenzo had a chance to react, Claudia reached for the instrument, asking Lorenzo to come to the flat, now, to talk.

The shiny bottle green Alfa was parked on the Via delle alpi within the quarter-hour. An agitated, concerned Lorenzo Bighilaterra was at the door. He had been in the middle of dinner preparations for Jane and himself and had not bothered to change from his old clothes. He was wearing torn blue jeans and a worn cotton shirt, now sprinkled with the homemade tomato sauce—a treasured Bighilaterra family recipe—he had just put on to simmer. He hadn't yet shaved. Claudia's heart went out to him. The stubble only accentuated the extreme youthfulness, she thought, of his otherwise smooth face.

She asked Lorenzo to sit down, handing him a cup of heavily sugared hot tea with milk, her sure-fire remedy for calming one down and alleviating shocking news. She then related to him what had apparently transpired, that Anna Maria, it seemed, had gotten Jane upset, that she had to go away for a few days to think things over, that she was somewhere in the vicinity of Borgetto, that she would be back, but that, right now, she couldn't bring herself to speak to Lorenzo about it.

* * * * *

Lorenzo had pushed the tea aside. "What do you mean she can't speak to me? What in God's name is she upset about?" Last night, he thought, last night she was fine, everything was fine, they were both fine. Had she had second thoughts about what had happened between them? No, impossible, he was sure of that, his pride, his manhood, denying that there could be any problem.

He had turned fiercely to Anna Maria, cringing in a corner of the silk loveseat, "What did you do to her, Anna Maria? What did you do, what did you say, to my darling Gianna to make her run off like this? I want to know the truth, now, nothing but the truth!"

And Anna Maria, before the double-barreled force of his anger at her and his deep concern for Jane Holland, had burst into tears.

"I'm sorry, I'm sorry, I didn't mean it . . . it was all lies, I was just teasing her! I didn't think she would take it all that way, I didn't!" She turned to her mother, beseechingly. "Please, Mama, forgive me!" Then to Lorenzo, "I'm so sorry, believe me. I'll never talk about you again, I promise you, I will never say anything about you as long as I live, I swear. Please forgive me, Lorenzo?"

Lorenzo sighed. He could not understand how two people like Aldo and Claudia Donzini, two of the dearest friends of his family, could have produced a child like Anna Maria, so unlike them. He had never liked her. Recently, at a big party in town, she had flirted outrageously with him, throwing herself at him with no sense of pride. He had left the party early, opting to catch the Naples Symphony Orchestra at the Opera House. They'd played selections from Mozart and Vivaldi, he remembered. It had been a peaceful evening.

This girl—he shook his head—if she had destroyed his relationship with Gianna, he would gladly strangle her with his bare hands. As if in response, his hands tensely clenched and unclenched.

"Claudia, what shall I do? I must speak to her. I care for her a great deal. This is no passing fancy, believe me."

Claudia had flinched at the pain in his intense blue eyes. She honestly did not know what to tell him. Anna Maria was still sobbing her mean little heart out. The door to the flat opened and closed.

Lorenzo ran out of the sitting room, calling out his beloved's name. "Gianna?"

It was Aldo, back from his restful day at the farm in Alcamo, ready to be taken into the bosom of his happy little family. As soon as he saw the faces that greeted him—Lorenzo, stricken, Claudia, brow furrowed with worry, Anna Maria still crying—he wished he had never left his vineyards.

"What now?" he had sighed.

All this went through Claudia's mind as she spoke to Jane. It had been a miserable afternoon. She had tried to persuade Lorenzo to let Jane come to her senses, repeating that she had no idea whatsoever how to contact Jane if she was in Borgetto, but she wasn't at all sure that determined young man was about to listen to her advice. He decided to leave, to sleep on it, to see what the next day brought in the way of settling this misunderstanding. He was gone scarcely two minutes when he was back at their door again, a beautifully wrapped square box in his hands.

"This is for Gianna," he said, "in case she comes back. I meant to give it to her tonight." Then he was gone. Claudia had not had the heart to return the gold chain Jane had left for him.

"Jane," she said now to the girl who had turned her once-peaceful household upside-down, "Lorenzo is very upset, there's no question of that, none at all, but he wants a chance to talk to you, to straighten out whatever misunderstandings have occurred between you two. Jane . . ." She hesitated. "He seems to care for you very, very much."

Jane wasn't so sure. Lorenzo didn't know that she was aware of what had transpired between him and that mysterious and beautiful older woman on the Cortile Santa Caterina; he had no idea that she had seen him carrying on with a woman with whom he was obviously on intimate terms. Jane was certain he was just putting up a front before Claudia. He didn't want Claudia, his champion, to have a bad opinion of him. Anna Maria had told her he was like that, always currying favor insincerely with her parents.

"Jane? Are you still there?" Claudia, hearing no response to her last statement, thought that Jane had hung up on her. But no, she was there. "Jane, I almost forgot to tell you, Lorenzo left you a present. What do you want me to do with it, my dear? Shall I return it to him? Is that what you want? Or shall I leave it here for you?"

A present? Jane was flabbergasted. Why would Lorenzo leave her something? This would be his second gift in two days, the gold chain for the amulet being the first. "What is it?" she wanted to know.

"Well, I don't know. It's all wrapped up. Pretty silver paper and a big, floppy white grosgrain bow. The box is medium-sized, kind of squarish in shape."

She had to know what it was. "Open it, Claudia, please."

"Are you sure? Well, all right, give me a minute while I put down the phone."

Jane could hear rustling sounds as the bow and wrapping paper were removed from the box. She heard Claudia exclaim, "Oh, my!" Jane was impatient. *Hurry up, Claudia, hurry up, tell me what it is!* She wanted to scream into the receiver.

Jane could hear Claudia picking up the telephone. There was awe in her voice. "Jane, I don't know what to say . . . this is superb . . . and I have no doubt that it is genuine, the real thing. It must be worth a fortune . . ."

Claudia, you are torturing me, Jane wanted to scream! The woman was a master of slow, subtle torture. "Please, Claudia, what is it? What has Lorenzo given me?"

"I think it's Greek, late classical Greek, quite sophisticated, utterly beautiful. It's a small marble head, of a young woman. Oh, it is just spectacular. I can't believe it, Jane, you will just love it." She sounded completely entranced and overwhelmed.

Jane, too, was utterly and completely overwhelmed. Another mysterious piece of classical statuary had suddenly turned up in her life. Too many strange, oddly coincidental things were happening, and all at once.

Jane felt a cold chill up her back. She shivered. When Jenny and Jane were children, Jane remembered, one of them would tease the other when one of them shivered or felt a chill up her back. "Someone's walking on your grave," they'd tease each other.

And tomorrow she had an appointment in a cemetery.

Chapter Eleven

The Vineyards at Dusk

Time weighed heavily all day on Jane. She was anxious and disturbed. Tomorrow she would meet with Margherita. The old woman had been so excited and happy; Jane wondered what it was she was so eager to show her. Whatever it was, it was extremely important to her. Jane could not help but like Margherita; she was a dear, sweet lady towards whom Jane was swiftly developing tender, protective feelings. She was a lady who clearly had suffered, surely undeservedly so.

And Claudia Donzini . . . Claudia was wonderful. Jane knew she should trust her more, confide in her. What was holding her back was the humiliation of having to admit that Lorenzo had made a fool of her, and that she had allowed it to happen despite the older woman's concern and warning. She sighed. It was too hard to keep it all bottled up inside her; she had to unburden herself to someone, someone who would care, someone who would be sympathetic. She should have told Claudia everything that had happened and asked for her help.

Lorenzo . . . the feelings he aroused were perhaps better left alone. They confused her, tore her apart. She could not seem to think logically. She knew that, in his eyes, she was probably just an unsophisticated little foreigner, unable to understand or to adjust to the way the world really worked. Why couldn't she simply accept the fact that he had a mistress—possibly more than one—and that she had no hope of changing him? He was used to his way of life; she was the one who had to make the adjustments if she wanted him. Or as much of him as he could spare for her.

Claudia's spirited defense of Lorenzo notwithstanding, she was a foreigner, too, Jane had to acknowledge, no matter how long she had lived on this strange little island. They were both outsiders in a closed society. And who was to say Aldo did not have his secret liaisons, girlfriends hidden away, also? Claudia had probably adjusted a long time ago, turning a blind eye to his affairs. Could any of these charming, too-handsome, lusty male animals be trusted?

Was trust even the issue? She was simply imposing her own banal sense of morality—her boring, solid, middle-class American values—on an ancient, sophisticated culture that had evolved differently. *What did she know about Sicily or Sicilians?*

It was no use. She was making herself crazy, and getting nowhere. She had to talk it out, try to make some sense out of the whole mess, and it was clearer by the minute that her confidante had to be Claudia Donzini. There was simply no one else she could talk to about this. She would ring her up again and set up a time to meet.

There was no answer at first at the Via delle alpi flat. The telephone rang and rang. No answering machine picked up the call. Her mind racing frantically, Jane tried to remember the conversation she'd had with Claudia early that morning. Was the family planning to go to Alcamo, to the Donzini vineyards? Did she have that number? She gnawed nervously at the edge of a fingernail, wondering what to do next. As she was about to hang up the phone in despair, Claudia's voice floated over the airwaves.

"Jane? Dear, whatever is the matter now? Has something

else happened?" she asked, alarmed.

Jane's voice sounded strained even to her own ears. This was so hard to do! "Claudia," she began, "I need you. I need to talk to you, now."

"Do you want me to come to Borgetto?" Claudia asked.

Jane panicked. As much as she was risking almost all by taking this step, by asking Claudia for help, she could not reveal her hiding place. Not yet. "N-no," she stammered, "I'll come to meet you . . ."

"Tell me where, Jane," Claudia responded.

"Not Palermo." No, she couldn't take the chance of running into Lorenzo. She was not that brave. She had an idea. "Alcamo? At the farmhouse?"

Jane could hear Claudia hesitate. "The farm? Well . . . I . . . I don't know. Oh, why not? Yes, the farm, tonight. Come just before dark. I have a thousand errands to run today. You caught me just as I was rushing out the front door."

"I'm sorry—"

"No, don't apologize. I just may be a bit late. You get yourself out to Alcamo and I'll see you there. *Ciaio,* Jane." She hung up.

Well, her begging had worked. Claudia had arranged to meet her at the Donzini farm, between Borgetto and Palermo. She would have to drive to the farmhouse, but it wasn't far. Perhaps Ninfina would go with her. She and Claudia would have a heart-to-heart talk. Her advice would be reasoned, good. She wouldn't let Jane feel like a naive little fool, and Aldo could be counted on to entertain her cousin in the interim. He was good with shy people and Ninfina certainly belonged in that category.

Yes, she would persuade her cousin to go to Alcamo with her late that afternoon, but it appeared that it wasn't going to be that easy.

"But, Ninfina, why can't you come? It's not so far away, and I have to see my friends. It's important." Jane, impatient, was acutely aware of the whiny undertone in her voice as she attempted to persuade her cousin. She winced. She hated whiners!

Ninfina's dangling gold earbobs bounced from side to side as she shook her head no. They had just eaten a late lunch—the store and *caffe* had been unusually busy that afternoon, well into siesta time—and both mother and daughter seemed frazzled.

They were committed to go to a wake, as it turned out, in a small village on the coast several kilometers from Borgetto. A distant cousin of Ninfina's late uncle. It would be unforgivable to be absent, according to her cousin. This, she explained, was how bad feelings among relatives started. Not that they knew the deceased well, she admitted freely, but they had to show respect, nonetheless.

"Gianna, of course we do not expect you to come with us—" *Thank goodness!* Jane thought, relieved, "—and we can travel to San Pietro with our cousins the Lupos. They have a Mercedes big enough for all of us. Cousin Gaetano Lupo worked in Stuttgart for five years, you know, and he brought it back with him."

Completing her careful explanation, Ninfina gravely offered Jane the keys to her car, passing them on to her as if the battered jalopy's keys were sacred objects of the Mother Church.

Recognizing that this was an act of genuine kindness, Jane gave the only appropriate response, taking the keys with a sincere-sounding *"grazie."* The thought, however, of her driving Ninfina's less-than-reliable-looking car over unfamiliar Sicilian country roads made her hesitate. She really didn't have the foggiest notion of how to get to Alcamo, much less how to locate the Donzini vineyards. She had been so agitated setting up the appointment with Claudia that she had neglected to ask directions. Worse yet, she knew the telephone number for the farmhouse was unlisted, and there was a busy signal, then no answer at the Palermo flat when she tried to ring back. Claudia had said she had a thousand errands to run and she had obviously left immediately to take care of them.

Ninfina was surprisingly astute. "Let's look at the map," she suggested gently. "I have been to Alcamo many times—we have cousins there, also—and I can telephone them for the exact directions to the farm of your friends. All right?"

What could she say? The matter was out of her hands. If she wanted to see Claudia, this was the only way she was going to do it. Stifling her fears of driving on bad Sicilian back roads and having to cope with aggressive Sicilian drivers, she could only nod her thanks.

Her first glimpse of the Donzini farms and vineyards was from between the cypresses that lined the winding road leading out of the town of Alcamo proper. Claudia had told her that it was a simple country place and had always been a family farm, part of the extensive baronial manor holdings that had once been in the hands of the Donzini clan. (The manor house and a good deal of land had been sold after the war to pay off debts.) But it was no ordinary farmhouse, not by any stretch of the imagination, Jane's critical eye noted. It was beautiful, the white stone exterior lovingly restored. Yes, she could see that it had been modernized, but discreetly, tastefully. It did not stick out as a jarring and anachronistic note in the rustic landscape.

Jane parked the car in the roundabout in front of the house. An old blue pickup truck was parked off to one side, its cab slightly dented, crates stamped Vino Donzini heaped haphazardly on its ample bed. No other vehicles were in sight. Although a number of outside lights—obviously timed—were beginning to come on around the farmhouse as dusk fell, there were no lights showing from within the house. It was, in point of fact, eerily quiet.

Jane hesitated, one hand clutching the car door handle tightly, and called out. "Aldo? Claudia?" No answer. Not one sound. How odd. Where was Claudia? Where was Donna Maria, the housekeeper? The farm laborers and other servants? The place seemed deserted. She glanced at her wristwatch. She was exactly on time. Making up her mind to take a better look, she released the handle and slammed the car door shut. She had come all this way. She might as well have a good look around.

Leaving the keys in the ignition and the Fiat's windows rolled down, she wiped her wet palms on her blue jeans and cautiously walked up the flagstone path to the front door. It was a screen door, and it was unlatched. The door behind it swung open. "Aldo? Claudia?" She called out again.

The room she entered was big and high-ceilinged, buttressed by ancient and massively wide oak beams. Glass-fronted wooden cupboards held glistening rows of what had to be Claudia's treasured collection of 18th century Sicilian blue opaline glass and majolica. There was a strong smell of paint in the air and white cotton dust covers were thrown over the furniture, which was bunched together in the middle of the room. The interior had recently been white-washed and the paint was drying. No wonder none of the servants was about, but where was Claudia?

With a frustrated sigh, Jane sat down heavily on a cloth-covered chair. Claudia had stood her up. *Why?*

Damn! She sighed again, frustrated. Leaning back in the chair, she steepled her fingers under her chin. *Double damn!*

Her eyes flickered around the room. Stacked everywhere were dark green glass bottles of Donzini red, the private label Aldo sold only to a few select customers, connoisseurs of small, estate-bottled vintages. Jane had sampled the red in Palermo. It was a fine rich wine, predominantly dry yet with a fruity aftertaste. Most unusual. It did not travel well, and so its fame was primarily local. Jane remembered its rich ruby hue, as pleasing to the eye as its aroma was to the nose and its taste to the palate.

Aldo Donzini had told her that the older vintages, kept in the farmhouse cellars, had paled in color with age, and that the taste had transmuted subtly, deeper yet lighter at the same time, almost a contradiction. A mysterious, many-faceted purple grape was the basis for the renowned Donzini private label.

Tommaso Donzini, Aldo's grandfather, had been obsessed with the wine grape. He had researched the history of grape growing in Sicily, delving deeply into ancient literature to find out what had flourished on these rocky hillsides long ago. He'd traveled widely all over the Mediterranean, to Crete, to Greece, even to the ancient outposts of Greek and Roman civilization in the Middle East, to find native Sicilian grape stock.

He went to Arne, described by the poet Homer as *"rich in vineyards,"* journeyed to Histiaia—*"rich in vines"*—and Epidauros—*"full of vines"*—and to Pedasos, the *"land of vines,"* and to Ithaca and Phrygia. A man obsessed, he searched in vain for the notorious Pramnian wine of the sorceress Circe, the wine that turned men into beasts and enslaved Ulysses' homesick sailors.

He rode on the backs of donkeys deep into Thrace to find the fabled, fragrant Maronea, the honey sweet wine so deep in color it was almost black, the very wine reputed to have intoxicated the giant Cyclops. He followed the trail of a purple, early-ripening grape thought to have come from Lemnos and investigated Hesiod's famed Lebanese Bibline, which had been introduced into Sicily by the ancient Greeks and was known to them as Pollian.

Bringing back as many grapevines as he could find and identify, Aldo Donzini told Jane, his grandfather Tommaso planted them and grafted the best results onto each other until he had achieved what he thought the ancients had described so effusively and lyrically in their poetry. He never ceased, even into his dotage, experimenting with grape stock.

The Donzini red private label was the living proof of his labor. The other grapes grown on the farm went into a good, plain white, what the French would call a *vin ordinaire,* their reliable cash crop, their bread and butter. Aldo still had acres of these grapes, which he sold at a good price for blending into other wines for the Common Market. The other, the red, was stored in old oak casks and bottled for a select and choice clientele.

Thinking of the story of Tommaso Donzini's quest made Jane thirsty for his red wine. It was a warm night. There was a slight breeze coming through the screened windows and doors, wafting the sweet smell of Claudia's heirloom rose bushes indoors. Jane wandered into the kitchen and turned on a light.

The kitchen was a cook's delight. High-ceilinged and wooden-beamed like the living room, there were walls covered with high-tech appliances cheek by jowl with glossy, shined-to-a-high-finish antique copper pots and sauté pans. The counters were green black-veined marble, the sink fittings burnished bronze. Off to one side was a wet bar, with racks of wine laid on their sides.

Jane selected a wide-bodied wine glass from the counter and chose a bottle of wine. She uncorked it carefully and poured herself a full glass. She was instantly warmed, her senses opening up to the pleasure of the fragrant, slightly fruity wine. She could feel herself glow. *With Donzini red,* she thought irreverently, *who needs a man? Even if he is a prince?* She giggled and poured herself another glass.

Her blood absorbed this sweet juice of sun-warmed Sicilian grapes and her skin tingled with a pleasant heat, not unlike the afterglow of lovemaking. The wine was extraordinarily delicious and she was amazed at how quickly it coursed through her veins. She'd never enjoyed a wine as much as she was enjoying this. Sipping her drink, she mused on what it might be like to be a grape just before harvesting, a big, sweet grape, bursting with rich juice.

The speculation, as she giddily imagined herself as a fat purple fruit about to split open, made her giggle yet again. She refilled her glass and opened the Dutch door leading out of the kitchen. A wood-planked path led straight and true into the vineyards.

The shimmering white sparkles of thousands of fireflies danced in the distance, drawing her attention with their staccato glow. Dusk had fallen, to be replaced by dark twilight. She looked upwards as she walked carefully down the wooden path, and blinked at the star-dusted sky, the stars twinkling back at her like heavenly fireflies. Her legs were a little wobbly; staring up at the stars had always made her unsteady on her feet when she was a little girl. She realized also, too late, that she had drunk much too deeply of that special, heady wine.

Chapter Twelve

The Dionysian Revels

The ground beneath her feet shifted. She braced herself, thinking she was surely tipsy and had lost her balance and was going to fall, but, no, it was just the sensation of a different texture under her feet: dirt, not wood. Somehow, unaware, she had lost her shoes and slipped off the path onto bare earth. She blinked. That wasn't possible; she wasn't that intoxicated.

And, she was still in the Donzini vineyards . . . wasn't she?

No, she wasn't. This was certainly a vineyard of sorts, but not Aldo or Claudia's. This was different, completely, amazingly, different. This vineyard was in the middle of an orchard. An orchard? *Where had all these trees come from?* She recognized olive trees, pear trees, evergreens, fig trees, laurel, bushes of wild rose.

At her bare feet three-leafed ivy was growing freely, unfettered, interspersed with the sharp purple presence of hundreds of tiny violets. Amongst all this lush, thick vegetation grew the grapevines, which were loosely-staked, propped up with short wooden sticks or trailing over the loamy, fertile earth and loaded down with heavy bunches of dark grapes, fragrant, bursting with juice.

Music. Faint. Growing louder. Coming her way. *Was someone having a party? A celebration?* She heard the sweet high music of flutes as revelers came dancing through the trees singing a song of the gods, the ancient ones, and of the sweet, sweet wine. Songs of the harvest. Songs of fertility and abundance.

"Evoe, evoe, evoe," they murmured softly. Women, *maenaeds,* came, garbed in flowing togas and *chitons* of white, yellow, blue, and red, their long, wild tresses loose, waving freely in the soft breeze. They sang of intoxication, of the wine, of Dionysus and Bacchus, the gods of the wine. Their bare feet beat a loud rhythm on the hard-packed, much-trodden earth.

Small boys playing lyres hopped and skipped among the reveling women. Men followed. Jane gasped in fright, her heart beating fast, too fast. *These were not men!* They were beasts—half-man, half-animal—their bottom halves covered in coarse, furry hair, their hips and legs narrowing into sharp hooves, their private parts enormous. Strange instruments, double flutes with a single mouthpiece, were between their fleshy lips, bringing forth a haunting tune, mesmerizing, liquid, honey-sweet to her receptive ears.

Possessed, the *maenaeds* danced wilder still among the boys and the beasts, weaving long wands wreathed with curling ivy and bindweed, trailing larkspur, roses, violets. Some wands were wrapped about with herbs, purple-flowered sage, yellow-blossomed oregano, fringed tendrils of dill. They came closer, much closer, singing, chanting, dancing. Dancing! Dancing!

Jane ran sweating hands over her thighs, crying to control her trembling. With a sickening chill, she brought her hands away in horror, realizing that her jeans and tee shirt had disappeared and that she was now clothed like these women, but even more elaborately dressed in a white linen pleated toga trimmed with gold *ribands.* A deep purple shawl trimmed in glimmering gold fringe caressed her bare shoulders. Her hands flew to her head as she suddenly became conscious of her tightly curled and braided hair, hair that was wound into a firm chignon. A delicate, hammered gold *fillet* encircled her forehead and temples.

She froze.

What was happening? Where was she? Who was she?

The words of the women's song floated on the soft, scented air of the fruit orchard like the delicate, gossamer wings of moths . . . and stopped. There was a ripple at the far edge of the throng of dancers and musicians and then they were stilled, their frenzied movements abruptly arrested, making way for someone. A man was approaching, parting the crowd as he came. No, not a man. A god.

A god was approaching.

The light from a thousand stars showered down upon the tall, radiant figure nearing Jane. A halo glowed about him, its aura almost blinding her. She held her breath and her body rippled in a long shiver. The revelers fell away to the side, parted, and came back together in his wake. He was resplendent, magnificent. Jane drew a quick, sharp breath.

She had never seen anyone so beautiful, so splendid, in her life.

The god was tall, slender, his oiled, well-defined muscles gleaming with good health and virility. His hair was long, black, and curled, softly waving over his broad shoulders. He wore a white pleated chiton that showed off sinewy, corded legs. Glittering, jewel-like blue eyes in a finely chiseled, aquiline face appraised her. She was transfixed by his brilliant stare. His face was sculpted, his chin firm and strong, his lips firm and curving. She thought, for a fleeting moment, that she knew him. He smiled at her in approval, nodding his head.

At a commanding signal from his right hand, two women separated themselves from the surrounding throng and came up behind Jane. They loosened the gold filigree clips that held her toga together at the shoulders. It fell to her feet in a soft, slithery movement, a puddle of fabric on the bare brown earth.

Low, hypnotic chanting began as the soft, warm night air caressed her naked, trembling flesh. The god came closer, his wine-sweet breath brushing her cheeks with sudden warmth. Involuntarily, she stepped back, feeling the cold marble edge of an altar cutting into the flesh of her bare buttocks. Two of the women rose up quickly and placed a curly-haired white sheepskin over the chilly marble, covering it completely.

More women darted forward, strewing the sheepskin-laid sacrificial altar with fragrant wildflowers and delicate, leafy vines. Dionysus placed his warm hand gently on her bare shoulder and slowly eased her down over the altarpiece. The chanting of the drunken revelers drummed intensely in her ears. She began to swoon as he lowered himself onto her. Before she fainted dead away, she felt the hardness of his muscular body and the sharp stab of pain that accompanied his deep thrust inside her.

The maiden Daphne, pursued by the amorous god Apollo, had begged the virgin goddess Diana for help and been turned into a laurel tree. She, Jane Holland, had been given no such charitable option this night.

She was lying back on a bed, an enormous four-poster dressed in crisp linen bed sheets and draped with gauzy white curtains. Her shoes were off, but she was otherwise fully clothed. Lorenzo Bighilaterra, his face pale and anxious, was hovering over her.

"Are you all right, Gianna?" he whispered, his voice husky. He was holding her hands tightly in his.

Jane was too taken aback to answer. What had happened to her? Seconds before, the god Dionysus had painfully penetrated her maidenhead, having his way with her before a throng of faceless strangers, and now . . . here was Lorenzo. Lorenzo. *Of all people!* She tried to rise up.

"No! Don't do that!" Lorenzo's voice was sharp and commanding, contrasting with the gentleness of his hands as he eased her back against the big, square pillows at the head of the bed. "Don't raise your head, Gianna. You fainted in Aldo's vineyard."

He smiled. "You looked at me as though you'd seen a ghost. I don't blame you for fainting. I am sure I am the last person you expected to see here, surely the last person you wanted to see."

He couldn't hide the hurt, the pain behind his words. Jane licked her lips; they were so dry. She tried to speak, to answer him, but she didn't sound at all like herself. She croaked, "I thought the Donzinis would be here . . . Claudia said she would meet me—"

"Oh?" he wondered. "Were you ready, then, to come home?"

She shook her head slowly, wincing at the movement. She'd had too much of that bewitching wine and she would pay dearly for it.

"What is this nonsense all about, Gianna? Are you going to tell me, or do I have to guess?"

She winced again at the tone of his voice, angry and injured at the same time. She lowered her head.

He released her hands and walked away, one hand thrust deeply into his trousers pocket, the other running through his already tousled dark curly hair.

Lorenzo turned back and fixed her with a cold blue glare, willing her to look at him. "You have to communicate with me, you know. This running away, this is what children do. You cannot continue to behave this way, *cara.* Tell me, please, when are you going to grow up?"

She was mortified, but she wasn't going to cry. More childish behavior, he'd think, as she disgraced herself further in his eyes. How he'd laugh if she told him why she had run away. She'd run far, run fast, but she hadn't been able to run fast enough or far enough to forget that she loved him.

Nor could she forget that woman. His mistress. He wanted her to grow up. *Grow up, Gianna, accept Lorenzo's other women, his mistresses, his peccadilloes.* No, she could never be that grown up. Well, then, to him she was immature, a child, so be it. She was what she was and she knew she could not change.

He had turned his back on her again and was pacing back and forth. Suddenly he whirled on his heel and squeezed her shoulders in a hard, hurting grip. "Say something, damn it!" he shouted hoarsely.

Surprised at his angry outburst, she cried out at the pain. Tears welled in her eyes and she couldn't stifle a sob. He'd hurt her . . . Lorenzo, her gentle lover had hurt her.

Had she been mistaken about his gentleness, also? Had it only been a facade?

His face crumpled. Tears were running down his cheeks. He clasped her to him, flattening her bosom against his hard, muscled chest. "Ah, God, I'm losing my mind! Please, *cara,* forgive me . . . I did not mean to hurt you . . . I would never hurt you, but you have torn me in pieces with worry. Please, I beg you, what have I done? What is the matter?" he pleaded.

The feel of him against her, warm, hard, brought back the hallucination in the vineyard. It was Lorenzo she had conjured up, her imagination running wild because she wanted him so much, her defenses down because of that wine. Of course she had fainted, because she had, she thought, truly conjured him up in the flesh.

The bizarre dream was a combination of too much wine and too little Lorenzo. How could she be such a fool as to think she could get over him so quickly? *It was pathetic; she was pathetic.* All the more so because right now, at this moment, she wanted him more than she had ever wanted him before. She was tired of running away from him.

He was still trying to reason with her. "I cannot believe that you do not care for me, Gianna. I do not think you could have faked your feelings so well . . . you are not that good an actress, *cara.* Everything shows on your sweet face." He stroked her cheeks gently with his thumbs. "There is something real and good between us, my love. Why did you run from it? What are you scared of now?"

Numbly, she cast her eyes down again, her fingers nervously playing with the linen counterpane. She couldn't look into his eyes, still glistening with tears; she would be lost.

He wasn't giving up. "Look at me, *cara.* Tell me yourself that we don't belong together. Tell me, and . . . and I will go away and stop bothering you." His voice was soft, low, caressing. Reluctantly, she opened her eyes.

"You are so lovely . . ." he began, gently tracing her chin, the side of her jaw, with two fingers. "I will be frank with you, Gianna. There have been other women in my life; I won't deny that. Lovely women, also, but none that I ever wanted the way I want you. Can you believe that? It's the truth. The Hindus have a word for it, *karma,* destiny, fate.

You and I belong together, *cara,* the two of us. I feel we were together in the past, perhaps more than once, and that we are meant to be together now. Don't turn away from me."

She looked at him without flinching, hearing his avowal, wanting to believe everything he said. Yes, there was that pull, from the first. They had teased about being lovers at Segesta, artisans working on the cathedral at Monreale . . . perhaps they had met once, too, on a forested hillside under the stars, with *Bacchae,* as revelers, with chanting all around them in the night. Perhaps, though, it was all foolishness, poppycock, and it was only the here and now of their being together that was important. Maybe he truly loved her now, and she would be enough woman for him in the future.

She felt the rational, logical girl named Jane Holland, the girl she had been for most of her life, slipping away without a fight. The new Jane, the one Lorenzo had christened Gianna, was putty in his hands. That Jane believed everything he said, took all his lies and half-truths as gospel. It was no contest. She wanted him so. The yearning, the love, the need to be loved, to believe all the lover says, took over.

She swayed towards him, nuzzling his neck, finding the sweet, hot juncture where his throat met his chest, pressing her lips lightly upon the pulse that throbbed there so strongly. His heartbeat. *Hers.* No, she couldn't run from him anymore. It wasn't the effect of the wine, either. *She wanted him.* It was that simple; it had always been.

Lorenzo was momentarily off-balance, startled by the change in her behavior, her seeming surrender in his arms. Warily, he took her face in both hands and looked into her eyes, staring her down, asking her directly. "Are you sure, Gianna? Is this what you want?"

Flushing slightly, her lower lip trembling, she responded huskily, "I want you, Lorenzo."

Lorenzo hesitated. He knew Jane had drunk nearly a full bottle of Donzini red, a potent wine with a high alcoholic content. He had driven up to the farmhouse after receiving a call from Claudia Donzini.

Claudia said that although she realized she was breaking a confidence—and that bothered her conscience not a little—that Jane and he had to get together and settle their differences. The situation between the two young people was ludicrous, immature. Lorenzo would be the one to meet Jane at the farmhouse, not her. Perhaps this would be perceived by Jane as a mean trick on her part, but if the girl had any sense she would understand that she could not keep running away from her problems; she had to grow up and face them.

He had been overwhelmed by Claudia's call, by her decision to let him know where Jane would be. She had cautioned him to get to Alcamo promptly, before Jane realized, from the state of the house, that it had been freshly painted and no one was in residence, nor had been for a while. She would deal with Jane's anger later. The sight of that strange little car parked outside and the light in the kitchen had made his pulse race. The acrid smell of paint was strong in the air. He had gone in quietly, seen the open bottle of wine on the counter, and had looked out the back door.

His breath had caught in his chest when he saw her. It was unmistakably her. He would recognize those long, elegant legs and that erect carriage anywhere. Except that she wasn't so erect. It appeared as though she was having trouble standing up. She had turned then, hearing him walk up the path, to stare at him in openmouthed surprise. She had dropped her wine glass, the red wine spilling and staining the unfinished pine planking, and fainted dead away.

He had no idea if she had truly been in Borgetto or elsewhere, or whose car that was, but those questions hardly mattered. He had sprinted to her side, picking her up before her head hit the wood planking, taken her up in his arms, and brought her to the master bedroom.

He smelled the faint scent of the sweetish wine on her breath, remembered the evidence of the almost drained bottle on the kitchen counter, and had come to the conclusion that she'd had too much to drink. He was surprised at her. On the two occasions he'd seen her drinking before, she had not over indulged in alcohol.

What was he to do now? Only a cad would take advantage of a woman when she was drunk. His body was crying out for her, but it would be a mistake. For one thing, he had promised Claudia that he would try to straighten out their problems. For another, she didn't know what she was doing. A woman doesn't run from you one day, Lorenzo thought, and throw herself at you the next. *Something was terribly wrong.*

Gently, he tried to extricate himself from her embrace. "No, *cara,* I think not . . . I'm going to make you some black coffee, you're going to drink it, and then we'll talk. Talk, *cara,* not make love."

Jane stared at him, not believing the words that were so calmly coming out of his mouth. *Talk?* Talk would solve nothing. Talk would expose her as a naive provincial; he would laugh at her innocence. She had too much pride for that. But not enough pride to deny she wanted him. Her bizarre dream encounter with Dionysus was a poor substitute for this flesh-and-blood man sitting on the bed next to her. She'd had enough of dreams.

She wanted him.

She was not drunk, but the wine had loosened her inhibitions considerably. In the cold light of morning she would probably reflect upon and regret her impulsive behavior, but that was hours away. The Jane in Claudia and Aldo Donzini's bed was not the rational Jane. She reached for Lorenzo's shirt and began to undo the buttons.

She wanted him.

Alarmed, he stopped her, grabbing for her hands. "No, stop it, Gianna. You don't know what you are doing."

She ignored him, putting her arms around his neck and pressing her mouth against his. She closed her eyes; the soft pressure brought back delicious memories of her in his arms, of a night of love without end. She groaned in anticipation of the delight their bodies would have in each other. His lips parted.

This was madness, but his body was suffused suddenly with heat. He wanted to resist, but could not. There was a quickening in his loins he could not ignore. With an inarticulate moan of frustration he opened his mouth and gave in to her sweet attack, tracing the soft flesh behind her lips with his tongue, running his tongue lightly over her teeth. He could hear her groan deep in her throat.

This was madness!

They had major problems to settle, things to discuss, problems for which lovemaking was not the solution, questions that needed answers. But Lorenzo's protests were feeble; in truth, his resolve was weak. He had spent too many nights alone in bed, dreaming of this, wanting to be with her like this. The abruptness of their parting, after a single night of passion, had been a hard cross for him to bear. They were healthy young people who strongly desired each other, who craved physical union. Sober discussion was a poor substitute for passionate lovemaking. He groaned. Claudia would lose all respect for him. He would lose all respect for himself.

He didn't care. Rational thought was quickly eluding him.

Greedily, Lorenzo's tongue had its way with Jane's mouth, ravaging every corner, leaving her breathless, wanting more, reveling in the sweet wetness. Her body was responding eagerly; she felt moist between her upper thighs. She dug her fingers in his thick curls, incoherent sounds coming from her throat. They were devouring each other like wild animals in heat. It was utter frenzy.

Coming up for air, panting, Jane finished unbuttoning Lorenzo's shirt and made for his belt buckle, unclasping it roughly and easing his trousers down over his briefs. He obliged her quickly, shedding the rest of his clothing, slipping off his shoes and socks. She raised her arms so he could slide her loose tee shirt over her head. There was no time to waste.

Now, her mind screamed, *now!*

He paused, drawing in his breath, his eyes taking in her round, perfect breasts. His hands went to them of their own volition, weighing their fullness; his thumbs encircled Jane's hardening nipples through the sheer lace of her flimsy bra. Her skin radiated heat. She threw back her head, her long, heavy hair flowing backward, covering the big, square linen pillows behind her.

Lorenzo eased her back on the bed and stripped off her blue jeans. They rustled as they fell in a heap over the low footboard of the four-poster. He paused before pulling down the lacy bikini underpants that clung low on her hips. Her belly was flat, the skin soft and warm. He passed a hand over the crotch of her panties and downward; she was wet, ready for him. *So ready.* He pressed his lips to a spot just below her navel. She moved sinuously, sensitive to every caress he bestowed, arching her back, groaning softly. Her underwear soon joined the rest of the clothes flung carelessly onto the bedroom floor.

A sense of urgency drove them, as if time was running out; it almost seemed as if they both thought if they did not have each other now they would never have each other again. It was a veritable frenzy of barely-controlled need and desire.

Lorenzo placed her long fingers on his groin. She stroked the hot, taut, silky flesh of his erect manhood and he felt himself engorging in her hand. Surely he would burst. It was too fast, too hot. He tried to slow himself down, knowing for a certainty he would explode the instant he slid inside her soft, wet, welcoming warmth.

He grasped her hands and pinioned them on each side of her head. She was tossing herself from side to side now, begging him to enter her. He willed himself to relax, willed himself to control his ragged breathing. He kissed her again, long and slow. She melted in his mouth. Her hips ground restlessly against his.

Lorenzo kissed her for a long time, deeply, thoroughly. She began to shudder; he could feel her body convulsing beneath him. Still holding on to her wrists, he moved down the long length of her, trailing moist kisses over her breasts, her belly, her parted inner thighs. She cried out as he buried his head between her legs and kissed her intimately, his tongue stroking her sweetness and conquering her there as completely as he had taken her mouth. She melted entirely then, engulfed by wave upon wave of longing and the promise of fulfillment.

As her orgasm crested, he raised her hips and drove deeply inside her. She cried out again and again as each thrust brought her closer to ecstasy. With one last, deep penetration, he gave her the release she sought and his own, finally, as well, clasping her closely. They climaxed as one, exhausted, coupled, momentarily at peace with each other.

"I love you," she whispered in a husky voice, much, much too low for him to hear.

The morning sun was persistent and already strong, infiltrating the big four-poster's gauzy white curtain screen. Lorenzo stirred. He had slept too long, over-tired, wrung-out both with the passion and intensity of their lovemaking and the emotional strain of the past week. But she was back now. That was something. *No, that was everything!*

Lorenzo reached over for her, hoping that whatever had been broken could begin to be mended, that things could be worked out between them instead of irrevocably put asunder. "Gianna?" he whispered, drawing himself up on one elbow.

The bedclothes were a catastrophe, standing up in peaks like stiffly beaten egg whites. *Where was she?* Not in bed. The bath? It was empty, a damp towel bearing traces of a distinctive lemon/rosemary scent. The kitchen? He padded barefoot through the silent house. There was the empty wine bottle, mute witness to Jane's intoxicated condition of the night before. He shook his head. Had she known what she really wanted when she had reached for him? Did she regret it now, in the harsh, demanding light of morning?

Far off, he heard the crowing of a cock on some peasant's farm. Lorenzo wondered, briefly, what kind of night the rooster had had for himself in the hen coop. *Ah, for an uncomplicated animal life!* Hoping against hope, he pushed the screened front door open. His Alfa was there, right where he had parked it last night, next to the strange car, the little Fiat that had seen better days. But the little Fiat was gone.

And so was hope.

She had run away from him again in the night, a night of intense lovemaking that had brought both of them to the brink of exhaustion. He was as much in the dark as ever as to why she'd behaved so strangely, the victim of his uncontrollable passion for her. Granted, she had made no promises, so he could hardly accuse her of having broken any. Indeed, she had not spoken more than a few words to him. In the depths of their lovemaking she had called out his name many times, but no other words had passed between them. He blamed himself for not finding out why she had run away.

And now she had run from him again.

Frustrated, Lorenzo angrily hit the side of the door with his fist. The sudden shock of pain woke him up completely. It wasn't over yet, he vowed, sucking on the bruise he had given himself on the side of his hand. He had found her once, thanks to Claudia's telephone call to come to Alcamo; he would find her again, in Borgetto. He knew he would. All the running in the world was not going to keep her from him. Not now, not ever. They belonged together.

He loved her. It was that simple. And he would find her.

Chapter Thirteen

Family Secrets

Every family has its secrets.

Margherita was telling Jane hers, in the quiet, green, glade-filled Borgetto cemetery where all her grandmother's kin lay long buried. She had reluctantly left Lorenzo's bed during the night and fled back to Borgetto, unable to face the unforgiving light of day. She was no closer to dealing with her problems with him than she had been the day before. But she was, she had to admit, fascinated, enthralled, as this hitherto unknown part of her family's saga unfolded. She forgot Lorenzo for a little while in the quiet of the cemetery, listening to her aunt's mellifluous voice.

Margherita held a photograph with both her delicate hands. It was framed with a dark, varnished, unidentifiable wood that was fancifully shaped in the form of convoluted, intertwined twigs. The old photograph showed Margherita as a young teenager and her older sister, the notorious and much-reviled Caterina, taken at the best photographer's studio in Palermo, Grifalcone, on the Via Liberta. Proudly, Margherita told Jane that Prince Maurizio Bighilaterra had arranged for the sitting, had paid for the photograph.

In the manner of studio portraits of that time, Caterina and Margherita posed somewhat stiffly, unnaturally to modern eyes, dressed in what must have been their Sunday best. Margherita wore a full-skirted sheer white cotton frock over voluminous petticoats. The skirt came to mid-calf; her shoes were a flat, shiny black. In her fluffy hair was a big white bow. She had a shy smile on her sweet, adorable face.

Caterina's looks were somewhat sterner, her outfit more severe. Her full-bosomed figure did justice to the form-fitting dark wool crepe dress, which flared out provocatively above her shapely, well-turned ankles. Her high-arched feet sported cross-strapped pale leather heels. One long-fingered, strong hand rested on her hip; her back was straight, her carriage proud. Intelligent eyes looked out from a handsome face: high cheekbones, generous full mouth, firm chin.

The shock of recognition had hit Jane Holland hard.

It was her face.

Her face, staring back at her over the long passage of time. Except for the hair, which Caterina had pulled back and combed into a thick bun lying low at the nape of her long neck, Jane and she were spitting images of each other. It was remarkable. No wonder Margherita had nearly had a stroke when she saw Jane at the church. She'd thought it was Caterina, come back from the dead.

But there were some differences between them. Caterina looked out at the world with no trepidation, no fear, no nonsense. She was all strength and feminine power. No insecurities unsettled or troubled that woman. It would be a long time, if ever, Jane knew, before she could achieve a look—so proud, so independent—anywhere near Caterina's, but, otherwise, the resemblance was there, a marked resemblance that anyone with average eyesight could see.

Jane squinted a little to make out what was dangling on Caterina's formidable chest. It was a necklace. Could it be? Yes, heavenly angels! It was the golden *trinacria* of the Bighilaterras, that costly bauble, hanging between her breasts. *What does it all mean?* Jane wondered. Then she realized that she was going to find out very soon, as she looked up from the dated photograph into Margherita's clear old eyes and her aunt began to narrate her long repressed story.

Caterina, Jane's great-aunt, and Maurizio Bighilaterra, Lorenzo's grandfather, had been lovers.

Yes, that lovely peasant who had figured anonymously in the Bighilaterra family lore, the one who supposedly had been presented with the gift of the *trinacria* amulet after a passionate and unforgettable night of love, was Jane's blood relative. That was the horrible, shameful scandal that still could not be spoken aloud, even down to the present generation. The women of the family had scrambled violently to disassociate themselves from the scarlet woman, the Prince's whore, and her no-doubt-tarred-with-the-same-brush younger sister.

As Margherita's soft, melodic, old woman's voice related the tale of the two star-crossed lovers, Jane fantasized, sitting on the cool stone bench in the cemetery facing the family plot, about what it had been like for them, so long ago, in that tightly-knit, too small community, strait-jacketed by rigid mores and codes of behavior. Convention had been thrown on its head and those mores flaunted. Jane was certain, however, that whatever horrible things Aunt Caterina had done, she had most assuredly done them with her own characteristic and individual flair . . .

Caterina asked the driver to stop the cart just before they reached the main gates of the Bighilaterra estate. The gently rolling hillock overlooked its great expanse, those thousands of acres sweeping down to the sea, to the Golfo di Castellamare. The Prince was very rich.

She turned to her timid younger sister. *Such a baby!* Caterina thought, but not unkindly. She had accepted the responsibility for her sister that no one else would assume. She thought of her other five sisters in Borgetto with contempt and loathing. Margherita's welfare was in her hands now. She smiled wickedly, remembering how she had lunged at the fat white throat of her older sister, Francesca, scarring her sibling's soft flesh deeply with her long, sharp fingernails. *Butana! The bitch!* Caterina thought, angry still at how they had all sent their delicate baby sister off to that sterile orphanage in Palermo, as if, as if—she seethed—there were no family members who could take her in.

The older sisters had all been jealous of the young girl, who had been so spoiled and so cosseted by their doddering old parents. Senile parents, who hadn't been aware of the hateful forces they had set into motion by making too much of their *vasteneddu,* their last child, the cherished seventh daughter. Francesca, the eldest, had been the worst; she had set the tone, convinced the others, and Caterina had despised her the most.

Returning to Borgetto after rescuing Margherita from the nuns at the Palermo orphanage had been a mistake. The act had publicly shamed the other Conigliaro sisters. People were talking, as they always did, secretly glad to have the opportunity to criticize that too-proud family, and she, Caterina, had given them a good deal to talk about, also.

No woman of that patriarchal culture, that time, that place, ever left her husband. So what if he had been brutal, had beaten her? Most women accepted the battery as part of their lot in life, and, more important, kept it to themselves. Maybe they spoke of it in confession to their parish priest, but he, most probably, would have admonished them for being the sort of wives who had to be beaten. It was always the woman's fault. But Caterina confessed to no one, apologized to no one.

No, I'm too outspoken, Caterina thought. That was something they—her family and that narrow-minded small town—could never tolerate. She told them what she thought, what she felt. She even—here she smiled, her full, ripe, generous mouth breaking into laughter—she even told that no-balled priest to get himself stuffed when he told her she should go back to her husband Giuseppe in America.

The priest, mightily offended, had bustled off angrily to her sanctimonious brother-in-law, Francesca's husband, to complain about her dirty mouth and her decidedly unmeek, unfeminine behavior. Caterina had refused to apologize, to accept penance. She'd made it worse by insulting the old fool once more.

Her brother-in-law. Simone Conigliaro. She winced. She had let him talk her into marrying Giuseppe Malatesta after the family's decision to separate her from her first cousin, Pasquale Polizzi. She and Pasquale had been strongly attracted to each other and, unbeknownst to their disapproving relatives, they had actually consummated a brief, sweet, adolescent love affair.

A disgrace, it would have been, to marry a first cousin, the son of her mother's brother. Ironically, her sister Francesca and her husband Simone were also cousins, but, although they shared a common surname, they were only distantly related. It was different. Glibly, the oily Simone had talked her into accepting the available but unhandsome Malatesta, persuading her that he had good qualities and worked hard, telling her that *"good looks don't put bread on the table!"*

She still didn't know why she'd allowed herself to be cowed by her brother-in-law, who was now the head of the family. It had been a horrible mistake. The family had arranged a quick marriage for Caterina, then a hasty send-off to America, to a man who turned out to be a wife-beater. *It had been hell.*

Caterina still had a long white scar across her shoulders from Giuseppe's last beating. He had used his belt, and the edge of the buckle had ripped open her skin, drawing blood. It was the last beating he ever gave her. She had thrown a heavy chair at him, rendering him unconscious, half-hoping that she had killed him, and had fled into the cold dark Brooklyn night with all the money in his wallet, all the silver coins hidden in the jars in her kitchen that she had saved from the household money. It had been a sizable amount. She and Margherita had been living on it while they pondered what to do with their futures.

Such a jealous little man, that Giuseppe, Caterina thought, shaking her lovely head. She hadn't been a virgin bride. The beatings were clumsy attempts to force the name of the other man from her lips. She had never betrayed her cousin Pasquale, but that adolescent romance was over. How could she still ever desire a man who had let her go so easily, with no regrets? Anyway, Pasquale had married. She dismissed him and Giuseppe from her thoughts.

The important question was: what were she and Margherita going to do with their lives? No home, no family, the money from America running out fast . . . *I could go away again, back to America,* she thought—*such a big country, not like Sicily, no one could ever find me if I didn't want them to*—or she could go to South America. Many Sicilians had emigrated to Argentina.

Then she had heard domestics were needed at the Bighilaterra estate, which was located between Borgetto and Montelepre. There would be room, board, a small monthly salary that could be saved. The work would not be hard. She was strong, used to working; Margherita was more delicate, but young. Then, maybe, when enough money was saved up, they could think again about Argentina or going back to America. Yes, they would become servants; Caterina thought it was an excellent idea.

"Look, *cara.*" She helped her sister out of the wagon, a conveyance sent by the Prince's major-domo to bring the two women and their pitifully few belongings to the estate. "See how beautiful it is!"

A soft, citrus-edged, sweet-scented Sicilian wind blew across the sheltered valley of the Bighilaterras' agricultural estate, rustling the big smooth leaves of the fig trees, the small shiny leaves of the trees in the extensive olive groves, brushing past the sweet lemon and blood orange plantations, gently waving through the fields of hard golden semolina wheat, blowing out to sea over stands of silver fir, sweet chestnut, spreading oaks, orchards of flowering almond and cherry.

The big stone manor house was surrounded by prolific wild rose bushes. Ample kitchen gardens stretched out on either side, planted with a variety of vegetables suited to the rich Sicilian soil, cardoons, artichokes, zucchini, tomatoes. Exotic produce was grown in glistening, glassed-in greenhouses adjacent to the rear of the house.

Margherita was taken aback by the sight of such beauty and plenty. "Oh," she breathed. "I think we will be happy here!" She embraced her older sister joyfully. They climbed back into the wagon to complete the last mile of their journey.

Caterina hoped that the work would not be too hard for her sister. Margherita was delicate, fragile, after that stay in the awful orphanage, but they were both from basically strong, healthy peasant stock. Although Margherita was not accustomed to the kind of hard physical work Caterina had done, she would soon find her way and her strength would come.

Luckily, the nuns had taught her to embroider, and young Margherita did meticulous, excellent work. There would be a lot of good, expensive linens to maintain, to mend, at that big house, and a servant who could embroider fine linens well was always treasured.

Caterina would work in the kitchen; she was a good plain cook and was ambitious to learn more. Prince Maurizio Bighilaterra was reputed to have a skilled French-trained chef, and Caterina was determined to learn as much as possible at his hands. And, maybe, some fine day perhaps not too far off in the future, she would be employable at a fancy restaurant in America, or Argentina. It didn't hurt to think ahead, nor to be ambitious for one's self.

The prince, Caterina mused, wondering about the sort of man her employer would be. Not that, she thought, she would be seeing much of him. She would be below stairs, in that great huge kitchen, learning to cook well. She would ingratiate herself with the chef. *They say I'm beautiful,* she thought—*but too headstrong and independent—and I know I have intelligence.* She was not ashamed to toil as a domestic for the time being. She thought, no, she knew, that one day soon, good things would come her way. She had great faith in herself.

Then Caterina worried that she must not be too obviously ambitious, or over-anxious to perform her job well. Despite her natural impatience she had to take her way slowly and carefully and not tread on anyone who might impede her progress. Listen. Observe. Learn. All these she had to do before she acted. She was all too aware that she had Margherita, her responsibility, to worry about. She could not, must not fail her. She had to be cautious and circumspect.

Over the next few weeks, Caterina and Margherita got used to the big house and its daily routine. The prince was not yet in residence, but he would be there soon, and there was spring cleaning and other preparation for the staff to undertake. The sisters for a time worked together, readying the upstairs rooms for the soon-to-come influx of guests and the steady entertaining that would commence and go through the social season.

The manor house of the Bighilaterras was built and furnished in the overwrought French baroque style so favored by the Sicilian aristocracy. All was heavily gilded, ornamented, richly brocaded in gold and silver. There were immense rooms floored in *parqueterie,* bursting with Old Master paintings and ornate, overwrought, dripping crystal chandeliers and candelabra.

The conservatory boasted three grand pianos and seating for over a hundred guests. Floor-to-ceiling windows in most of the rooms provided open access to the elements, the strong, golden Sicilian sun, Apollo's own, the clear blue sky, the soft sea-scented Mediterranean wind. Although Caterina and Margherita worked harder than each of them ever had, those first weeks they thought that they were truly in a kind of paradise.

The staff was large and amiable, carefully selected by the prince's major-domo. The prince himself was a fair and generous employer, paying the best wages in the region. An intelligent man with cultivated, European tastes, he was an intimate of many of the lesser crowned heads of the continent as well as the Sicilian upper crust.

He was related, by blood or by marriage, to Western

Europe's wealthiest families. He was fond of reading, conversation, riding, the hunt, fine food and wine, beautiful women. He had been a great catch, and mothers wept when he finally married, at the ripe age of thirty-five, a Tuscan heiress, the daughter of a prince.

This had been two years before. The northern Italian prince, who claimed kinship with the Borgias, was a large landholder. The daughter, Princess Fiammetta, was an exquisitely beautiful blue-eyed blonde who had been spoiled by her father for any other man. She loathed Sicily, longing instead for the charms of her gracious Tuscan palazzo in the soft green hills outside of Florence.

Maurizio found her unresponsive and frigid; she shrank from his lovemaking, and the marriage had swiftly disintegrated. She fled back to the north, to be with her beloved father, and Maurizio did not bother going after her, seeking his sexual pleasures elsewhere. There were no lack of companions for a handsome, wealthy Sicilian prince who was generous with his gifts and who knew how to treat a woman well.

Margherita, an inquisitive child, was fascinated, if a bit in the dark, about the below stairs gossip that flourished concerning the relationship of the Prince and his Tuscan Princess-bride. She would repeat it, verbatim, to Caterina, and speculate out loud. Caterina had absolutely no interest in any of the gossip or speculation. She pretended to listen, but her thoughts were somewhere else. (On Italian restaurants in the Argentine, for example.)

"The Prince and Princess had separate bedrooms, Gina the upstairs maid told me," Margherita announced to her sister one day, as they were sorting linen to be mended.

Caterina, half-listening, held a tea towel with frayed edges closer to the light, frowning. "That is the way of the rich, *cara,*" she commented absently. I *would have not minded a bedroom separate from Giuseppe's,* she mused, shuddering at the memory of his gross and repulsive touch.

"Caterina . . ." Margherita was whispering now, bending her fair head closer to her sister's ear, "what is it that men and women do in bedrooms? The nuns, they never told us anything about this."

Caterina smiled. The nuns! *Her poor little sister.* Well, there were certainly things Caterina thought she could—things she probably should—tell the child. Who else could? At least, she reflected, she had had the experience, both good and bad. So many young girls never knew what to expect, and the wedding night was not the time to become enlightened. She thought of Giuseppe's rough groping and shuddered involuntarily again. He had known nothing of how to please a woman. He had not even cared to try.

Now, Pasquale . . . she felt a stab under her heart thinking of her cousin. They had both been so young. It had been sweet, so natural, so loving. Not at all what it was with her husband. *What could she tell Margherita?*

What she told her were the facts, stressing that it only made sense, only meant anything, if there was love, also. But Margherita had trouble believing her older sister. She giggled! "No, Caterina, you are making this up!" Caterina reminded her that she had been married.

"I never liked Giuseppe," Margherita admitted.

"I did not either, *cara,* that's why I left him!" Caterina laughed out loud. It wouldn't do to tell the girl that Giuseppe had been brutal in bed. He hadn't made love; he'd raped her. Repeatedly.

The thing you have to do, she'd advised Margherita, is to marry someone you love, someone who cares deeply for you in return. She knew she could have been happy with

Pasquale, but that was past, over. Would she have another chance, ever again, with someone else? Ah, but it was something she wasted no time thinking about; actually, it was quite low on her current list of priorities.

"*Cara,* believe me, with someone you love, I tell you it is heaven." She squeezed her sister's hand affectionately and tossed the tea towel on the mending pile.

It was then that Margherita realized that there must have been someone else for Caterina once, besides Giuseppe. Maybe more than once, else how would she know the delights of the bedroom? The thought was worrying. *Just what kind of woman was her older sister?*

The prince had come home in the middle of the night. All was in readiness for him. The major-domo congratulated the staff on their hard work; the manor house shone. Vincenzo Volta, the prince's Paris-trained chef, was already inspecting the clean, gleaming kitchen, making lists of foods and preparing menus for the many dinner parties that would take place that spring. He looked over his staff critically, noting especially the tall, striking, chestnut-haired, hazel-eyed woman who had told him she was honored to be working for him.

Vincenzo Volta was as vain as anyone else, and although not partial to women, preferring young men, appreciated her fresh, extraordinary beauty and her obvious intelligence. *My dear,* he gloated to himself, practically rubbing his hands in glee, *wait until my master the prince sees you just you wait!*

Volta, although well aware that the prince did not as a rule dally with servant girls, and that he did not lack the love and companionship of beautiful women all over Europe, had a special feeling about Caterina Malatesta, nee Conigliaro. She was striking, definitely someone to watch, he thought. Yes, she would bear watching.

Volta was right on the mark. Over the next few days, Prince Maurizio Bighilaterra caught tantalizing glimpses of a tall, brown-haired young servant who carried herself regally, very much like a queen, her back straight and strong, striding to and fro from her chores with an inner pride that belied her lowly status in his household. *And that face!* She was lovely. *These peasants,* thought the prince, *every now and then they produce someone so exquisite it was hard to be believed. This was a woman to die for.*

The image of Caterina soon began to haunt and disturb his sleep.

It was troublesome, something he could not control. One particularly sleepless night, he had slept in, waking up late in the morning. Getting out of bed, embarrassingly erect, like an adolescent boy unable to forget an erotic dream, he had gone to his window, which faced the back of the house. Opening the window and breathing in great salubrious inhalations of air, he saw her, the woman of those disturbingly erotic dreams. He did not even know her name.

Caterina was pegging out just-laundered snowy white damask tablecloths and napkins upon one line of the kitchen's extensive clotheslines. Behind her, row upon row of empty lines stretched out like furrows of just-turned earth, straight and long. The wind coming in through the prince's windows, ruffling the linens on the clothesline, whipped Caterina's long cotton skirts about her rounded hips and long, slim legs, teasing her glossy nut-brown hair in soft wisps and tendrils around her proud, beautiful face, outlining and holding taut her full, high breasts under the thin white cotton lawn blouse she wore.

Maurizio caught his breath at the splendid sight. Unaware of his intense blue eyes taking in the vibrancy, the sensuality of her face and form, Caterina unselfconsciously went about her chore, bending easily and naturally against the background of the glorious spring day, stretching her arms high to secure the cloths to the line.

The prince's hand, holding back the lace curtain at the window, trembled slightly. He drank her in hungrily, like a man stranded in the desert who has no oasis within reach. Then he was furious with himself, turning away angrily. He thought he must be mad, leering at a mere servant girl, a peasant! He was Prince Maurizio Bighilaterra, after all!

It was all because of Fiammetta. It was time to end his folly of a marriage. He needed a wife with him, at home. That would end his lustful yearnings in preposterous directions. If Fiammetta was still unwilling to be his wife, to share his bed, well, then, he would take the necessary steps to secure an annulment through the Church.

Europe was full of other young, beautiful heiresses who would more than willingly take his wife's place. It had all gone too far, this nonsense, when he couldn't tear his mind and eyes away from the body of one of his lowly female servants.

Yet, yet, for all he argued with himself, for all he despised himself for his low animal lusts, he could not get the lovely young woman out of his mind. He dressed hurriedly and went to question his chef, Volta. He knew the woman worked in his kitchens.

He wanted to see her face, close up, to look into those light eyes, brown eyes so pale they were almost not brown, to be near those full inviting lips. He wanted to hear her voice. He would have to be careful, very careful, if he was not to make a fool of himself. It would be unseemly for a prince to make a fool of himself over a servant.

Vincenzo was not surprised when the prince walked into his kitchens, unannounced, that morning. He had been expecting him, wondering at the man's masterful restraint, his steely self-control. *What had taken him so long?* He had been impatiently awaited.

And now, here he was, at last! Vincenzo crowed silently, triumphantly.

Caterina, under Vincenzo's tutelage, was beating egg whites for a vanilla soufflé. She looked up, curious, from the bowl. There was a tiny smear of egg white, foamy and delicate, at the corner of her mouth. The prince's heart beat loudly in his chest; he longed to lean over and lick the white fleck from her lips, to trace the outline of that succulent mouth with his tongue, to take her in his arms and enfold her willing body to him.

He nodded coldly at Caterina, his eyes blue ice, belying the intensity of his emotions, and beckoned Volta outside. He had managed to look into those rich, sweet, amaretto-hued eyes, to drink them in. His thirst was beyond relief. He realized he was a little dizzy.

Caterina wondered why the prince had come to see Vincenzo; surely, it was more appropriate that the servant go to the master, and not the other way around. She shrugged at the ways of masters and servants and went back to her soufflé. She had taken a cursory glance at him, not wanting to stare, but noting that he was a good deal younger than she'd assumed, and that his eyes were a beautiful, bright, surprising blue. He was also strikingly handsome.

"Vincenzo," the prince came right to the point, "who is that woman?" He avoided looking into Volta's eyes.

"Her name is Caterina, your highness. She and her sister are new to the staff. They are both from Borgetto. Is there something wrong?"

"No, no." Irritably, he waved away the suggestion. "It's just that . . . I have noticed her. She carries herself well. Are her talents such that we could take her to Palermo with us? Would she be suited for the palazzo staff? What do you think?"

Well, this was something new. In the past, it had always been Vincenzo who had pointed out which servants showed promise, who was good enough to be installed in the prince's Via Loro palazzo in the city, where only the most experienced and talented hands were welcome. Never, never, had Prince Maurizio Bighilaterra taken a personal interest in a servant. *Never.* Vincenzo, a romantic at heart who abhorred Maurizio's wife, the cold and arrogant northern-bred Princess Fiammetta, was delighted.

"Caterina is excellent, your highness. She learns fast, absorbs all she is given, never complains, a hard worker . . . and decorative, too," he could not help adding.

From under his dark eyebrows, the prince shot Vincenzo a warning look. "Is she? I hadn't noticed. That's all, Volta, thank you." He stalked off, angry with Vincenzo's last, gratuitous comment. *The man sees too much,* he thought, *sometimes he goes too far.*

Not noticed? Volta smirked. Oh, my dear prince, you have noticed, yes, you have noticed our lovely Caterina. Now, the question is, what are you going to do about it? Oh, this would be a most entertaining spring and summer, Vincenzo chortled to himself. The prince, the sophisticated, worldly Prince Bighilaterra, was displaying the classic symptoms of lovesickness.

Reluctantly, Vincenzo Volta turned his attention back to kitchen matters. In a few days, the first round of dinner parties would be commencing. There was a great deal to do. Caterina was going to be a valuable asset; she had strong culinary instincts. He, Volta, who had, as he liked to remind people, been trained by the great Escoffier himself, was making her his protégée, sure she would do him proud. She would contribute to making his dinner parties—that is, the prince's dinner parties—successful and talked-about.

Volta was highly-strung. Like an actor or an opera star before an important performance, he would experience bouts of nausea similar to stage fright. He was used to the feeling. So, when the first wave of malaise hit him, he put it off to the usual pre-performance jitters, that unsettling surge of adrenaline that momentarily destabilized the system. But the attacks, rather than abating, grew stronger, until, finally, he collapsed in the kitchen in front of Caterina.

She took over immediately, without hesitation. Over Vincenzo's feeble protests, she called for one of the farm laborers and had him carried to bed. She sent another of the farmers to fetch the doctor. Not wanting to alarm the prince on the night of his first important party, she thought, unfazed, *I can do this all myself.* Some dishes had been prepared in advance. If she remained calm, organized, she thought, it could be accomplished easily.

After the doctor had left, giving Vincenzo sleeping-draughts to alleviate his fever and rest his aching body, Caterina went in to see the head chef. Refusing to take the sleeping potions, Volta had asked instead for hot chicken soup and strong red wine. He ordered Caterina to have a cot set up in the middle of the kitchen floor so that he could supervise the dinner preparations. Caterina, faced with his stubbornness—recognizing a character trait they both had in common—did as he instructed. While another servant fed him spoonfuls of rich yellow chicken broth and fortifying shots of the local blood-red wine from the neighboring vineyards of Tommaso Donzini, they managed to turn the dinner party into a rousing success.

His voice enfeebled, but his determination strong, Volta guided Caterina through the last steps in the preparation and presentation of great chaud-froids of farm-raised veal, fois-gras in tomato-basil flavored aspic, snipe impaled on their own beaks in the French style and served on crisp toast spread with their own chopped, seasoned livers, fresh fish—spada, white-fleshed swordfish, sarde con finocchio, the Sicilian specialty of sardines and wild fennel, lobsters alla diavola, appetizers of salted tuna Trapanese—just-picked vegetables from the kitchen gardens and hothouses, asparagus, slender and white, broccoli di rape studded with minute yellow florets, artichokes alla Romagna—hand-made, hand-shaped pasta, speckled with green bits of basil and sage—delicate deserts, both French-inspired and of Sicilian origin, sfinci ammilati, lemon souffle, minni di virgini, all shape and variety of freshly-formed and realistically-tinted marzipan fruit.

Caterina herself was near collapse by the end of the long evening. Margherita, who had been pressed into kitchen service, was worried by the paleness of her sister's face and the dark circles of fatigue now beginning to show under her eyes.

Vincenzo had finally been persuaded to take the sleeping-draughts and was sleeping like a baby, having been deposited by a strong manservant into his comfortable bed. No such rest was in store for Caterina yet. The burden of supervising the cleaning-up and the organizing of the Sunday brunch had yet to be done.

So it was that the prince, delighted with the fine showing his chef had made in front of his first weekend guests, came into the kitchens to congratulate Volta personally and to present him with an expensive hand-rolled cigar and a glass of his finest French brandy.

He came upon a sparkling, well-scrubbed kitchen, all leftover food stored away, clean crockery and shining glasses washed and draining in rows of wooden racks on the kitchen counters. And the girl, the girl he had been aching for, was all alone, having sent the exhausted help to their beds.

She looked exhausted, too, so weary, but pleased with a job well-done. Tendrils of long dark hair had come loose from the bun on top of her head; her arms from the elbows down and her hands were red from the hot, soapy dishwater. Depleted she was, but strangely triumphant, unbowed. Proud. She turned to see who had come into the kitchen.

"Where is Vincenzo?" the prince asked, surprised to see Caterina so obviously in charge.

"He is . . . unwell," she answered.

"Unwell? Then, how?" And he knew, he knew she had done it all, done it herself. She smiled. "But . . . you must be exhausted!" He blurted out.

She shook her head, even as the weariness caught up with her, and her long, tired legs gave way, and she felt herself sinking to the floor. In an instant, the prince was at her side, his strong arms and back lifting her, keeping her upright. *She is a feather,* he thought, as she lay, relaxed, in his arms. He savored the feel of her, the slight lemon and rosemary smell of her that wafted towards him.

She was embarrassed. *How silly this was! I never faint,* she chastised herself, *I'm not a delicate, swooning woman.* She attempted to free herself from his tight grip. "It's quite all right, your highness, I am fine, really," she insisted, trying to move away from his closeness.

His eyes, she thought, momentarily disconcerted by his nearness, how blue they are. *Yes, I was not mistaken,* she thought, *he is a very handsome man.* Her cousin Pasquale flashed across her mind; no, not Pasquale, rather, what she had felt like in Pasquale's arms. She was suddenly disoriented, frightened, pulling away from him.

Maurizio did not feel like letting go. He had been struck by lightning, *un colpo di fulmine.* Love at first sight, but he didn't realize it right then and there. All he knew was that he wanted this woman. He wanted his servant. His cook. *I am crazy,* he thought, as he drew Caterina closer to him and kissed her soft, full mouth, the mouth he had imagined kissing for days, long and passionately.

Caterina stiffened. *No,* she thought wildly, *no! I am not your whore!* For what else could the man be thinking? What else could he possibly want from her? She had recognized that look in his eyes. It was a look she'd seen often, from many men, many times. She struggled to free herself, but his mouth was insistent, his kiss deep and demanding. She felt herself drawn in by his desire, his need. It was becoming her need. No, no, she couldn't succumb! It mustn't happen.

Maurizio was half out of his mind with the physical closeness of the woman, with the sweet wetness of her mouth, the yielding softness of her breasts, the warmth of her belly against his jutting manhood seeking to claim her for its own. He placed an arm under her knees and began to scoop her up, planning to carry her up the back stairs and into his wide, waiting bed. It yawned empty and cold. He needed her to fill it.

She would not allow it. With the considerable strength she possessed, notwithstanding her fatigue, she fought back his desire, pushing him away, making him lose his footing on the black and white tiled floor. He stumbled, and she fled.

The prince caught himself on the edge of the porcelain sink. Behind him, the crystal brandy glass fell, bouncing, to the floor, spilling its rich amber contents. *Damn!* he thought, *damn!* He'd let his lust lead him into a regrettable and unsavory situation. He had behaved badly and not in a particularly princely manner.

He was ashamed. And then he was angry at her, for rebuffing him, as if he were a serf, a lout, pawing her after imbibing too much wine. *Damn the girl!* Who did she think she was? She should have been overwhelmed by his attentions, not fought them off! He had been insulted, pushed away by a mere peasant woman.

Over the days that followed, Volta, now fully recovered from his bout of fever and basking in the compliments on all sides on the first dinner party, noted a coolness in the prince's demeanor and an uncharacteristic depression on the part of Caterina. Something was wrong. Something had happened between the both of them—and he had missed it! It was no good trying to get anything out of Caterina, let alone his master, the prince. He would have to watch them both, to wait and see.

The prince was possessed. He could think of nothing but the girl. Her rebuff had only fired his passion. He was angry at her, but, perversely, more determined to have her. She, on her part, went about her duties unobtrusively, deliberately keeping out of his way. These days, her younger sister appeared at her side more and more, as if chaperoning the elder. It was a tense situation.

And the prince had abruptly cancelled the next few dinner parties. Volta wondered if he were planning to go back to Palermo for the season, but, no, it seemed he wanted simply to be alone. He put off the impatient, amorous messages from his sometime paramour, the voluptuous Costanza Bellini, wife of the elderly Count Bellini; suddenly her charms had ceased to interest him.

Most mornings, he took long and solitary rides through the countryside on one of the handsome thoroughbreds from his extensive stables. But he would rather have been riding another handsome animal, a chestnut-maned two-legged beauty for whom his loins ached.

It was on one of these solitary rides, as he followed the course of a stream that he had often fished, scarcely two weeks after that memorable night of the dinner party, that he saw her, alone.

Caterina was on the grass beside a small, bubbling rivulet, a tributary of the main flow. Her high, laced-up shoes were on the ground beside her, her black cotton stockings neatly rolled up and stuffed inside them. That glorious fall of long, glossy hair was down, and she was brushing it slowly, with careful, measured strokes.

She is a nereid, he thought, taking in that lissome form on the long grasses at the water's rim, a beached water nymph, one of the fifty beautiful daughters of the sea god Nereus. (The prince's classical education served him well on all kinds of occasions.) He urged his mount forward, riding slowly towards her, the riding crop in his hand lightly flicking the horse's withers.

Caterina had turned at the sound of the animal's advancing hooves. She was startled. The color rose in her pale face. She stopped brushing her hair, pulling it back with one hand, the other still holding her brush. She had frozen. Noting the tenseness of her body, Maurizio thought she was poised for flight.

She cannot stand the sight of me, he thought, in despair.

His thought could not have been farther from the truth of Caterina's feelings. She was strongly attracted to him, had thought of little else but him all these long warm nights. He was a handsome, sensuous man, in his prime. She knew he desired her; she desired him, also.

But the last thing she would do was become the prince's whore. That must not happen. She wanted him, but not that way. But what other way could a peasant have a prince? She twisted on the horns of her dilemma, becoming more and more depressed.

The fine twill of the prince's riding breeches tightened across his flat belly as his manhood, aroused by the sight of her, swelled against the hard pommel of the leather saddle. He slowly removed his riding gloves, placing them carefully into the pockets of his coat. He spoke, his voice cruel, as cold as his eyes; his leather crop, clenched tightly in his hand, was now flicking the top of his thigh.

"So, Caterina, you are without your little companion today?" he asked, referring to her blonde, adolescent sister, always in her wake.

Caterina was surprised she could speak, surprised she could dare to answer him. She could sense the iciness of his anger towards her. Her mouth was dry. "She is looking for wild strawberries in the woods. She is not far."

Far enough not to hear you call out, he hoped, as he dismounted from his steed and, holding the snaffle and curb reins loosely in his bare hands, approached her. He would take her here, now, on the grass, as his need directed him to, as his right asserted itself. He would push her body down against the grass, lift up her skirts, have his servant woman. The relief would come then, and he could forget her, go on with his real life, snuff out this bizarre fantasy, this inappropriate desire. It would happen, now, and be over. He came towards her, dropping the reins on the grass. The horse would stay, chewing at the green field, for as long as it took. It wouldn't be long, not with the urgency of his need.

Caterina, looking at his ice-blue eyes, her face reddening at the obvious bulge below his belly, knew what was on his mind. He would ravish her here on the grass. *No!* She was fierce, though afraid, afraid of his strength, his power over her. *It would not happen!* She scrambled to her bare feet, the brush in her hand.

Noting that she was about to brandish her brush like a weapon, the prince smiled. She had spirit, this woman. If she relaxed, this could be an enjoyable interlude for both of them. Maurizio preferred it when his sex partners took pleasure in the act. An experienced, enlightened lover, he knew that the woman's pleasure would only enhance his.

He could pleasure this woman, if she'd let him. It wouldn't be so bad for her. Quickly, he stepped forward, his English leather riding boots gliding swiftly over the long grass, and in one motion he took the brush out of her shaking hand, threw it to the ground, and pinned both arms behind her.

Caterina gasped in surprise. He was too fast, his swift reflexes were too good for her. She was a strong woman, but he was a man and stronger. His mouth claimed hers and she succumbed, briefly, to the wonder of his kiss. He was in absolute control of her mouth, his tongue expertly exploring its soft recesses, finding her rebellious tongue, taming it, bending it to his will, as he sucked it greedily.

The warm sweet wetness of that angelic mouth distracted him, as it had done before. He loosened his hold on her arms, intending to force her back slowly, to savor these final moments before he possessed her totally, before he brought her down to the inviting green lawn beneath them that would serve as their bed. The blood was coursing rapidly through the prince's veins now, in anticipation of his sweet conquest.

His relaxation was the opening Caterina needed. She drew a knee up, kicked him accurately and hard between the legs, scooped up her shoes and stockings, and fled towards the woods.

He bellowed in pain and surprise. No one—especially not a woman!—had ever dared . . .

As he doubled over, the waves of nausea dizzying him and rendering him helpless, he swore revenge. *The bitch would pay.* She would pay dearly for this second rebuff of his attentions.

The next morning, a pale and still angry Prince Maurizio Bighilaterra asked his major-domo to bring Vincenzo Volta to him. He was no longer in physical pain from Caterina's blow to his genitals, but the affront to his manhood smarted still. His anger at the woman partially transferred itself, irrationally, to his chef, who had never missed an opportunity to praise her.

He had half a mind to sack him, too, as he would sack the woman. He instructed Vincenzo to fire Caterina. "Here." He tossed a leather pouch bulging with heavy coins towards the chef. "Three months' wages. This is for the sister, too. I want them both gone by tomorrow morning, do you understand?" His eyes and voice were glacial, steely.

"No, your highness, I do not understand. The women are good workers, they give satisfaction"—the prince, Volta noted, winced at his choice of words—"I will not be a party to this. Tell Caterina yourself." Vincenzo, realizing his insubordination could cost him his job, but refusing to be part of the sordid game the prince was playing, dropped the money pouch on the prince's desk, turned on his heel and walked out.

Maurizio was stunned. He had known Vincenzo Volta for years; Volta had worked with Caterina a scant few weeks. What inspired this stand of his, this loyalty to a non-entity, someone he scarcely knew? He barely had time to collect his thoughts. Caterina was at the door of his office, her face pale, her back unbowed, asking, "Did you send for me, your highness?"

She was terrified. He could, she knew, have her arrested for assaulting him. What he had been about to do, of course, didn't matter; it would have been her word—a peasant's word—against his, the lord of the manor and all he surveyed. Vincenzo had sent her to see him, squeezing her cold, bloodless hands, whispering, "Coraggio, Caterina, courage!" into her ear. And so she had come, terrified but unbowed.

"I ordered Vincenzo to fire you," the prince began, his anger at his servant barely under control, his hands clenching the edge of his mahogany desk in a tight, ferocious grip. "He refused. Can you imagine that, Signorina? I suppose, now, that I will have to fire him, too."

"Signora," she whispered, her eyes on the floor. She could not look at him. He was so angry, and she deserved it. She had hurt him, body and soul, and he would make her pay, her, her sister, and now Vincenzo, too.

"Signora?" He was puzzled. He looked at her hands. No wedding band showed. "You are married?" My God, what had he done?

She was a married peasant woman in his employ. His lust made him sick.

"Where is your husband, Signora?" he asked, his voice low, calmer.

She looked up defiantly, her light amber eyes flashing with fire. "In America. I left him!"

Maurizio didn't know what to say next. This woman continued to pull the rug out from under his feet. No Sicilian woman, especially not one from the lower classes, left her husband. *What kind of a woman was she?* "But why?" he asked, intrigued despite himself.

Caterina brought her hands to the top button of her thin cotton shirtwaist. Slowly, she began to undo the buttons, down to the waist. The prince stared at her as she stripped, unable to move, to keep her from doing this.

She removed her blouse and turned her back to him, dipping her head forward and lifting the heavy bun of shining chestnut hair off her neck so that he could see clearly. The long puckered scar gleamed whitely and malevolently against her bare shoulders, across the length of her back. She heard the prince draw in a sharp, hissing breath.

"Madonna mia," he whispered, aghast at the cruelty, at the beautiful, disfigured flesh. Maurizio's voice shook. "He . . . your husband . . . he did this to you?"

Caterina nodded. She turned to face him, her blouse wadded in her hands, clad from the waist up only in a plain white cotton chemise, her high, firm breasts thrusting the thin batiste forward, the twin aureoles of her rosy nipples clearly visible beneath the fabric. She was surprised to note that the prince's eyes were wet. *For her?* Was Prince Maurizio Bighilaterra weeping for his lowly servant girl? She felt a tightening, a pang, in her heart.

The prince was bitterly ashamed. He had attempted to force himself twice upon a woman who had clearly had her share of violence, who had suffered dearly—the ugly scar made him sick to his very core—at the hands of a man, her lawfully wedded husband. The man deserved to be killed.

And what do I deserve? Maurizio wondered, for he had sinned against her also.

He spoke again, gently, his voice low. "Why did this happen, Caterina?"

She shrugged wearily. Nothing mattered anymore. Why not tell him? She'd be gone from his sight soon enough. "Because he knew I didn't love him. It made him angry."

Maurizio shook his head, visibly moved by Caterina's suffering. "Forgive me," he said. "I had no right to try to . . ." He stopped, unable to go on, his shoulders bowed in humiliation.

Involuntarily, greatly moved by the pity and shame in his voice, Caterina moved forward, dropping her blouse onto the desk that stood between them, her hands, tentatively, awkwardly, brushing his face. He grasped them in his, looking into her eyes. The rawness of what they saw there, looking deep into each other's souls, shocked them both. Desire. Need. Love. Now. Yes.

Now.

He skirted around the desk quickly, on pure instinct, not thinking, bruising his hip on a sharp corner, drawing her to him, and she came unhesitatingly, wanting him as much as he wanted her. No thoughts, no fears, no worries distracted her now. This was a purely instinctual, animal reaction to him, to this man who could weep for a woman. Who could weep for her, his servant.

The reality of her in his arms was overwhelming. She was warm, soft, yielding, her body yearning against his. He covered her face and neck with kisses, loosened her abundant, fragrant lemon and rosemary scented hair from its pinned-up bun, so that it fell, covering the puckered ugliness of the scar across her back.

In his eagerness to possess her, he tore the chemise down

from her breasts, the skirt from her waist. The magnificence of her body enraptured him. Her breasts were so full, her waist so slender, her belly flat, the rounded hips slim but curved, womanly, and those legs, so long and shapely. He was overcome.

He drank her in, thrilled by the whole of her, the living, breathing, here and now of her. Her arms were draped around his neck. She was suddenly shy, this proud woman, as the man she desired more than she had ever desired any man looked at her face and body with such joy, such naked longing, such—dared she name it?—love. *He was so beautiful.*

He looks like one of the ancient gods of the Greeks, she thought, lovingly. She no longer cared about what would happen next, after what was surely to occur between them, this morning, was over. This was enough. She had been a silly fool to reject what he had to offer her—what was now jutting hard and insistent against her naked belly—because she wanted him. That was enough. It would have to be enough. "Maurizio," she ventured, daring to call him by name.

"Yes, my love?" he whispered, softly, his strong hands running through her thick hair, his lips worshipping at her breasts, searing her erect, rock hard nipples. A lifetime would not be enough to savor all this woman had to offer, he realized, as he held her in his arms, marveling at her beauty, her tenderness.

"I'm so sorry . . . I always wanted you . . . but I was . . . afraid," she had to tell him, to let him know that those feelings were always there, from the very beginning, that fateful night of the dinner party.

Her words inflamed him. He would burst if he didn't have her, now, in this very room. He scooped her up in his arms and carried her to the leather couch against the wall. He lay her down and hurriedly stripped off his clothing. They would be totally naked together, as God had made them.

They forgot they were still married to other people, in the eyes of that very same God. Now, there was only need, a great, urgent need that made them breathless with too-long-pent-up desire and passion.

Maurizio was inside her in a minute, her welcoming wetness absorbing the sizeable length and breadth of him easily, her back arching to meet that first thrust and the ones that followed rapidly, in quick, deep, passionate succession. She moaned in ecstasy as his virility satisfied her need, again and again, as she opened up to him more and more, her body writhing, until there was nothing left of her to offer him and he possessed her entirely. Her long, strong legs tightened about his buttocks, his back, as she urged him on, deeper, harder. She was so moist, so welcoming, so insatiable.

His, finally, his!

He stroked her flanks, her breasts, her flushed cheeks. He kissed her mouth, thrusting his tongue in deeply as she moaned from her throat. He drove in hard and expertly to her center, her femaleness, with a hoarse cry, collapsing on her body, exhausted, spent, exhilarated. She jerked upwards once, as she shattered completely in silvery shards of satisfaction. She called his name, then was still, her breath shallow. They were drenched in sweat, clinging stickily to the leather couch and to each other, oblivious to everything, their souls locked together in love and great, unexpected joy.

Chapter Fourteen

The Threads Are Cut

Old Margherita paused in her long narrative. She turned to Jane, asking her, "Do you know the story of those goddesses of old who control our lives, the one who spins, the one who weaves, the one who cuts the threads?"

Jane nodded. She was still transfixed by the immediacy and passion Margherita had brought to the story of her sister and the prince, but, yes, she vaguely remembered. She thought that the names of the goddesses were the Three Fates. They were old and ugly and dressed in black—she recalled seeing a painting once that depicted the terrifying-looking crones.

Her great-aunt nodded, continuing. "Well, the thread had been spun and woven. The story that was our lives had taken shape. Little did we know how soon the thread-cutting that would end our lives would commence. We had been in paradise, my sister and I, but it was a paradise for fools. It was not going to go on forever. When Caterina and Prince Maurizio became lovers, when he set her up in the *palazzo* and the manor house as his mistress, when they thumbed their noses at society and the Church, it was the beginning of the end."

Caterina was alone with Margherita in the kitchen gardens, in the back of the manor house, picking out fresh new peas, *pisilli,* for the Prince's dinner that night. It was the day after they had become lovers. Afterwards, he had told her she was no longer a cook, but his mistress. Caterina had accepted it, as she had so joyfully, finally, accepted his love.

She knew that below stairs and in the villages and towns—including her own, Borgetto—there would be another name for her, the prince's whore. It would be harder on Margherita than on her. Caterina asked for some time, so that she could break the news to her little sister gently, before she heard crude remarks from others.

So now, it was time. Caterina was strangely tongue-tied. Her sister had been under the influence of the nuns for such a long while; they had filled her young head with notions of sin that Caterina had rejected years ago. Margherita would be shocked, unhappy, but there was no one, nothing, that would make Caterina give up the prince. She was madly in love; she had not known such strong, wild feelings existed; she would not have believed it if anyone had told her that she would be so overcome by him. Her lover Pasquale had swiftly become an old memory.

"Margherita, *cara,* we are no longer to be servants to the prince." The girl's big eyes widened. Taking a deep breath, Caterina spewed it all out, succinctly, truthfully, looking directly into her sister's eyes, which were now even wider.

"*Sorella* . . . you are both married! This is a great sin . . ." she began, tears starting to form in her eyes.

Caterina took both of Margherita's hands in hers, pushing aside the garden *trug* full of tender young green peas. "No, *cara,* no. Not a sin. We love each other. Truly, we do. I did not love Giuseppe; Maurizio does not love his wife. We made mistakes, but they are in the past. Now, we are together. That's what matters. I want you, *sorella,* little sister, to stay with me, with Maurizio. We will take care of you; he will take care of us. Trust me, *cara.* I know what I am doing. I love him, I do. And he loves me."

Margherita, confused, empathizing with her sister's sincerity and passion, nodded in agreement. Whatever Caterina wanted, she would do. If Caterina had not come for her, had not rescued her from the orphanage, she would be dead. She owed Caterina her life. It was as simple as that. She put her arms around her sister and hugged her hard, laughing and crying at the same time.

The unbidden thought, out of her deeply entrenched Roman Catholic upbringing, overlaid with the fatalism endemic to the Sicilian peasantry, came to her, jabbing at her heart. *There would be a price to pay for this sin, one could count on it.* Caterina and the prince were experiencing great happiness, but also committing a very great sin. They would have to pay, Margherita knew and feared it. She feared for her brave sister; she feared for the prince.

Volta was puffed up with his own importance. He had seen it all coming. He had known that the prince would find the lovely, aloof Caterina irresistible. He knew his master well. He hoped that Maurizio would rid himself of his dreadful wife, the odious Princess Fiammetta, and install the beautiful peasant in her place. He couldn't wait. Oh, this was delicious!

The prince moved back to his palazzo in Palermo, with Caterina and her sister and a few select servants, to give the estate staff time to get used to the changes he had made. In Palermo, Caterina shared his bed, took charge of the *palazzo*'s household staff, and was at his side at social functions both in his home and in the city. They traveled abroad, like honeymooners, leaving Margherita in Volta's capable hands. He was teaching her how to cook. (She didn't have the innate talent Caterina had in the kitchen, Vincenzo thought, but she did show promise.)

Palermo society reeled at the happenings on the Via Loro. It was delicious gossip—for a very short time—until more shocking, lurid events cast it to one side. The decadence of upper-class Sicilian society demanded more titillating stuff than the installation of a peasant woman as the mistress of a prince, and no one would dare to snub a Bighilaterra, no matter whom he installed in that position. Tongues were soon wagging with more exquisite tidbits, among them the suspected poisoning of old Count Bellini by Costanza, his beautiful, young, promiscuous wife. Maurizio and Caterina soon became old news, the kind a worldly sophisticate yawns over and dismisses.

Caterina was happy, happier than she had ever been at any time in her life, happier than she thought any person could ever be. She enjoyed living in the elegant *palazzo* and was learning to run it well, earning Maurizio's respect and praise.

Margherita had started cooking lessons, under the tutelage of Caterina's good kind friend, Vincenzo Volta, and was also embroidering pieces of her own choosing, no longer having to toil at someone else's mending pile. And she had also, or so Caterina suspected, fallen in love. With a young footman named Carlo Mannino, who was from, of all places, Borgetto.

And Maurizio . . . how could she describe what she felt? Her skin warmed at the very thought of him, her arms and neck tingling, her legs growing weak, her head dizzy. He was an unbelievable lover and a caring, tender human being. She wanted it to last forever. She knew she could never leave him. Sometimes she worried he would tire of her. She was, after all, just an uneducated, unlettered peasant woman.

To that end, she was honing up on her reading skills,

working her way through the formidable collection of volumes and manuscripts in the Bighilaterra library. The multisyllabic words in all those big, leather-bound books both terrified and fascinated her. She tore through them hungrily, pleased when she could converse with Maurizio—yes, in-between bouts of frenzied lovemaking, they did converse, she laughed to herself—and almost on his level. And he seemed delighted with her determination and her growing prowess. Every day, he told her, he loved her more, his bright, beautiful peasant.

She was in the library one afternoon in late summer, when he entered the room frowning, asking her to sit down. They had important things to discuss, he told her. He seemed agitated, on edge. Dear God, she thought, thinking the worst, it's over. *He doesn't want me any more. So soon!* What did she expect, though? She could amuse him for only so long. His tastes were more refined. How could a woman of her class . . .

He spoke. "Caterina, please, listen to me, pay attention. This is important."

Now she noticed that he had some papers in his hands. One looked like a telegram. He was going away. She was sure of it. All the color drained from her face.

"Caterina? Please, stop daydreaming. I have news for you. You are a free woman."

What a way to put it, she thought; he is throwing me out of his life and telling me that I am a free woman. Now she began to get angry.

"I've always been a free woman, Maurizio. I chose you freely, now—"

He stopped her before she could say more. "What are you going on about, woman? I'm trying to tell you that your despised husband, Giuseppe Malatesta, is dead." He waved the telegram in her face. She seemed dazed.

Dead? Giuseppe, the grotesque, hateful Giuseppe, dead? "But how . . . when?" she stammered, almost incoherent.

"Dearest one, let me finish, please. Now listen, don't say anything. I had contacted . . . certain people . . . in New York, Brooklyn . . . to find your husband, to let me know what he was doing. They reported back to me by telegram today."

He held up the yellow sheet. She could see the small cut out rectangles of words glued onto the thick square sheet of paper, bearing news meant for her. Words of freedom, her freedom. Giuseppe, dead! It was a miracle, praise be to God!

Maurizio read from the tersely worded document. "Giuseppe Malatesta unavailable for interview as per your request—stop—Said Malatesta run over by trolley car in accident last month—stop—Caterina Malatesta a widow—stop—We await your further instructions."

Caterina licked her dry lips. "What does that mean . . . what kind of . . . interview . . . were your people planning to have with Giuseppe, Maurizio?"

The prince leaned back against the edge of his desk. "They were going to persuade him to divorce you, *carissima,* on the grounds of desertion, or perhaps, get him to file for an annulment. Following my instructions, they were prepared to offer him a great deal of money—which, happily, I can now use for other purposes—the primary one being the filing of my annulment papers with the Vatican. The money meant to pay off your late husband will now line the pockets of an agreeable, bribable priest or two at the Holy See, so that my farce of a marriage to Fiammetta can be dissolved."

She looked at him in wonder, her amber-hued eyes wide,

shaking her head from side to side. "You never told me you were planning to do all this, Maurizio."

"Well, I did not want to say anything until I was sure these things could be accomplished. I didn't want you to worry, my love, and I thought that you would have no objections."

But she did not understand, not fully, asking, "Why couldn't we just go on as we are? There's no need for you to waste your money, devote your time to these pursuits."

"How else will we be free to marry, *cara?* Your late husband has been very obliging, but we still have my wife with whom to contend."

He could say no more. Caterina's face was strangely contorted. She looked as though she were about to burst into tears. She never cried; she'd told him that more than once. "What's wrong now?" he asked, exasperated.

Her voice was so low he had to bend to catch her words. "You never said you wanted to marry me."

His arms were around her in an instant, holding her sweet, trembling body close to his. Caterina willed back the tears that were beginning to form in her eyes. She held him fiercely, her heart pounding against his.

With a groan, Maurizio scooped her up in his arms and took her upstairs, back into the master bedroom, back into their bed. He made love to her that afternoon with a ferocity and passion that exceeded the intensity of all their previous couplings, celebrating her freedom, his soon to come.

They made love through dinner and into the night. Margherita ate at the long, polished mahogany table in the dining room by herself, embarrassed by the knowing smirks of the household staff, wondering what could possibly be going on that would cause her sister and the prince to miss one of Vincenzo's excellent meals. But Carlo the young footman was being especially attentive to Margherita that night, and she soon dismissed the couple's antics from her mind.

Antics, indeed. Caterina and Maurizio were exploring and plumbing the depths of their passion in his enormous bed. Caterina was an apt and eager pupil in that bed, just as she had been apt and eager in Volta's kitchen. She learned quickly; she learned well. She sought out everything that would give him pleasure and performed enthusiastically.

He, in turn, drove her to heights of ecstasy that left her gasping in wonder and delight. He had put his head between her legs, kissing her intimately and carnally, thrusting his expert tongue deep inside her, driving her mad with desire for him.

Madonna mia! she thought, trembling, this is something I could never share with Margherita! He had asked her to touch him and she had wrapped her strong, slender hands around the root of his manhood, stroking him until he came in a great burst of seed. Nothing they did with or to each other was shameful, and they did it all, into the long night.

Long afterwards, Caterina had time to reflect, to think, telling herself that they were too happy that day, that night, rejoicing over someone's death. *We angered the heavens with our joy,* she thought, *with our animal delight in each other's bodies. Perhaps that was why the price we paid in the end was so high,* she mused ruefully.

Meanwhile, back in the neighborhood of Maurizio's estate, in the Conca d'Oro, unbeknownst to him or Caterina, other wheels had been set into motion. Months ago, the prince had been approached by the swarthy representative of a group of ruthless extortionists who had been demanding payments—*i pizzi*—from all the wealthy landowners and aristocrats in the region. Maurizio had sent the extortionist away with a warning not to return; the man had replied with a vicious threat. *La Mafia* was not to be trifled with.

Headquartered in Partinico, a nearby town, they had begun to carry out their threats seriously, with no interference from *i caribinieri,* the police. According to some, these police were hand-in-glove with the *Mafia;* at the least, they were ineffectual. The Italian government, based too far away in Rome, was useless in local Sicilian disputes. The canny Church, always looking out for its own interests, was neutral.

Many frightened aristocrats had caved in and paid. The prince, a man of pride and honor, had been the only one, so far, to refuse outright. They were not going to let him get away with it. He would be made an example so that others would not dare vacillate.

In Tuscany, more wheels were spinning. Fiammetta's father was getting tired of his frivolous daughter, thinking that it was high time that the silly girl went back to her too-tolerant husband and produced an heir. As he was preparing to lecture Fiammetta on the neglect of her wifely duties, word came from a family emissary at the Vatican that Maurizio had filed for an annulment of his marriage.

Substantial bribes, it was rumored, had already changed hands. It seemed as though the powerful Prince Bighilaterra would have his way. The emissary further added that the prince was willing to fix a generous settlement on the wife who had deserted him, although he was clearly the injured party.

It seemed a cut-and-dried issue. Fiammetta had behaved stupidly and would have to suffer the ensuing consequences, the ignominy of being cast off. But then a so-called friend in Palermo had written to the princess, desirous of being the first to let her know that Maurizio was openly flaunting a live-in mistress at the smartest levels of Palermo society. There were always those who were gratified grinding salt into a raw wound, whether they call themselves friend or foe.

But this was the best part: the woman was a servant, a menial, a mere domestic, a peasant from the Bighilaterra estate. This lowly creature was Fiammetta's replacement, sharing the prince's bed, his life. The knife had been driven into Fiammetta's back and neatly turned so as to cause the most pain. It made its bloody point. She ran crying to her father.

Maurizio had shamed the proud Tuscan prince's baby girl with one of his own lowly servants! That put a different light on the matter of his and Fiammetta's estrangement. This was now a question of honor. The Tuscan aristocrat's family would not be the laughing-stock of Italy, not for a mere Sicilian, no matter how princely or distinguished his family.

Fiammetta's father fired off a missive to his papal emissary. Bighilaterra's bribes would be matched, *lira* for *lira,* even if he had to mortgage all his extensive landholdings. It would take some time to gather the money. The emissary was instructed to try to delay the annulment proceedings as long as possible. The money, he was assured, would be forthcoming.

"What was it like in Palermo? At the Prince's *palazzo?*" Jane asked her old aunt, who, remembering those glory days, seemed radiant and yes, even young, once more.

Margherita smiled. "It was magnificent! The most beautiful house on the Via Loro." She turned to Jane. "That is near the Piazza Garibaldi, maybe you know it?"

Jane shook her head no. *I could have seen it, Zia, I could have. But I was too proud, too proud and angry after seeing Lorenzo with another woman that horrible afternoon. Now I'll never see it,* she realized, bitterly.

Margherita was going on with the rest of her story, fired up now, eager to tell it all. "The servants at the Palazzo Bighilaterra were mostly city people, not country folk like us, like Caterina and I. But there was a footman . . . ah, he had beautiful, refined manners, although he was from Borgetto, too, like us. His name was Carlo, Carlo Mannino . . ." Now she was crying, softly. "He became my husband."

It was a shy, adolescent courtship, this sweet, slow dance that Margherita and the footman Carlo engaged in that summer at the Palazzo Bighilaterra. Caterina was amused to note them making cow's eyes at each other, blushing red when they passed in the hallways, which seemed to happen countless times during the day. Margherita was in love, Caterina knew. She remembered the sweetness of her brief love affair with her young cousin. She wanted Margherita to be happy and to secure that happiness quickly. She spoke to Maurizio.

The prince was amused. "What are you talking about, *cara?* They are both children—"

"No, not so young. They are ready for each other. Young love is very sweet, *caro,*" she cooed softly, pressing the young couple's suit with him.

"What are you suggesting?" he asked her fondly, caressing her with his eyes. She was getting more beautiful every day. He was on tenterhooks waiting for his petition to be approved by the Vatican. He wanted to make her his bride.

Caterina smiled, getting her way. "Talk to him. I will talk to her. Let's see what they have to say. Maybe we will have a wedding!" *Not ours, my dearest,* she thought, tenderly, *but that will come, too, I know it!*

So it was that a lavish wedding and reception took place very soon. The staff outdid themselves, getting the *palazzo* in order, serving up fabulous food creations. It was a dress rehearsal for the wedding they all wanted to take place next. The staff knew, thanks to Vincenzo, that the prince had filed for an annulment, and they were waiting, too. But, for now, the young bride was lovely, the young bridegroom handsome, and happiness was in the air.

Margherita, having been apprised by her sister some months ago (and by the upstairs maid Paolina quite recently) of how babies were made, was eager to start a family right away, to surround herself with loving children. But her big sister beat her to it. Caterina was expecting a child.

Always in abundant good health, Caterina had been feeling poorly and out of sorts, and could not understand why. Not that she was unaware that what she and the prince had been doing, so eagerly, so intensely, every night and usually during the day, was known, in most circumstances, to bring on pregnancy. She was hardly naive about the sex act and its consequences. No, Caterina had presumed she was barren.

Her history seemed to bear this out. First there was the affair with her cousin, Pasquale Polizzi; then her two-year marriage to Giuseppe Malatesta. Since she had never conceived, it surely had to be her fault. It was never the man's. But Pasquale, who had since married, was not yet a father. It was possible that both of those men had been sterile. More than possible.

Maurizio took the confirmation of Caterina's pregnancy

with great joy; joy tinged with great sadness. Joy that they would have a child to bear witness of their love for each other, sadness that it would be a bastard who would never have his name. Unless the hoped-for annulment came through, he and Caterina could never marry.

As summer passed into fall, and Caterina's pregnancy advanced, they decided to spend the hunting season at the estate. This was the first time they would be back since leaving the manor house in the late spring. Caterina was coming back as the mistress of the house, although not yet Maurizio's wife.

Maurizio let it be known that he expected Caterina to be treated, nonetheless, as his lawful wedded wife. She was that in the prince's eyes . . . and heart. The staff took its cue from Volta and the prince's major-domo, and, if there was gossip or speculation, it was strictly a below stairs activity.

Margherita shook her head sadly in recollection. "We all overlooked the fact that they had sinned. We pretended that they were husband and wife because that was what the Prince wanted. But we feared it would soon be time to pay the awful price.

"Once, the priest from Borgetto dared to come, the same one who had failed to persuade Caterina to return to her husband in America. He had been sent by our family. They were shamed in the town, shunned because of Caterina's doings.

"The priest called her *una butana,* a whore, and cursed the unborn child in her womb. The prince had to be restrained from tearing the priest apart. Then he set his dogs on him and chased him off his property."

Margherita chuckled, remembering the fat, obnoxious priest, rolls of flab shaking as he ran for his life from the hunting dogs, hot and howling on his trail. It had been very funny. Then she hesitated, as if unable to go on.

Jane prompted her. Margherita sighed and continued, shaking her head sadly. "Ah, *cara,* I wish you had known him, the prince. He was a real man, a good man, an honorable man, but too many people were conspiring against him, the church, its priests, the princess's father, *la Mafia.* Yes, he had sinned—we all sin, *cara,* but he did not deserve what happened to him. Nor did my Carlo." Here the tears started to roll down her wrinkled cheeks, and she whispered, "Nor did Carlo deserve what happened to him."

All along, *la Mafia* was there, waiting to for the right time to make its move, to teach that proud prince a lesson; like a fat black spider in the middle of an enormous, well-constructed web, ready to spring. The prince, yes, he would be caught, Caterina, his paramour, also, but their first victim would be the innocent Carlo, Margherita's young husband.

The *Mafia* had waited a long time for the prince to deliver *i pizzi,* those extortion demands, to them. He had insulted them by ignoring their request, by kicking their representative out of his house. A few times, when he was bird hunting, engaged in *la caccia,* potshots, warnings, had been fired at him. Maurizio never went for quail and partridge without being surrounded by a retinue of bird dogs and retainers, so the interlopers had been so far frustrated in their pursuit of him, unable to get close enough to make their bullets count.

And then, one fine fall day, the air crisp and clean with the cool smell of the winter to come wafting in the breeze, Maurizio and Caterina were caught by surprise, off-guard. He had just returned from rabbit hunting, his long-barreled antique shotgun was hanging at his side. She was there to greet him at the front door. She had kissed him and he had placed his hand tenderly on her swollen belly, feeling the child kick strongly.

Carlo had come running up to the prince, a letter secured with an important-looking large red seal in his hand. The prince turned, expectantly, to face Carlo. Shots rang out. Carlo was dead instantly, shot in the neck and back. The prince was badly wounded. Caterina, instinctively, had fallen to her knees as Maurizio's body had buckled with the impact of the shots, saving his head from hitting the hard stone of the front entryway and incidentally saving her own life by moving down out of range of the shooters.

"Help me! Help him!" she had screamed in her grief. Later, Margherita said, they claimed that her pitiful cries for help could be heard for miles, echoing in the deep valleys. She'd thought for a certainty that he was dead.

"My love, my dearest love," she wept, she who never wept, over his prone, seemingly lifeless body. Volta sent for the doctor. Nothing could be done for Carlo, taken cruelly in his young manhood. The valet Alfonso took the blood-soaked letter out of his stiffening hands. Gianni the majordomo pulled Caterina gently but firmly away from Maurizio so that the farm laborers could carry him to a bed. They assured her that he was still breathing, but she was a wild woman. The doctor feared for her unborn child's life. He made her swallow a sedative.

Volta was there when they brought Carlo's body to Margherita to bathe. She could not react, she could not cry, she could not move. She sat paralyzed, repeating his name over and over again, as if he would hear her and come back. Pitying the girl, Volta asked the physician to administer a sedative to her, too. *The poor, poor child,* Volta thought, *the poor children.*

The prince's wounds, the ones that could be seen, were patched up. When he regained consciousness, he immediately asked for Carlo. His last memory was of the young man holding an important-looking letter out to him and then crumpling as the bullets tore through his body. The stunned silence told him everything. He shut his eyes in pain. He knew why all this had happened. He was to blame. Only *he* was to blame.

Caterina, at his side, held his hands tightly, her eyes fierce. Maurizio asked for the letter Carlo had been about to give him. *Why?* Caterina thought. *What does a letter matter now, at a time like this?* But, of course, she realized, it was the letter the prince had been waiting for and young Carlo had known it, too. That's why the footman had raced so eagerly to bring it to his prince. It was the news they were all waiting for from Rome.

Caterina, hands trembling, read it to her lover, the raw bloodstains and their memory of death and the long, difficult words tripping her up, causing her to stumble as she read. It was, indeed, from the Vatican. The long-hoped-for annulment had been denied.

"It was the end, *cara,* the end of everything. Our earthly paradise was gone. The despair of the prince at the bad news, combined with the severity of his wounds . . . well, he never truly recovered, not in his body, not in his soul. And he was suddenly frightened for the unborn child, for Caterina. The curses of that stupid priest rang in his ears . . . ah, he was afraid, then, that strong, brave man. He sent Caterina away."

Jane was aghast. "He sent her away? But he loved her!

What kind of man was he?" She couldn't believe Maurizio, the Maurizio she thought she had come to know so well through Margherita's poignant narrative, was capable of separating himself from his great love, Caterina.

"*Cara,* he feared the *Mafia* would return and kill her, too. That day, they had come so close. They knew what would really hurt him. He sent her to Paris with the chef, Volta. Vincenzo had good friends there from his student days. The prince was confident that the *Mafia* would not be able to track her down, and that Vincenzo would see that she was well looked after. But we never saw her again, nor Volta, either."

"I don't understand." Jane was near tears herself. It couldn't end this way. "Why? What happened?"

Margherita looked at her sadly. This had all happened such a long, long time ago. What could the child know of what was happening then? Of how the world was falling apart? "The Great War, *cara,* World War I, you Americans call it. We all lost touch."

She shook her head. "I was no good to anyone. I think I had what they call now a nervous breakdown. I was too distraught over Carlo; I was not myself. I took to my bed; time was meaningless. I was not aware of anything. And, when I finally recovered, it was too late. I wanted to try to get to Paris, to join her, help her with the baby—which, by now, had to have come, so much time had passed—but it was too late. We all lost touch. No one ever knew what happened to her."

Jane was upset. Margherita's life had fallen apart. Her husband dead, her sister . . . dead? Missing? And the child? What of that poor baby? Jane's soft heart ached for them all.

Margherita had more to tell. "And of course, Princess

Bighilaterra, Fiammetta, she came back. The Vatican had turned down the petition for annulment. She was still Maurizio's lawful wife. She came back, and took over. The prince . . . well, he was too unhappy, too weak, to protest. I don't think he ever got over it, *cara*. Depression, that's what they would call it now. He was such a sad, changed man, never the same."

She reached out to touch Jane's face tenderly. "I wish you had seen him, Gianna. Such a handsome man he had been, such wonderful, kind blue eyes. You would never have forgotten him, never. You would have fallen in love with him, just as my beloved sister Caterina did."

Ah, Zia, I will never forget the blue eyes of his grandson, Jane thought, *his grandson, whom I do love so much.* Jane blushed at the memory of how much she had loved Lorenzo the night before in the Donzinis' bed at Alcamo. She had driven back after midnight, exhausted, falling into a deep sleep and waking up just in time to meet her old aunt at the cemetery. Her body ached with the memory of Lorenzo's fiery lovemaking. Reluctantly, she turned her attention once more to the sad story Margherita was telling.

"And the princess, well, as I said, she took over. Almost losing him had taught her a lesson. Not that she cared for him that much—I think she always preferred the wealth to the man, which gives you an idea of the shallow kind of woman she was—but I have to say that she took care of him. Yes, she tried very hard to be the perfect wife. No one ever heard her complain about having to live in Sicily again, and she was willing, this time, to share his bed.

"She even . . ." Here Margherita looked directly at Jane, her lips in a sneer. "She even went so far as to have his child. Anything to keep him. But the child he longed for—although he was a good, kind father to the other one—was

Caterina's child, his and Caterina's. He used to tell me that when I saw him."

Lorenzo's father, the one who had perished in the car accident, so then he was Fiammetta's child, named Maurizio, too, after his father. Jane pursued this. "No one ever found out about Caterina's child? He—or she—never turned up, never came back to Sicily?"

"*If* there was ever a child." Noting Jane's puzzlement, Margherita explained. "In those days, *cara,* many women died in childbirth. We thought that was probably Caterina's fate. And remember that it was wartime. Things were so very bad in Paris. We thought she and the child had both perished."

"But that doesn't explain what happened to Volta," Jane persisted.

"No, you're right." Margherita frowned. "That was a mystery, Volta's disappearance. But, you know, he hated the princess. Perhaps he had gotten word she'd returned; he would never have come back to work for her, and, too, there was always the possibility that Vincenzo and Caterina had been killed in the war. So much to think about, to wonder, and none of us ever found out."

"What did you do, *Zia?*" Jane pressed the old woman's hands.

"Ah, well, I had a problem, you know. I couldn't stay in the *palazzo* anymore, nor go back to the estate. Seeing me around would make it unpleasant for the princess, remind her of my sister, the prince's lover. I had to go.

"The prince was very kind; he found me work with friends of his, another aristocratic family in Palermo. But then, I decided to come back here after a few years. Carlo's family took me in. Mine . . ." She shrugged. "Mine would have nothing to do with me. Ah, *cara,* sometimes . . . I don't know, sometimes I think that my life has been wasted . . . I am like a lemon that has been sucked dry." She wept again, softly.

She stopped, dabbing at her bright, wet eyes with a beautifully hand-embroidered handkerchief. "I have to stop feeling sorry for myself. I had love, once, in my life, my sister and my husband. Some poor souls never have any. And the prince, *cara,* let me tell you about the prince. He never forgot me. He sent me money every year.

"The annuity still comes, after his death. He used to tell me that he had been a great fool, that it was only money the *Mafia* wanted, only money. He could have given it to them and saved us all this misery, all this pain. He never forgave himself for that. He suffered for his sin. He had to pay for it; we all did."

Now, she was angry, her soft eyes ablaze. "And was it such a horrible sin, to love someone so much? Over the years, and I have had a long time to think about it, I thought not. No, there are worst sins, *cara,* many more worse sins.

"But I could not persuade him that he had really done no wrong, that it was just our fate, that it had been time—who knows why—time for those threads to be cut. He died still blaming himself, still yearning for Caterina and the child. Ah, *cara,* he died so young, too young, only in his forties, he was."

"So, we always pay the price, whether it's fair or not . . . we have no control over such things," Jane commented, depressed.

Margherita stroked the girl's thick glossy chestnut brown hair, so like her sister's. "Yes," she agreed, "we pay. Always." And then they wept together, over this unfair thing called life, in that graveyard, in the cool air of morning.

And do the dead hear us, Jane wondered? *Do they weep also, with us?*

Margherita dabbed at her eyes again, and at Jane's. She had been saving up her story for years, and she wasn't finished yet. Jane thought: *she is like the Ancient Mariner of the poem, and I am the wedding guest, doomed to hear her out. But I want to hear it. This is no fictional soap opera. This is my family. This is their sad Sicilian saga.*

"Lately, I have had such strange feelings, *cara,* such dreams. I went to the Madonna di Romitello to pray. I have prayed for many years, but now I prayed harder. I thought that something was about to happen, and then I saw you, Caterina, come back from the grave. I am happy now, Gianna, truly I am, despite all the tears that have been flowing out of me. My sister has come back to me once more before I die. I am grateful. You are here, with his gold charm, his amulet, the one she always wore as his token of love. My proud sister! She would never take any other jewelry from that wealthy man, not one other thing, just this." Margherita pointed to Lorenzo's *trinacria* amulet, dangling from the gold chain around Jane's neck. She took it in her frail hands and turned it over, seeing the initials incised on its back. MB.

"Cara mia," she asked gently, her soft eyes boring into Jane's skull, intent, "I must ask you, please, how did you come by this?"

Chapter Fifteen

Finding the Answers

"Zia," Jane told her great-aunt, "this was given to me by Lorenzo Bighilaterra. Yes, Maurizio's grandson. It belongs to him. I have to return it."

"But how do you know him?" she asked, her soft brown eyes wide in amazement.

"I met him at the home of the people I am staying with in Palermo—the Donzinis—friends of my mother's. I . . ." Jane took a deep breath. "I love him." It was the truth, Jane realized. She really did love Lorenzo. Nothing had changed that. Last night had only confirmed it. She could run from him, but not from her love for him.

The sweet-faced old woman, not all that different from the adorable teenager in the framed studio portrait that Jane still held in her hands, her newly-discovered, so quickly dear great-aunt, smiled. Hearing those words, which Jane suddenly realized she meant with all of her heart, Margherita broke into a truly beatific smile. Holding out her thin arms, she embraced Jane with a surprisingly firm grip for one so bird-like and small.

She cupped Jane's young face in her wrinkled hands, looked deeply into her hazel eyes—so like Caterina's that they broke Margherita's heart—and blessed her, praying, "Make this love story, your love story, have a happy ending, *cara*. We need some happy endings in this unlucky family."

Well, that did it. Jane broke down completely at the old

woman's words, continuing the flood of tears that had overtaken her at the *caffe* with Anna Maria, soaking Margherita's dress at the shoulder, making a bitter lie of her promise that she would not ever cry for Lorenzo again.

Margherita waited her out, then handed her the damp hand-embroidered hanky. "Keep it, my dear," she said. "These tears . . . they have a habit of coming again and again."

How true, Jane thought, blowing her nose.

Margherita patted her cheek. "Will you be here tomorrow?"

Jane nodded, handing the old framed photograph back to her. As they took their emotional leave of each other until the morrow, Jane thought she saw, out of the corner of her eye, a black-clad shape dart around one of the small stone mausoleums. Frowning, she dismissed it as a trick of the light.

Jane had a good deal to ponder on the long dusty walk back to her Aunt Maria's *caffe*. About people with too much pride who couldn't forgive, who couldn't talk about what was troubling them; about people who gave up on the loves of their lives because they lost heart; about having to live with grief and disappointment for the rest of one's life because you've made the wrong choices. Who did that describe? Maurizio? Caterina? Or her, Jane Holland?

Jane made up her mind that she would go back to Palermo and seek Lorenzo out, talk to him, explain how she felt about love and relationships, before it was too late for them. He'd kept telling her he cared, that they belonged together, and he'd made love to her so exquisitely. How could that all be an act? And there could be a perfectly rational explanation for that overly intimate scene she witnessed on the street—couldn't there be? Had she over-reacted?

And the proud, brave Caterina—there was one possibility it seemed that Margherita could not face, did not even deign to address—there was the possibility that Caterina had made the deliberate choice never to return. That it was *she* who had given up on Maurizio, the love of her life, on Margherita, the sister she cared for so strongly, simply leaving the whole mess behind her. She had lost heart. Could she have done that to them? They loved her so much!

Am I doing this to Lorenzo? Jane wondered. Do Caterina and I resemble each other in more than our looks? Are our inner selves—our stubborn, prideful selves—very much the same? Can I learn from this unbearably sad story before it's too late for me? She was tormenting herself with all these questions.

Ahead of her were three big black-clad workmen, dented shovels across their shoulders, oversized feet raising great balls of dust into the air. *I Schifosi.* Funny how they always turned up, Jane thought. She slowed down her pace considerably and let them get way ahead of her.

She was still quite nervous about what had happened two nights before, when she'd discovered the purloined Greek antiquities in her grandmother's house. Had one of the brothers seen her scrambling out of the front door? Who did they suspect of uncrating the *nereid*-on-a-dolphin statue? They had to have noticed, as dim as they appeared to be. She could be in trouble.

Rats! Jane exclaimed to herself. They were heading towards the *caffe,* too.

Jane ducked around the corner of Number Four Corso Roma, peeking carefully out at the *caffe.* Only one end of the outdoor coffee shop was visible, but that was where the Schifosi clan always chose to sit, their favorite table. Jane had a clear view of all of them. Alfredo, the youngest, seemed to be trying to flirt, in his heavy-handed manner, with Ninfina. She looked annoyed—or was she simply flirting also, being coy? Everything, Jane thought, has a double meaning these days. Now Ninfina was waving Alfredo away with her hands and tosses of her head. She went behind the bar.

Now someone else had appeared, quite unexpectedly, into her line of vision. Someone she knew. That walk, that proud tilt of the head. The sun flashed into her eyes, high overhead, the bright light temporarily blinding her. It was just past noon. She looked again at the man approaching *i Schifosi* from the other end of the *caffe*. She blinked.

It was Lorenzo. *Lorenzo, her love.* The lover she had abandoned early this morning. He was in Borgetto. He hadn't given up. Unbelievable! He had tracked her down. Did he truly love her, after all? Was it all going to be all right forever after? Happily ever after?

Shaking, Jane leaned back against the stone facade of the house. Her heart was beating rapidly. She wanted to dash out and run to him—run *to* him, this time—not away from him. Did she dare?

Still shaking, Jane peered around the corner of the house again. Lorenzo was in animated conversation with the despicable Schifosis. Jane was puzzled. Did he know such low-life? Of course, he probably did, she reminded herself. The Bighilaterras probably knew all the peasants from miles around, had employed them and their relatives for gencrations on their estates. Now, Lorenzo was patting the shoulder of the oldest, ugliest Schifosi, Guido, and laughing. What was the joke? Jane wanted to know. *Was it on her?*

Lorenzo reached into his pocket and pulled out a fat wad

of *lire,* placing it on the table in front of the brothers. Was he staking them to a few hundred rounds of their favorite liquid refreshment, *espresso con grappa?* Or . . . was he paying them off for a certain late classical Greek antiquity, the head of a woman?

Jane's mind was racing wildly, remembering the Schifosis were antiquities robbers and that Lorenzo had left an expensive piece of Greek statuary with Claudia for her. What connection, if any, did Lorenzo have with *i Schifosi?* Was he their fence? Their silent partner in crime? Was he here in Borgetto for her . . . or for the Schifosis? She was confused. Just what was going on? She fretted, paranoia getting the best of her.

From her hiding place, she wondered what chance she, a naive, innocent *Americana,* had to sort out all the nefarious and devious relationships that abounded in this small town. Should she have confided what she'd found in her grandmother's house to Margherita? She'd been so caught up in Margherita's story that there'd been no time to tell hers. Tomorrow. She'd tell her tomorrow; maybe she could give her some good advice. Lord knew she needed it, needed it badly.

And Lorenzo . . . what of her decision, reached just a few moments before, to try to patch things up with him, to apologize for her childish behavior, to tell him she loved him, to hear his side of the story? Things were too complicated, moving far too fast. She needed time now, more time to think. She peeked back at the *caffe.* Lorenzo had gone.

Did she imagine the roar of his Alfa Romeo heading east, back towards Palermo? Her heart sank. The sight of him had thrilled her, she could not deny that. It had torn her up to leave his bed that morning; she had wanted nothing more than to lie there with her arms around him forever. She wanted him, still, more than ever; as much as she had wanted him last night, as she would always want him.

But who was Lorenzo? What was he? Which Lorenzo had she fallen in love with? Did that Lorenzo really exist? Or was he only a figment of her over-active imagination, subject to hallucinations in vineyards, now put into fast-forward, thanks to Margherita's romantic tale of princes and peasants and tragic love affairs?

All bets are off, Jane promised herself, *until I figure out just what is going on around here!* She sauntered casually, or so she hoped, across the Corso Roma, her sneakers making no sound on the worn-down cobblestone street, and sauntered into the courtyard of the *caffe.*

She saw Guido Schifosi cock a straggly black eyebrow at his brothers, Nino and Alfredo. Ignoring all of them, she went in search of her cousin Ninfina. Could she trust her? Could she trust Aunt Maria? *Guardate, Jane, guardate,* she cautioned herself.

Halfway back to Palermo, Lorenzo Bighilaterra pulled over sharply to the side of the autostrada. He hit the steering wheel hard with the flat of his palm. He had just remembered someone who might help him, someone more reliable than those *malandrini,* the Schifosis, to whom he'd just paid a considerable amount of *lire* to find out if there was a tall American girl in the vicinity.

The brothers got around, doing the occasional odd job; the word was that they would do anything, legal or not, for an extra *lira* or two in their pockets. Lorenzo's uncle and his friend, Aldo Donzini, had, however, stopped giving them work on their properties, as too many things tended to disappear when those boys were around. He'd probably made a mistake in hiring them.

Now he had another idea. Turning the Alfa around, he headed straight back to Borgetto. There was an old woman there who'd done some work for his aunt, some embroidery work. She'd been asked to repair some fine work she'd done years ago for his grandfather that had been damaged by careless laundering. He thought hard and came up with her name: Margherita Mannino. A widow. She lived on the Via Reggio. She might know if anyone fitting Jane's description had passed through the town.

Jane had joined Ninfina in the kitchen, taking up a serrated-edged knife and slicing red ripe tomatoes with her for the noon meal. Their knives were sharp, making neat, angled slices from the big tomatoes, spurting little juice. Jane arranged them all artistically on a thick white china plate in overlapping rows.

"Ninfina," she asked innocently, licking sweet tomato juice from her fingers, "the Schifosi are such regular, good customers . . . were they very good friends of your father's?"

Ninfina seemed a little surprised by the coming-out-of-the-blue question, wondering at Jane's inquisitiveness, putting it down to the natural curiosity of Americans.

She nonetheless answered without hesitation. "My father and Guido worked together once, a long time ago. Guido tried to court my mother after my father died, but she would have nothing to do with him. Now . . ." She wrinkled up her small nose, making a wry face. "Now Alfredo is getting those same ideas about me."

"You don't like him, do you?" Jane asked. Certainly, to all outward appearances, she didn't seem to; she was not very pleasant to him. But Jane worried that Sicilian mating rituals were quite different from those in the States. What Jane had experienced so far herself had left her in some confusion.

"Gianna, you may think me unnatural, unwomanly, but I am not at all interested in getting married or having a family. Life is too hard for women here, and I don't want to be under any man's thumb. *Certo,* I don't want to be under the dirty thumb of one of the Schifosi!" Ninfina slammed her small fist on the kitchen counter for emphasis, and then she giggled.

Jane thought: *my cousin is a feminist!* Throwing aside all caution, she decided to take a chance on Ninfina's honesty and forthrightness. "Ninfina," she began, "is there any way—please think about this—is there any way at all that the Schifosi could have gotten the key to Number Four Corso Roma, across the street?"

Ninfina looked at Jane with some surprise. It seemed that her cousin was full of questions this afternoon. Did it have anything to do with her drive to Alcamo last night? She had come back very late. "Why do you ask that, Gianna?" She was wiping her tomato knife carefully with a damp washcloth.

"Because I saw them in there, two nights ago, when I went to look at the house and you and Aunt Maria were here working on your account books." *There,* thought Jane, *now it's all out, let's see what she does with it and where it gets me.*

Intent, her brow furrowed, Ninfina questioned Jane closely. "Did you see what they were doing in there? Were they taking anything?"

"I saw what they were doing, Ninfa. It wasn't good," Jane answered.

Now she was clearly worried, her eyebrows knit together. "Shall I tell Mama?"

"Not yet," Jane cautioned her. "First, please come with me, to the house. I want to show you exactly what they are up to." Jane took Ninfina by the arm to lead her across the street. "Let's go, *andiamo . . . ammonne.*" Unthinking, she had started to speak to her cousin in the Borgetto dialect.

"But," Ninfa was protesting, "how will we get in? You know we have no key. How will we unlock the door?"

"The back door was open the night before last. Let's pray it's open this afternoon, too. First, let's make sure the Schifosi are still at their table." Jane and Ninfina peered through the glass beads that separated the house from the *caffe.*

I Schifosi were sitting somberly, sullenly, drinking espresso and munching on hard cheese and *pane di casa.* They were also sharing a plate of sesame biscuits. They'd be there for a little while longer, Jane thought. She noted that the pile of *lire* that Lorenzo had placed in front of them was gone. She gestured to Ninfa. "Okay, let's go now."

Like two thieves, but in broad daylight, they slunk across the road. Most *Borgettani* were behind their doors, at their mid-day meal; no one noticed them. Or so they thought.

Jane pushed gently but firmly on the old wooden back door. The hinges squeaked softly and the door swung open. They quickly entered the house, shutting the door behind them. Jane looked around in amazement and disbelief. All of the boxes had disappeared. The black and white tiled floor had been swept clean.

Ninfina was perplexed. "Well, what is it? What did you want to show me?"

Jane was desolate; she felt like a fool. "They're all gone." She turned to her cousin. "Believe me, Ninfina, they were here two nights ago. Crates full of Greek antiquities, statues of the gods and goddesses from ancient times. Stolen goods, all of them. The question is, what happened to them?"

Jane looked more closely at the swept tiled floors. Well, the Schifosis had not been able to cover their traces completely. There was a long, deep scrape all the way from the center of the room to the back door, such as could have been caused by dragging a very heavy box across it. But would a scratch on the floor, which could have been there from times before, convince Ninfina that Jane's story was true, that she hadn't made it all up?

Ninfina looked skeptical as Jane pointed out the scraped floor, repeating her story of the Schifosis and their cache of stolen goods, the priceless Greek statues. "I did see the statues; I touched them. I ran away when I heard them coming. In fact, I'm worried that one of them—Alfredo—might have seen me as I went out the front door."

Ninfina reacted instantly, grabbing Jane by the hand. "Oh, God, if he saw you . . . Gianna, let's get out of here before they return."

"Why would they come back, though?" Jane asked her. "There's nothing left. Unless . . ." A thought came to Jane. "Unless there's something upstairs, too, something they forgot. Ninfina, you go check. I want to search this floor carefully."

Ninfina hurried towards the stairs, eager to take a quick look and then get out of there. Jane heard her light footsteps overhead. She circled the area, eyes intent, vowing not to miss a thing. There had to be something the Schifosis overlooked.

Jane looked into the other room that made up the downstairs, a tiny, completely tiled kitchen. It looked like majolica, green and yellow tiles that ran from floor to ceiling and over the sink and oven. She remembered her grandmother Benedetta telling her about her mother's fancy, tiled "English" kitchen. *This must be it,* Jane thought, wondering what was particularly English about it. Goodness, it was tiny.

All those stories *Nonna* told, Jane mused, all those tales of the old country. And, somehow, she had forgotten the most intriguing story of all, the tragic story of Caterina and her prince. There was a lot she would ask *Nonna* the next time she saw her in New York; there was a lot she'd have to tell her, too.

Well, no trace of any goddesses here, Jane decided, extremely downcast. She walked back into the main room, the area where she'd made her startling discoveries that night, and saw, swept into a corner with leavings of straw and dust, the thing that would prove she was telling the truth. It was a marble finger—much like the finger that had beckoned her, in such a sinister way, in her dreams—broken off, no doubt, in the Schifosis' hurry to get out of the house with all their loot before she, the intruder, returned.

Excited, Jane ran to the staircase, calling up to her cousin, "Ninfina, I've found something! Come quickly!"

"What?" Ninfina responded faintly, as Jane knelt down and picked up the finely sculpted marble finger, the digit of a god, admiring its realism and artistry. She had a big smile on her face. Which soon turned to terror.

Nino Schifosi had just entered through the back door. Again, in her excited admiration of fine art, Jane had neglected to hear the warning squeak of the un-oiled hinges. Nino's filthy knuckles, smashing with brute force against her jaw, were the last things Jane saw before falling backward into unconsciousness.

Chapter Sixteen

La Mattanza

The battered blue pickup truck avoided the arterial highways, the *autostradi,* sticking instead to little-used back roads and rutted country lanes. Three men in black crowded the cab of the vehicle. They were in a hurry, having an important rendezvous to make at nightfall. Their precious cargo—and one unwanted interloper—had to be passed over to their employers.

The cargo, rich pickings plundered from archaeological sites in Sicily over the last several months, was eagerly awaited by wealthy and unscrupulous collectors of antiquities all over the world. It was as fine a haul as *i Schifosi* had ever dug up. They would be well compensated for their thieving efforts.

The unwanted intruder, the interloper, the too-curious *Americana,* was a problem. They couldn't leave her there, in Borgetto, to tell all she knew to the local police or to Interpol. Neither did they have the time—nor the inclination—to dispose of her. They would leave that to the Arabs, their partners. Their problem would simply be transferred. They would soon know if the Arabs would be willing to accept the transfer. At any rate, the brothers Schifosi knew it was time for them to disappear, to go underground, until things cooled down considerably for them in the area.

In the back of the pickup truck, Jane was trussed tightly in a foul, slick piece of oilskin. She had been knocked unconscious, and was only now slowly coming around and trying to identify her whereabouts. She hoped that her cousin Ninfina had managed to remain hiding upstairs in Number Four Corso Roma and that the Schifosi trio thought that Jane had been acting alone. Jane hoped that Ninfina had not panicked, that her cousin waited until it was safe for her to leave and then raced to the *caffe,* where she no doubt breathlessly instructed her mother to call the police, and, as an afterthought, the Donzinis in Palermo.

Jane knew none of this for sure, but as she slowly regained consciousness and could not sense the presence of anyone else in the space she was now occupying, she hoped it was true.

Meanwhile, she was acutely aware of the smells about her, particularly the fishy smell of the slimy wet oilskin wrapped around her stiff body. The air was fetid with the ghosts of long-dead sea creatures and their recently gutted relatives. The oilskin had probably been stolen from a fishing boat in the vicinity. The slimy residue lining the rough material had a vile, nauseating stink. Jane gagged, tasting bile in her throat; she was going to throw up, she was sure of it. A bout of dry heaves wracked her body and made her stomach hurt. She had to keep from actually vomiting; the way she was so tightly bound she could choke and suffocate on the vomit all too easily. She tried to concentrate, get her bearings, attempt to figure out where she was, where she was going, and leave off thinking about what was happening in Borgetto and Palermo. It was her survival now that had to be uppermost in her mind, not the aftermath of her kidnapping.

She'd quickly realized that she was rolled in oilskin, yellow slicker stuff. Like the raincoats she and her little sister Jenny wore to school on rainy days—oh, it seemed so long ago—in Newton. And she was being jostled severely in some sort of moving vehicle. A car? A truck? A van? The driver was going over some exceedingly bumpy terrain, and too fast. Her spine felt bruised. She was frightened and disoriented, but she knew that she had to keep her wits about her.

Her jaw hurt. It hurt so much she could hardly open her mouth. Her lips were very dry. She remembered that Nino Schifosi, the middle brother, had decked her. He'd put her out like a light, sneaking up behind her in her grandmother's house as she'd knelt on the floor marveling at the workmanship of that single marble finger, stupidly oblivious—she rebuked herself now, but it was too late—to the real danger of being discovered by the dangerous, felonious Schifosis. She had put herself into this situation. *Fool! Fool!* She screamed silently at herself, realizing how little good it did to berate herself now.

But how incautious, how naive, she had been. How could she have imagined that the trio would not be watching for her, that they would be content to munch bovinely away at their snack of cheese and bread while she searched for clues in the old house? They were stupid, but not that stupid. She'd misjudged them badly.

She should have had her head examined. Perhaps she had brains, but little common sense. The two didn't always go together. The Schifosi brothers were thieves, now kidnappers, perhaps worse. She'd soon find out the worse part. It terrified her. No, better she put off thinking about that for a while longer.

Her thoughts came back to Ninfina. She didn't really know what had happened to her cousin, whether she had been discovered or was safe and had gone for help, but as she rolled around this space, she knew that there was no one else in here with her. Entertaining the notion that, somehow, Aunt Maria and her cousin Ninfina were even now getting help was helping her state of mind. She did not want to consider that her relatives had some connection with the thieving activities of the Schifosi brothers, though it had been a possibility. Lorenzo's connection with them was also a possibility.

Claudia Donzini had described the gift he'd left for her, the precious head of a Greek statue. With her very own two eyes Jane had seen Lorenzo in Borgetto in conversation with the Schifosis and he had passed them a great deal of money. Was his turning up just as the Schifosis were transferring their goods a coincidence? Was that head, that gift for her, part of this recent cache of stolen objects?

Lorenzo knew a great deal about Greek antiquities. His grandfather had amassed a magnificent collection, he'd told Jane, of Greek gold and silver coins. She was wearing a reproduction of one of them now, around her neck, the *trinacria,* that ancient symbol of the island of Sicily. Lorenzo loved beautiful things.

Would he steal to have them? Would he see her sacrificed to keep his dark dealings secret? What was worse, she agonized, his infidelity, his insincere lovemaking, or his thievery? No, she couldn't believe, wouldn't believe, he'd allow these thugs to kidnap her. He loved her. Didn't he? Last night, that night on the beach . . . he could not have been acting. Could he?

The thoughts, each one more awful than the one preceding, crowded into her frantic brain. Now she was trying to figure out the connection, if any, between Guido Schifosi, the one-time cigarette smuggler, and her late uncle, Salvatore Modica, his former smuggling partner. Cigarette smuggling. A trade that was controlled by the *Mafia.*

Did her relatives and the Schifosis have ties to the *Mafia?* Did Lorenzo? Should she lend any credence to Anna Maria's claim that the Bighilaterras were allied with the *Mafia?* Good Lord! Jane got hold of herself, thinking: *who is it I don't suspect?* Next it would be the Donzinis themselves, and her poor sweet Great-Aunt Margherita.

This is nonsense, Jane thought shakily, trying to calm herself. *These silly conspiracy theories will get you nowhere, my girl,* she admonished herself. She had to, instead, concentrate on getting out of the mess she was in. Her survival instincts had to take center stage. She had to get that adrenalin pumping. Fight or flight, she thought, wasn't that how it went? She was fully aware that in the here and now she was in plenty of trouble. She had to utilize her considerable brainpower to help herself.

It's up to you now, babe, just you, she encouraged herself, visions of cheerleaders dressed in Newton High's blue and white shouting: "Go, Jane, fight!" dancing through her head.

Except that I can't fight like this, Jane thought, knowing in her gut that trussed up as she was she was completely helpless. She could neither fight nor fly. She was disabled. Her jaw ached, her back hurt, her knees were stiff . . . *oh, jeez!* she screeched silently, *if I don't stop this ridiculous whining, I am dead meat!* So her mouth wasn't functioning, she couldn't see, her hands were tied. But her brain was functioning fine, if teetering on the edge of delirium. It was fine. *Your brain is fine, girl, use it!* That little voice inside her head had gotten louder, was giving her hell, not letting her wimp out of this dangerous situation. And she had ears, too. She had to keep them open and listen for any clues that would help her out of this deplorable situation. She also had to figure out a way to untie her hands.

So Jane's first cogent thought was: *your hands are not tied together. They are pinned to your sides, yes, but not tied together. You have been rolled into an oilskin and wrapped over that with heavy rope, but your limbs have not been bound. So, try to move them, now. Oh, yes!* Jane almost wept. By sliding her right arm, ever so slowly, gingerly, holding in her stomach, she could pass her arm over from her side and free it. Yes, it was free! Jubilation! Now try the left arm. Yes! Her arms were loose.

Now, she tried to flex her knees. They were so stiff. Ouch! Something had just jabbed her thigh. One of her freed hands felt around, patting down the pockets of her jeans. It was a knife. There was a knife in the front pocket of her jeans. One of the serrated knives she and Ninfina had been using to slice those tomatoes for lunch. She must have slipped it into her pocket when they had left the house. Had that been a subconscious survival instinct? No matter, she now had a weapon. No, better than a weapon. She now had a tool.

How to use this tool most effectively? She gripped the wooden handle of the knife and inched it upwards, carefully, towards her face. One bad bump now, one false move, she thought, and she'd put out an eye or slice a nostril. Nasty thought, that. No, her luck had returned, and was still holding. There! She started to jab that sucker of an oilskin—ugh, it was thick—with the sharp blade. No, she discovered, a sawing motion was better. She concentrated, all of her energy flowing into that blade's very sharp serrated edge.

Yes, it was coming, just a slit, but that was all she needed now. It would allow her to see where she was going. If the cut were too wide someone would notice it, and her luck would run out too soon.

She moved her arm back down and tucked the knife into one of the waistband loops of her jeans. She would need it again. Now, turning her head, she could clearly see, looking out through one eye, that she was indeed in the open back of a pickup truck, surrounded by wooden crates of all sizes. Dirt and straw had spilled out from the boxes and was covering the back of the truck. There was nothing but her and the boxes. She felt better: her cousin had not been captured along with her, as she'd worried. She was the only live creature in that space.

She was in the middle of the stolen statues, she realized, amongst cases and cases of purloined antiquities which had been wrested from the earth, their resting-place for thousands of years. Just as she'd been wrested, taken unwillingly, from her grandmother's childhood home. Jane and the statues were all on this hellish journey to God knew where together. And where were they now?

Another sense had returned. Her nose. Either she had gotten accustomed to the fishy smell of her oilskin container, or she had begun to notice that fresh air was coming in through the tiny slit she had cut. It was the sweet, welcome smell of the ocean. They had to be driving down a beach, on densely packed sand. The rutted road had been left behind; she could feel the difference in surface.

Jane was emboldened by the fact that no one else was in the back of the truck with her. None of the Schifosi boys were riding shotgun; they had all to be squeezed together in the truck's cab. It was a break. She attempted to move her entire body, to hoist herself up, as it were, to try to see where she was. It didn't work. She was still too tightly lashed and couldn't flex her knees yet; her legs seemed to be thoroughly out of commission.

They had come to a sudden stop. Time to play possum,

Jane decided quickly, slipping down and slumping amidst the crates, moving her face back from the clean gash she'd made with that tomato knife.

Voices. Coming from the beach. Men. *Listen carefully, Jane,* she told herself, *activate your keen hearing.* The Schifosis were meeting someone—more than one person, from the sound of it—on this mysterious beach. Jane wished she hadn't been unconscious for part of the ride, as she had absolutely no sense of how long a ride it had been, of how much distance had been covered. No time to cry over spilt milk, she reminded herself. She had to concentrate now, concentrate on those voices on the beach. What were they saying?

Her heart sank. They were not speaking Italian. Nor Sicilian. Nor English. That was not a Romance language she was hearing. *Oh, Lord, what was it?* She panicked. How was she going to decipher it if she didn't know what it was, what the words meant? Had her luck run out again, so soon?

But wait, the Schifosis were responding to this language, whatever it was, in Sicilian, at least some of the time. Unfortunately, the Schifosis spoke a corrupt kind of Sicilian dialect, harsh, slurred. They were from Borgetto, though, and Jane knew that dialect well. She thought that she had a chance to make it out if she listened carefully. *Concentrate!* She commanded herself. *Listen to what those louts are saying and save your life.*

They were all men. Their deep voices had risen; they were angry, arguing. The other language had a pleasant cadence; it was musical. Somewhere, Jane had heard it before. Maybe it would come to her if she kept calm. *Listen!* An agitated voice, Alfredo's, saying no, they weren't late, they were right on time, with all the merchandise, but that they had run into a slight complication. More discussion; lowered voices. Then a word, *hiya,* and another, *bint.*

It was Arabic! They were speaking Arabic.

No wonder it had sounded familiar to her. She'd heard Arabic before, years ago, when she was a little girl in Newton. She had a friend from Morocco named Miriam al-Dawi. They had been best friends from the second to the fifth grades, when Miriam returned to North Africa with her parents, who'd been graduate students at BU. She was going to help Miriam with her English, and Miriam would teach her Arabic words. It never worked out that way, of course. Miriam was a quick study and had learned English too fast; Jane's Arabic had never kept pace.

But she knew *bint.* She'd gotten that far. It was the Arabic word for girl. Those folks on the beach were talking about her, Jane. *She was the complication.* What exactly were they saying? What were they up to?

Their next words made Jane's blood run cold. She froze. *Mayit,* she heard, then *la mattanza.* Killing. The Schifosis and their Arabic friends were planning to kill her.

Jane's bowels started to loosen with fear. She managed to control herself in time, but she was completely panic-stricken. She overcame her panic and forced herself to listen harder. This was no game, this was life and death. Her life . . . or her death.

Paying acute attention to the conversation on the beach gave her the name of a city: Trapani. Quickly, Jane remembered that the large city of Trapani, on the Mediterranean west and a bit south of Palermo, was the Sicilian city closest to North Africa. Of course! It made sense; the Arabs had to be from North Africa. That was probably where the smuggling ring was based.

Were the antiquities going there first? That had to be a

strong possibility. Jane had no idea how closely patrolled these waters were. Would a boat full of Greek antiquities—so many boxes of them—escape notice? How where they going to do it? And where did she come in?

If she weren't so terrified, she would be fascinated to learn all the details of this business. It made sense that the Schifosis were simply the hard labor, the grunts, merely diggers-up of the treasures. The Arabs probably provided them with sites and a shopping list, waited for the stuff to come in at this spot near Trapani or at other coastal locations, paid the brothers off, and went their merry way.

This was a lucrative trade. Millions of dollars were involved here. Private collectors would pay willingly for the high quality antiquities she had seen in those crates. Jane's life mattered not one iota on the profit/loss sheet maintained by these men.

I Schifosi had graduated from penny ante cigarette smuggling to the big time. They were in Fat City. And where, Jane thought bitterly, was Interpol when you needed them most? She giggled. *Oh, Lord, I'm losing my mind,* she panicked. *This is not funny.*

Pay attention to what's going on now! She ordered herself.

Mattanza again, that deadly word. No, *la mattanza.* The *"la"* made all the difference, Jane realized with a start. They weren't talking about killing her at all. Maybe she still had a chance, a way out.

They were referring to *La Mattanza,* the huge tuna kill that took place in late June, the annual harvest of the big fish in Sicilian waters. The fishing fleet out of Trapani was the island's biggest. Guidebooks touted it as a tourist event, though it was hard to believe any tourist in his or her right mind would want to be in the middle of that bloody slaughter.

Jane remembered descriptions of the kill from one of her more colorful guidebooks. It was an event with an old history, replete with rituals. The fishing boats, small and wide-prowed, were similar to those that were used in the 9th century by the Arabs. Certain Arabic terms, such as the title *rais,* for captain, were still in use among Sicilian fishermen. Enormous nets, designed like those of old, were utilized to trap the tuna.

When the time was ripe, when the huge schools of fish were spotted in the open sea, all the boats which had been at the ready for days set out. The struggle was long and hard; the tuna were netted, hooked, and bludgeoned. With the battalions of fishermen, nets, boats, and weapons, the fish didn't stand a chance. The massacre stained the sea dark red for days. It was a spectacularly bloody event.

According to what the men were saying, the tuna kill would be excellent cover for their deeds. Theirs would be one boat among hundreds. They'd go only so far, then veer off and head for the North African coast. With all that nocturnal activity occurring, no one would notice the smugglers' ship. They were just about ready to go.

But the Arabs were not about to let the Schifosis go that easily. They were asking about the girl. The gist was—Jane struggled to figure it out—why should the Arabs do the Schifosis a favor? Jane was their problem, it seemed, not the Arabs'.

Nino Schifosi was trying out some crude Arabic on his bosses. *"Al-bint al-jameelah,"* he wheedled, as his brothers, like back-up singers in a band, supported his statement, and then guffawed coarsely. Jane could only imagine, blushing deeply, the vulgar gestures that accompanied the conversation. Because Nino was telling the Arabs that she was a pretty girl—*al-bint al-jameelah.* Miriam's father, Mohammed, had called her that many times, Jane remembered nostalgically—and that it would be worth their while to take her. And if they didn't think she was that pretty, Alfredo's voice chimed in, speaking Sicilian, then they could throw her overboard. Her blood would mix, unnoticed, with that of the tuna.

Jane trembled in the oilskin, but the Arabs were interested. They asked for more details. Nino supplied them, letting them all know that she had very large breasts. Guido and Alfredo broke into crude snorts of laughter at that, Guido commenting that he knew for a fact that a certain very rich Sicilian prince was quite interested in her breasts. He had given them money to find her for them. Obviously, he had sampled her wares, Guido added, and wanted more. The Arabs liked that. They all burst into coarse laughter, passing sexually crude remarks.

Jane was devastated, shaken. Her choices were death or dishonor. Probably both, with the dishonor first. But she, luckily, was not their priority. The antiquities were. The Schifosis were quickly instructed to get her on board, along with the crates of statuary. Once they hit the open sea, they'd turn their attention to Jane, but, right now, they were anxious to join the fleet of ships already underway. Night was falling and time was wasting.

The only good thing, she realized, that had come of this is that she now knew that Lorenzo was no thief and had nothing to do with this evil enterprise. He had simply given the Schifosis money to look for her. He had been undaunted by her second episode of running away from him; he had picked himself up and continued to look for her. The Arabs obviously didn't know him and the Schifosis were making fun of his interest in her. No pun intended, she realized, but Lorenzo—and her aunt and cousin—were off the hook.

The realization perked up Jane's dampened spirits considerably. Lorenzo cared. He had come looking for her. He wanted her. And now there was a strong possibility that she would never see him again. The thought was a punishing one and it almost did her in. She pushed it out of her mind fiercely.

Goodbyes were being exchanged on the sands. *"Tawasal bis-salaamah,"* Guido called out. One of the Arabs wished him well, also, *"Allah yusalimak fee amaan illah. Salaam."* Arabic was a courteous language, even when spoken by lowlifes, Jane thought.

Suddenly she was being hoisted roughly over someone's shoulder, taken off the truck, and trundled down to the softer sand of the beach near the water's edge. She could hear the soft hiss and pop of the waves lapping at the shore. The sweet smell of the Mediterranean was stronger now.

Whoever was carrying her was sinking into the sand under her weight and cursing her in Sicilian under his breath. Jane guessed it was Alfredo, the one who was pursuing Ninfina so aggressively. She imagined herself a ton of bricks, mentally attempting to make her body heavier, hoping it would affect him and that he'd sink in further, preferably up to his thick bull neck. His brothers, too. For a minute or two, she enjoyed the image of all the Schifosis buried up to their necks in the sand as the swift tide came in. It was the most relaxing thought she'd had yet, and she savored it.

All along the beach she could hear the crates being dragged hurriedly, pulled unceremoniously towards the waiting boat. Poor old things, Jane sympathized, feeling for the precious antiquities. They were, together, suffering the same indignities, all literally about to be in the same boat. They were bound for unknown ports, for rich Arab art collectors, connoisseurs of priceless artifacts, and, perhaps, young women. That was, if she didn't get thrown overboard first. *What is my fate to be?* Jane trembled, pondering the worst.

Her bearer was walking clumsily up a rope ladder and onto the bridge deck of the fishing boat. He hesitated. Jane prayed he would not bring her down to the hold. She had a plan, and it could only work if she was on the top deck, and if she had no company there. He set her down on what felt like ropes. Then the Schifosis' heavy footsteps died away. The ship's anchor was being raised. Jane heard the powerful outboard motor go full throttle, heading the vessel towards the open sea.

They had set sail.

Jane waited impatiently, not moving, until she was sure there was no one on deck with her. The sailors' voices, the voices of the Arabs, had drifted away; their footsteps padded downstairs, in the direction of the ship's galley. Spicy cooking smells wafted up to her. It was suppertime.

North African cuisine was delicious and she realized she was very hungry, but first things first! She peered out of the slit she'd cut in the oilskin. The black night was illuminated only by several hanging oil lanterns and the cold glitter of stars. Jane spotted Venus, the North Star, bright in the sky.

Bringing herself, by dint of sheer will power and inner strength, to a sitting position, Jane found and gripped her precious tool, the sharp serrated knife. In one quick movement, she ripped the oilskin cage from top to bottom, freeing her body. Luckily for her, it was rotted; she knew she wasn't really that strong. She saw that she had been set on a pile of thick, braided rope and netting. The familiar crates were all around her. She saw some of the other fishing boats ahead; some of them had floodlights hanging over their sides, bouncing reflections over the calm, still water.

I'm free!

Jane was jubilant as she wriggled out of the oilskin and its confining ropes. *Oops!* she thought, as she tried to stand on legs through which blood had not been circulating well for a long while; *it's not going to be that easy.* She persevered, rubbing her stiff, aching limbs, refusing to acknowledge the bruises on her body calling out for liniment. *Survival.* That was uppermost in her mind now. That was the goal. Her only goal. First, she would try to stretch and bend her legs and arms, get them working, and then, then she was going to jump into the sea and swim back to Trapani.

Yes, it was desperate, but it was also her only chance for escape. She had little time. Once the smugglers got hold of her—she shivered at the thought—her fate would no longer be in her own hands. She was a good swimmer. She was certainly motivated. She knew she had a chance. If she had to, she could swim ten miles. She had been a swimmer all her life and anchor for her swim team in the 440-meter relay at Newton North High School. She swam every day in the Vassar College swimming pool, her answer to aerobics class. She had stamina and endurance. She would play it like another swim meet, only in this case the stakes were a little higher—she would be swimming for her life.

She put aside the fact that her body had never ached so much as it did now as she quickly and quietly shed her jeans and her sneakers and secreted them behind one of the crates. They were heavy and would weigh her down in the water. She would jump into the sea wearing only her underwear and her tee shirt. And her determination. She could not give up now; she was not going to lie down and die. She would fight. She had to see Lorenzo again. Mouthing a quiet vow to the Madonna and thinking of Lorenzo, she slid silently into the warm, inviting sea.

It was like stepping into a bath. The Mediterranean, *Mare Nostrum,* welcomed her. Filling her lungs with air, she made a shallow dive into its depths, propelling herself forward, legs scissoring in unison, heading for landfall. It was still possible to make out the lights of Trapani; she knew she would not get disoriented in the dark, limitless expanse of water and swim in the wrong direction.

Calmly, keeping her wits about her, concentrating solely on the evenness of her swimming strokes, refusing to acknowledge the hurts in her jaw, her limbs, and her spine, she paddled towards land. She psyched herself by repeating a mantra she made up on the spot: *Every stroke brings me closer to shore, every stroke brings me closer to shore . . .*

She thought back to her swim meets, to how wonderful, funny old Coach Lanoue always told them that first you had to win the mental race, the one in your head, and then you could win the one in the water. She remembered how her parents and sister went to every one of her meets and how they encouraged her from the stands, petite Jenny hopping up and down in her seat in her enthusiasm.

Jane would tear through that Olympic-sized swimming pool, carrying the colors for good old Newton North High, hearing her little sister's high, clear voice saying, "Come on, Janey, come on! You can do it!" *Yes,* Jane repeated to herself, *I can do it. I can do this. Every stroke brings me closer to shore, every stroke brings me closer to shore . . .*

This mantra that would carry her through.

She was moving easily through the wine-dark sea, her arms and legs scissoring in rhythm. The warm salt water, full of life-giving nutrients and minerals, the place from whence the human race came millions of years ago, was massaging and repairing her abused body. Never, even when she was in the most rigorous aspects of her training for swim meets, had she ached so much. She had to put that negative thought behind her.

She concentrated on winning the mental race, reciting her mantra, thinking of her loved ones. She could not believe that once upon a time she had taken her life for granted. When this was over, she would take nothing for granted any more.

She smiled to herself thinking of how her romantic little sister Jenny would react to her story of falling in love with a handsome prince, of being kidnapped by three thugs, of swimming the big wide deep Mediterranean to freedom from possible death by drowning or bludgeoning or white slavery in a harem in North Africa. She chose not to think of what her mother's reaction to all this would be. Therein, madness lay.

I am going to make it, she thought. *Every stroke brings me closer to shore . . . I . . . am . . . going . . . to . . . make . . . it . . .*

She continued to push herself forward, toward the lights on shore that teasingly flickered and beckoned like a monster swarm of fireflies cavorting in early summer. She was stroking cleanly and evenly, taking deep lungfuls of the sweet night air.

Far behind her, echoing through the depths of the sea, she thought she could hear—or was it an illusion, a trick of her over-active imagination—the brutal, killing sounds of *La Mattanza.*

Even as she swam to safety, those big, peaceful schools of Mediterranean tuna were being netted, strangled, and clubbed to death in that so-called tourist attraction of northwestern Sicily's coastal waters. She thought of the sea red with blood. Sometimes dolphin, fond of swimming with tuna in these waters, were also caught in the heavy nets and suffocated to death.

She was tiring. *Too soon!* The muscles in her long, powerful legs had started to cramp up. Her lungs hurt with each breath she was taking. She decided to tread water for a while, floating on her back, varying her stroke. She tried not to panic. The mantra had flown out of her head. The hasty vow she had sworn to the Madonna of Romitello before jumping ship came back to her. She had meant it.

If I survive, she had promised the Virgin, *if I survive, I will find out what happened to Caterina and her child.* For old Margherita's sake the family tragedy had to be laid to rest. It was important for her to know where that child was, that baby conceived in great love with Maurizio, Lorenzo's grandfather. Caterina and her child had been lost to all of them for far too long. They were blood kin . . . both hers and Lorenzo's, another bond between them.

"I promise!" Jane screamed out loud, taking in an unexpected mouthful of water and starting to go under. And now the sinister whirlpool of her nightmares was stirring madly beneath her, under her poor, struggling body, furiously gripping her ankles with mad, wet claws of death. *No! No!* She screamed silently. She had come too far, this could not be happening to her now. She couldn't, she wouldn't, allow this to happen.

The pulling of the whirlpool had reached her knees and was spiraling upwards. Bubbles were beginning to foam and churn around her hips, her waist. She was frantic with fear and despair. It was all over. She was done for . . .

And then . . .

The sea lapped her lovingly, with a soft, moist, salty tongue. She was on the broad back of a very large sea creature. A dolphin. He had come under her and scooped her up, tossing her into the air like a disjointed, floppy rag doll. She had landed serenely, painlessly, on his big smooth shining back as he streaked through the ocean, which was, once again, calm.

Companion, protector, his long snout bottle-shaped, his taut skin gray and gleaming in the dark, he comforted and soothed her. She was no longer afraid. She put her small head close to his large one and they chattered in the high-pitched syllables of a language common to them both. They understood each other, perfectly, completely.

Around them, his fellows leaped in their wake. Some, like her dolphin, were bottle-nosed, others were striped, shading from the darkest charcoal gray to ivory white. And the spinner dolphins, longer and sleeker than the rest, were there too, skipping and hopping over the lightly rolling waves. A phalanx of great fish were aiding her flight to shore, on guard, protective, her saviors. They had suddenly appeared, out of nowhere . . .

She was surrounded by love, her heart full to bursting, limbs rejuvenated and pain-free. Her jaw no longer ached. She could smile, laugh, she could call out in joy. She would make it. There was no longer any room for doubt. She *would* make it.

The dolphins moved without visible effort though the sea's dark ruffled waters, moving out of formation only to jump joyfully as they came closer to shore. Jane marveled at the scores of dolphins, some in family groupings, in twos or threes together, some solitary, by themselves.

There were dolphins with *nereids,* those graceful water nymphs, on their backs. The statue come to life a hundredfold, Jane thought happily. And she was a *nereid,* too, on the broad back of the biggest dolphin in the sea. And then she saw the land . . .

She had made it to shore. She fell upon the white, sandy, inviting beach, safe. The nightmarish whirlpool had not devoured her.

Chapter Seventeen

In the Arms of My True Love

The sharp, slightly astringent smell of rosemary interwoven with a sweet, teasing aroma of lemon filled her nostrils when she awoke on the spit of sandy beach that had been her bed the night before. She yawned and stretched, her muscles still a bit tight, her jaw slightly tender, reminding her of her ordeal. But she had been miraculously rejuvenated during that dreamlike swim to shore from the fishing boat. How could that be? Jane wondered.

Then she remembered the fantastic school of dolphins that had accompanied her to safety. Had she imagined them? Were they another hallucination, another Sicilian dream? She would never know for sure. It was a mystery. But she was alive. Safe. And she felt wonderful.

She had no idea where she was. On one side of the beach was an eroded stone formation that looked like an elephant with its trunk in the sea. It was craggy and grayish white in the early morning sun. Past her bare feet was the Mediterranean surf, gently kissing the shore with its white, foamy mouth. The water was clear.

She could see, in its depths, the spiny, rugged porcupine heads of purple sea urchin, the orangey-red of five-branched starfish, the iridescent blue of mussels clinging to stones by their grassy beards. Fingers of green seaweed were washing onto the sand. She stepped delicately into the sun-warmed water, her toes sensing the sharp edges of barnacles on a rocky underwater ridge. She bent down and washed her face.

She was practically naked. Her long tee shirt covered her only to mid-thigh. Underneath, all she wore was a bra and panties. She felt anxiously around her neck. The gold chain and *trinacria* amulet were still there. The amulet, her good luck charm. The sea had not claimed it on that mad swim last night. She ran wet hands through her tangled hair and thought hard.

She needed to get to Trapani, the city whose lights had guided her towards shore. She needed to speak to the police. She needed to contact her family in Borgetto, the Donzinis, and Lorenzo. She trudged up the beach, hoping to find a road into town.

She saw a rutted country lane and followed it for a while, her bare, sensitive feet conscious of each sharp stone, each pebble cutting into the soft flesh of the soles of her feet. Luck was still with her. The lane connected with a road that led to what seemed to be a major *autostrada*. She was determined to hitch a ride in the first vehicle that came by. Her state of dress—or, rather, her state of undress—made her uneasy. She wasn't too eager to meet up with a pervert. A white van put-putted towards her.

LATTE was painted on the side of the van in big black letters. It was a milk truck. Who else would be out so early in the morning? she reasoned. The driver, an older man, was kind and concerned. He asked Jane if she had had an accident. "Yes," she told him, "I fell off a boat."

He clucked sympathetically and helped her into the front of the van. Before starting up again, he reached into the back and handed her a half-liter bottle of fresh milk. She thanked him profusely. She had forgotten when she'd last taken nourishment. Now, the milk, whole fat and creamy, was delicious. She drank it, ravenous.

The kind milkman was going to Trapani for his early morning rounds, and, yes, he would drop her off at the police station. In addition, concerned for her modesty, he had fished around in the van and come up with an old, patched pair of white pants that had been used as a rag. Jane accepted them gratefully. The pants were, in addition to being dirty, quite short, coming to her mid-calf, but they did the job of covering her up. She pulled the drawstrings tightly about her waist and tied them into a double knot.

The night shift was just leaving the police station when Jane walked in, disheveled, hair a wild tangle, and barefooted. The day shift looked at the night shift, then they all stared at her. Someone wolf-whistled. Jane blushed, then, in slow, precise Italian, asked to see someone in charge. A Captain Amato ushered her into his office, and she began to explain her situation.

With barely concealed skepticism, Captain Amato telephoned his colleagues at the police station in Partinico. Jane heard him ask for Captain Gambino. An animated conversation, in dialectical Sicilian, so fast that Jane could barely catch it, was soon underway.

One of the young subordinates brought her a steaming cup of *caffe latte* and a buttered roll. She could have kissed him in gratitude, but settled for a wide smile instead. Turning her attention back to the captain, she caught the name Schifosi. Amato signed off, with an *"Ah, bene,"* to his colleague.

Captain Amato now turned to Jane. He noted that her mouth was full of roll, and that big white crumbs were dotted up and down the front of her wrinkled tee shirt. He sniffed delicately, folding his hands on his neat, orderly desk.

The captain told her that she had been reported kidnapped by her cousin, a Signorina Ninfa Modica, and that an all-points bulletin had been sent out immediately for the arrest of the Schifosi brothers, but to no avail. *I Schifosi* had so far apparently eluded the police with ease.

Amato then took a statement from Jane, telling her she would have to repeat it in Partinico. He added that Captain Gambino had told him that two of her relatives had insisted on coming to Trapani to pick her up. She was to wait for them. They should make it in an hour or so.

The captain asked Jane if she would care to use the staff showers. He was apparently eager—his pinched nostrils evidently did not care for odd things that washed in from the sea—that she did so. She accepted his offer with thanks, and then she asked him which of her relatives were coming for her. Amato apologized for not noting their names. Did she want him to call Gambino back? No, Jane responded, that wouldn't be necessary. She thought it was probably the Donzinis, Claudia and Aldo. Gambino had just assumed they were her relatives. It made sense; Maria and Ninfina would have gotten in touch with them immediately. She would be so very glad to see them.

Meanwhile, she took advantage of the police station's shower room, lathering up and washing her hair with the plain soap that was her only choice. Poor Captain Amato! She had smelled like a dead fish. She changed back into those deplorable clothes, but she was decidedly cleaner and looked more presentable.

She checked her face in the shower room mirror, and was pleasantly surprised that her ordeal had not made more of a mark on her. There was some swelling along her jaw line, and an ugly purplish-yellow bruise there, but otherwise, she looked fine. Not gorgeous, but okay. The nurturing sea had brought her back to life.

Her relatives had arrived by the time she'd cleaned herself up. They must have flown along the *autostrada,* making it to Trapani from Borgetto in world-record time. She had guessed it would be Claudia and Aldo.

But it was Margherita . . . and Lorenzo.

Before Jane had a chance to react, both of them had taken her into their arms. Margherita was sobbing quietly, Lorenzo's heart was beating so fast she thought it would break out of his chest. "You two know each other?" she asked, stunned.

Lorenzo nodded. He was touching her bruised face tenderly, his blue eyes glowing with love. *"Povera bella,"* he cooed softly.

He kissed her cheek gently. She closed her eyes and let him hold her tightly. She loved him so much. How could she ever have left him? Once was bad enough, but twice? And how could she ever have imagined him to be in league with the murderous Schifosis? *She was an idiot!* He enveloped her with his love, his caring. She let it all wash over her, relaxed, happy.

"Will they catch the Schifosi brothers?" she whispered.

Lorenzo stroked her hair, pushing it back from her face. "They will, in time, don't worry. They're not going to hurt you again. Forget about them. You're the one we're concerned about now, *carissima.*"

Jane melted. Her legs were weak. She sat down on the hard wooden bench in Captain Amato's office. Margherita sat down next to her, taking her by the hands.

"I want to know everything that happened since yesterday," Jane told them both.

Lorenzo leaned back against the standard-issue steel case desk in the captain's office. Jane noted that his dear,

dear face looked tired, as if he had been up all night, but he still looked wonderful, handsome in fact.

He started to explain. "I was furious at myself for having had the great good fortune to find you at Alcamo, thanks to Claudia Donzini's telephone call, only to lose you again, so I came to Borgetto to try to find you, knowing you were there, somewhere—even though Claudia was discouraged, saying I should let you be, that you obviously still had things you had to think over—and I ran into the Schifosis at the little *caffe,* not having the least idea, then, that it belonged to your aunt, and gave them money to look for you."

Jane nodded; she knew from what the Schifosis had told the Arabs on the beach that what he was saying was true. She hadn't realized, though, that Claudia had sent him to Alcamo. *Bless her,* Jane thought, *bless her!*

Lorenzo continued his narration, running his hands wearily through his uncombed hair. She remembered those hands all over her body on a recent occasion and shivered deliciously, but now she had to focus on what he was saying. She riveted her attention onto his story.

"Then, I remembered that my aunt knew someone in Borgetto, someone who had done some embroidery for her. I went to the home of this lovely lady—" he smiled that lazy, seductive smile at Margherita, who smiled back "—only to find out that you were related to her, that you were also related to the owners of the *caffe,* that you and I shared a common past."

He shook his head, puzzled. "Why did you never tell me that you were half-Sicilian, *cara?*"

Jane steeled herself. It was time to ask that terrible question, to risk destroying this sweet, miraculous reunion, to blow it all, and her fragile heart, to pieces. "And why didn't you ever tell me about your girlfriend in Palermo, Lorenzo?"

Lorenzo reeled as if he had been struck in the stomach. "Girlfriend? Gianna, what are you talking about? Did you get hit in the head, too?"

Jane's face smarted with his tactless comment, but she couldn't stop now. It had to come out, all of it. "The woman who kissed you goodbye several mornings ago at the Conca d'Oro restaurant, on the Cortile Santa Caterina. The morning after you and I went dancing, Lorenzo. You can't have forgotten her. That beautiful, blonde, older woman, my dearest."

Lorenzo looked at Jane incredulously. Guiltily? And then he shook, all over, shook with great whoops of laughter, almost choking in his merriment.

Margherita and Jane looked at each other in alarm. Jane was stricken, Margherita angry. She spoke firmly to Lorenzo in her best Great-Aunt tones. "*Figlio mio,* stop that! After what you told me in the car, coming over, that you would kill yourself if anything happened to Gianna, that your life would be over, how can you laugh at her like this?"

Lorenzo was wiping his eyes. He had laughed so hard he was actually crying. "Zia, you're right. I apologize, I'm sorry . . . but . . . I can't believe . . . oh, this was all so stupid . . . I have been tearing myself in two wondering what had upset you, and it was such a stupid, stupid, ridiculous misunderstanding."

Jane was livid, the bruise on her jaw glowing angrily. "Misunderstanding? That disgusting old bag had her hands all over you, *Signore Principe!*"

Lorenzo reached over and folded Jane into his arms. He buried his face, now composed, into her hair, caressing her back and shoulders gently. *"Cara, cara,"* he explained, whispering softly, "that disgusting old bag was my aunt."

Jane stood back from him in amazement, her hazel eyes wide, shocked. "That disgusting old . . . your aunt?" she repeated, her voice squeaking.

Lorenzo nodded, his eyes never leaving her dear, sweet face. "My aunt. Luisa's mother. The woman who brought me up, *Tante* Marie-Claude Strelli. My uncle's wife." He was trying to make the relationship painfully clear to her, explaining things as if she were a child, a slightly demented child, she thought, or someone who had indeed suffered a severe head injury.

He shrugged nonchalantly, explaining further. "She's French. She always kisses me goodbye like that." His eyes crinkled up with laughter, "Now, don't tell me you are going to be jealous of my old aunt . . . or, as you so nicely put it, that old bag."

Jane wanted to hit him. She never wanted to hurt anyone so badly in her life. How dare he speak to her as if she was an idiot! How dare he laugh at her! Then the stupidity of her misunderstanding hit her. She *was* a total idiot. She had jumped to a quick conclusion with no proof, giving him no chance to explain. Her strong feelings for him had made a complete fool of her and she had nearly destroyed the most meaningful relationship of her life. She was stunned at what she had done. She hid her face in her hands.

Lorenzo thought he had gone too far teasing her. She'd had a horrible ordeal; she was in a fragile state. He was a fool. "Gianna? *Cara?* I'm sorry. I didn't mean to make fun of you, of your feelings . . . I'm just so relieved that this is all it was. Oh, dearest, I thought you didn't care for me any more."

He took her hands from her face, cupping that adorable face in his strong hands, kissing her softly on those full, delicious lips. He sighed. "I love you," he whispered.

"Oh, Lorenzo, I love you, too, so much!" she put her arms around his neck and began to cry softly, all the pent up emotion of the long ordeal of the last few days finding release.

He patted her gently, held her tightly, closing his eyes in relief that all the silly, dangerous misunderstandings had been laid bare, that they were together again and that nothing had ever been so good for him. And he realized that he could not bear to have her leave him again, not ever again. "Gianna?" he whispered, kissing her neck, her cheek.

"Yes, Lorenzo?" They were the only people in the world now, in that rather seedy little office in the Trapani police station. All time had stopped.

"Don't go back to America," he pleaded, looking directly into her eyes, holding them, mesmerizing her with his intensity, his devotion, the sincerity of his love. "Stay here, please. Marry me."

Chapter Eighteen

Cops and Robbers

Franco Gambino, captain of the police detachment at Partinico, had a head much too small for his body. He resembled Stan Laurel's sidekick, Oliver Hardy, with his snub nose, small blue twinkling eyes, and fat ruddy cheeks. His reddish-brown hair was thinning on top, and his uniform jacket strained to stay buttoned over his mound of stomach. For all that, Gambino seemed remarkably nimble on feet that were also too small for his body. He greeted Jane, Margherita, and Lorenzo with effusive friendliness and warmth, springing up to shake hands with alacrity.

"Ah! The brave *Signorina* 'Olland!"

Jane smiled. Nope, the Sicilians could not manage her last name; good thing it would soon be changed. She smiled at the captain as he peered closely at her face, gravely noting her bruised jaw. He shook his head in sympathy.

"*Que cosa!* What a shame! What a thing to do to such a lovely face!" He spat on the floor, a bulls-eye into a shining brass spittoon. "May *i Schifosi* rot in hell!"

That passionate show of emotion over, he immediately got down to police business. "You know, *Signorina,* you have been very helpful to us. We have suspected *i Schifosi* for a long while. What we did not know was where they were hiding their stolen artifacts. They acted quite boldly, hiding those boxes right in the middle of Borgetto. And, frankly, we were not so sure that the

Modica women were not their accomplices."

Jane made a small sound of protest, but Gambino continued, commanding center stage. He ticked off his points one by one. "We knew that Guido Schifosi had once been in partnership with Salvatore Modica. We knew that they had both been cigarette smugglers. We knew that Guido had attempted to court the widow Maria Modica soon after her husband had died. We knew that Alfredo was friendly with Ninfina Modica, that he had boasted in public places that she was his *inamorata,* as you Americans say—" he turned a hundred-kilowatt smile in Jane's direction "—his girlfriend."

"But that wasn't true. Ninfina can't stand the sight of Alfredo Schifosi," Jane interrupted.

Captain Gambino stilled her with one pudgy, sausage-fingered hand. "*Si, si,* that's what she stated, also, to us, but we were not so sure, then, that she was telling us the truth." He continued pontificating, jabbing the air as each point was made, circling the three of them, who were seated on chairs in the middle of his tiny office, as he paced the floor energetically on those too-small but oh-so-nimble feet.

Lorenzo, Jane could tell, was thoroughly enjoying the show that the amiable policeman was putting on for their benefit. Margherita was frowning, paying careful attention to the role the Modica women, her nieces, had played in this bizarre drama. She leaned forward in her chair, intent.

"But!" He jabbed one of his sausage fingers with zeal at the flaking plaster ceiling. "We were on to them! Eventually, we knew we would have them, that all would be revealed! We have our modern methods, our, how do you call them? Ah, yes, our new technologies."

Lorenzo was going to lose it entirely if the good captain continued in this vein, Jane thought. He had covered his mouth with his hand, managing so far to stifle his laughter. Margherita, on the other hand, was most impressed with the showmanship of *il Capitane* Gambino. She nodded vigorously at his last statement.

Captain Gambino turned to his desk, moving surprisingly fast for such a fat man. He whipped out a raggedy-edged newspaper clipping from a bulging file. "Here!" he exclaimed. "*This* is what we did!"

Lorenzo, Margherita, and Jane pored over the clipping Gambino had handed to them. They read it, looked at each other in amazement, then at the grinning policeman.

"You wiretapped the cemetery?" Lorenzo was incredulous.

Gambino smiled broadly. "Modern technology! As you can see." He took the newspaper from them and started to read it aloud. The article was about the enterprising tactics of the Naples police force, who, in order to get information on a vicious gang of drug dealers, had bugged several key cemeteries, especially zeroing in on the tombs and mausoleums containing the mortal remains of prominent *Camorra* families. The *Camorra,* Gambino explained for Jane's benefit, were the Neapolitan equivalent of the *Mafia.* (Same bad guys, different organization and name.)

"So, as you can see, we did exactly what they did, taping the conversations of *Borgettani* we suspected might have *Mafia* connections, now, or in the past. We thought we saw the *Mafia*'s black hand in this affair of the robberies of archaeological sites. Now, we know this was not the case, thanks to the *signorina.*" He bowed to Jane. "But we suspected *i Schifosi,* and they had once been involved with the *Mafia.* Still, even with what we did know, we had to catch them red-handed, as you Americans say, with the goods."

"Did you actually hear conversations where the Schifosis

talked about what they were doing with their accomplices?" Jane innocently questioned the captain.

"Well, no, not really." Gambino gestured, his arms wide, as if apologizing. "But . . ." His round rosy face brightened, "We did overhear many, many other interesting and enlightening conversations, such as who really might have fathered Inspector Vitale's last bambino, that Gennaro Pacienza at the gas station overcharges his customers, who the Mayor's wild young daughter is currently having an affair with, and, of course, that truly sad, sad, conversation you had, *Signorina* 'Olland, with your *Zia* here." Gambino took Margherita's tiny hands in his, engulfing them entirely, kissing her fingertips lightly.

His face was stern now. "Your relatives, the Modica women, have been truly unkind to you, *Signora* Mannino. I took it upon myself—I hope you do not mind—to lecture them on their unseemly and disgusting lack of respect towards you. I believe, if I may say so myself, that they were extremely chastised.

"And I let it be known that, if there are no apologies to you, and no visible changes in their public and private manner toward you, well, let's just say that they would soon receive regular, costly, and humiliating visits from my men to their *caffe*. We would, I told them, be looking for many kinds of irregularities and violations, of the sort that could lead to the losing of their licenses, both in the *caffe* and the general store."

Margherita's old face crinkled into a smile. She reached up and gave the captain a peck on the cheek in gratitude for his trouble on her behalf.

Jane shook her head in amazement. The Partinico police were going to lean on Maria and Ninfina and get them to show respect to Margherita. *Bravo,* Captain Gambino! She smiled to herself. That's the ticket! Life was too short—and too precious—to play out in such petty feuds and grudges. Maria and Ninfina hadn't even been there, Jane thought, yet they willingly accepted the Conigliaro legacy of hate unto the next generation, shunning a sweet old woman who had already suffered so much. *Too much.*

Jane stood up and shook Captain Gambino's hand. "*Mille grazie, Capitane* Gambino," she thanked him.

He beamed with pleasure; just a small-town cop doing my job, his manner indicated. But, no, he had done much, much more. The so-called high tech methods he'd tried to use hadn't gotten any results, Schifosi-wise, but they would accomplish, Jane hoped, a good deal for Great-Aunt Margherita.

They all rose to take their leave, but Jane had one more question to ask. "Do you really think you have a good chance of catching *i Schifosi?* And their Arab partners?"

Gambino nodded in reply. "*Signorina,* your information on that Arab connection—which was the clue we needed badly—and on the use of that fishing boat to smuggle the statues under the cover of participating in *La Mattanza* was most important. We alerted our coast guard immediately. Perhaps we have lost, for now, the Arabs and that lot of statues, but we supplied the description of the antiquities you managed to see to Interpol. Your sketches, also, will be particularly helpful, if you can get them to us. If these works of art turn up on the international art market, their provenance will be questioned immediately.

"And *i Schifosi* . . . Well, they cannot hide forever. When that fishing boat returns to Trapani, we will take the crew into custody. I think they will have much to tell us, no? It was especially brilliant of you, *signorina,* to note the name of that vessel. They will not know that now we know it too, they will not think they will have to change the lettering on its side, to cover it up before we spot it."

Jane blushed at Gambino's compliments. Heck, she thought to herself, modestly, it was no big deal. The light from the oil lanterns and from the floodlights of the other boats had clearly illuminated the name on the side of the craft as she had slid soundlessly over its side into the sea. It had just been another of the strange coincidences that had plagued her this week in Sicily.

The name of the phony fishing boat was *La Trinacria,* the same as the amulet that still gleamed, golden, at her throat.

Chapter Nineteen

Reunion in Borgetto

On the long ride to Partinico, and again on the short one back to Borgetto, Jane and Lorenzo couldn't stop talking. She was curled up close to him in the front seat of the Alfa, nestled as close as humanly possible to his dear, much-beloved body. She couldn't touch him enough, as if reassuring herself constantly that he was really there, that they were together, that they would never be apart again, not in this lifetime and perhaps not in those to come.

Of course, Jane had accepted Lorenzo's proposal even before it was out of his mouth. No maidenly hesitation or coyness there, Jane recollected, not at all embarrassed. Lorenzo had let out a whoop of delight that startled Captain Amato, in the next room, and brought him to the door. Margherita didn't know what was going on.

So it was that Captain Paolo Amato of Trapani and Margherita Mannino of Borgetto were the first to know of the betrothal of Miss Jane Holland to Prince Lorenzo Bighilaterra. Not exactly the *Boston Globe* or *The New York Times*, Jane thought, but it really didn't matter.

Margherita, ever at the ready, had started to cry. No one had a handkerchief. Amato ran out and brought back tissues. Margherita started to jabber in Sicilian at Lorenzo and Jane, calling them Maurizio and Caterina, vowing that she'd make it to their wedding this time.

Lorenzo looked at the old woman fondly, then turned to

his dear Jane—thinking to himself that she'd never looked so beautiful to him, battered face, dirty clothes, bare feet and all—saying, "She told me all about my grandfather and her sister, Caterina."

Jane took a deep breath. "Did she show you the photograph?"

Lorenzo nodded. "It is absolutely amazing! Do you recall that day, at Segesta, when we talked about knowing each other in another life? Gianna, do you think it's really possible? You do look so much like Caterina and Margherita told me I was another Maurizio."

"She said you looked like him?" Jane sat down on the wooden bench again with her great-aunt. "*Zia,* does Lorenzo look at all like his grandfather, Prince Maurizio?" She had wondered about this after the old lady had first told her the story.

Margherita dabbed at her happy tears with the tissues. She nodded. "When he came to my door, I knew right away who he was. Prince Maurizio was older when he met Caterina—she was older than you, also, Gianna—but the resemblance is there. Lorenzo is thinner, perhaps a bit taller, but those eyes, that face, it's there. It is a miracle of the Madonna. She did this in response to my prayers all those years. I am so blessed, *cara.* I am so very happy."

A miracle of the Madonna.

Jane was reminded now of her vow, her promise to that same Madonna. She was sure she hadn't made it to shore on her own last night. Something, someone, some spirit, had accompanied her on that swim. Whether or not the dolphins were real or another one of her bizarre hallucinations, they had saved her . . . and the Madonna of Romitello had sent them. She had been rescued by a power greater than herself, *that* she truly believed. Now the other shoe was waiting to be dropped. She had to fulfill her promise, her equivalent of the dried-out *fava* bean.

Lorenzo noted that Jane's face had become very quiet and still. "Gianna, are you all right, dearest?" He was concerned, thinking that her old aunt had spooked her with all this talk about their resemblance to Maurizio and Caterina. He was not so much interested in that old story—although it was an eerie and unexplainable coincidence—as he was in the opening chapters of a new story, the story of their lives together.

Jane turned an earnest face up to his. "Lorenzo, we have to find out what happened to Caterina, to her child with Maurizio. Whatever it takes, we have to do it."

Lorenzo smiled. She was so pretty with that serious little face of hers, that furrowed brow, the anxiety in her beautiful eyes. He would humor her. Anything. He would promise her anything. "Yes, *cara,* whatever you say."

She could tell that Lorenzo was not taking her altogether seriously. She couldn't tell him that she had made a vow—not yet—and that was why she was still alive. Later, when they got to know each other better, later, she would tell him all about it. And enlist his help in her quest.

She addressed her old aunt. "*Zia,* Lorenzo and I will find out what happened to Caterina and her child. We promise you."

Margherita's face was wreathed in smiles. She threw away the damp tissues.

Now, in the car heading home, Lorenzo heard from Jane the whole terrifying story of her kidnapping ordeal. He was considerably impressed with her bravery in jumping overboard and attempting the arduous swim back to Sicily. He could not imagine his cousin Luisa or any of her silly friends—or, incidentally, any of the numerous women he had dated—doing such a thing, not even to save their own lives. They couldn't have coped with getting their teased, jelled, and sprayed hairstyles wet, much less their makeup and designer clothing ruined.

"Darling Gianna, were those scum planning to throw you over the side of the ship, tied up in those ropes?" He hated to ask, but he felt he had to know the worst.

"I think I was destined for a harem in North Africa," Jane told her lover, in English, not knowing quite how to explain white slave traffic to him in Italian.

Lorenzo, that oh-so-careful driver, almost went off the side of the road. Jane could see Margherita making the sign of the cross rapidly in the back seat of the Alfa.

"Jesu Christo!" he exclaimed, gaining control of the sports car and safely in command of the wheel once more. "Those infamous bastards! How dare they!"

"Well, the Schifosi brothers were all for dumping me in the middle of *La Mattanza,* where I'd be drowned or harpooned by those zealous tuna fishermen, but, after some discussion—" Jane didn't want to tell him how raunchy and incredibly degrading to her sensibilities that conversation had been "—it was thought that I could serve a more useful, time-honored purpose in the household of a rich Arab. I quickly decided," Jane told Lorenzo, "that the ocean could hold no danger greater than the fate the smugglers had in store for me in North Africa, so, over I went, but of my own free will, untrussed."

"Believe me, *cara,*" Lorenzo's fine white teeth were clenched, his jaw set in a grim line, "when those pieces of filth are caught, I will personally see to it that they spend the rest of their sorry lives in one of our best Sicilian penal institutions."

Poor Schifosis! thought Jane, suddenly sympathetic. From what she'd heard, a firing squad was kindness itself compared to the rigors of life in a Sicilian prison. And no *espresso,* either. Or *grappa.* Or her cute little cousin Ninfina to serve them both.

Lorenzo took a swift glance at Jane's bruised jaw. "And I would relish the opportunity, *cara,* to even the score with the one who did that to you."

She loved him. Life was good, life was wonderful. She squeezed Lorenzo's upper thigh in love and gratitude. *Oops!* Bad move! The Alfa skidded off the road again. From the back seat, Margherita rapped Lorenzo on the shoulder. He apologized profusely to her in abject Sicilian.

He straightened out the car and turned to Jane. "That was lovely, *cara,* but not here. Later, all right?"

Jane blushed, thinking of the "later" and of all the marvelous "laters" that were to come in their lives.

And she remembered that she and Lorenzo had one more tiny bit of unfinished business to discuss, now that he had identified the older woman, his aunt, whom she'd so stupidly mistaken for his mistress. Her voice serious, in English again, this time so Margherita would not understand what she was saying, she began, "We have to talk about that girl, the one who went to Switzerland."

A pained expression came over Lorenzo's face. "That gossip." He shook his head. "It went everywhere. There was nothing to it, *cara.* She was a friend of Luisa's. I consented to go on a date or two because Luisa was seeing—I think she is, unfortunately, still seeing—her brother. It was a way to keep an eye on Luisa and this man. It was ill advised. I should have kept out of it. It's time, I think," he turned to Jane, "that I step out of my little cousin's life. She will have to make her own decisions, unguided by my opinions. I have better things now to occupy my time."

Jane smiled and nodded. "So it was a complete fabrication on the part of Luisa's girlfriend?"

Lorenzo was adamant, his pride at stake. "It was completely false! I did nothing with that young woman that could, even remotely, lead to pregnancy. And, besides, even if I had slept with her—and I assure you, *cara,* that I didn't—I would have practiced what you Americans call 'safe sex.' I am a careful man." He grinned.

Jane couldn't resist teasing him. "Ummn, Lorenzo, that's not true. I know for a fact that you are not always so careful, my love. I recall two recent occasions."

He remembered, also. She was absolutely right. In the wildness of those two nights of passion they had shared, he had completely forgotten to be careful. That had never happened before. He was thirty years old and had never been so careless. "I think, then, that we had better get married quickly, *cara,*" he deadpanned.

She played along with him. "Yeah, I guess we had better." The prospect of having a baby so soon, with him, was not altogether unpleasant. She didn't think it would happen, actually, but it wouldn't be awful. Time would tell, but she wanted to marry him quickly nonetheless. This was as good a reason as any, if she needed a reason. She touched his cheek gently, not wanting him to lose control of the car again. "I love you, Lorenzo."

He smiled and whispered, his lips against her ear. "And I love you, my angel."

As they approached Borgetto, Lorenzo, casually, too casually, breaking the spell, told Jane, "Oh, by the way,

Gianna, your mother arrived from America last night."

Blam!

Jane's heart sank. She thought: *I'd rather go back into the ocean, now, and face that whirlpool again than face Joanna.* She caught herself up sharply. *That is really wimpy, Jane Holland,* she admonished herself. She knew that nothing her mother could say or do was of the least importance right now. If she had not grown up enough to face her in the last week, after all she had been through, then there was no hope whatsoever for her, none.

"Did you meet her, Lorenzo?" She was thinking: *oh, my poor lover, and I never even prepared you to face that woman. Yipes!*

Lorenzo laughed, a hollow sound at best. "She is an amazing woman, your mother. Yes, we met. We talked. That is, she talked, I had to listen."

Jane winced. "I'm sorry, *caro.*" She squeezed his hand sympathetically.

They had drawn up in front of the *caffe.* Lorenzo was parking the car. He turned to Jane. "She is nothing like you, Gianna, and, believe me, I have thanked God for that, since last night, many, many times over." He laughed again, a real laugh this time, adding, "Nothing she said means a damn to me, you know? I told her I loved you, my darling, and that I would marry you, if you'd have me, and that I cared for no further discussion with her. I will respect her as your mother, but I will not allow her to ruin our lives."

Way to go, Lorenzo! He was her hero! Jane beamed at him. Everything was going to be all right. She knew it. Lorenzo had stood up to Joanna Holland's bullying, and now it was Jane's turn. She hoped she would do as well.

Lorenzo helped *Zia* Margherita, then her, out of the Alfa. An unusual sight greeted their eyes. The *caffe* on

Corso Roma was bustling. It was a party. Jane remembered it was her birthday. But how did they know? She hadn't told anyone. Gosh, were there really this many people in Borgetto? She marveled, looking over the festive crowd. It seemed as though the whole town had come out to celebrate her safe return.

There was *Zia* Maria, busily hustling demitasse cups of her strong *espresso* at *la macchina,* handing them over to young Stefano, and Ninfina, balancing trays of what appeared to be freshly made pastries—chocolate *cannoli, sfinci, bocconetti*—reminding Jane that she was incredibly hungry, simply ravenous. And, suddenly, all eyes were on her, the birthday girl, the girl saved from the sea.

It was as if someone had pressed the pause button on the VCR, stopping the cassette that was playing her life. Then the video shot back into action, and there were lights and music and noise and people—relatives, friends, strangers—all over Jane, hugging her to their bosoms, kissing her on the cheeks, brimming over with good wishes, happy that she'd been returned safely from her ordeal. No one, of course, had any idea it was her birthday, that she'd just turned twenty-one. She made a point of remembering to tell Lorenzo, though.

Surrounded by love, just as she had been in the midst of her dolphins, she returned each greeting warmly, shrugging aside concern for her bruises, telling everyone she was okay. She really was okay. Never better, in fact. Neither white slavers nor whirlpools from hell had had their way with her. She'd come through.

And then she saw her mother. The jig was up. Or was it? She glanced back towards Lorenzo, suddenly a little panicked. He winked, signaling to her to have courage, to get it over with. He was right, she agreed. The sooner, the better, but it was not going to be easy. "Easy" was not a word that had any meaning in any context whatsoever involving Joanna Holland.

"Hi, Mom," Jane greeted her mother, who came running over to her, dear Claudia Donzini in her immediate wake.

Joanna Holland, a trim, handsome, youthful-looking dark-haired woman in her mid-forties, embraced her tall daughter. There were tears in her eyes. Claudia's eyes were wet, too. "Oh, Jane, we've all been so worried about you!"

"I'm all right, Mom, I've never been better, really. It's good to see you, but, you know, you really didn't have to come all this way to bring me back home."

Joanna wasn't listening; she was staring at Jane's bruised jaw.

Claudia nudged her. "It looks all right, Joanna. She can talk. Nothing's broken."

Joanna Holland turned to her friend. "We really should have it X-rayed, don't you think? Is there a decent hospital in Palermo?"

Claudia Donzini sighed deeply, exasperated. "Yes, there's a decent hospital in Palermo, and no, I don't think it has to be X-rayed. Give it a rest, Joanna, please. Jane looks great."

Jane's mother scrutinized her daughter closely. "Hardly great. She's a mess! Just look at her, those pants, bare feet . . ."

Faced with the two women fussing all over her, Jane giggled and then called out to Lorenzo. "Lorenzo, save me, please, from all this fuss, love, and concern!"

Lorenzo came to her side, taking her arm, holding her close, possessively, to him. Joanna Holland and Claudia Donzini stopped their argument and turned their attention to him.

Claudia, a big smile lighting up her warm, pleasant features, spoke first. "Well, *caro,* I guess you two have made up, no?"

"Yes!" the couple shouted in unison.

Claudia grasped Jane's hand, apologizing, "You're not angry that I sent Lorenzo to the farmhouse to meet you?"

Jane, one hand grasping Lorenzo and the other, Claudia, was overwhelmed by their love for her. "I'm grateful you cared that much about the both of us, Claudia. Not that anything got settled . . ." She looked over at Lorenzo, who had the grace to blush slightly, remembering their night at the farmhouse in Claudia's big, wide bed.

Joanna, left out of the conversation, scowled at the secrets it implied. "Jane, come inside the house with me. You have to change, and we have to talk." She was implacable, stone-faced, her dislike of Lorenzo showing clearly in her angry dark eyes.

Jane faltered, turning to Lorenzo. "Lorenzo," she started to say.

He hugged her close and then pushed her towards her mother. "Go, *carissima,* I shall be right here."

Claudia followed Jane and her mother into Maria's house. In the guest bedroom, Jane pulled a clean red tee shirt and white Bermuda shorts out of her duffle bag. She rooted under the narrow bed and came up with her sandals, remembering that was the only footwear she was down to. Her sneakers were probably still on the fishing boat. Quickly, she stripped off the milkman's soiled trousers and the sea-changed tee shirt.

Her mother was staring at her lace underwear, the bikini briefs and the underwire bra. "Where on earth did you get those, Jane?" she asked her, recalling that her daughter Jane only wore the plainest cotton underwear at home.

"This is the new me, Mom. Like it?" Jane pulled on the clean outfit hurriedly, slipping on her sandals. She reached for her hairbrush and attacked the wild tangle that was her hair.

Joanna did not rise to Jane's flippancy. "We have some serious things to discuss, Jane."

Jane was glad that Claudia was still with them. It made it easier, facing Joanna, with Claudia's support so evident. Jane sat down on the bed, brushing away at her hair. "What do you want to know, Mom?"

Joanna Holland leaned back against the oak dresser facing the bed. "Your relationship with that man, I think, for starters."

Jane looked at Claudia, who smiled at her encouragingly, then at her frowning mother. A simple answer, Jane thought, for a simple question. "We're lovers." She continued to brush her hair. She could hear Joanna's surprised, indrawn breath.

Before Joanna could put her shocked reaction into words, Jane had leapt into the breach. "And we are going to get married. He loves me and I love him. I'm not going back to Boston with you, Mom, nor am I going back to school. I'm staying here with Lorenzo."

Joanna turned to Claudia, who had also been caught off-guard by Jane's retort. "Thank you so much, Signora Donzini, for the wonderful care you took of my daughter," she lashed out at Claudia, her voice raspy and sarcastic.

Claudia would not be cowed. "Oh, come on, Joanna! Jane's a big girl and she's mature enough to know what she wants. Lorenzo is a wonderful young man . . ."

"That's not what your daughter Anna Maria told me. She says he is a notorious womanizer and playboy, that he has a bad reputation—"

"My daughter wanted the prince for herself. She's jealous, a common enough emotion. What Anna Maria said has nothing to do with the reality of this situation." Claudia was trying to get the conversation back on an even keel.

"Jane is coming back to Boston with me, as soon as we can book a flight. She's not going to be one of those dizzy American women who are dazzled by Eurotrash, by phony foreign titles—" Joanna had the good grace to stop when she saw the stricken look in her friend's eyes. "Oh, goodness, Claudia, I didn't mean you," she tried to explain.

"Mom, how could you?" Jane whispered.

"Claudia, I'm so sorry, really. I didn't mean that. Please, it's just that Jane has made me crazy." Joanna reached a tentative hand out to her friend. It was an awkward, unpleasant moment. Over twenty-five years of friendship hung in the balance.

Claudia took both of Joanna's shoulders in her strong hands and pushed her down on the bed next to Jane. Claudia's blue eyes flashed with anger. "Sit down next to your daughter! Talk to her, find out how much she loves Lorenzo and try to understand her, Joanna. And, for the love of God, stop your damned bullying! It's always been your least attractive feature." Claudia turned on her heel and left mother and daughter together.

Joanna, subdued, didn't know what to say. She tried to begin. "Jane, I don't want to bully you, honestly I don't, but you're so young, so inexperienced. How long have you known this man?"

Forever, Mother, Jane wanted to tell her. *He is my soul.* Aloud, she responded, "It can't be judged that way, Mom. This is the first and only time I've ever felt this way, I can't just turn around and let him go."

"If it's really love—and not just raging hormones, you

little innocent—he'll wait for you. At least until you finish your senior year at Vassar. Jane, you love school, how can you give it up?"

Joanna was trying to be reasonable. Claudia had cleared the air between them. It was going to be possible to have a grown-up discussion. Jane shook her head. "I'm the one who won't wait. You have no idea how much I want him." She didn't believe she was having this kind of conversation with her conservative mother. "Yes, I've slept with him, and yes, it's wonderful. I want more. I want a lifetime of it."

"Jane, there's more to a marriage than sex. You're smart enough to know that. You can't go off with the first man who makes love to you."

"And what was Dad for you, Mom? How many men did you have to sleep with before you settled for him?" Jane asked boldly, not believing she had the nerve to say all this to her mother.

Joanna Holland smiled, remembering, suddenly, her own passion for her husband, undimmed by the passage of time. "*Touche.* You hit the right button. Okay, so you've found your prince, but why hurry it? Can't you both wait a bit and get to know each other more? Jane, it's only been what, five, six days? Not even a week! That's insane! At least I knew your father four months!"

"I know him, Mom, and he knows me. We're good for each other. And," she continued, gently, "if it is a mistake, well, it's my mistake. I'm entitled to make my own decisions now, I think. I'll finish school in my own time. You have to let go, Mom. You know you do."

Joanna Holland looked at her child. She knew what day it was, that turning point parents both look forward to and dread. Jane was an adult. She was, indeed, capable of making her own decisions, and she had just made a very important one. Joanna Holland wasn't at all sure it was the right one for her. She feared for her daughter's innocence, her naivete. She knew the traps that lay in wait for her beloved child in the big bad world, but the decision was Jane's to make, and it would have to do. She would have to accept it.

She reached out and touched the brand-new adult's cheek with tenderness. "Happy Birthday, Jane," she said, seeming to remember what first love was like, accepting her daughter's decision.

Later, as the party was breaking up and all the guests drifting away into the dark, starry night, Jane, safe inside Lorenzo's strong and caring arms, was happy to note that her mother and her betrothed had forged a peace, of sorts. Well, they were no longer staring at each other like a pair of savage fighting cocks, the one ready to lunge and tear at the other's throat, the other prepared to disembowel with its sharp claws.

They even managed to smile at each other once or twice. Jane knew that her mother would be one of Lorenzo's greatest challenges, but he was a charmer and she had a feeling that Joanna Holland didn't stand a chance.

Yes, Joanna was in a better mood, mellowed, perhaps, by the couple of shots of the *grappa* Aldo had dared her to down. She was talking about telephoning Jane's father and sister tomorrow and getting them over for the wedding, which she had to allow was inevitable and would take place very soon.

And, she confided to Jane, the way she had stood up to her, not backing down an inch, reminded Joanna of how she had stood up to her own difficult parents when she had made up her mind to marry Neal Holland, whom she'd fallen madly in love with, a WASP, a non-Catholic, non-

Sicilian. She had even gone so far as to drop out of her first year at Harvard Medical School to marry him, never to return.

That was why she was so worried Jane would never go back to finish up her degree, because she hadn't. It was something she had always regretted. Jane had never known that. Her mother had been in medical school? She could still go back, Jane thought. Joanna would make a great doctor. She was a smart lady. And she hadn't known her grandparents had tried to keep her mother from marrying her father! No wonder she was still so angry at her family after all these years. But she had to get over that, too. It was a waste of energy. She and her mother had a lot to talk about before she flew back home.

All these secrets, she mused. Tomorrow, Jane promised herself, she would sit Joanna down and start telling her a few. The family stories, the secrets that *Nonna* had, for some reason, never seen fit to share with them. Yes, there were a lot of things to tell her mother. Joanna, the new Joanna, who was now Jane's friend as well as her mother, would be amazed.

Chapter Twenty

The Temple of Concord

From the open floor-to-ceiling window on the second floor bridal suite of the hotel, Jane could see the naked stone of the Doric temple, gleaming honey gold in the early morning sunlight. She and Lorenzo would be married there today.

Lorenzo stirred in his sleep on the wide double bed, one strong bare arm thrown over his head. His wiry black curly hair was tousled. There was a half-smile on his full, sensual lips. Jane moved closer to his naked body under the thin, fine linen sheet. The initials VA, for the hotel, the Villa Athena, were worked on the counterpane in white silk embroidery thread, flowing in a Spencerian-like script.

"Good morning, love," Jane whispered in his ear. The half-smile turned into a full, wide grin, and she was instantly engulfed in both his tanned, muscular arms. She sighed in perfect contentment.

"Ah, bella, che ore sono?" He was asking the time, his voice lower and huskier than usual from sleep.

"Early . . . very early. Look at the temple, Lorenzo, isn't it beautiful?" She nudged his head towards the direction of the open window. He yawned and nodded, his blue eyes darkly smudged with sleepiness. Then he opened them wide, laughed, and pointed to the railing of the balcony that encircled the window.

A pair of very sexy, very lacy underpants (once the property of Anna Maria Donzini, now Jane's) lay draped over the railing of the balcony, carelessly tossed and caught by the railing and more than apparent to any other early morning riser at the Villa Athena. Jane jumped out of their marriage bed, her rear view of bouncing bottom and long shapely legs drawing much admiration and a meaningful wolf-whistle from her new husband, as she quickly grabbed the sexy, albeit possibly offending, lingerie.

They had behaved with great abandon the previous night, all night, and there was clothing strewn haplessly over the suite. Luckily, the railing had snagged the lace of the panties and they had not fallen to the recessed first floor terrace below them. Nor had they wafted into the sparkling, clean water of the Villa Athena's swimming pool, a shimmering rectangle of blue nestled in the shade of the sweet lemon trees.

But then, Jane realized, the Villa Athena was an old, well-known honeymoon hotel. Over the years the staff had probably witnessed many more provocative things than a stray pair of white lace bikini briefs.

After the short civil ceremony at Palermo's city hall yesterday afternoon, Jane and Lorenzo had gone to Claudia and Aldo's flat for a marvelous and memorable reception. Donna Maria, aided and abetted by one of Palermo's best caterers, Ferrara's, had set forth a splendid feast topped by a wedding cake baked and iced according to a recipe Great-Aunt Margherita said had been one of Chef Vincenzo Volta's favorites. It was topped by a colorful and fanciful variety of *marzipan* fruit. (All those years, the old lady had saved a book of Volta's recipes, the ones she and her sister Caterina had set down during their training with him. Jane had been extremely touched when Margherita presented it to her as a wedding gift.)

It was a simple reception. There would be a bigger one

at the *Palazzo* Bighilaterra when the couple returned from their wedding trip in ten days. They had just wanted to get married quickly, get away, and be alone together for a while, just the two of them.

Over *hors-d'oeuvres* of Beluga caviar, smoked salmon, and *tuna carpaccio,* everyone present had toasted the bride and groom, the new Princess Bighilaterra and her prince, with magnums of Moet et Chandon champagne. (Jane had instructed her mother to send the wedding notice to Vassar. She thought all her friends would get a real kick out of it. She still couldn't believe it herself, Princess Gianna Bighilaterra, nee Jane Holland. If that didn't boggle the mind, nothing would! She felt like Cinderella . . . or Snow White.)

Jane and Lorenzo basked in the love and company of their family and friends. The Strellis were there: Lorenzo's uncle, the Count, aristocratic, mustachioed; his aunt, the beautiful and too-young-looking Marie-Claude (forever to be referred to by the newlyweds in their secret code as "the old bag"); his giggly cousin Luisa, leggy in a very short beige lace dress, her tawny hair swooping along one side of her lovely face (unaccompanied by her beau—she'd realized Lorenzo was right about the man and had dumped him).

And the Hollands: Jane's slightly jet-lagged lawyer father, Neal, tall, handsome, blond like Jenny, with distinguished streaks of gray at his temples; her precious little sister, Jenny, seventeen and already dreamy-eyed and half-in-love with Jane's prince; her mother Joanna, reconciled to her daughter's hasty wedding (taking her aside the night before and asking her if the reason for the rush was because she was pregnant, Jane answering, "Mom, you really should've stayed in med school, then you would know it's really too early to tell," both of them laughing over the incident afterwards.)

And the Borgetto relatives! Together, forced into a truce by the decisive and energetic Captain Gambino, actually speaking to each other and trying to make an effort to be friendly after the tragic and unfortunate estrangement of so many years. Maria, Margherita and Ninfina, dressed in their Sunday best, a bit ill at ease among all the aristocrats, their new relatives by marriage.

The Donzinis appeared so proud and happy, as if Jane and Lorenzo were their own children; Claudia weeping during the ceremony into one of Margherita's fancy embroidered handkerchiefs; the Baron handsome and worldly in a morning coat, reminding his wife that he'd seen from the first what a good-looking couple Jane and Lorenzo were, so obviously made for each other. All the Donzini children were present, too. Even Anna Maria had put off her pouting sulkiness for the occasion, no doubt mindful that her parents had still to decide on an appropriate punishment for her inappropriate behavior, and endeavoring to get into their good graces. (That process, Jane thought, could take years!)

Before Jane and Lorenzo departed on their wedding trip, Jane threw her small beautiful bouquet of night-blooming jasmine, orange blossoms and tiny white rosebuds over her shoulder to the females in the group. Margherita caught it, giggling uproariously—she'd enjoyed more than one glass of that fine champagne—at the thought that she would be the next bride. She handed it over to her niece, Ninfina, who took it, blushing.

The Villa Athena had been Lorenzo's suggestion. He had always loved the hotel, which was literally in the Via dei Templi, the valley of the temples, a 5th century B.C. Greek complex occupying a shelf of land below the modern city of Agrigento, nestled in a hilly spot among arbors of almond trees and bushes of *fighi d'Inde,* the Sicilian prickly pear cactus. Clinging tenaciously to the upper slopes of the hills rising to the temples were the gnarled, ancient trunks of long un-pruned olive trees.

When they arrived, Jane and Lorenzo walked from the hotel up the hillside and through the fertile almond orchards for a quick look at the temple site. They gazed happily upon the two-mile square temple precinct, which shimmered like an ancient mirage under the hot July sun. Lorenzo squeezed Jane's hand in delight as he pointed out the closest building, the Temple of Concord.

He had made arrangements beforehand for a priest from Agrigento to marry them there. His idea was to secure the ancient blessings of the old gods of Sicily as well as the new. It was a long-adhered-to custom for local newlyweds to visit the Temple of Concord for good luck, and to pose there for wedding pictures.

Lorenzo would go them all one better by actually having him and Jane married there in a religious ceremony. She would wear the same white, close-fitting filmy silk dress that his cousin Luisa had found for Jane at one of her favorite Palermo boutiques. Lorenzo would again don his tuxedo. The hotel florist would fashion another wedding bouquet for Jane, and the best photographer in Agrigento would snap away like mad. (The choicest photo would go to Aunt Margherita to set next to the one of her beloved sister, Caterina.) It would be truly glorious. Lorenzo, it seemed to Jane, would never run out of different and wonderful ideas.

That evening, in the outdoor portion of the hotel's restaurant at the edge of the blue-tiled swimming pool, they dined on *orrechiette alla Norma,* ear-shaped macaroni in a typically Sicilian tomato-basil-eggplant sauce, a simple salad of goat cheese with shredded *radicchio,* and a tart lemon sorbet garnished with the mint-like leaves of citrusy bergamot.

The main restaurant was given over to a wedding party. The couple graciously asked the waiters to pass out slices of their wedding cake to all the diners outside, too. Lorenzo and Jane had admired their cake, which had been on display when they passed through the restaurant, with its exquisite spun sugar replica in miniature of the Temple of Concord crowning the topmost tier.

When the time came to toast the bride and groom, Jane and Lorenzo took up their wine glasses and stood with the other guests, looking into each other's eyes and toasting themselves, too, for it was indeed their wedding day as well as the other couple's.

As night fell, floodlights illuminated the temples, playing on their ancient crevices and scarred pillars. It was magical, Jane thought, being there with Lorenzo, who had turned to her and was kissing her forehead, smoothing back her hair. She sighed in complete and utter happiness.

It was still a matter of deep wonder to Jane that her life had changed so in the matter of a few short weeks. She had come to Europe, just another average, ordinary American college student on holiday, only to be plunged into death-defying adventures, dark family secrets, and a torrid love affair with a prince.

Had her actions been guided by some unseen force? Great-Aunt Margherita would call it fate. Lorenzo was her fate. Their families had been linked tragically in the past. It was almost as if it was now up to Jane and Lorenzo to set it all right.

Lorenzo had told her that when he saw her at Segesta that first morning he had felt a thrill of recognition. He had not wanted to leave her. And then, when he went to the

Donzinis, a dinner party he had not been all that eager to attend, he had locked glances with her again, their visitor from America, and thought, *Ecco bella* . . . behold, beauty . . . I know you . . . and I know you are meant for me.

An impulse had made him hand over his *trinacria* amulet to her on their first date. He didn't know why; it certainly was nothing he had ever felt moved to do before. And to find out that Jane's Great-Aunt Caterina had been given a *trinacria* by his grandfather, Maurizio . . . it was strange, bizarre, but wonderful, too.

Now they were together, and nothing would part them. He had learned the hard way, having searched for her through the rural byways of the Conca d'Oro, that Jane was a jealous lover, and that he would have to reassure her constantly of his fidelity and his love; it was a challenge he was only too happy to meet, for he had no doubt that she would learn to trust him. They would have all the time in the world now, together.

"Come." Lorenzo, her husband, her lover, was whispering into her hair at their table. "Come." It was, after all, their wedding night.

Jane's heart was beating wildly as Lorenzo led her up the hotel's main stairs to their second floor suite. She was nervous, nearly as nervous as she had been with him the first time, that blissful night of love they'd shared at Capo Gallo, on the beach. Save for the passionate interlude at the Donzini farmhouse in Alcamo, they'd had precious little time together those days before the civil ceremony. There had been so much preparation, so many insignificant but time-demanding things to do. Their desire had had to take a back seat. They had yearned for each other terribly.

Now they were alone, legally man and wife, alone in the hotel. It was overwhelming. Jane trembled with growing sexual excitement. Lorenzo, ever sensitive to her youth, her inexperience, her needs, cupped her face in his strong hands and kissed her eyelids. "Relax, *bella mia,*" he whispered, "everything will be all right." He had made sure she hadn't imbibed too much wine; he liked her better when she was slightly shy with him.

As if he were unwrapping a precious, priceless gift, Lorenzo undressed Jane with a delicacy that came, she thought jealously, from long years of practice. He peeled off her light summer dress, leaving her in her revealing lacy underwear. Jane slipped off her sandals as he disrobed swiftly, throwing his garments carelessly asunder.

When he was completely naked, he leaned over her as she stood before him, licking and kissing the cleft of her full, swelling breasts. She nearly swooned, groaning softly, her hands clutching at the curly hair on his head. He tossed her lace-trimmed bra to one side; Jane saw it catch and drape itself on the lavatory doorjamb. Not through with her breasts, he cupped them in his hands and caressed their round fullness, circling each nipple with a thumb and forefinger, transmuting them into diamond-hardness. His touch was searing her skin, burning her nerve endings. She wanted to scream, but could only moan, deep in her throat. Her belly tightened.

Now he was kneeling before her in the softly-lit room, kissing the insides of her thighs, drawing down her lace panties. She was moist with anticipation. One of his hands was rubbing her belly, stroking downward, expertly, until she groaned again, this time louder, as he touched the sweet and secret entrance to her female core. The other hand disposed of her underpants, throwing them somewhere beyond her line of vision. Her legs had begun to give way, to tremble.

Swiftly, he got up from his knees and grasped her under her buttocks, lifting her to the level of his hips. She started to freeze, not knowing what he planned to do next. "Relax, darling one," he whispered in her ear, "I'm not going to hurt you."

She was overcome with passion at the sound of his exciting, husky lover's voice. She begged him to take her, now. "Please, Lorenzo, please."

"Ah, now you're impatient, now you want it," he laughed, his arms tight around the small of her back.

"Yes, I do, I want it, I want you," she murmured back, not so shy after all.

He didn't mind. "Then, carissima, bella mia," he responded, huskily, "you shall have me."

And, with that, he brought her hips down gently over his hard throbbing shaft.

"Oh!" she cried out, as he levered her downwards and upwards in the primordial rhythm of love. She cried out again, maddened with the need for him, for all of him, inside her.

Her arms were wound around his neck. Her mouth found his and held it, her tongue thrusting inside his mouth even as he was thrusting inside her. His mouth was so soft, so sweet, so warm. Her desire for him threw her into a frenzy. Her body was on fire as she arched her back and met his every movement with her own.

Their tongues grappled wetly, even as he moved faster and thrust deeper; she was with him, riding him, riding this physical and spiritual union out to its dizzying, glorious climax, when they shuddered together, exploded together, trembled in wave after wave of aftershock . . . and were still.

His strong legs had not buckled, not with the weight of her, impaled on him, not with the magnificent, thundering disorientation of his senses as his seed burst deep inside her warm wet body.

Holding her to him with one arm, he stroked her neck with a free hand, crooning soft, gentle endearments, words of love and passion that he'd never said, never meant, before. He was overcome by her, totally and unreservedly. *A lifetime is not going to be enough to savor this woman,* he thought.

"*Ah, Gianna, lei voglio bene* . . . I love you so much," he whispered, holding her close. He released her from love's grip, scooping her into his arms, carrying her to the wide double bed in the center of the room. *No, a lifetime is not enough,* he thought, as he laid her down gently, *but tonight I—we—will make a good start.*

Jane held up her arms to him, drawing him down, covering her naked body with his, insatiable, wanting more, needing more, needing him as she was certain Caterina had once needed Maurizio. Love doesn't die, she thought. What those two lovers felt would always be a part of them, she knew, and she was glad. As long as she and Lorenzo lived, and loved, so too would their star-crossed ancestors. That love would not die.

Later, spent with loving, they lay against the white crumpled clouds of their bunched and scattered bed linen, dreamily trailing their hands over every curve, every bend, every fold and opening of each other's bodies, as if they were memorizing each little bit with their gentle, caressing movements.

In a few short hours they would arise, meet the priest, repeat their marriage vows, the promises they would never stop keeping, against the dappled, lacy shade of the gnarled old olive tree in front of the ancient temple that they had seen that afternoon, the sole survivor of the groves that had once flourished on those hillsides. Under the clear, bright Sicilian sky they would pledge their love before the old gods and the new, before that enduring temple, buttressed by its tall, straight, honey gold columns.

The hired photographer would snap away. Tourists walking by would reflect on the handsomeness of the young couple, obviously so much in love. Perhaps one or two would notice the gleaming gold amulet hanging from the bride's neck and remark on its unusual configuration.

Jane half-dozed against the big square pillows, thinking about her wedding day. Lorenzo stroked her cheek, knowing what she was thinking about now, anxious to tell her the next part of their honeymoon.

"*Cara mia,* listen," he said as she nodded, sated with love, pressing her hand to his. "Tomorrow we drive to *Siracusa,* the place where your amulet was minted so long ago by the Greeks. We will see *Ortygia,* the old city, and the Ear of Dionysus. Then we will journey up the coast to one of the great Goethe's favorite Sicilian towns, *Taormina.* It's a favorite of many Europeans and I have booked rooms for us in an out-of-the-way pensione that I was told had the best view of *Mt. Etna* in all of *Taormina.*

"It's owned by a German family that settled there after World War I. They are interesting, too. The German was an excellent photographer, only now being rediscovered by historians of the art. When I called to book the rooms, I was told by the grandson that the family had recently come upon a secret cache of his negatives and prints, which should be mounted by the time we arrive.

"It will be a little something extra. Then, of course, we will see all the famous tourist attractions in *il teatro Greco*, the Cathedral of San Nicola, the—"

Not sated after all, and not at all shy, Jane had silenced

Lorenzo by gently rolling over his body, adjusting her curved contours to his. Not sated either, and enjoying her more aggressive style of lovemaking, Lorenzo smiled, ran his hands through her hair and kissed her temples. Then he pressed his mouth on hers, parting her soft lips, teasing her tongue with his, claiming it for his own, rolling her on her back and into love's old sweet rhythm. He melted into her, easily, smoothly, as she sighed and called his name. The waves of pleasure began to undulate through their entwined bodies. They were lost in each other.

Soul, body, they were one. *As before.* But this time, nothing would ever part them.

Chapter Twenty-One

Found

Lorenzo parked the Alfa in front of the pretty pink *pensione.* He opened the car on Jane's side and helped her out, then unlocked the trunk to take out their luggage. They had traveled light, a soft leather bag for each of them containing the bare necessities: toiletries, bathing outfits, casual wear for day and evening. It was an informal honeymoon.

Jane hooked her hands in the back pockets of her white duck pants and admired the breathtaking harbor view and the looming volcano. It was still morning, and *Etna* was shrouded in a white, smoky mist. The *pensione* was situated at the top of a hair-raising hairpin drive up to *Taormina* from the two-lane *autostrada* below. The little Alfa had hugged the dangerously curvy road easily, but Jane had been a bit nervous. She would not have wanted to drive that stretch all by herself.

Lorenzo, a valise in each hand, nodded towards the entrance of the *pensione,* a wide, screened door outlined in charming white wood gingerbread carving. Jane held the door open for her husband and then stepped in behind him, into a small entryway lined with scores of framed and matted photographs. A familiar and distinctive aroma assailed her senses: lemon and rosemary. She heard Lorenzo make a startled exclamation and drop their suitcases.

"*Caro,* what is it?" she asked anxiously. He turned to her, his face white, drained, as if all the blood had rushed out of it. He couldn't speak. Mute, he gestured at the walls.

She looked around her, comprehension growing even as amazement took over. She was dazed, no, dazzled, by dozens of faces—dozens of *her* faces—staring back at her. But it wasn't her. It was Caterina. Caterina . . . on the walls of this tiny hotel on the top of the cliff that was the town of *Taormina,* Caterina, garbed in Roman togas, Greek tunics, and dozens of other fanciful costumes for the German photographer whose family ran this guesthouse. Caterina . . . alone, nude, gracefully posed, her beautiful body forever young, Caterina . . . and a young child with masses of dark curly hair and clear, light eyes. Eyes that even in the black and white photographs were unmistakably the very same blue of Lorenzo's.

Caterina! My God, they had found her.

Epilogue

Taormina

Etna was always there, mantled in snow, fuming, smoking, hiccuping balls of orange flame. When they had first moved from Paris, she had been sure she would never get used to seeing a live volcano from her bedroom window, her first sight of the day, her last at night. She'd suggested to Klaus that they take a look at other inns for sale, but he'd fallen in love with the pink *pensione,* dramatically set against *Taormina*'s exposed black volcanic cliff.

His artistic eye had also been enraptured by the cascading blooms of pale ivory and deep purple bougainvillea that hugged the house's stony facade. So she'd given in to him, as she was wont to do, and now the active volcano was simply another constant in her life.

She cooked, cleaned, looked after their guests and the child, and, of course, Klaus. Klaus, who had taken her back to Sicily—"I know you want to go home, Caterina"—and who had promised to care for her. Caterina needed someone to care for her.

It was an unusual *menage,* the three of them: an aristocratic German homosexual, engrossed in his art of photography, a Sicilian peasant trained as a cook, and her love child, the result of her liaison with a married Sicilian aristocrat. To the townsfolk, she was Klaus von Krenski's "wife," her child, their child.

Klaus took his other pleasures discreetly, if at all, seemingly content with adding to his private photographic collection of nude, well-muscled young Italian men wrestling in the old Graeco-Roman style or adolescent and pre-pubescent boys cavorting like Pan in the ruins of the old temples dotting the hillsides.

Her pleasures? She had the child, Maurizio's child, and her memories, the good ones and the bad ones. She broke her vow never to go back to Palermo only once, upon hearing from her old friend and mentor, Vincenzo Volta, that Maurizio had died.

She'd wept at her lover's grave in the rain, a solitary figure, a tall woman wreathed in black, and lingered outside his *palazzo* on the Via Loro only long enough to catch a glimpse of the child he'd fathered with his legal wife. The young boy's clear blue eyes matched those of her child . . . exactly. In fact, they could have been twins, save that hers was older.

Margherita. She missed her sister. But Caterina bore the guilt for the death of Carlo, her sister's young husband. In the convoluted logic of sin, guilt and retribution that is the Sicilian heritage, she blamed her adultery with Maurizio for the young man's death. With that knowledge, how could she ever face her sister again?

She had finally come to realize, those lonely days in Paris waiting for the child to be born, that she'd been wrong. She'd been too glib in her dismissal of sin and its consequences. Margherita had said someone always had to pay . . . well, it was she, Caterina, who had paid the price. She realized that when she heard the prince's wife had returned to Palermo and come back to her husband.

The news that Fiammetta was expecting Maurizio's child shattered her. She surmised from that fact that he'd made his choice. She still loved him fiercely; indeed, he had been the great love of her life. But now there was no place for her with him any more, either. (Poor Caterina! She was never to know how wrong she was.)

Prince Maurizio had sent her for safekeeping to Paris, accompanied by his chef Volta. He'd feared that the Mafia, having tried and failed, to kill him, would try to kill her and their unborn child. Vincenzo saw that Caterina was well taken care of, ensconced in the lively bohemian circle of his student days, where no one cared that she was an unwed mother.

She'd found employment, too, and was happy to be able to use her culinary skills in a small Left Bank bistro. The German was a regular customer at that restaurant, delighted to find Sicilian dishes on the menu from time to time. He had spent a year in Sicily and had always been drawn to its rustic charm and beauty, its handsome, unspoiled people, its remoteness.

One night he asked to meet the cook. Caterina's natural beauty had blossomed after becoming a mother. Von Krenski's aesthetic sensibilities warmed to her good looks and gentle demeanor, and he'd noted the deep-buried sadness in her fine, amber-colored eyes. He had always wanted to go back to Sicily, to live there and set up a photographic studio. Caterina would be an excellent cover for his aberrant proclivities, and a good companion as well. He'd make her a business proposition, he decided.

Rutiger von Krenski, Klaus's father, sent him a substantial monthly allowance on the condition that he never return to their Bavarian estate. Klaus had been living in Paris and biding time, waiting for the long depleting war to end before deciding what to do next. Meeting Caterina, he'd made up his mind. He was frank with her, she equally frank with him. She accepted his proposition. They shook hands to seal their unusual bargain.

Klaus was an excellent photographer. People began to collect his work. There were some small museum exhibits. One of his most popular series of photographs was a cycle he had taken of Caterina attired in a white toga, her long chestnut brown hair streaming down her back and over her shoulders, playing with her beautiful dark-haired, blue-eyed young child in a meadow of wildflowers. He called this cycle "Ceres and the Young Persephone," and he printed up a set to be displayed permanently in the lobby of their *pensione*.

To his private collection of nude male studies, he added nude photographs of Caterina alone, catching her wistful face and still lush body in artistic attitudes. These gently erotic pieces were neither for sale nor display.

Klaus had introduced Caterina to the pleasures of the mind, encouraging her to explore literature and the ideas of the great philosophers and thinkers. She'd once made a tentative start in that direction in the prince's fine library. They spent many a quiet evening at the inn, after the child and their guests had settled down for the night, talking about life and the meaning of their own existence, breathing in the lemon-scented Mediterranean air, idly noting the volcano's spewing under the cold light of the star-pierced sky.

Klaus was intelligent and always intrigued by new ideas. Some German intellectuals, friends of his who had journeyed to the east, to India, had come by to stay at the *pensione* on their way home, bringing fanciful ideas about reincarnation and the transmigration of the soul. Caterina was strangely fascinated. If it were true—and who was to say, for certain, that it was not—perhaps she and Maurizio would meet again in another life, in a better time for them and for their love. She kept this idea locked in her heart. It was one of the few things she never shared with Klaus.

All her long life she wore the golden amulet that the prince had given her. After her death, a sharp-eyed descendant, coming upon the secret cache of Klaus's private photos, noted that she wore it even when she wore absolutely nothing else. It was obviously something very special to her. But what did it mean? *Nonna* had not left anything behind by way of explanation, just the golden *trinacria* itself, in a box containing a few pieces of cheap jewelry and trinkets to be passed on to the next generation. She had never had much in the way of good jewelry.

About the Author

As the descendant of Sicilian peasants, this fanciful story set in Sicily and based on tales Jo Manning heard as a child is close to her heart.

The character of Caterina Conigliaro is based on a great-aunt who did, indeed, have a free and independent life at a time when few women of her time and class did. She really was unhappily married to an abusive husband who beat her and who met his just demise under the wheels of a trolley car in Brooklyn. That much is true.

The places in *The Sicilian Amulet* are real and the anecdotes and stories about miracles and Madonnas are those many Sicilians know by heart. All of the characters, of course, are fictional and bear no resemblance at all to anyone living or dead—except perhaps for the above incidents in the life of the real Caterina Conigliaro. All else is coincidental.

Sicily is an ancient and magical island where all things—including perhaps reincarnation—are possible and the unusual quite often happens. The story of Jane and Lorenzo and Caterina and Maurizio is fiction, but the story of Klaus, the homosexual German photographer who befriends Caterina, has some grounding in fact. There *was* a German photographer, a homosexual, who settled and worked in Taormina between the first and second world wars. Coincidence? Serendipity? Certainly spooky, if nothing else!

Jo Manning lives in Florida with her husband Nick, who

makes films. They have two grown children and four grandchildren. She's written a number of short stories, an audiobook, two Regency novels, and is currently working on a third Regency as well as the biography of a celebrated 18th century courtesan who was a mistress of King George IV.